J. N. Chaney

Copyrighted Material

www.jnchaney.com

1st Edition

THE AMBER PROJECT

BOOK 1 IN THE VARIANT SAGA

J.N. CHANEY

STAY UP TO DATE

Chaney posts updates, official art, previews, and other awesome stuff on his website. You can also follow him on Instagram, Facebook, and Twitter.

Search for **JN Chaney's Renegade Readers** on Facebook to join the group where readers can come together and share their lives and interests, especially regarding Chaney's books.

For updates about new releases, as well as exclusive promotions, sign up for the VIP mailing list. Head there now to receive a free copy of *The Other Side of Nowhere*.

https://www.subscribepage.com/organic

Enjoying the series? Help others discover the Variant Saga by leaving a review on Amazon.

BOOKS BY J.N. CHANEY

Renegade Star Series:

Renegade Star

Renegade Atlas

Renegade Moon

Renegade Lost

Renegade Fleet

Renegade Earth

Renegade Dawn

Renegade Children

Renegade Union

Renegade Empire

Renegade Descent

Renegade Rising (July 2019)

Renegade Prequel Series:

Nameless

The Constable

The Constable Returns

Warrior Queen

The Last Reaper Series:

The Last Reaper

Fear the Reaper

Blade of the Reaper

Wings of the Reaper

The Orion Colony Series:

Orion Colony

Orion Uncharted

Orion Awakened

Orion Protected

The Fifth Column Series:

The Fifth Column

The Fifth Column: The Solaras Initiative

BOOK DESCRIPTION

THE AMBER PROJECT: VARIANT SAGA #1

Everything is a grave.

In 2157, a mysterious gas known as Variant spreads across the globe, killing or mutating most organic life. The surviving humans take refuge in an underground city, determined to return home. But after generations of failures and botched attempts, hope is beginning to dwindle. That is, until a young scientist makes a unique discovery—and everything changes. Suddenly, there's reason to hope again, and it rests within a group of genetically engineered children that are both human and Variant.

Terry is one of these children, modified and trained to endure the harsh conditions of a planet he cannot begin to understand. After years of preparation, Terry thinks he knows what to expect. But the reality is far stranger than anything he can imagine—and what he will become is far more dangerous.

For Lori
Who read stories to children
And taught them to believe

ACKNOWLEDGMENTS

I'd like to take this time to thank all the people who helped make this novel a reality. To my family, whose kind words and support have proven to be an essential asset throughout my entire life; to Sarah and Geoff, whose advice and creative insights helped shape the finer points of this tale; to Rob, without whom the science in this sci-fi novel would not be nearly as accurate; to James, my friend of twenty-four years, who always believed in the dream, even when I didn't; to Dustin, Dan, Leslye, Brad, and Valerie for their encouragement; to Chase Nottingham, my editor and wordsmith, whose meticulous work kept me humble; and to everyone else whose name I left out. Thank you all for everything.

Here's to the beginning.

CONTENTS

PART I

A scientific man ought to have no wishes, no affections—a mere heart of stone.
–Charles Darwin

The future belongs to the few of us still willing to get our hands dirty.
–Roland Tiangco

It worked!
–Robert Oppenheimer, father of the atomic bomb

1

Documents of Historical, Scientific, and Cultural Significance
Play Audio Transmission File 021
Recorded April 19, 2157

CARTWRIGHT: *This is Lieutenant Colonel Felix Cartwright. It's been a week since my last transmission and two months since the day we found the city…the day the world fell apart. If anyone can hear this, please respond.*

If you're out there, no doubt you know about the gas. You might think you're all that's left. But if you're receiving this, let me assure you, you are not alone. There are people here. Hundreds, in fact, and for now, we're safe. If you can make it here, you will be, too.

The city's a few miles underground, not far from El Rico Air Force Base. That's where my people came from. As always, the coordi-

nates are attached. If anyone gets this, please respond. Let us know you're there...that you're still alive.

End Audio File

April 14, 2339
Maternity District

MILES BELOW THE SURFACE OF THE EARTH, deep within the walls of the last human city, a little boy named Terry played quietly with his sister in a small two-bedroom apartment.

Today was his very first birthday. He was turning seven.

"What's a birthday?" his sister Janice asked, tugging at his shirt. She was only four years old and had recently taken to following her big brother everywhere he went. "What does it mean?"

Terry smiled, eager to explain. "Mom says when you turn seven, you get a birthday. It means you grow up and get to start school. It's a pretty big deal."

"When will I get a birthday?"

"You're only four, so you have to wait."

"I wish I was seven," she said softly, her thin black hair hanging over her eyes. "I want to go with you."

He got to his feet and began putting the toy blocks away. They had built a castle together on the floor, but

Mother would yell if they left a mess. "I'll tell you all about it when I get home. I promise, okay?"

"Okay!" she said cheerily and proceeded to help.

Right at that moment, the speaker next to the door let out a soft chime, followed by their mother's voice. "Downstairs, children," she said. "Hurry up now."

Terry took his sister's hand. "Come on, Jan," he said.

She frowned, squeezing his fingers. "Okay."

They arrived downstairs, their mother nowhere to be found.

"She's in the kitchen," Janice said, pointing at the farthest wall. "See the light-box?"

Terry looked at the locator board, although his sister's name for it worked just as well. It was a map of the entire apartment, with small lights going on and off in different colors depending on which person was in which room. *There's us*, he thought, *green for me and blue for Janice, and there's Mother in red*. Terry never understood why they needed something like that because of how small the apartment was, but every family got one, or so Mother had said.

As he entered the kitchen, his mother stood at the far counter sorting through some data on her pad. "What's that?" he asked.

"Something for work," she said. She tapped the front of the pad and placed it in her bag. "Come on, Terrance, we've got to get you ready and out the door. Today's your first day, after all, and we have to make a good impression."

"When will he be back?" asked Janice.

"Hurry up. Let's go, Terrance," she said, ignoring the question. She grabbed his hand and pulled him along. "We have about twenty minutes to get all the way to the education district. Hardly enough time at all." Her voice was sour. He had noticed it more and more lately, as the weeks went on, ever since a few months ago when that man from the school came to visit. His name was Mr. Huxley, one of the few men who Terry ever had the chance to talk to, and from the way Mother acted—she was so agitated—he must have been important.

"Terrance," his mother's voice pulled him back. "Stop moping and let's go."

Janice ran and hugged him, wrapping her little arms as far around him as she could. "Love you," she said.

"Love you, too."

"Bye," she said, shyly.

He kissed her forehead and walked to the door where his mother stood talking with the babysitter, Ms. Cartwright. "I'll only be a few hours," Mother said. "If it takes any longer, I'll message you."

"Don't worry about a thing, Mara," Ms. Cartwright assured her. "You take all the time you need."

Mother turned to him. "There you are," she said, taking his hand. "Come on, or we'll be late."

As they left the apartment, Mother's hand tugging him along, Terry tried to imagine what might happen at school today. Would it be like his home lessons? Would he be behind the other children, or was everything new? He enjoyed learning, but there was still a chance the school might be too hard for him. What would he do? Mother had taught him some things, like algebra and English, but who knew how far along the other kids were by now?

Terry walked quietly down the overcrowded corridors with an empty, troubled head. He hated this part of the district. So many people on the move, brushing against him, like clothes in an overstuffed closet.

He raised his head, nearly running into a woman and her baby. She had wrapped the child in a green and brown cloth, securing it against her chest. "Excuse me," he said, but the lady ignored him.

His mother paused and looked around. "Terrance, what are you doing? I'm over here," she said, spotting him.

"Sorry."

They waited together for the train, which was running a few minutes behind today.

"I wish they'd hurry up," said a nearby lady. She was young, about fifteen years old. "Do you think it's because of the outbreak?"

"Of course," said a much older woman. "Some of the trains are busy carrying contractors to the slums to patch the walls. It slows the others down because now they have to make more stops."

"I heard fourteen workers died. Is it true?"

"You know how the gas is," she said. "It's very quick. Thank God for the quarantine barriers."

Suddenly, there was a loud smashing sound, followed by

three long beeps. It echoed through the platform for a moment, vibrating along the walls until it was gone. Terry flinched, squeezing his mother's hand.

"Ouch," she said. "Terrance, relax."

"But the sound," he said.

"It's the contractors over there." She pointed to the other side of the tracks, far away from them. It took a moment for Terry to spot them, but once he did, it felt obvious. Four of them stood together. Their clothes were orange, with no clear distinction between their shirts and their pants, and on each of their heads was a solid red plastic hat. Three of them were holding tools, huddled against a distant wall. They were reaching inside of it, exchanging tools every once in a while, until eventually the fourth one called them to back away. As they made some room, steam rose from the hole, with a puddle of dark liquid forming at the base. The fourth contractor handled a machine several feet from the others, which had three legs and rose to his chest. He waved the other four to stand near him and pressed the pad on the machine. Together, the contractors watched as the device flashed a series of small bright lights. It only lasted a few seconds. Once it was over, they gathered close to the wall again and resumed their work.

"What are they doing?" Terry asked.

His mother looked down at him. "What? Oh, they're fixing the wall, that's all."

"Why?" he asked.

"Probably because there was a shift last night. Remember when the ground shook?"

Yeah, I remember, he thought. *It woke me up.* "So they're fixing it?"

"Yes, right." She sighed and looked around. "Where is that damned train?"

Terry tugged on her hand. "That lady over there said it's late because of the gas."

His mother looked at him. "What did you say?"

"The lady…the one right there." He pointed to the younger girl a few feet away. "She said the gas came, so that's why the trains are slow. It's because of the slums." He paused a minute. "No, wait. It's because they're *going* to the slums."

His mother stared at the girl, turning back to the tracks and saying nothing.

"Mother?" he said.

"Be quiet for a moment, Terrance."

Terry wanted to ask her what was wrong, or if he had done anything to upset her, but he knew when to stay silent. So he left it alone like she wanted. Just like a good little boy.

The sound of the arriving train filled the platform with such horrific noise that it made Terry's ears hurt. The train, still vibrating as he stepped onboard, felt like it was alive.

After a short moment, the doors closed. The train was moving.

Terry didn't know if the shaking was normal or not. Mother had taken him up to the medical wards on this train once when he was younger, but never again after that. He didn't remember much about it, except that he liked it. The medical wards were pretty close to where he lived, a few stops before the labs, and several stops before the education district. After that, the train ran through Pepper Plaza, then the food farms and Housing Districts 04 through 07 and finally the outer ring factories and the farms. As Terry stared at the route map on the side of the train wall, memorizing what he could of it, he tried to imagine all the places he could go and the things he might see. What kind of shops did the shopping plaza have, for example, and what was it like to work on the farms? Maybe one day he could go and find out for himself—ride the train all day to see everything there was to see. Boy, wouldn't that be something?

"Departure call: 22-10, education district," erupted the com in its monotone voice. It took only a moment before the train began to slow.

"That's us. Come on," said Mother. She grasped his hand, pulling him through the doors before they were fully opened.

Almost to the school, Terry thought. He felt warm suddenly. Was he getting nervous? And why now? He'd known about this forever, and it was only hitting him *now*?

He kept taking shorter breaths. He wanted to pull away and return home, but Mother's grasp was tight and firm, and the closer they got to the only major building in the area, the tighter and firmer it became.

Now that he was there, now that the time had finally come, a dozen questions ran through Terry's mind. Would the other kids like him? What if he wasn't as smart as everyone else? Would they make fun of him? He had no idea what to expect.

Terry swallowed, the lump in his throat nearly choking him.

An older man stood at the gate of the school's entrance. He dressed in an outfit that didn't resemble any of the clothes in Terry's district or even on the trains. A gray uniform—the color of the pavement, the walls, and the streets—matched his silver hair to the point where it was difficult to tell where one ended and the other began. "Ah," he said. "Mara, I see you've brought another student. I was wondering when we'd meet the next one. Glad to see you're still producing. It's been, what? Five or six years? Something like that, I think."

"Yes, thank you, this is Terrance," said Mother quickly. "I was told there would be an escort." She paused, glancing over the man and through the windows. "Where's Bishop? He assured me he'd be here for this."

"The *colonel*," he corrected, "is in his office, and the boy is to be taken directly to him as soon as I have registered his arrival."

She let out a frustrated sigh. "He was supposed to meet me at the gate for this, himself. I wanted to talk to him about a few things."

"What's wrong?" Terry asked.

She looked down at him. "Oh, it's nothing, don't worry. You have to go inside now, that's all."

"You're not coming in?"

"I'm afraid not," said the man. "She's not permitted."

"It's alright," Mother said, cupping her hand over his cheek. "They'll take care of you in there."

But it's just school, Terry thought. "I'll see you tonight, though, right?"

She bent down and embraced him tightly, more than she had in a long time. He couldn't help but relax. "I'm sorry, Terrance. Please be careful up there. I know you don't understand it now, but you will eventually. Everything will be fine." She rose, releasing his hand for the first time since they left the train. "So that's it?" Mother said to the man.

"Yes, ma'am."

"Good." She turned and walked away, pausing a moment as she reached the corner and continued until she was out of sight.

The man pulled out a board with a piece of paper on it. "When you go through here, head straight to the back of the hall. A guard there will take you to see Colonel Bishop. Just do what they say and answer everything with either 'Yes, sir' or 'No, sir,' and you'll be fine. Understand?"

Terry didn't understand, but he nodded anyway.

The man pushed open the door with his arm and leg, holding it there and waiting. "Right through here you go," he said.

Terry entered, reluctantly, and the door closed quickly behind him.

The building, full of the same metal and shades of brown and gray that held together the rest of the city, rose higher than any other building Terry had ever been in. Around the room, perched walkways circled the walls, cluttered with doors and hallways that branched off into unknown regions. Along the walkways, dozens of people walked back and forth as busily as they had in the train station. More importantly, Terry quickly realized, most of them were men.

For so long, the only men he had seen were the maintenance workers who came and went or the occasional teacher who visited the children when they were nearing their birthdays. It was so rare to see any men at all, especially in such great numbers. *Maybe they're all teachers*, he thought. They weren't dressed like the workers: white coats and some with brown jackets—thick jackets with laced boots and bodies as stiff as the walls. Maybe that was what teachers wore. How could he know? He had never met one besides Mr. Huxley, and that was months ago.

"Well, don't just stand there, gawking," said a voice from the other end of the room. It was another man, dressed the same as the others. "Go on in through here." He pointed to another door, smaller than the one Terry had entered from. "Everyone today gets to meet the colonel. Go on now. Hurry up. You don't want to keep him waiting."

Terry did as the man said and stepped through the

doorway, his footsteps clanking against the hard metal floor, echoing through what sounded like the entire building.

"Well, come in, why don't you?" came a voice from inside.

Terry stepped cautiously into the room, which was much nicer than the entranceway. It was clean, at least compared to some of the other places Terry had been, including his own home. The walls held several shelves, none of which lacked for any company of things; various ornaments caught Terry's eye, like the little see-through globe on the shelf nearest to the door, which held a picture of a woman's face inside, although some of it was faded and hard to make out. There was also a crack in it. What purpose could such a thing have? Terry couldn't begin to guess. Next to it lay a frame with a small, round piece of metal inside of it. An inscription below the glass read, "U.S. Silver Dollar, circa 2064." Terry could easily read the words, but he didn't understand them. What was this thing? And why was it so important that it needed to be placed on a shelf for everyone to look at?

"I said come in," said Bishop abruptly. He sat at the far end of the room behind a large brown desk. Terry had forgotten he was even there. "I didn't mean for you to stop at the door. Come over here."

Terry hurried closer, stopping a few feet in front of the desk.

"I'm Colonel Bishop. You must be Terrance," said the man. "I've been wondering when you were going to show up." He wore a pair of thin glasses and had one of the larger pads in his hand. "Already seven. Imagine that."

"Yes, sir," Terry said, remembering the doorman's words.

The colonel was a stout man, a little wider than the others. He was older, too, Terry guessed. He may have been tall, but it was difficult to tell without seeing his whole body. "I expect you're hoping to begin your classes now," said Bishop.

"Yes, sir," he said.

"You say that, but you don't really know what you're saying yes to, do you?"

The question seemed more like a statement, so Terry didn't answer. He only stood there. Who was this man? Is this how school was supposed to be?

"Terrance, let me ask you something," said the colonel, taking a moment. "Did your mother tell you anything about this program you're going into?"

Terry thought about the question for a moment. "Um, she said you come to school on your birthday," he said. "And that it's just like it is at home, except there's more kids like me."

Colonel Bishop blinked. "That's right, I suppose. What else did she say?"

"That when it was over, I get to go back home," he said.

"And when did she say that was?"

Terry didn't answer.

Colonel Bishop cocked an eyebrow. "Well? Didn't she say?"

"No, sir," muttered Terry.

The man behind the desk started chuckling. "So you don't know how long you're here for?"

"No, sir."

Colonel Bishop set the pad in his hand down. "Son, you're here for the next ten years."

A sudden rush swelled up in Terry's chest and face. What was Bishop talking about? Of course Terry was going home. He couldn't stay here. "But I promised my sister I'd be home today," he said. "I have to go back."

"Too bad," said the colonel. "Your Mother really did you a disservice by not telling you. But don't worry. We just have to get you started." He tapped the pad on his desk, and the door opened. A cluster of footsteps filled the hall before two large men appeared, each wearing the same brown coats as the rest. "Well, that was fast," he said.

One of the men saluted. "Yes, sir. No crying with the last one. Took her right to her room without incident."

Terry wanted to ask who *the last one* was, and why it should be a good thing that she didn't cry. Did other kids cry when they came to this school? What kind of place *was* this?

"Well, hopefully Terrence here will do the same," said Bishop. He looked at Terry. "Right? You're not going to give us any trouble, are you?"

Terry didn't know what to do or what to say. All he

could think about was getting far away from here. He didn't want to go with the men. He didn't want to behave. All he wanted to do was go home.

But he couldn't, not anymore. He was here in this place with nowhere to go. No way out. He wanted to scream, to yell at the man behind the desk and his two friends, and tell them about how stupid it was for them to do what they were doing.

He opened his mouth to explain, to scream as loud as he could that he wouldn't go. But in that moment, the memory of the doorman came back to him, and instead of yelling, he repeated the words he'd been told before. "No, sir," he said softly.

Bishop smiled, nodding at the two men in the doorway. "Exactly what I like to hear."

April 14, 2339
The Academy, Central

"STICK OUT YOUR ARM," said the nurse.

The needle pierced Terry's skin, and he flinched. The nurse filled a small vial of his blood. "What's it for?" he asked.

"Tests," the nurse said, detaching the vial and replacing it with another. Once it was full, she handed the vials to a young man. "Mark, hurry and label these. Put them with the rest."

"Yes, ma'am," said Mark. He picked up the vials, and disappeared into the back room.

"What kind of tests?" Terry asked.

"Easy, honey," she said. "We do it for every new student."

"But why?" he asked.

"Because we just *do*," the nurse said plainly. "Now why don't you go tell the boys in the hall that you're ready, okay? We're all done here."

Terry nodded and went to the door. He opened it to find the same two men who brought him here still standing in silence. Had they been waiting for him this entire time?

"Finished?" one of them asked.

"I think so," Terry said.

When it was time for sleep, they led him to a room with two beds. "This is your room," one of the men said.

"When can I go home?" Terry asked.

But there was no answer, only a closed door. They had left him alone. All alone for the first time since he awoke that morning and saw his sister and—

Janice. She must be so confused right now, wondering where he was, why he never came home. *She'll cry*, he thought. *Cry and plead with Mother until she falls asleep or passes out because that's how she is. She's so little, and now she's alone. Sure, she's got Mother, but when was that ever enough?*

Suddenly there was a loud flushing sound. It came from

the other side of the room, behind a wall with an open door where a light shone. Terry walked to the door, staring at the knob, waiting. After a moment, the knob turned and another boy stepped through.

He was taller than Terry, his chin a little thicker. He had short black hair and looked as surprised as Terry to find another person on the other side of the door. "Uh, hi," he muttered. "What are you doing in my room?"

Terry looked around at the two beds. He felt like an idiot for not seeing them both before. One had a bag at the end of it, with the sheets and blanket already laid out. Of course somebody was already there. How could he not have noticed? "They told me this was my room."

"Oh, I thought it was all for me."

"Sorry," said Terry.

"That's okay," said the boy as he walked to the side of his bed and sat. "To be honest, I was getting kind of bored. All the other kids got roommates, but they stuck me in here all by myself with nothing to do."

"What other kids?" asked Terry.

"You know, the other students. Didn't you see them?"

Terry sat on his bed. "No, you're the first kid I've seen all day."

"Really?" asked John. "There's about twenty of us, I think. Most got here early this morning. You're kinda late."

"Am I the last one?" asked Terry. He didn't like being late.

"Dunno," said the boy, shrugging. "They stuck me in

here hours ago, and sent the rest to their own rooms. Anyway, I'm John."

"I'm Terry," he said. "How long do we have to stay here? They told me it was ten years. Is it for real?"

John nodded. "Until you're seventeen."

Terry stared at the floor.

"How long did you think it was?"

"I thought I'd be back by the end of the day."

John didn't say anything.

"Why didn't my mother tell me?"

"Maybe she didn't want to," John said.

Terry gripped the edge of his bed with his hand, squeezing it. "Well, she should've said something. Now my sister thinks I'm coming back, and I'm not. She's going to think I left her alone."

"You have a sister?"

"Yeah," nodded Terry. "Janice. She's four."

"I never had a sister," said John. "Just an older brother. He graduated from the academy last year. When he came home, I got to meet him for the first time, and he told me all about this place."

"You're lucky," muttered Terry.

"Lucky?"

"Yeah, you knew before you got here."

"I guess," said John, his voice a little softer. "But I only got to know my brother for a year. I won't see him again until I'm seventeen. You got to spend four whole years with your sister. That's lucky."

"Sorry," said Terry. Of course John didn't think he was lucky. He was probably hurting as much as Terry.

"It's okay," said John. "And happy birthday, by the way."

"Thanks," said Terry. "Is it yours today, too?"

"Sure is. Me, you, and everyone else in our class."

"Really?" asked Terry. "Seems like a lot of birthdays."

John paused for a moment. "Actually, yeah, it kind of is."

"What do you mean?"

"My brother told me before I got here everyone starts school on their birthday. But he also said when you get here, your class is already going on, because different kids are born at different times. The classes are based on what time of the year you're born in."

"So?"

"So if all of us have birthdays today, isn't it kind of weird?"

Terry shrugged. "All my mother said about birthdays was you went to school on them."

"It's weird, though," insisted John. "My brother said kids get here at different times, not all at once. It doesn't make any sense if we're all on the same day, does it?"

Terry thought about this for a moment. "Maybe a lot of mothers just had babies all at the same time. Maybe our class is smaller than the other ones."

"So many maybes."

Terry sighed and leaned back against the wall. His feet

dangled off the side of the bed. "What happens tomorrow?"

"Orientation," John said. "And we start our classes. That's what they told me earlier."

"Nobody told me anything," said Terry.

"Probably because you were late," said John. "When we got here, they lined us all up and explained it. Tomorrow's orientation, then our first class."

"Anything else?" asked Terry.

"Dinner," said John, pointing to a clock next to his bed. "Ten more minutes until we eat."

2

**Documents of Historical, Scientific, and
   Cultural Significance
Play Audio File 109
Subtitled: Re: Cheer Up
To: SE_Pepper
Recorded February 20, 2174**

*CARTWRIGHT: I wish I shared your optimism, Sasha. I really
do. But the sad truth of the matter is that there is no going back. We've
spent the last two decades trying to figure out a way to fix what's
happened, to pull ourselves out of this tomb, but we still have nothing
to show for it.*

   *We need to accept our fate. We're never leaving this city. It's been
decades since the gas came, but nothing's changed. There's still no
word from the outside, no responses to the hundreds of transmissions*

I've sent out into the void. The six hundred surviving humans in this cave of a city are all that's left. No one else is out there. No one here is leaving. As far as our species goes, this is it. We're at the end of the line. The planet's dead and rotting, and the rest of us are waiting in the grave.

End Audio File

April 14, 2339
Central

Mara boarded the platform and waited for the train to arrive. Now that Terrance had been dropped off, it was on to the mothers' lounge. A few minutes on the A line and she'd be there. *Can't be fast enough*, she thought.

Metal clanked against the rails, echoing through the station, followed by a veil of dust that seemed to cover everything. It was coming from a set of vents nestled high above the train line. A group of contractors dangled nearby like puppets on strings, shouting and laughing as they worked. One of them kept hitting the side of the vent with his wrench, scattering wave after wave of dust with each loud smack.

Everyone called it the purifying season, though it was hardly a season at all—more like a month of air purification coupled with manual routine maintenance on several of the major systems. The whole process used to only take a week or two, but thanks to recent problems in other parts of the city, including an ongoing quarantine over in the slums, the contractors were spread pretty thin.

Still, the purifying season had its silver lining. Most of the mothers rarely had a chance to meet any men, especially when it came to the contractors and soldiers, who spent the bulk of their time in Central. But with the annual repairs came potential contracts. The season didn't last very long, so if a mother didn't pick a sponsor now, it meant she'd have to file for one later through the official channels, and nobody wanted to do that. It might take anywhere from three to six months, all with the possibility of a rejection letter. If a mother met a sponsor in person, it became much easier to persuade him to sign his seed away.

If a mother got lucky enough to land one of the level-9 contractors, a high ranking soldier, or (God-willing) a council member, it could change everything. A contract like that meant prestige and higher living, but more importantly, it meant a seed with a future, not just some other worker in the factories.

Mara always had a knack for the job, picking and choosing the right sponsor for the best contract. All of her children came from the highest quality donors—officers, scientists, and even a council member or two—something many of the other, more inexperienced mothers aspired toward.

But then, everyone had always called her special.

When she was still new to motherhood, the doctors told her about a new birthing standard called *Archer's Genetic Profile*. The AGP worked like a points system, ranking genetic traits and compiling them into an overall score. This score not only determined the candidate's eligibility to become a mother, but also how many children they were allowed to produce. Depending on a woman's genes, the AGP could give them everything—decent pay and housing, access to Central, and above all, respect. The system functioned solely to keep humanity alive, and the mothers were its lifeblood. They were the only ones allowed to reproduce —a harsh but necessary rule, given the need for genetic diversity.

Mara became a mother when she was fifteen. She still remembered her first time with a sponsor, before she had a grasp on the fundamentals—the expressions of sex and the grinding rhythm of warmth and flesh. The instructors simply told her to lie there because the veteran sponsor would know exactly how it needed to be done. It was his job, after all.

She remembered pain, forceful and unpleasant— nothing like it is now. And there were people watching— scientists with clipboards who claimed it was for the betterment of mankind, rather than what she suspected all along: they wanted a show to re-imagine later when the lights went out.

But now she and the world were both a bit older, and the circumstances had changed for each of them. That scared little girl on the table had since vanished, replaced by someone else—a veteran mother who raised twelve children.

Most of Mara's boys had gone on to be contractors, while a few others were selected for the medical field. After graduating the academy, the boys underwent an additional four years of schooling, covering anything from engineering, medicine, agriculture, military science, and construction. Afterwards, they were placed into positions that reflected their personal abilities and aptitudes. Each of Mara's males had displayed impressive results. Her daughters, on the other hand, had all become mothers—the cost of having such wonderful genes.

There was never a choice, not for any of them. Nothing in this world revolved around choice. If the government said a boy would be a contractor, that was the way it went. If the administration wanted a girl to be a mother, she became one. There was no getting around it.

The train arrived, clearing the tunnel of dust as it sent gusts of wind through the platform. Mara climbed aboard, taking a seat near the back. Her apartment would be so empty now that her son was gone. *Gone forever,* she thought. *I doubt I'll ever see him again.* She scoffed at her own arrogance. *Why would he even want to see me? I'm horrible.*

But maybe it was all for the best. The program was in full effect now, and the children had to do their part.

It had only been eight years since she learned about a new initiative, a different approach to the way people looked at the world. "The city's falling part, but it doesn't have to be this way," Colonel Bishop, then a major, had told her. "We can save our children from all of this. We can make a better world. We just need mothers like you." At first she embraced the idea. Save the human race—what better calling could a mother have?

But that was then, back before they started using her womb as a glorified incubator for their experiments. Back before the seven stillborn infants they pulled from her body.

And then Terrence. Yes, he was the lucky one, the one who somehow managed to pull through and live. But Mara knew the cost of that—the price her son would pay when he eventually came of age. When he inevitably died, his fate would be the same as the billions who came before— victims of the gas...of Variant.

Mara had so many regrets, but helping Bishop had to be the worst. Despite all the seductive words and promises, all they'd really wanted was a human incubator—some- thing to practice on until they got the formula right. She had gone along with it, believing in the possibility of saving humanity, but after witnessing Variant's wrath firsthand, such a prospect seemed impossible. After all, being born was one thing. Surviving direct exposure to the most toxic gas on the planet was something else entirely. Could little Terrance actually live through that? Or would he perish like all the rest?

She trembled at the thought.

Mara was forty-two years old, an age when most

mothers began to think about their retirement—sneak away from the maternity district to find another, less restricted section of the city where it didn't matter who a person bedded, whether they matched a certain genetic profile or not, because everyone went there for a reason, and no one wanted to talk about the *why*.

Maybe that was what she would do someday, when the fineness of her skin had dried itself to lines, and her hair grew thin and lost the shape of youth. Maybe in that distant moment, she could tell stories of a life that wasn't hers, and the people there would listen and believe it. She'd tell them of a girl who never was a mother, never drowned herself in thoughts of dying boys becoming men.

As USUAL, the accounts clerk was taking an extended amount of time trying to do what should have taken no time at all, but thanks to the naturally unbiased standardized tests that determined a person's lot in life, the little fool was stationed at this desk on this day, most likely by the council—at the suggestion of Colonel Bishop, no doubt—to do nothing other than annoy and pester anyone and everyone who walked through the door, namely Mara.

She sighed inwardly as the lanky, bookish man-child swiped desperately on his pad. "How long is this going to take, Mr...?"

"Rolstien, ma'am," he said, almost hesitantly. "I've got your documents right here. Miss Echols, right?"

"Yes, that's me," she said, pressing the "Accept" button on her pad. The files loaded instantly.

"Sorry about the wait, Miss Echols," said the boy.

Obviously new, she thought. *He's probably fresh out of training, maybe even still enrolled. He'll probably get replaced in a few days.* After all, she never encountered the same clerk more than a few times. They eventually got transferred, one after the other. On to bigger and better desks with bigger and better paperwork. *What a dull life*, she thought. "Thank you, Mr. Rolstien, I suppose, but try to be a little faster next time, will you?"

"Y-yes ma'am," he answered. "I'm sorry."

She turned away, leaving the poor boy with the nagging question of whether or not he pissed off the wrong person. *Ah, to be young again.*

At the end of the nearby hall lay her destination, the mother's lounge. It usually teemed with the new inductees, an occasional veteran among them, though that wasn't always the case. They held the meetings here—discussions and debates over which of them had developed the better method. Naturally, the youngest were the most enthusiastic, never in short supply of smiles and compliments.

Mara took a seat on one of the green chairs. There were several tables, dozens of seats, and a podium. Potted plants were scattered throughout the atrium, brought in from the botanical gardens and maintained by local volunteers—rejected applicants and retirees, mostly. But the plants made the air a little sweeter than it should have been, and most would say they enjoyed it.

The truth was that the lounge was always meant to be elegant, its seats lined with different colors—green, blue, purple, red—hardly a hint of the gray murk that infested the rest of the city. There was a reason the older mothers grew tired of this place—it reminded them of all the things they could never have, an echo of another life outside the closed off silver walls of their hidden metropolis.

The whole thing gave Mara a headache.

"Oh, Mara!" called a voice from across the room. "Happy Mother's Day! I wasn't sure you were coming."

"Hello, Rayne."

"Bring your documents?" She said as she scurried over.

"Of course." Mara pushed the pad across the table. "This isn't my first time, you know."

"Oh, come on." She snorted. "You know I'm only teasing." She took the pad and sorted through its files, her eyes widening a bit as she found the right one. "So…this is him?" She showed the picture to Mara, revealing a smiling young boy with dirty blond hair and green eyes. Short for his age. Quick to learn. Quiet. Her son. "He looks quite handsome, Mara. Oh, you always make the prettiest babies!"

"His name is Terrance," she said.

"Terrance? That's a nice name. Was he a good boy? I'm sure he was! Oh, but you've still got the girl, too, right?

Has she been asking about him? Seems like she would be. Oh, it's always so hard on them when they're separated, but that's the way it works, right? Give them attachments when they're young so they develop into perfect law-abiding citizens."

"Was there something you needed, Rayne? I have a bit of a headache right now and—"

"Oh!" she exclaimed. "Did you hear about the quarantine? I can't believe all those poor people died! Honestly, you'd think the contractors could do a better job insulating the city, but I suppose mistakes happen when you're way out in the slums like that. Imagine living that far from Central. It's no wonder the maintenance crews barely make it out there."

"If you say so," said Mara.

"Anyway, I need to get to my table. Just wanted to swing by and say hello to my old friend." She giggled and slid the pad back to Mara. "Can you believe it's already been seven years? Just think, both our boys are finally together, going to school. Isn't it wonderful? Oh, but I'll leave you to it. Feel better, okay? And let's get together sometime soon. It's been so *long*."

She left smiling, heading back to her table. Poor, annoying Rayne. The woman was always so happy—so full of that tiring, high-pitched banter that never seemed to end. She and Mara had been close once, a long time ago before the program.

Back when Mara took the AGP tests, she and several

mothers were placed into a special bracket of mothers. Each of these women had scored within the tenth percentile, which meant they had first rights to all sponsors and were allowed to produce as many children as they wanted. Mara scored higher than all the other mothers in her age group. Rayne, who was only a few months younger, scored second. A woman's AGP score became her shield, her authority. A golden ticket.

A few years later, a young officer named Bishop came to them with a request. When he asked to run his tests, nobody argued. When the injections began, they welcomed them. Embryos, part human and part Variant, became the building blocks of the future. "We're making a better world," Bishop told them.

Months later, a group of soldiers and doctors took the mothers to an exclusive wing of the hospital and had several of their eggs extracted. The eggs would be frozen for safekeeping.

"No more babies," Bishop had explained. "Not until it's time."

"Why?" Mara had asked.

"We need you ready at a moment's notice. You can't be pregnant when the time comes."

"How long will it be?"

"Not long," he had said. "Maybe a year. Two at the most."

So they waited.

It took three years, but eventually a man came to

Mara's door and told her the day had come at last. Mara and Rayne, along with several other women of varying ages, were brought to the hospital and implanted with the seeds of strangers. They had no idea who the fathers were, nor would they ever know.

Mara's stomach turned at the memory. *Why did it have to be me?* She pushed the thought out of her mind.

The lights dimmed after a moment. Mara leaned back in her cushioned chair, trying to relax. The ceremony was about to start. The matron would begin with a standard introduction, which would immediately be followed by opening and closing contracts. Today, Mara would present her closing contract to the others for review. Today, she would tell them about her son. Not everything, of course, because certain things surrounding him were classified, but she would give them the fodder they wanted—tell them stories and reflections of a boy she didn't really know, couldn't know—and it would be a lie.

A moment passed, and the matron Ava Long stood before the auditorium of whispering youths. She was eloquent, her silver-lined curls bobbing as she stepped toward the microphone. How long had it been since this woman birthed a child of her own?

"Today we meet again," Ava said. Her voice was just above a whisper. "Some of you are here for the first time. Others are nearing their last. But here we've gathered, not an empty seat among us. All of you with your busy lives and schedules and children, you've still found the time to convene together to discuss what really matters…the future of the human race. Because isn't that why we're here together now? To bring even more living and breathing *people* into this world so that things go on? And look at all of you, nearly three hundred, isn't it? I remember hearing stories from *my* mother of when there were only sixteen." She took a breath and smiled. "My, just look at how the world has *grown*."

3

Amber Project File Logs
Play Audio File 187
To: Ava_Long, William_Archer
Recorded February 12, 2327

BISHOP: We can't just sit around underground like a bunch of gophers, sticking our heads out every few decades to see if anything's changed. This city's falling apart. It seems like every morning I'm getting briefed about another riot, a gas leak, some broken maintenance systems, or a personnel shortage. I'm tired of it. Human beings were never meant to live in a bottle forever.

I'm giving Archer the go ahead for phase one. It's about time we got the ball rolling on this project. Ava, I'm requesting a list of candidates—send me your best mothers. The children will need to be at the peak of what we can manufacture, which means following the AGP to the letter—no exceptions or special treatment. Archer, let me know what else you need to finish your work. I'll try to send you some extra help, at least what I can spare, but it won't be much. I'm still running a school after all.

End Audio File

April 15, 2339
The Academy, Central

The auditorium was the biggest room Terry had ever seen. The walls, comprised mostly of large white tiles, stretched up a dozen feet. Blue mats covered most of the floor, except for the areas closest to the walls. The only piece of furniture was a single podium, which sat a few feet away, close to the entrance.

Terry stood beside John near the center of the room, facing the podium. They were standing about, all the boys and girls, at least a few dozen. Several men—soldiers, John had called them—stood motionless around the walls, facing the children. "Line up in rows of six," said one soldier. "Wait there and be quiet."

Wait for what? Terry wondered. None of the soldiers gave a reason, but Terry could tell it was important. With so many men in the room, it had to be.

"Hey," whispered John. "Whatcha think? Maybe they'll tell us what's going on."

Terry shrugged. "I hope they tell us more about school or something."

"Yeah, one of the girls said that's what it's for."

"One of the girls?"

"There," he said, leaning and pointing down the line. "That one on the end."

Terry bent forward to look. There weren't very many girls in their group, so he spotted her easily. He noticed her skin right away—a golden shade of brown—and her shiny black hair hung gently from her head to her waist. She looked very serious—a narrow brow, her eyes focused and staring toward the door behind the podium.

"Her name's Mei," John said.

"What else did she say?" Terry asked.

"Not much. I only got to talk to her for a second or two when we were standing outside." John paused, looking around. "I think I hear something."

They both grew silent and listened. Sure enough, there was a rumbling sound, like doors slamming one after another in the distance. And it was getting louder.

"What is that?" asked one of the boys behind Terry.

But there was no time for an answer. Instead, the doors beyond the podium crashed open, and a line of soldiers entered. As they filed in from the outer hall, the soldiers took up positions surrounding the podium. They faced the children and slammed their feet against the floor. Their bodies were stiff, and their chests pressed out, with arms gripping both their sides. They looked like plastic toys.

Finally, one of the soldiers moved behind the podium and stepped up so he was above the rest. To Terry's surprise, it was the same man he'd met yesterday. Two streaks of gray ran through his dark brown hair. He wore a uniform that was similar to the other men, except it had brown in the places where the blue should be, and there were more pins on his chest and along his neckline. Colonel Bishop, the man in the gray suit had called him. He looked like an old memory.

Bishop stood quietly at the front, staring at them. A long hush of silence filled the room. It wasn't until the old man cleared his throat that Terry let himself relax.

"Listen up," Bishop shouted, his voice booming. "You're all here right now because it's the first day. Yesterday was a test run, just to make sure none of you were sick or half-dead. Lucky for us, you're all perfectly fine." He paused a moment, slowly looking from one side of the group to the other. Was he looking at each of them? Was he looking at Terry? "But make no mistake. We aren't here to coddle you. That was your mother's job, and she's not here anymore. All of that is over. Instead, you'll stand on your own two feet, fully capable of doing what needs to be done. By the time this is over, you *will* be better," he said. "The very best we can make you."

AFTER BISHOP'S SPEECH, a few other speakers talked about discipline and day-to-day expectations. When orientation finally concluded, the soldiers escorted the children to a classroom. The walk from the auditorium was shorter than Terry imagined—only a few hallways—but the soldiers kept stopping to reform the children's lines.

"Stay together," one of the soldiers said. "Everyone walks in two lines."

When the gaps between the children grew too wide, or if one of them accidentally tripped or swayed too much, the entire group had to be stopped and the lines reformed. "Halt halt halt," the soldier would say, holding up his fist. "Reform the ranks. The trainee has fallen out." Everyone would stop and look and wait until it was time to move again. By the time they reached the classroom, the group had stopped a total of twelve times.

"Hold," the soldier in the front said when they arrived. He held up his fist again.

Everyone waited quietly for a moment.

"Is that them?" asked a voice from inside the room.

"Yes sir," said the soldier.

"Well shit, bring them in already. I haven't got all day."

The soldier turned to face the children. "Fall out, quickly. Everyone inside."

The children scurried into the classroom. Terry stayed as close to John as he could, but the shuffling of so many bodies in such a small space caused him to get pushed aside. Before he knew it, Terry was at the back of the crowd.

"Hug the wall with your backsides," said the soldier. "Line up and face the middle. Hurry!"

Everyone moved as quickly as possible. Terry found a spot between a blonde girl with freckles and a chubby boy with dark hair. He'd learn their names later, if he could, but right now he had more important concerns.

"Sir, the trainees are ready," said the soldier. He was speaking to a man behind a desk on the other side of the room.

"Great. Now move out, so I can get on with it." Terry tried to see who was talking, but with so many soldiers in the middle of the classroom, it was impossible.

"Yes, sir," said the soldier. He held up his hand again, but this time he didn't make a fist. Instead, he pointed his fingers out and moved his entire arm in a circular motion. Without a word, the soldiers left the room.

"Finally," said the man behind the desk. "Talk about unnecessary." Terry couldn't help but look at the man's face. His eyes were narrow, surrounded by wrinkles and spots, and he was balding. Shorter than the soldiers, he had a thick gut on him, which made his shirt tight.

But after a moment, Terry's eyes moved to the man's right arm. It didn't quite look the same as the left one, he realized, although it was hard to tell because he wore long sleeves, keeping his right hand tucked inside his pocket. But there was something about the sleeve that drew Terry's eye more than anything else, a look that reminded him of home, of his room, of something familiar. And then he remembered: it looked thin and empty, like a shirt left hanging in the closet.

"Jesus," said the man, looking around the room. "You're all still babies."

He sighed and picked up a digital pen. "My name's Henry Nuber, and I'm your teacher." He made a few swipes with the pen on his desk, tapped it a few times, and his name appeared behind him on a translucent screen.

"I'll be your teacher for as long as you're in this school. It won't be easy," he said. "I'll tell you that right now, but if you do exactly what I say, you'll have a better time of it. Now, there are twenty-two of you in this room and twenty-two desks." He started writing with the pen, pausing briefly to stare at the children. "Well, what are you waiting for? Sit your asses down!" He shook his head. "I can't believe I agreed to do this."

John and Terry found each other near the front of the classroom and without a word sat in adjacent desks, Terry on the right and John on the left. Mei took the seat next to John, directly in front of the teacher.

Once everyone found their place, Nuber continued. "Since your curiosity will no doubt get the better of you, I'll go ahead and let the secret out now, so it saves me the trouble later." He jerked his right sleeve out of his pocket, revealing an absent hand. Using his shoulder, he waved the sleeve in the air. "As you can see, I'm missing something."

He gripped the sleeve with his left hand, and squeezed. "All the way up to my shoulder. It happened several years ago before any of you were born. I was working as a contractor and my team was sent to the surface to work on one of the riggies, which are basically power stations that cycle electricity all around the city. I got injured on the way back and lost the arm. It was careless, plain and simple. I was stupid. You all remember that, you hear? Carelessness can get you killed. The outside world is a *dangerous* place, full of a thousand new and frightening ways that can kill you. Trust me. My missing hand could write a thesis on the subject."

So that was it. Terry had noticed there was something wrong with his arm, but he never would have guessed the rest. He tried to imagine the story Nuber told, tried to put pictures to the words he was hearing. But the more he thought about it, the more afraid he became. Terry slouched down in his seat, gripping his right arm. *Why would he tell us that?* Terry thought. *What's wrong with him?*

"Let's move on," said Nuber, tapping his desk again. The screen behind him quickly changed. This time, instead of his name, a list appeared, covering the entire display. As Nuber tapped his desk, the screen scrolled on and on, and for a moment it seemed like it might never stop.

"This is our schedule," he said. "Pay attention." He scrolled to the top and zoomed in on the first line. *Modern History*, it read.

"This is your life now, what's on this list. Nothing else is going to matter. When you wake up in the morning, you'll come here. When you leave, you'll go to your dorms and study. There will be two hours of recreational activity every day, but the rest will be filled with this. Any questions?"

Everyone stared at the display, completely silent.

The old teacher sighed again. "I swear to God," he said. "Bunch of babies."

Nuber spent the rest of the day going over the lesson plan and summarizing everything about it. It was a day filled with introductions: modern history, mathematics, literature, geology, biology. Terry got to know them all.

"Modern history covers the past two hundred years, approximately," Nuber explained. "We'll spend most of our time touching on the events that led up to the Jolt, and then we'll talk about how our ancestors settled this happy little underground city.

"Mathematics is exactly what it sounds like, except I'm sure your mommies all covered the basics, so I'll save my breath. What *we'll* be studying will be a bit more advanced. The main focus will be geometry and, by the end of the year, physics.

"If you look in your desks, you'll find a pad with a list of books. The pads are filled with all your textbooks, along with several reading assignments, which will be automatically updated and downloaded onto your pads every time I send in a request. These aren't like the ones you had back home; they were made specifically for this class, which means you can't download just anything to them."

Terry opened the top of his desk and found the pad. It looked identical to the one Mother used for her work, except smaller. He pressed the power button at the top and watched as it came alive. Within a few seconds, he was sorting through a collection of textbooks and novels, moving from one to the next with a slide of a finger. *So many weird books*, he thought. *Argonautica, The Odyssey, The Method of Mechanical Theorems, The Red Badge of Courage*, and *Meditations*. He'd never heard of any of them. What was an *Argonautica*? He didn't have a clue. He could barely pronounce it. Was Mr. Nuber serious about this stuff?

"Next, we'll be discussing geology, which, for those of you still in diapers, is the study of rocks. If you haven't been paying attention for the last several years of your lives, you may not have noticed that we live underground and are therefore completely surrounded by rocks. Thus, it would *behoove* you boys and girls to learn as much as you can about them. Finally, there's biology, which is the study of living organisms, past and present. Mostly past."

There was a sudden knock at the classroom door. Nuber stopped lecturing and walked to it. After a brief exchange with whomever was on the other side, he turned toward the class and cleared his throat. "I have to step out for a moment," he said. "None of you are to move an inch until I get back. Do you understand? And don't say a word. If you do, I'll know. There are voice recorders in this room.

Now, go over the reading material until I get back. Or sit there and look stupid. I don't care. Just don't talk." He left and shut the door.

If ever Terry needed some kind of confirmation that school would be harder than his home lessons, this was it. Geology and biology? *Argonautica*? He didn't care about any of it. He only wanted to go home and sleep—run upstairs to his bed and collapse and forget this stupid dream about Colonel Bishop and Mr. Nuber and a school full of strangers and children and books he couldn't pronounce.

He closed his eyes for a moment and took a deep breath. *Relax. I have to relax or everyone will see.*

Something tapped his foot and he opened his eyes. It was John, kicking him and trying to get his attention. Terry looked with his best *what-do-you-want* face.

John stared at him for a moment, arching his brow. *You okay?* He mouthed.

Terry shrugged and nodded, hoping he was giving John the right response. He didn't want to lie to him, but there was no way to explain how he felt, not without words. He couldn't say he was trapped, or how he missed his sister, or that everything about this place was strange. All he could do was nod.

John returned the nod, but this time he did it with a smile. A wide smile, like he knew a joke but couldn't say it. What was so funny?

Suddenly, there was a giggle from the other side of

John. The sound was light, hard to hear, but it was close enough that it pulled him away.

That's Mei's voice. Terry leaned forward to see her. She was looking at John, and smiling, her face a little pink as she held her palm against her mouth. Mei shook her head, still grinning.

John's smile turned into a snort as he covered his face with both hands. When he finally removed them, he was biting his lower lip and crossing his eyes, making an awkward, silly face.

Another boy snickered behind Terry, followed by another. Finally there were several. Before long, it didn't even matter that John had stopped making the face or what the joke had been in the first place. The laughter had become contagious, trailing through the room, jumping from one child to the next. By now it was clear there was no real joke, that there never had been one, except for the thing inside each of their heads, the one they made for themselves.

As Terry turned to look at them, he felt his body relax. He looked at John and Mei, at each of their smiling faces. He watched as they laughed at nothing in particular, at the simple idea of it all.

And then, despite himself, Terry smiled, too.

April 15, 2339

The Academy, Central

MARA SAT QUIETLY in Bishop's office, waiting for him to show. He'd called her in for a last minute appointment but didn't give the reason.

Naturally, this irritated her, but she knew better than to show it. *Sit still and wait,* she thought. *Everything in time.* She blinked her dry eyes a few times and swallowed. It had been a long week with all the running back and forth to Central, submitting her closing contract to the mothers, and now this. If only she'd been born a man, none of this would be happening.

Mara glanced around the office at the display cases on the walls and the artifacts they contained. After years of coming here, she'd memorized most of the trinkets in the colonel's exhibit. In the decades she'd known him, his fascination with the old world had only grown. So, too, had this collection.

There was a time decades ago, when she'd been impressed by all of this, when she'd cooed and swooned over Central's rising star. His ideals, his dreams—every convincing word. The whole thing drew her in.

But no longer. The two barely spoke now and never how they used to. There were no private flirtations, no passionate nights of whispered possibilities. She let go of that a long time ago.

Besides, Mara was middle aged, and scandals were for the young.

The office door suddenly opened, and Colonel Bishop stepped inside. "Hope I didn't keep you waiting, Miss Echols." Bishop's voice had a hint of a joke in it.

"A little over an hour," Mara answered. "You'll have to do better than that if you want to get a reaction."

He shut the door. "I'm not sure I know what you mean."

"Of course not. Now tell me, James, is there a reason behind this, or did you simply miss seeing me?"

Bishop eased his way to the desk, far from the door, and calmly took his seat. "Of course there's a reason," he said. "I promised you a meeting, and this is it."

Mara stared at him. "You mean the one we were supposed to have when I dropped off my son? You realized that was supposed to happen yesterday. Are you going to apologize for making me look like a fool?"

He clasped his hands. "I'm truly sorry, Miss Echols. Please forgive my rudeness."

"No," she said, turning her nose away.

"Please?" he begged.

She shook her head. "Nope."

He chuckled. "Well, I tried."

She smiled. "That's why you'll never make it very far, James." It was an old joke. Something his old supervisor had told him many years ago. Since then, she'd repeated it often, whenever he did something that displeased her. It'd been a few years since she'd said the words, but they still felt as natural as they once had so long ago.

Bishop returned the smile. "Good to see your sense of humor hasn't changed."

"Only when I'm here," she said. "I'm usually quite boring."

"I find that difficult to believe."

She could see where he was going, flirting with her, so she didn't answer. Instead, she glanced off, feigning disinterest.

After a lingering silence, Bishop cleared his throat. "About the boy," he said with a serious tone. "I had a look at him. Talked to him and everything."

Mara tensed up. "And?"

"Seems like a good kid," he said, shrugging. "Small for his age, but obedient. You did well."

It was nice to hear him compliment her son, but she didn't let it show. "I did my job."

"Right, of course," he said. "Anyway, we ran some tests on the class. It's promising."

"That's good."

"Yes, it is."

A short pause.

Bishop leaned forward. "Look, Mara, I wanted to ask you something. Pending another test, which won't take place for a while—pending that, I'd like you to donate again."

"Donate?" she asked. "Donate what?"

He shifted in his seat. "Eggs," he said. "Like you did before."

Mara scoffed. "I can't believe you just asked me that. Did you forgot about the contract I signed?"

"No, of course not. It's why I'm asking you now."

She rolled her eyes. "Only because you have to."

"What? You think I'd force you if I could?"

She sighed. "I don't know, James. Probably not. But Archer might. That rat doesn't care about anything but his work and that lab."

"Archer isn't here," he said. "The burden is all mine."

"I'm too old to do that kind of thing anymore," she said. "My body couldn't take another one." It wasn't a lie. As soon as she sent Janice to the academy, she'd retire. No more experiments, no more sponsors, no more contracts. "Besides," she went on. "The whole thing's a waste of time."

"What the hell is that supposed to mean?"

She blinked at him. "Oh, come now, Colonel. We both know where this experiment of yours is going to end."

"Do we?" he asked. "Because from where I'm sitting, everything's going pretty well."

"Lie to yourself if you want, but I'm no fool. Those children don't stand a chance. You might as well pull the trigger yourself."

"You sound so certain."

"I think the research speaks for itself, don't you?"

"You're oversimplifying things. None of the others survived the birthing process, sure, but these did. They're walking around like any other group of kids."

"So that's it?" she asked. "Seventh time's the charm?"

"Archer seems to think so."

"And what do you think?"

"I think if it doesn't work, we'll know soon, and that'll be it. You can say, 'I told you so' as much as you want." He smiled a wide smile, the same one he always used to give when he thought he was right. "But if it works, Mara, if this group really is the one that pulls through and *lives* all the way to the very end, well, the future might not be so bleak after all." Bishop leaned back in his chair. "But we've still got a few years left before we start the gene-activation process, so I guess we won't know for a while."

"I'm not giving you anymore eggs," she said. "After Janice, I'm done. I'm sure you can find more mothers to help you. I'm not the only one around, you know."

"But you're the only one with a near perfect AGP," he pointed out. "No one else even comes close."

"Be that as it may, I'm done," she said. "For all my years, I'm finally out."

He didn't speak at first. Instead he sat staring at her, considering. She didn't look away from him, either. She was serious about this, and he was going to know it.

"Alright," he said, after a while. "You win. No more after this. I promise. If that's how you want to do it, that's how it'll be."

"Thanks," she said, standing. She started gathering her things.

Bishop stood with her. "Hold on," he said. "Before you go, I have a deal for you."

She sighed. "What now?"

"It has nothing to do with what we discussed," he insisted. "It's about the boy."

"Terrance?" She set her bag down in the chair she'd been sitting in. "What about him?"

"How would you like to meet with me again?" he asked. "About your son. Meet with me to see how he's doing?"

This was unusual. Mothers generally didn't follow up with their children once they left for the academy. It wasn't illegal or against any particular rule—it simply wasn't done. Mothers were supposed to stay detached, otherwise they'd never manage to let the children go. What James was proposing now was uncommon, to say the least. The prospect seemed intriguing. "Why would you do that?" she asked, trying to appear resistant.

"You want the truth?" he asked, walking to the display case nearest to his desk. He stopped in front of two-hundred-year-old baseball.

"That depends," she said, watching him. "Will I hate you more or less afterwards?"

He touched the glass case. A translucent display appeared. It asked for a code. James entered four digits. There was a light click as that particular section snapped open. He pulled the glass back, took the baseball and held it in his hand. "I honestly don't know," he said, gripping the ball. He examined it, turned it over in his palm. "I don't know you well enough anymore to say."

She knew he was right. They'd barely spoken in recent years, only passing remarks. They were each so busy. She had her children, and he had his school. "The truth," she finally said. "I won't hate you if I can help it."

He smiled at the words. "There's two reasons," he said. "The first is simple: I like seeing you. I'd forgotten how much before today."

He was buttering her up, of course. She could tell that much. James always used to throw out a compliment before the big reveal.

"The second," he continued. "Is that I still want your help. I know you're against it, Mara, but maybe you'll change your mind once you see your little boy's doing okay."

She paused, letting the anticipation build. "I'm not sure," she said at last. "I'll have to let you know about it. You understand."

"Of course," he said, tossing the baseball a few inches in the air and catching it. "I'll be here."

Mara left without another word. She closed Bishop's door behind her, and made her way through the foyer and out into the street. Her thoughts circled the recent conversation.

She didn't know what to do. The prospect of keeping tabs on Terrance was enticing. As James had said, Terrance was the first of her Amber children to live, the only survivor. None of the others had made it beyond the first trimester. When the boy was born, everyone knew they'd entered uncharted territory. During his first few years, doctors came and went, examining and re-examining, but after a time they stopped. They'd begun to relax but not Mara. She never stopped worrying, never let herself forget any of the other failures. And now she had a chance to keep an eye on her little boy—something that none of the other mothers could claim. The real question was should she take the offer? And if she did, what would happen if the rest found out?

She'd be shunned, ostracized. All her years of garnering respect and prestige would be thrown away. She'd be a laughing stock.

So what if she was? It wasn't like Mara had any real friends anymore, and soon enough, she'd be retired. All the gossiping fools in the city meant nothing in the grand scheme of things.

James had certainly given her a lot to think about.

The train station was nearly empty when she arrived, with the exception of a young woman and a teenage boy. Mara recognized the girl as one of the newer mothers, not fresh out of the academy, but new enough that she'd yet to sign a contract. She wore a small purse over her left shoulder—blue with a black trim, the kind they sold in the plaza nearby. The boy, on the other hand, was a stranger. Near the back of the platform, dressed in dirty clothes (probably from the slums), he sat silently on the bench.

What was he doing all the way in Central? He didn't have anything with him, at least as far as Mara could see. Was he visiting someone? Why so late?

The train soon rolled in, filling the platform with thunder and a swirl of hot air. As it came to a stop, the raggedy boy on the bench rose and made his way closer to the other woman. The girl, intently staring at her pad's screen, paid him no mind.

The doors slid open, and Mara approached the one closest to her. She watched as the boy and the girl both entered through another door down the platform. The train was completely empty, aside from the three of them.

Mara took a seat close to the front. The boy inched closer to the girl, who still had her eyes glued to the pad. As he drew near, the doors began to close. Suddenly, he launched himself at her, snatching the purse from her shoulder and dashing back to the platform. The girl screamed and fell back, catching herself on the handrail and dropping her pad.

Mara snapped to her feet and ran to the girl. "Are you alright?" she asked.

"He took my purse!" she yelled, still on the floor, pointing at him through the glass.

The train rumbled as it began to move. The boy stood and watched as it left the platform.

The girl kicked the floor with her heel, cursing. "Jerk! That was my only purse."

Mara helped her stand. "Relax. At least you're okay."

"My mother gave it to me, though," she said, her voice quivering. "What am I supposed to do now?"

Mara didn't know what to say. The girl could file a report, but the chances of her getting that purse back were basically nonexistent.

Mara leaned against the window, and watched the buildings begin to slide away.

As the train passed through the tunnel between Central and the neighboring district, the cab's lights flickered, and finally dimmed.

Mara folded her arms, and she closed her eyes. She tried to clear her thoughts, to set everything aside, but she kept picturing the look on her son's face the last time she'd seen him when she'd said goodbye.

She trembled. *What's wrong with me?*

She put her forehead on the seat in front of her and felt the warmth of the blood as it rushed to her cheeks. She wanted nothing more than to forget about the boy she'd sent away—the son she'd given up all for the good of her race.

"Please don't die," she whispered, her voice shaking. "Please just stay alive."

4

Archer's Personal Logs
Play Audio File 06
Subtitled: Initial Testing
Recorded August 22, 2316

ARCHER: I can't believe the level of stupidity I've had to deal with on this project. Just because I'm twenty-nine, it doesn't mean I don't know what I'm talking about. And yet that's the perception around here. My ideas are constantly ignored, not because they're flawed, but because of my youth. My vigor. My passion.

I went to Doctor Mayhew yesterday afternoon with an idea, but he rejected it outright. Oh, yes, he nodded along the same way he always does, but I could tell he wasn't listening, and I knew what the answer would be even before he opened his mouth. What an arrogant fool. I swear he's already turning senile. And I used to think so highly of him.

I suppose it doesn't matter. What truly matters is that I record what I know to be the solution. I need to get it all out. I need to have proof that it was mine first, just in case the old fool steals my idea or if something happens to me. I need the record to show the truth.

So here we go:

Regarding compound R2-16V, commonly known as Variant, the airborne catalyst, I, Doctor William Archer, present my findings and hypothesis.

As the record shows, the solution originally proposed was to modify the cell membranes to block the foreign bodies before they had the chance to infect the cells. Despite all attempts, the results were always the same. Moments after the initial injections, the germ-lines of the embryos appeared to be stable, but a few hours later, the accelerated replication of the cells would ensue. As the cells began to replicate, they would change, sometimes drastically, until eventually deterioration would set in. This process consistently resulted in the death of the cells. Before even a full day, the human cells became completely dead, while the catalyst remained intact, ready to move on to the next organic compound it could find.

These experiments were being conducted under the presumption that the solution was to strengthen and modify the cell membranes, blocking the catalyst before it could even enter. It was a theory based on centuries of traditional science. And it failed. Why? Because deep down in the back of our minds, we are fundamentally afraid of change.

But Nature operates on change, on adaptability. If we cannot adapt, we cannot progress. And if we cannot progress, we will die. If we can accept this fundamental truth, we can move forward.

First, we must accept that the cell membranes are going to be invaded, regardless of any modifications that we make. After hundreds of different scenarios, this has always happened. What I propose, instead, is a forced cellular adaptation, a complete redesign of the cells. The catalyst's only goal is to modify the organic tissue, but if we beat it to the punch, if we change the cells so that they've already modified —a variation that is both Variant and human—the catalyst will move right through the tissue, ignoring it completely. It will essentially look at the cells, see that its work has already been done, and move on.

The end result of this will be a new race, a new breed of human, but it will be one capable of survival. We'll be able to breathe the air again; we'll be able to walk the Earth again. The next stage of human evolution is before us.

We just have to get out of our own way.

End Audio File

April 09, 2341
The Academy, Central

It had been twenty-four months—two rough, exhausting years in this pit of a place they called the academy.

Terry's eyes burned with sleeplessness. Nearly an hour

had passed since the last group left, John being among them. Mr. Nuber had gathered them together in a hurry, threatening referrals to anyone who wandered off or trailed behind. When the class finally arrived at the quad, the nurses called the first two groups in. The rest waited.

Of course it wasn't the first time this sort of thing happened. A year in a place like this was no less unpredictable than the first day. They were still pushed around, taken from one appointment to the next with little to no explanation. Even when it seemed like things were settling down, when a few weeks passed by without any interruptions, something always happened that turned them all on their heads.

Terry sighed, hunching over to rest his head on his knees. It was a little after four in the morning, three hours before the alarm normally went off. *It's too early for this*, he thought, but he knew the adults didn't care. All that mattered to them was that the children were on their feet and ready to go.

The room they waited in was shaped like an octagon, with nearly all of its sides connected to other, smaller rooms. These rooms, Terry had learned, were originally intended to be labs and offices back when the city was still supposed to be a scientific research outpost. Now, however, the rooms had been converted to storage units, filled with broken hospital equipment and old desks. Terry often wondered what places like this would have been like had things not gone the way they did. How many discoveries might have happened here? How many wonders born between these walls? How many miracles?

So much for good intentions.

"This is so stupid," Alex barked as he continued to pace. His voice jerked Terry's mind back from the edge of oblivion. "Why are we even out here?"

"You know as much as we do," Mei answered. She sat next to Terry, swinging her short legs below the bench. "Why do you care so much?"

"Because," he snapped, "I have to know."

Mei nodded while he continued to walk around. Terry knew she could argue with him now, tell him he was being stupid or impatient, but it wouldn't do any good. He'd only get worse. That was the problem with Alex. Instead of learning how to handle his problems, other people had to handle *him*.

Mei turned to Terry. "Hey," she said, placing her palm on his back. "You alright?"

"What's wrong Terry?" Alex asked, approaching them. "You gonna cry?"

"No," Terry muttered.

"Looks like it to me," he snickered. "What a baby."

"Leave him alone," said Mei.

"You his mother now, too? Guess he needs one since he's so little." Alex kicked Terry's shoe. "Poor little boy can't talk for himself, huh?"

"Leave me alone," said Terry.

"Or what, huh? What you gonna do?"

Mei leapt forward off the bench. "I'll tell Mr. Nuber if you don't stop it."

"Like I care," snapped Alex. He pushed Mei. She shuffled backwards, nearly falling. "Goober Nuber doesn't scare me."

Terry gripped the edge of the bench. If Alex came at him, at least he'd have a bit of leverage. "Leave us alone."

Alex stepped closer. "What did you say, turd?"

"I said stop it."

"Or what? You gonna do something?" He kicked Terry hard in the leg.

The pain shot through Terry's limb and into his gut. He squeezed the metal lip of the bench, trying not to make a sound. He wouldn't give Alex the satisfaction of knowing he'd hurt him.

"You like that, huh? Feels good?"

"It's great," said Terry, biting his lower lip. He forced a smile.

Mei stomped the ground. "Stop it, Alex. You're acting stupid!"

"Stupid? I'm not the one who likes getting hit. Right, Terry?" He kicked again. Same spot, same leg.

Terry flinched but suppressed the need to scream.

"I wanna know why little Terry's got two moms. How'd you get so lucky, huh?" He pulled his foot back, readying the kick.

Here it comes, thought Terry, tightening his grip and anticipating the pain. But as Alex's foot began to move,

Terry slid to the side, avoiding it. Alex's ankle smashed into the bench, and he let out a sharp cry. He fell forward, cursing repeatedly. Terry scrambled away from him, leaping from the bench and toward Mei.

Alex's face went red immediately as he gasped heavy breaths, clasping his ankle with both hands. "You idiot! You made me hit my leg."

"You tried to hit him first," said Mei.

Alex cradled his leg with his hands. "I wasn't even hitting him hard. He knew I was kidding!"

The door on the other side of the room suddenly opened, and Mr. Nuber walked through. "What the hell's going on out here? I can hear you kids all the way inside."

Alex got up from the ground. "It was nothing, Mr. Nuber," he said quickly. "I fell. That's all."

"You fell?" asked the teacher. He looked at Mei. "That right?"

"Yes, sir," said Mei.

Nuber stared back at Alex. "What'd you fall on?"

"I tripped over my shoe and hit the bench. It's not a big deal."

"I swear if I have to come back out here, you're all getting referrals, you hear me? I don't want to hear anything out of you. Alex, sit down on that bench." He shot a look at Mei and Terry. "And you two, go sit over there and be quiet. No talking." He stormed off, back toward the hospital doors, slamming them as he exited.

Terry didn't dare look at Alex as he marched to the

other side of the atrium. *I bet he's mad,* thought Terry. *I should've taken the beating and let him do what he wanted.* But it was too late for that now. He couldn't change it. All he could do was prepare for the next fight, whenever it might come.

Mei furrowed her brow. "What a jerk. If John were here, Alex never would've done that."

She was right, of course. John was the toughest kid in class. If he'd been around, it never would've gotten so far. But he couldn't protect them forever, no matter how hard he tried. Eventually something was bound to happen. Terry had to learn how to stand on his own feet. That was how you became a grown up.

Nobody talked again, not at the risk of upsetting their teacher. Even Alex stayed quiet.

Footsteps filled the quiet atrium as the receptionist returned from down the hall. "All of you come with me," he said, snapping his fingers at them. "You're the last group for the morning."

The students rushed to their feet. He led them through the double glass doors, stopping when they reached a group of men in white coats. "I'm afraid we have to separate you all now," said the receptionist. "These other gentlemen will escort you to your individual rooms. They'll ask you a series of questions and run some tests to see if you're in good health."

One at a time, the men approached the children, taking

them each through a separate hallway. There appeared to be one adult for every student.

One of the men approached Terry. "This way, young man," he said, motioning to another glass door to their left. "Your room is through here, third door on the right. Come on."

Terry followed him toward the back of the hall. Along the way, he watched as many of the other children entered their own rooms. As they arrived, the man checked his pad, tapped the screen and muttered to himself.

"Is everything okay?" asked Terry.

"The doctor will be right with you. Wait inside, and it won't be very long."

"Why did they bring us here?" asked Terry.

But the man didn't answer. Instead, he nudged Terry into the room by his shoulder, closing the door.

The room was small but not at all cramped. There was enough room for two chairs, a bed, and some cabinets. The walls were bright and uncommonly blue. In all the time that Terry had gone to school, in all his many months spent at the academy, he'd never seen a wall with such a color to it.

After a moment, the door opened. To Terry's surprise, a woman with glasses entered. She looked at him and smiled. "Hello there," she said. "What's your name?" She wore the same coat as the men in the hall, only there was a bit of red on the collar and an extra pocket near her waist. She had her hair in a bun behind her head, the same as his mother often did.

"I'm Terry."

"It's nice to meet you, Terry," said the lady. "My name's Doctor Sanders. This is where we get to talk."

"Talk about what?"

"Don't worry. It's nothing serious. We're just going to talk about school. Is that okay?"

"Yeah."

"Good," she said, sitting in the other chair. "Now, Terry, why don't you tell me a little about how things are going for you? Are you getting along with your classmates? Any complaints to speak of?"

Terry had more than a few complaints about school. The food, the teachers, the other students, the way they dragged them out of bed in the middle of the night so a lady in a white coat could ask him a few silly questions. There was plenty to hate, but somebody else, one of the other students, would probably say the same things. Why should he be the one to talk about it? Better to speed things along so he could get on with his day. "No. No complaints."

"Are you sure? There's nothing at all?"

He shook his head.

"Well, alright," Dr. Sanders said. "Let's get on with the physical. You've had one of these before, I'm sure, so I won't bother explaining, but if you have any questions you can certainly ask."

They went on with it for a while, the doctor poking and

prodding, asking questions as she went. She inquired about each of his classmates, how they all treated him and what he thought of them. She asked about how Terry was coping with the school and the change in scenery. She even wanted to know how the blue walls made him feel.

"Fine, I think," said Terry.

"Do you know why they're blue?" asked Doctor Sanders.

"No."

"Well, because the sky used to be that color."

Terry considered this. "But not now," he said, remembering how Variant had made the color different. "The pictures they showed us in class were purple."

"Right. Now the sky's purple. It's a shame, really."

"What are those white things at the top?" asked Terry.

"Those are clouds. Of course, I've never seen a cloud, personally, but the historical vids all say there used to be all sorts. Big, small, thin, fat. A little like people, I guess."

"I saw different vids. Not like this."

"And now that you've seen these, what do you think?"

"I think I like these better," he said.

Sanders nodded. "Okay, Terrence, let's move on. I have to take your vitals now, if it's alright. It should only take a minute or two." She didn't wait for an answer. Instead, she took his blood pressure, checked his heart rate, and scanned his stomach with a small handheld machine which beeped occasionally.

"What's that do?" Terry asked.

"Checks your lungs and other organs," said the doctor.

"Checks them for what?"

"Nothing important," she said. "We have to make sure you're breathing alright. Your body's very special, and we have to take good care of it."

"Special?" Terry asked.

The doctor smiled as she put the machine away. "Everything seems to be in order," said Dr. Sanders. "Follow the hall to the right and you'll find the exit. Your instructor will be there waiting." She stood and went to the door. She paused before leaving, then beamed another smile his way. "Hurry up now, Terry. This isn't your only stop today."

A CROWD of people had filled the foyer in the time that Terry had been in the blue room. Adults walked back and forth from the hospital entrance, oblivious to Terry, small as he was. Strangers now gathered, sitting where his classmates had sat before. He didn't recognize anyone.

He stood there for nearly a full minute before the realization hit him that everyone he knew had left. Where could they have gone? Or was he the first one out? His face went warm as his eyes darted around the atrium, jumping from face to face, searching for familiarity. Had they truly forgotten him? Terry had never been alone outside the school before. What was he supposed to do?

"Terry!" called a familiar voice from the crowd. A few people separated and went about their business, and a fat, bald teacher revealed himself. He waved to Terry with the only arm he had, and Terry waved back. "Don't just stand there like an idiot," said Mr. Nuber. "Come on. Let's get going."

"Where is everybody else?"

"In a classroom, waiting for us. We had to move when the crowds started forming. You're the last one out." He grabbed Terry's shoulder, nudging him to start walking. "Get a move on, kid. We're trailing behind."

As THEY ENTERED a section of the school he'd never been before, a smell like rust and eggs made Terry gag. He clasped his hands over his face in a futile effort to breathe. It was no good. The smell was everywhere.

"Yeah, I know," said Nuber, not even bothering to look at his student. "Just try to ignore it."

Easier said than done, Terry thought. "Where are we?"

"This is Facility Twelve, otherwise known as the Rat Maze, where all the crazy science types work, and where you're going to be spending most of your time during the next phase of your blossoming education. Aren't you excited?"

Nuber had to be joking. The smell alone was like breathing nails, not to mention the fact that it was in a restricted area, far from the dorms and the other facilities. In order to even get there, they had taken the elevator to the sub-section of the school, which had always been a red zone, meaning *No Students Allowed*, as the signs would say. Not that any of the kids could reach it, anyway. Nuber had to use some kind of card on the scanner in the elevator to get it to take them there.

They walked along a few corridors until they came to an open door. "After you," Nuber said.

On the other side, there was a room full of a few dozen chairs in a square pattern facing a large computer screen. Half the seats were filled with other students. Mei and John were also there, calling him to sit with them.

"Hurry up and wait," said Nuber. "That's the golden rule." He turned and opened the door again. "Somebody should be along in a few minutes to fill you in. Go have a seat." He closed the door and left.

Terry did as he was told and joined the other students. "What's going on?" he asked.

John shrugged. "Guess it's supposed to be a new class or something."

"I don't think so. Remember when we first got here, and Mr. Nuber said he'd be our only teacher? Why would he say that and then stick us in here?"

"Maybe it's some kind of advanced program," said Mei. "We won't really know until they tell us."

"You're all *lost*," a voice erupted from behind them. "Like little rats trying to figure out what to do next."

"What do you know about it, Alex?" asked John.

"More than you three, that's for sure."

Mei rolled her eyes. "Ignore him. He's just acting tough. He doesn't know anything."

"The hell I don't! *Goober Nuber* told me all about it."

"Well, why don't you clue in the rest of us? No point in keeping secrets," said Mei.

Alex leaned back and crossed his hands behind his head. "You'll find out soon enough," he said, staring off to where the wall met the ceiling. "Learn some patience."

Before any of them could argue, the door opened, and an older-looking man with balding red hair entered. He took the terminal at the head of the class, waiting until the screen powered on before he spoke.

"Here we are now, children. Sorry about the delay. My name's Doctor Walter Byrne. Now, I know this might be difficult to follow for a few of you, but try to bear with me, and we'll all get through this relatively unscathed." He pressed a button, which sounded like a hard *click*, and a picture appeared. It was Earth. "Do you all know what this is?"

Everyone nodded.

"Good. Now who can tell me how this thing relates to all of us?"

A boy named Roland threw his hand up. "It's the planet we live on. There are seven continents: North and South America, Asia, Australia, Europe—"

"Your basic facts are correct, young man, but I was

looking for more than what the textbook says. I'd like you to tell me what *you* see when you look at this *thing* on the screen?"

None of them said anything.

"Anyone?"

This time it was Sarah, a blonde girl in the back. "Well, we can't go outside, so we don't know that much about it except what we read in the books. A lot of people died two hundred years ago and now we can't go up there anymore. At least, that's what we learned in our last class." A few of the other students nodded along.

"Alright, good," said Dr. Byrne. "And who can tell me what happened to make it that way?"

"We can't breathe the air," said one student. "It got corrupted in the Jolt."

The Jolt. The great disaster that destroyed the world. Mr. Nuber had told them all about it, and about the day it happened—how a great storm erupted in the sky, and people started dying. Not all at once, of course, but fast enough that it was hard for most to understand what was happening.

It was the air that was killing them, Mr. Nuber had said. But no one knew it at the time.

Doctor Byrne smiled a little at the answer. "Correct, but what's in the air, exactly? And how is it killing them? Here, I'll tell you." Another *click* and the picture changed. This time it was a drawing of a bunch of circles, different colors connected to one another with a few numbers and letters in each of them. "*This* is what happened. Most people call it Variant, a catalyst."

The room was completely quiet. Finally, they were going to learn the truth. Maybe this class wasn't going to be so bad after all.

"Catalysts are things which cause a reaction or a transformation. Some like this one aren't consumed by the reaction, so they keep going, moving on to the next thing they find. In this case, Variant latches onto living matter, tricking the cells into thinking it's friendly and invades them. Here's where it gets interesting."

He changed the slide to show a human cell, with labels scattered throughout the image to show what was what. "Variant has a particular chemical structure making it very peculiar. You see, when it contacts the cell membrane, the cell acts like a friendly body, letting it in without any resistance. Once Variant is inside, however, it changes. And not only itself—it changes the composition of the cell, too. It negatively interferes with cell division, causing an explosive growth of altered tissue. This has the tendency to kill most of the modified cells, generally resulting in the death of the organism. In extremely rare instances, however, Variant actually succeeds in its attempt to transform the organism. When this happens, the specimen changes, adapting to the gas in the process and essentially becoming an entirely new lifeform."

Doctor Byrne looked around the room and sighed. "None of you understand this, I take it, but that's okay. It's why you're here today." He smiled. "But to summarize: if you go outside, you'll die. And it will hurt."

Another click, and this time there was a picture of a baby. "But what if we could fix this problem? What if, one day, children like you could walk on the surface without the need for purity suits? Would you want to go?" The doctor smiled. "My, what wonders would befall us, children? A whole new world of stories."

Most didn't say anything, but there were a few kids whispering in agreement.

"If you're lucky, some of you might get your chance to find out. But you have to be strong. You can't be afraid to do what we ask of you. You can't be unwilling to take risks. If you can do what I say, and if you think you can handle it, you might just get your chance."

Again, the slide changed. This time there was a picture of a man in a white coat, sitting on a stool. His hair was gray and thin, dark spots dotting the edges of his face, and he hunched a little. *Another doctor, just like Doctor Byrne,* thought Terry. But he wasn't like Doctor Byrne, not really. This man, the one in the picture—there was something about him. His eyes. They were looking right through him.

"Doctor William Archer," said Byrne, turning toward the screen. "Thirty years ago, he discovered a cure for Variant, or as close to one as we're ever likely to get."

The screen went black. "The problem is, you see, the cure to Variant isn't something you can take. It's not a pill or an injection we can simply put into somebody and watch it take effect. It has to be *bred* into you, into your very DNA, all before you're even born. To do this, we have to get hold of you while you're still a bunch of chemicals swirling together inside of a petri dish. When you're still a mere embryo."

Embryos. Mr. Nuber had taught them about embryos. It was one of their early lessons. It was part of a two week course about the human body's growth cycle. They studied fetuses, infants, cell replication, and even mutation. It seemed so useless at the time, but now the lessons made sense. It was all building to this.

"Some of you might be wondering what all of this has to do with you. 'Why is this man telling me about embryos and cells and Variant?' The answer is simple. *You* are one of those embryos, boys and girls. You've already been cured. In fact, you were born that way. Congratulations."

Several students shifted in their seats. A tentative voice in the back of the room asked what many were undoubtedly thinking. "What does that mean?" Cole asked. "I don't get it."

"Does it mean we can go to the surface?" asked Alex.

The doctor raised his hand. "Yes and no," he answered. "You can go there soon, but not right now. We have a lot of work to do before you'll be capable of surviving the transition."

Mei raised her hand. "If it's dangerous, why are we doing it?"

"Because we don't have a choice," said Doctor Byrne.

"In order for the human race to survive, we have to get out of the city."

"What's wrong with the city?" asked Sarah.

Doctor Byrne frowned. "Well, like any machine, it's breaking down," he said. "Eventually we'll need to replace it. This means finding a new home—one where our lives don't depend on whether or not the vents break down or the solar fields start malfunctioning."

He clicked off the display. "The future is going to be hard, I assure you. But make no mistake. There will be a reward. Such is life. You work hard enough, and you'll get what you deserve, so stay the course. That's all you need to know. If you do everything we say, if you stick to the plan we've made and follow the rules, maybe you'll do what no one else has been able to do in almost two hundred years: stand on the surface and take a breath of fresh air."

5

Archer's Personal Logs
Play Audio File 43
Subtitled: A Possible Solution
Recorded March 22, 2318

ARCHER: How luck seems to be on my side! After months of trying alternatives, I finally managed to stabilize one of the cells for more than a few minutes. Variant took a full three and a half minutes to destroy the cell, beating out the previous record of two minutes and thirteen seconds. The increase is remarkable, and it proves I'm on the right track. Soon enough, I'll have all the proof I need…and there'll be nothing Doctor Mayhew can do to silence me.

Speaking of which, the old fool gave me an order last week to attend the status briefings we give the military each week. I suspect he's simply trying to get rid of me, but the joke's on him. If I hadn't been at the briefing, I never would have met Captain Bishop or the other officers. They all sounded rather displeased with the lack of progress we've been making, which is exactly the kind of talk I need right now.

After the briefing, Bishop approached me with questions. He seemed very interested in Variant and the progress we were making. It was the first time a member of the military ever asked about my work. Naturally, I answered every question with great interest. I didn't detail all of my thoughts, of course, because that would be stupid, but when he asked how I felt about the lack of viable solutions thus far, I couldn't help but dig into it. I said I felt the project was meandering, possibly due to poor leadership and a lack of new ideas.

Innovation, he said to me. That's what we need around here. A little outside the box thinking!

End Audio File

August 05, 2343
The Maternity District

Mara took another sip from her drink. She wasn't drunk, but her face was warm, and her fingers tingled, which meant she was well on her way.

Ava Long sat before her. She slouched, crossing her legs, a calmness in her eyes. "You know," said the old woman. "I don't recall you being much of a drinker."

Mara swirled the glass in her hand, reflecting the dim

light of the nearby lamp. "I suppose I never was," she said, taking another sip. She flinched at the taste of it but swallowed anyway. "God," she gasped. "Disgusting."

"Why drink it, dear?" asked Ava.

"There's a payoff at the end."

"There are better tasting drinks, you know. I see two bottles of synth wine right over there in the corner. Expensive stuff. What you're drinking here is about as cheap as it comes." She paused. "Well, unless you count the toilet stuff they make in the slums."

"It's sentimental."

"How so?"

"One of my early sponsors gave me this bottle when I was still a new mother. He didn't have the money for the quality wine, but I didn't care. He was sweet, attractive, and he knew how to wear that uniform." She giggled at the thought.

"How nice of him," said Ava.

"We couldn't keep seeing each other once the contract was over, of course, and he knew that. So he bought me this bottle and promised one day, when I retired, we'd drink it and be together. Would you ever believe such a thing?"

Ava smiled. "Sounds like love."

"Maybe. But here I am, retired, drinking this awful bottle like I said I would, and where is he?" She snorted into the brim of her cup. "So much for happy endings."

"I don't know if I'd agree. You got a bottle of cheap wine out of it, didn't you? It's something."

"Oh, Ava," she said. "Is that the best you've got?"

The woman sighed. "Alright, fine. Pour me a glass, dear," she reached for a cup and held it out. "Unless you want to keep it for yourself."

Mara tipped the bottle into the matron's glass. "There you have it, Madam Mother."

"You know," said Ava. "I haven't drank in ages. You should feel honored."

"You don't have to drink it if you don't want to. I'd hate to break your sobriety."

"Now, now. Don't assume so much of your friends." Ava stared into the glass for a moment, blinking. She put the cup to her lips and flung her head back, shooting the alcohol down her throat. She smiled a crooked grin and let out a light burp. "Pardon, dear, and another, please. If you wouldn't mind, of course."

"You've surprised me. I never knew we shared a vice."

"It was before your time."

"Apparently."

They sat in silence for a while, hardly looking at one another, waiting. Mara hadn't expected Ava Long today, or any other visitors for that matter, but here they sat drinking synthetic wine and making small talk.

The matron rarely came to visit Mara during her mothering days. But ever since her retirement, the two had grown close. She didn't know why, precisely. When she asked about it, the old woman said, simply, "I was looking for a new friend and you didn't seem to have much going on at the time." She often joked like that, and Mara loved her for it.

Ava came to visit frequently, often once a week. It had taken some getting used to, but now Mara felt comfortable enough to tell her anything. Well, almost anything.

"So," said Ava suddenly. "How are things?"

"Fine," said Mara. She forced a smile. "You?"

"It's been busy. Mother's Day is almost here. Lots of contracts to approve."

"Sounds rough," said Mara.

"Yes, I suppose so," said Ava.

They each took another drink.

"So, dear," said Ava. "Is this how you want to do it?"

"What's that?"

Ava cocked her eyebrow. "Is this how you're handling the news about your son?"

Mara shrugged. "I don't know what you mean."

The woman giggled. "Come on, Mara. I know he told you."

"And you've been spying, have you?"

"Of course I have," she said. "But I was surprised, honestly. Bishop's never been one to share that kind of information, although I can certainly see *why* he did it. You're the child's mother, after all. Well, it's *one* reason." She grinned, winking. "I have to admit I was excited for the boy. To hear he's at the top of the compatibility list... always a good sign. If the procedure works, and I'm fairly certain it will, he'll make history. Hell, he and the rest of those children have already made history, if you think about it."

Mara didn't answer.

"Ah, you don't want to talk about it. Strange, considering it's been four years since you gave him up. That's time enough to move on, don't you think?"

"You're right," she said. "I don't want to talk about it."

Ava Long cocked an eyebrow and stared at her for a moment. She had always been so calm, so professional. For decades, she'd been the idol of the flock, a woman whose influence was vast, who, despite having retired many years ago, continued to be a force in the world. Even Mara had envied her once. "Remember what I said to you the day you agreed to be a part of the project?" asked Ava.

"You'll have to be more specific. You said a number of things."

"I said you were doing important work. I had faith in you."

"I believed it, too," said Mara, a bit of contempt in her voice.

Ava ignored the tone. "We were *all* excited in those days," she said, running her fingers through the tips of her silver locks. Her eyes grew distant as she spoke. "We had the dream to drive us. A dream, I think, no one truly believed in. But that's the way it is with dreams. You rarely expect them to come true. And when they do, we're shocked.

"At first, you're happy, because it's a miracle. You think

it can't be real and you question if you're worthy. Why this time? You ask yourself. Why was this one different? But rarely do we get an answer.

"Before long, you start to doubt it. You think the dream's going to come crashing down on you. Maybe it's going to explode, killing you in the process. You might even lie to yourself, say you'll never get attached, but when you can *see* it and you can *feel* it and it speaks to you and it laughs and it cries, everything about your life changes. You watch it grow, and as it does, so too, does the fear of losing it. But you can't stop yourself, because you're already in love." She paused suddenly and cleared her throat, shifting in her chair. "It isn't such a bad thing."

Mara took another sip from her drink and sighed. "Let's talk about something else."

"If that's how you want to do it." She reached out with an empty glass. "Would you mind?"

"So that's it? You're dropping it?"

"Look, I didn't come here to preach to you or convince you. I came here to lend an ear, and if you don't want to talk about whatever the hell it is that's bothering you, that's fine too. It saves me the hassle." She tossed the poison back into her skull and let out a small hiccup. "Now let's have another, sweetie. I think I'm starting to remember how all of this is done."

August 12, 2343
The Maternity District

MARA SAT QUIETLY in Ava Long's office, her thoughts scattered. The matron had called for her earlier that morning, but she could hardly think of a possible reason. The other night, they'd sat together in Mara's apartment, drinking thoughtlessly and hardly speaking. In all that time, Ava never mentioned anything important. She never said a word about a meeting. Yet here Mara sat, without any explanation, waiting in the matron's office.

The door behind her opened, and she turned to face it.

"Please hold my calls, Julia," Ava said beyond the cracked door. "I'll let you know when I'm done."

"Yes, ma'am," said the secretary.

Ava entered the office, closing the door and smiling. "Sorry for the wait. I got held up."

"It's okay," said Mara, standing to greet her friend.

"Now, now, you sit right back down, young lady," said Ava, walking behind her desk. "Were you waiting a long time?"

"Only a few minutes. I was late getting here. The train got delayed again."

Ava giggled. "Good. That's less guilt for me."

Mara watched as Ava casually swiped her fingers across the edge of her desk. "I'm sorry about the other night. I didn't mean for you to see me like that."

"What are you going on about? All you did was have a drink."

"It was unprofessional," she said.

Ava nodded. "That might be true if you still had a profession...or did you come out of retirement when I wasn't looking?"

"No, of course not. It's just that—"

"It's okay, Mara. You don't have to explain anything to me. That's not why I called you in." Ava paused, grabbing a pad on her desk. She started swiping through a collection of images. After a moment, she smiled and looked at Mara. "I never told you how I got to be in this position, did I?"

"No, but I've heard stories about it. Rumors, mostly."

"I'm sure they're all scandalous lies," she said, still grinning. "But go ahead and tell me the version you're familiar with. I'd like to hear it."

Mara sighed, immediately filled with regret. Embarrassing the matron wasn't something she'd planned for today. "I barely remember it," she lied.

"Try, dear. Don't worry. I'm sure I won't be angry. I've developed quite the shell for gossip."

"From what I remember, the story goes you tagged a high level sponsor, and he helped you out a little."

Ava chortled. "How did he help me?"

"He had political pull, so you went to him whenever you needed assistance. It made you look good to have that kind of influence. After a few decades, it paid off." She shifted in her chair. "At least, that's what I've heard."

"An interesting theory."

"But everyone knows it's not true. None of the mothers believe it. Well, maybe one or two, but none that I know." She folded her hands on her lap. "I'm sorry. It's so silly."

Ava smiled, glancing at the pad once more. "I see. So you don't believe the story?"

"Of course not," said Mara. "Everyone knows you'd never do that kind of thing."

"But why not? Is it really so hard to believe? How do you know it's not true?"

Mara paused before she answered. "I guess I don't. But I've seen how you are with the girls and even with me. You're good at this job. You earned your way."

"That doesn't mean I didn't have help. Haven't you ever taken advantage of a situation before?"

"How do you mean?"

"Well, think about it, Mara. A few evenings ago I asked if you'd heard the news about your boy, and you admitted to it. You're not supposed to know anything about him, right? But you knew plenty. His compatibility rating, his health. I'd be surprised if you weren't keeping tabs on his grades, too. And all because you know a certain colonel, yes?"

Mara didn't answer.

"Don't be ashamed," said Ava. "I'd have done the same thing in your place. In fact, I commend you for taking advantage of the situation like you did...and for being the mother you are. So many others give up their babies to that school and forget all about them until they come back. But not you, Mara. You don't forget. It's what makes you a good mother."

"I don't know what to say, matron."

"You don't have to say anything, dear," said the old woman. "I was only curious about it. Don't worry, I won't tell anyone about your arrangement with the colonel. It's your own business."

"Thank you, matron."

"How many times do I have to tell you not to call me matron? We shared a bottle of alcoholic piss together. I'd say we're more than simple friends now."

They both laughed.

"Right," continued Ava. "So back on point." She flipped the pad in her hand around so that the screen was visible. It was a portrait of a man. Middle aged, gray hair, a mustache. He wore a military uniform, though the style was outdated. "His name was Alvin," she said.

Mara recognized him immediately. General Alvin Stone, ten years deceased, but once the most powerful man in the city. For the better part of a century, he'd controlled everything from the top down. It wasn't until a few decades before his death that he completely restructured the city's leadership. He split the mothers and the science department into their own divisions, disseminating responsibilities and power to key individuals. Before that, everything was unified. If it hadn't been for General Stone, the mothers would still be under the control of the military. Granted, the military still controlled the academy, but they couldn't tell a mother what sponsor to take or which contract to acquire. Now, they had to go through the matron if they needed anything.

They had to go through Ava Long.

Mara blinked, staring at the screen. "Are you telling me that you're the reason General Stone gave up the mothers?" She leaned forward. "You can't be serious."

"I'm afraid it's true, dear." She set the pad down, patting it with her palm. "And I'm quite proud of it, too."

Mara was stunned. The implications of such a thing—did Ava even understand what she was saying? For her to have that kind of power over someone like the general and then for her to manipulate him into completely reshaping the government—it was outrageous. "I can't believe this," she muttered. "You're telling me it was your idea?"

"Of course. You don't really think Alvin had the brains to come up with such a bold proposition, do you?"

"What about the rest of the government? The science department? Did you ask for that, too?"

"Sort of," she said. "I couldn't go to Alvin and ask for special treatment. He'd never do it. I had to plant a few seeds, you know, talked to him about overhauling the system. The science department was part of it, but I didn't give two shoots about them. All I cared about was the motherhood."

"And it worked."

"Sure did, honey. No more forced contracts, no more unexpected births. Now, we control our own lives."

Mara leaned back in her chair and sighed. "I never knew."

"And you can't tell a soul about it, either."

Mara's eyes drifted to the floor. She scratched her hand with the tip of her nail, uncertain of what to say. "I don't even know why you're telling me all of this."

"A few reasons," said Ava. "First, I knew about Bishop, so it's only fair you know about my Alvin. We're friends, aren't we? I trust you not to spread this little rumor around."

Mara nodded, but she wasn't stupid. If she told anyone about Ava and the general, there'd be nothing stopping her from revealing Mara's clandestine dealings with Bishop. It was blackmail, pure and simple. Then again, she didn't have to tell her anything. She could've said she knew about James and left it at that, but she didn't. She confided in her. *It doesn't make any sense*, thought Mara.

"Then, there's the other reason," said Ava, grinning. "The same reason I called this meeting." She leaned forward. "I'm retiring, dear."

The words lingered in the air like steam.

"Mara? Honey, did you get all that?"

"I don't understand. You're…retiring?" In all Mara's years of mothering, Ava Long had always been the matron. She and the motherhood had nearly become synonymous. It was hard to imagine one without the other.

"Any week, now," Ava said. She ran her fingers through her silver hair. "I've been at this game long enough. I think it's time."

Mara didn't know what to say. The idea of the motherhood going on without its matron was difficult to imagine. Ava had a hand in almost everything in the organization, while also acting as its representative to the rest of the local government. Her absence would leave a gap in both the motherhood and the political power pool—a gap that, given the chance, Bishop and Archer would undoubtedly try to exploit. If the mothers weren't careful, they'd lose the autonomy that Ava Long had fought so hard to win them all those years ago.

"Tell me what you're thinking," said Ava. "Go on. Don't keep it all to yourself."

Mara hesitated. "It's a mistake. You're too vital to the program. What are we supposed to do without you?"

"*We?* And here I thought you were retired."

"I am," said Mara. "But that's not the point."

"Isn't it, though?" The matron stood, pushing the chair back with her thighs. "You say you're done with the job, but you certainly don't act like it. You're more involved now than ever before."

Mara scoffed. "Maybe I'm fitting into retirement, then, growing old and having opinions about politics. That's normal."

"Maybe it is," Ava mused. "Or perhaps you've got regrets about leaving."

Mara rolled her eyes. "Hardly."

"No?" taunted Ava. "You're spending so much of your newfound freedom talking to Bishop and me, discussing things retirees shouldn't be talking about. You're more a part of this world now than you ever were before. Don't you find it interesting?"

"Maybe I'm just bored."

"Or maybe you're hungry," said the matron. She walked around to Mara, gliding her fingertips across the surface of the desk. "I'll need a replacement, you know. Someone who understands the system, who knows how to get things done. I've got my eye on someone, but I haven't asked the question yet."

Mara wanted to stop her right there, to tell her no before she even asked. Instead she said nothing, only watched and listened as the old woman said what was already floating in the air.

Ava nodded at her. "I'm talking about you, Mara."

There it was, plain and unmistakably clear. If Mara was going to turn her down, now would be the time to do it. She stared down at her palms. They were trembling. She was so nervous.

Ava went on. "I'll admit, dear, I had ulterior motives for visiting your apartment. I wanted to see how you were handling retirement…to gauge whether or not you were right for the job. I wasn't sure at first, but I am now."

Mara clasped her hands and shook her head. "How can you say that? I was a wreck the other night."

"A wreck?" Ava asked. "Hardly. You were restless. Don't pretend with me, dear. I'm not your colonel or your child. I'm your matron, and I have been your whole life. Do you think I don't see what's going on? You can't handle retirement. It's not who you are. Even now, the gears in your head are turning, trying to figure out how to deal with this situation…what you should do. You can't stop thinking, and so you can't stop acting. It's the reason you still have those meetings with Bishop, and it's why you won't decline my offer. You care too much about this world, Mara, and the cracks in your armor are starting to show."

"Doesn't sound like you've left me much of a choice," said Mara.

"Would it make you feel better if I asked you directly? Alright then, how about it? Do you want to become the most powerful woman in the world or don't you?"

6

Amber Project File Logs
Play Audio File 225
Recorded November 18, 2343

BISHOP*: Are we fully prepared for the next phase?*

ROSS*: Yes, sir. The gym is being converted as we speak. We've also outfitted the battle gear with bio-sensors in order to monitor their vitals. Everything should be completed by the end of the week.*

BISHOP*: Good. Tell Henry to start the combat training as soon as it's done.*

ROSS*: Are you sure we shouldn't wait until after the exposures?*

BISHOP*: We need something to compare our results with. We put them in the arena now while they're still normal, then watch what happens once they're exposed to the gas. It's the only way to see how drastic the changes are.*

ROSS: Does Archer actually expect them to change all that much?

BISHOP: Not at all. In fact, he's expecting minor physical changes.

ROSS: Then why put them through the drills, sir?

BISHOP: Two reasons. The first is that placing them in a situation where they're forced to test themselves is the best way to see where their limits are, both now and after the exposures begin. We need to see what they can do under stress. You can't get those results by sticking them in a classroom. We need their hearts pumping, their muscles aching. They have to be pushed.

ROSS: And the second reason?

BISHOP: Simple. They need the training, Ross. Remember where we're sending them.

End Audio File

January 11, 2344
The Academy, Central

The new classes were different. Completely different and not in a good way. They had jumped, maybe even d*i*ved, from subjects like algebra and basic history to others like genetics and physics. What was even stranger was the fact that the students were now required to pass a combat efficiency class. It was a break from the books, sure, but why did they have to learn how to use a gun or a knife? When would they ever have to kill somebody with them? John said maybe it was for when they got to the surface, but if nobody was actually there, which was probably true, what would be the point?

That was all assuming they even let Terry *go* to the surface. The instructor said it *could* happen, but never that it *would*. Despite Doctor Byrne's optimism, there was no guarantee that the children could make the transition. It might all be a pipe dream.

"It's not good to think so much about it," John said one afternoon in class. "They told us it probably wouldn't happen anyway, right?"

"Right," Terry said. Besides, he didn't know if he even *wanted* to go.

Mei's head popped out from behind John. "Hey, what are you talking about?" she asked. "*Of course* we're going to go."

John let out a sigh. "Come on, Mei, don't get your hopes up."

"It's not a matter of *hope*, John. It's a matter of *fact*. Use your head and you'll see. I've got the highest GPA in the class, and Terry's right behind me. *You're* the best athlete, and your grades aren't *that* bad."

"Gee, thanks," he said.

"Look, I'm just saying we've each got a pretty good chance of getting chosen."

"Why would they care about our grades?" asked Terry.

"Because you need all kinds of people," she said. "Once we're up there, someone has to use the equipment." She looked at John. "Smart people. You know, so they won't mess it up."

John frowned.

"It's okay," said Mei, patting him on the shoulder. "You can be there to protect us while we do the important stuff."

"You think they'd let me?" he asked. "Would I get a cool gun, like the soldiers?"

"Probably, but I don't know what you'd use it on."

"Yeah," said Terry. "It's not like there's anybody there."

"Maybe there's other stuff," said John.

"Like what? There's nothing around but dirt and rocks," said Mei.

"Rock monsters, duh!"

Terry laughed. "Makes sense."

"They'd be ten feet tall, big and tough," said John. "Some would even have boulders for heads."

Mei covered her eyes. "Oh, no!" she cried. "What should we do?"

John pretended to hold an invisible gun. "Don't worry, guys! I'll protect you."

Mei giggled. "Thanks, you're the best."

"Don't mention it," he said, grinning. "Somebody's gotta protect you little geniuses."

July 19, 2344
The Academy, Central

TERRY MOVED with the gun across his chest, pointing the barrel toward the ground. He was having an easier time today. The rifles were new designs—less bulky than the last ones—and he quickly discovered a better way to carry them. Each of the weapons had a small hook near the trigger, making it possible for Terry to attach the weapon to his vest. He wasn't holding it so much as he was *wearing* it on his chest. It was still heavy, but now at least he could gather enough strength to aim and move. The hook made everything so much easier.

He lowered his visor and moved into the arena. It was darker than the last time, meant to simulate the night. There wouldn't be much light on the surface, Nuber had said, so of course they'd need to practice using the goggles, otherwise known as the MX-09.

The MX-09s were a set of goggles that allowed the wearer to switch between several kinds of vision, including infrared, night, and standard vision. It was the first time Terry had ever used them, but it didn't matter. The basics were simple. Infrared only showed warm bodies and nothing else, leaving most of the room in darkness. It was only really useful in open areas. Because of this, some of the other students seemed to be favoring night vision. It let the wearer see everything in shades of bright green—disorientating at first, but bearable once you got the hang out it.

Terry flipped between the three views and began to plan his attack. He'd begin in infrared so that he could find his opponents, then back to the night vision when he decided to move around. He fumbled with the controls at first, sometimes forgetting which direction he needed to spin the wheel to get the type of vision he wanted, but after a while, he got the hang of it. Once he thought he was proficient enough, he found a post and watched the others move through the battlefield. He spotted four opponents total. They moved frantically, mostly without any purpose. He wondered which setting their goggles were on, but as he observed them, it became more apparent. *The one on the left is using infrared. He's just sitting there, ducked behind a cube. The other one to the right is using night vision because he's staying low and moving, but he has no idea where anyone is.* Had none of them thought to use both?

Oh, sure, the others were probably changing them every few minutes, but Terry had taken to switching every few seconds. Between that and the newly discovered hook he'd found on his weapon, things were looking up. Now all he needed was a kill.

The one using the infrared—he'd be the easiest. He and another student were currently exchanging fire. If he hurried, Terry might be able to steal a kill without getting caught.

He dashed, his gun still hooked to his vest. He stopped quickly, switched his vision back, and saw the glowing red of the enemy, still in the same place. *He's pinned*, thought Terry. *Now's my chance.*

He ran to the rear of the target, unhooking his weapon and setting it on the cube nearby. He aimed it at the unsuspecting student's backside and felt his hands trembling. Terry was clumsy with the gun, the metal difficult to grasp, and it was heavier now in his arms, heavier than when it was on his vest. He was careful, though, and he waited until he had the shot. He switched between the two visions a few more times, trying to decide which one provided the easiest kill. He decided on *night* and fired.

There was a loud buzz over the intercom, and Terry heard the computer say, "Player Three retired." The "retired" soldier threw his arms up in a fit of aggravation and walked toward the exit. Once he departed the arena, another signal to continue followed.

He watched the remaining two soldiers, their sights now turned on one another. Terry moved the wheel to infrared and ducked behind the cube. He watched the red blur shift and move a little, placing his weapon on the mount and facing the other player. The student didn't appear to be worrying about Terry at all. Perhaps he didn't view him as much of a threat. *Maybe I can use this*, Terry thought.

He switched back to green, hooked his weapon, and moved along the outer wall of the arena, staying as far out of the others' views as he could manage.

About halfway to the next cube, the buzzer rang and the computer's voice erupted from the speakers. "Player

One retired." Another dead, but not his target. The signal to continue followed quickly, and Terry dashed to his next cube, his point of attack.

He made it, but he immediately took a knee and unhooked the metal weight he called a gun, placing it on the floor. He panted for a moment and once composed readied his position, switching to red and locating the target.

He took aim, carefully, slowly, and fired. He missed. The other player returned fire, sending several beams of light in his direction. Terry fell to his knees, dodging them. *Almost lost it*, he thought.

The enemy continued firing light beams a foot above his head, making it impossible to get a view. He flipped to green and scanned the area. The cube nearby extended to another, which had a mount in the middle, allowing for some firing cover. *I need to keep him focused on this spot.* Terry lifted the rifle above his head and fired blindly in the other direction. The enemy returned fire overhead.

Terry moved along the little walls until he found the elevated mount and switched between red and green. He focused his aim and fired at the unsuspecting student.

The buzzer sounded. "Player Four retired," the digital voice announced. The lights immediately came on.

"Alright, everyone out of the arena," said Mr. Nuber.

Had Terry actually won? He decided not to ask. Using the hook might be a violation, which meant he could get into trouble.

He placed his weapon on the rack and approached the rest of the group as it formed. Mr. Nuber was already talking. "It went alright, this being everyone's first time with the new goggles. I won't ask you how they felt, because frankly it doesn't matter. You'll have to get used to them. What I *will* ask is how many of you stuck to only one viewpoint for most of the battle? Don't lie to me, because I have recordings of each and every one of your feeds from the drill." Most of them raised a hand. "That's what I thought. Now, how many of you rotated them? And I don't mean once or twice or even five times. I mean often. At least once every ten or fifteen seconds." He looked around. Only a few hands went up, including Terry's. "One, two, three. Seems about right. Three out of twenty-two used those goggles correctly. And according to the data I've got, those three were also the winners in their designated arenas. Interesting, don't you think, class?" They all nodded. "Of course it is! Now you'll have about two days to get used to switching between those two types of sight. Afterwards I'm gonna enable a third. A few days after that, a fourth." Some of the students gasped. Terry couldn't blame them. It was difficult enough to switch between two, let alone four.

"It doesn't end there," said Mr. Nuber, almost grinning. "You'll get to experience some other upgrades in time, and you'll need to learn how to utilize them all without question. No stopping to think about if it's the right situation or if you have enough time. You'll just do it and that'll be it. We're gonna rewire your little brains to do all kinds of things. Believe me when I tell you that multi-tasking is everything in combat. If you can't keep up, you're dead, so you gotta be quick about it."

After that, and to Terry's surprise, he dismissed them. Not a word about the hook. *Maybe he'll talk about it tomorrow, once he looks at the feeds.*

But when the next day came, Terry used the hook again, and Mr. Nuber acted as though it didn't matter, going on instead about how they needed to be faster and less clumsy. Move around the battlefield. Don't stand in one place the whole time. You can't hit a target if you're only using infrared. Think of night vision like it's your normal vision, and then switch to red and do a quick sweep to verify your enemy's position, and do it often. Come on, idiots. You can do this!

So Terry didn't stop…and Nuber never brought it up. *Maybe it really is fair*, he thought on the third day. *Maybe that's the point, to do whatever you can to win.* So he started trying other things he wasn't sure about, other tactics and tricks to give him the upper hand. He left his shoes and other pieces of his gear behind a cube in order to move quietly and faster through the arena. The others still saw him with the infrared, but he didn't get so exhausted from all the extra gear anymore and he was able to go longer without stopping. As a result, he got more kills. Another day he moved a few of the smaller cubes around to form a kind of structure, hiding behind them and observing the others as they fought their little battles. At the end of the fight, when only one remained, Terry emerged and grabbed the kill, winning the match.

He was never criticized for his tactics. Every time he tried another scheme, a way to beat the system, Nuber said nothing and let him go on cheating. So Terry began to win. Not often, but still enough for it to matter. Enough that he wasn't the slowest or the weakest in the class anymore. Instead, he was somewhere in the middle. Better than terrible. Worse than okay. It was mediocrity. Wonderful, beautiful, unnoticeable mediocrity.

December 23, 2344
The Maternity District

BEING the matron was hard work.

Mara had never been a part of the administration, even in her later years as a mother. Her only experiences were with raising children, organizing, performing and closing contracts, and being the occasional mentor to a younger sister. In all that time, she'd never been asked to play the politician.

Now things were different. Now she was the matron. Every day when she arrived at her newly furnished office, two or three dozen emails awaited her attention. They ranged from contract approvals to additional supply requests to petty complaints and even gossip. Nearly all of them claimed to be an emergency.

It didn't take Mara long—little more than a week—to learn how to filter the letters. Grouping the contract approvals together, for example, streamlined her work and made it easier to quickly and efficiently respond to each and every email. Within the month, once she'd managed to establish a routine, it only took an hour and a half to get through the entire inbox.

This was a necessity, she quickly realized, since she was also required to attend several weekly meetings. Every morning, she met with her senior staff who oversaw the everyday work required to keep the wheels in the organization turning. She had meetings with the science department and the military separately, then she had joint meetings with the science department and the military. Bishop and Archer never came, claiming they were too busy to be pulled away. Gone were the days when the three heads of state gathered together to discuss their business. Now Archer and Bishop met privately without Mara, or so she had heard. In their stead, they sent subordinates, usually Captain Avery Ross and Doctor Byrne. Each was pleasant enough, but every meeting became a reminder of the other leaders' disapproval, and it made Mara hate them all the more.

Byrne seemed fine, but he sometimes rambled a little too much and lingered a little too long. Mara suspected it had something to do with his age. He was nearing seventy-five and was rapidly losing his capacity to give a shit.

Ross wasn't bad, not like some of the other military officials—or brats, as the mothers liked to call them. The captain carried herself well, acted respectfully to everyone she met, no matter the person's designation, and always spoke in a manner that was both direct and dignified. The fact that she was a female had surprised Mara, given that most girls were adopted by the motherhood when they were still in the academy. Not many women were chosen for the military arm of the government, and the few who were either had defective reproductive organs or bad genes. It was unclear which of the two categories Ross had fallen into. Either way, military women didn't make it very far in the ranks, generally never getting above a first lieutenant. Ross, however, reported directly to Bishop, the most powerful of all the brats, and she'd been doing so for several years now.

Today, Mara was meeting with Captain Ross alone. The topic of discussion, according to the email she'd received, was to be the further acquisition and relocation of mothers for the Amber Project. The Amber Project being, of course, the very same one that Mara had once been recruited into, herself. Now, it seemed the military wanted more.

Mara supposed it must be a good thing. After all, if their confidence was high enough to warrant such a request, the children must be doing well. And ever since she'd taken over the role of matron, her meetings with James had stopped. There was no explanation for it. She'd simply shown up one day at Central, waited over an hour, only to be turned away by Captain Ross. "The colonel can't meet with you today, ma'am," she had said. "He sends his regrets and promises he'll contact you for a follow up." But the meeting never came. Bishop had completely phased her out.

The surface of Mara's desk brightened, and a display screen appeared. There was a flashing icon in the center —a white telephone receiver—indicating a call. She tapped it. "Matron?" called the receptionist. Her voice was coming through the speaker at the corner of the desk. "Matron, your ten o'clock is here. Shall I send her in?"

"Yes, Julia, please do."

A moment later, the office door opened and in marched Captain Avery Ross. She was wearing the blue and white dress uniform, same as she always had and probably always would. The uniform was pressed, smooth, and seemed to fit her like a glove. Ross was a bureaucratic soldier. She sat in meetings, answered emails, and worked behind a desk. There was never a situation in which she didn't—where she *couldn't*—look her best.

And today Captain Avery Ross looked wonderful. Her hair, a chocolate brown, was pinned up so as to adhere to the strict military dress code, though anyone could tell how much care had gone into its maintenance. The woman's eyes were large and innocent, a seductive shade of cerulean blue.

Ross would have made a wonderful mother. She could have had any man she wanted, procured any contract she desired. Instead, through the irony of nature, her biology had betrayed her.

Even beauty had its price.

The soldier closed the door, stood silently in a position known as parade rest and waited to be acknowledged. She would wait, Mara knew, for hours.

"Sit down, Captain. It's good to see you again."

"Yes, ma'am," said the soldier. She took the only seat there was to take, right in front of Mara's desk. "Whenever you're ready, we can proceed."

"Go right ahead," said Mara.

"Yes, ma'am," said Ross. She took out a pad and handed it to Mara. The pad had a list of several names on it. "These are the candidates we're requesting."

"I see," said Mara, staring at the screen. The list included twenty names in total, many of whom she recognized. Tara Combs, Christina Medley, Sabrina Patterson, Patricia Dewey, and Lilian Summers, to name a few.

In that moment, Mara couldn't help but picture Ava Long sitting where she sat now, looking over the same desk, staring at another bureaucrat, at a very similar, very familiar list with Mara Echols among its candidates. What thoughts did the first matron have when the messenger from Central had handed her that pad, showed her the list, and asked for her approval? Did she waver, as Mara did now, at the thought of signing such a thing? Did she falter?

Mara stared with empty eyes at the text on the pad, the words blurring as her thoughts began to trail and circle.

After a moment, Ross continued. "Once you sign off on the transfer, and pending their own agreement, the candidates will be moved to the northern wing of Stone Hospital, third floor. They're to stay there for a total of three weeks, long enough to get through the initial tests and injections. Afterwards, they'll be returned to their living quarters in the maternity district."

Mara didn't answer, didn't look away from the pad in her hand. Ross had said "pending their own agreement," implying that the women had a choice in the matter—the same they had given her when she was in the program. But still, propaganda was propaganda, and Central would tell the mothers whatever they needed to in order to get them to sign their lives away. "It's for the greater good," they would undoubtedly say. "We're building a better world."

The thought turned her stomach.

"If you'd like, I can call for Doctor Byrne. He can give you a detailed summary of the procedures, as well as the improvements he and his team have made since you were… since you were part of the project. The candidates will be very well taken care of, I assure you."

"Mothers," muttered Mara.

Ross hesitated. "Ma'am?"

Mara finally set the pad down. She stared at Ross.

"They're mothers, not *candidates*," she said. "Hell, call them women, call them girls, call them anything but that."

"I'm sorry, ma'am," said Ross, with a sincere tone. "I didn't mean to offend."

Mara sighed. "No, I don't suppose you did," she said.

Captain Ross shifted in her seat. "If you'd like, I can come back another time."

"God, no," said Mara. "Tell me what you're here to tell me, and let's get this whole thing over with."

"There's not much else to tell, ma'am," said Ross. "They need your authorization for the transfer of the candidates…the women, I mean, and that's it."

"I'm sure," said Mara, flatly.

Ross was noticeably uneasy. "I can tell you're upset," she said. "What would make you feel better about this?"

Mara looked back at the pad on her desk. She wanted to pick it up and throw it across the room, break the damned thing to pieces. Each of those girls—none of them had been a mother for more than five years. They were more like sisters than mothers, hardly wise enough to make the right decision. They didn't know anything.

But Mara knew. She'd lived their lives already or at least the hypothetical version of it where they said *yes*, where the system stripped them of any sense of morality—turned them into government incubators.

A sudden flash of a hospital bed floated over Mara's eyes. Blood poured out from between her legs as the doctor pulled the baby out. She had cried, screaming in pain from the torture of this failure. "Let me see him!" But the doctor didn't answer. Instead he'd placed the lifeless form in a bag and handed it away. That had been the first and the most difficult.

But it's for the greater good, James' voice said in the back of her mind. Even in his absence, James Bishop still haunted her, begging for more and more of her soul. She imagined being in his office, sitting across from him, listening to him argue passionately, authoritatively, bellowing words in a voice she could listen to for hours. He spoke with such conviction that it was easy to understand how so many, including herself, had been enchanted by him. He was a born leader, an alpha male in a den of jackals, looming over them all with a welcoming hand, offering promises of a better tomorrow. Part of her agreed with every word he preached.

After all, everything about his plan had made sense. That was why she had originally agreed to it. Humanity needed this. It required the sacrifice. It required *all* the sacrifices—every one of those children's lives. How else was mankind ever going to rise from its crumbling ant hill? But even though she understood it, even though it was all perfectly logical, in her heart she didn't care, didn't give a damn. She'd witnessed the fruits of this program firsthand, along with several other mothers, and she wasn't about to let those tragedies repeat themselves. The pain and trauma of what she'd endured—no one deserved to repeat that.

"I'll tell you what would make me feel better, Captain.

How about your boss comes down here and talks to me himself? Or better yet, how about some disclosure on what he's doing over there?" She picked up the pad with the names and extended it to Ross. "Here," she said. "Take this back. I'm not signing it."

"Ma'am?"

"You heard me, Captain. Take this back to your master and tell him the motherhood declines his offer."

Ross stood quickly, grabbing the other end of the pad, but Mara grasped it even harder. She stared into her eyes. "There will be no transfers," said Mara. "No more military incubators. Understand?"

"Yes, ma'am. If that's your decision."

Mara released the pad. "It is."

Ross paused. "You're protecting them. I get it. You're responsible for them now."

"Just tell him what I said, please."

Ross nodded slowly. "The colonel will want to know why," she said, placing the pad under her arm.

"If he needs a reason, he can ask me himself," Mara said. She didn't like being mean to Ross. The woman had never done her any harm. But Mara couldn't let up. She had to send a message to Bishop, and the messenger had to believe it was true. *These words aren't meant for you,* she thought. *Take them back and deliver them like bullets.*

Captain Ross went to the door. She held the knob. "I'll tell him for you, and I'll do my best to make him understand."

7

Archer's Personal Logs
Play Audio File 58
Subtitled: A Possible Solution
Recorded April 04, 2319

ARCHER: Unbelievable. The embryo has accepted the cocktail! Not only that, but it is already beginning to show signs of molecular fusion. If the process continues to proceed at the rate I expect it to, the subject should achieve an acceptable level of atmospheric tolerance by the time it reaches the implantation phase.

Ava Long has expressed concern about the mother's health in this…whether or not the foreign half of the embryo's DNA will somehow "infect" the mother's…but I have assured her that there is nothing to worry about. Even if there was, one would think it would be an acceptable risk, given the scale of such an endeavor. We aren't trying to cure some silly disease, like the measles or chickenpox. We're changing the very way the human race is going to exist. After listening to the old woman preach her little sermons, talk about how the future depends on us, I thought she would understand. Of course, as has always been the case, I appear to be the only one who truly knows what is at stake here.

End Audio File

January 09, 2345
The Academy, Central

"Today, there will be no class," said Mr. Nuber. "Today, we are going on a trip. I'm sure you'll all enjoy it." There were several moans of disappointment, because of course it would not be enjoyable. Trips never were. The last one they took was to the doctor a week ago, and it wasn't fun or enjoyable in the slightest.

They walked through the corridors for nearly twenty minutes, passed the other classrooms, the dorms, the medical bays. Before Terry knew it, they were in a place he had never seen before, a part of the school that wasn't a school, the part that was something else.

They entered a room with several chairs but no desks. "Sit down," said Nuber.

They did. Nobody said anything, not even Alex or Cole. They sat for what seemed like forever.

Then, there was a sound—a door opening. It pierced the room like a child's scream, quick and sharp, and a man walked in—balding white hair, wrinkled, spotted skin, and a set of eyes that Terry instantly recognized from the slides he'd seen all those years ago.

Nuber looked at the man and nodded. "This is Doctor Archer. He's gonna talk to you all for a while, so listen up and pay attention. It's important. *Very* important, so if I see any one of you acting up, even a little, I'm gonna walk over to your seat, quietly pull you out of the room, and positively, absolutely beat the stupid right out of you." He walked to the back of the room and sat down.

Archer approached the podium at the head of the room. He cleared his throat. "First, let me explain where you are," he began. "This is a lab, but it isn't like the other labs you've been to, where you had your blood taken or the doctors looked into your ears and asked how you felt. We don't do any of that here. This lab is special, designed specifically to test your DNA. We do this in order to see whether or not you are capable of surviving on the surface."

The children stirred.

"What you will experience will be unpleasant," he continued. "Of this I have little doubt, but you must endure it. I will not stop because you are afraid or because it hurts or for anything. What we are about to do is far too important for that." He paused a moment, looking at them, scanning them, until his eyes caught Terry's, and they lingered for a moment longer than they should have.

In that moment Terry saw a kind of—awareness, maybe. These eyes knew something more than what the doctor was letting on. This was the person to watch, the one Terry should listen to. Not the teachers or the soldiers, but this man, this Archer.

"I shall call you in shortly," said the doctor. "One at a time, beginning in no particular order, until each of you has experienced the chamber."

The chamber. The words seemed to linger in the air like an old smell. Archer had spoken them with such finality that they were all Terry could remember, even as the doctor left the room. What was this chamber? What purpose did it serve?

Mr. Nuber coughed to get everyone's attention, the way he did in class sometimes. He was once again at the head of the room, waiting patiently. "The doctor is going to call you individually using the intercom. When he does, get up and walk on in. You don't have to wait for anyone to come out or anything. Just go."

The intercom system roared to life, and Terry heard Archer's voice enveloped in static. He was calling for the first student, Bradley, who quickly stood and walked to the door.

Every eye in the room watched him go, including Nuber's, and in a moment, he disappeared through the same door Archer had taken.

Slowly the others were called in. Next came Michael, and then John and Roland. The wait between names was agonizing.

Perhaps it was nothing, another test like all the rest. Maybe the only thing on the other side of that door was a room with a nurse and a needle. Nothing to get worked up about.

Terry shook his head. There was no way. Archer wouldn't call something "the chamber" for no reason. He'd explained it would help them go to the surface, but what did he mean? How could a room do something like that?

Four hours passed before they called Terry's name over the intercom. He wasn't the last one—Mei, Everett, and Sarah were still waiting—but he might as well have been. Terry rose from his chair, went to open the door, and walked in.

He immediately noticed the smell, like burnt plastic and —something sweet. Fruit, maybe. He wriggled his nose as he walked, but the odor only grew stronger.

At the end of the corridor, he found a room. He entered and found Doctor Archer hunched over a desk, staring at a computer screen. A long glass window covered most of the wall before him, overlooking a large and empty chamber. "Come in and take off your clothes," said Archer, without taking his eyes off the screen. "Once you disrobe, enter through the other door." He knocked against the glass in front of him. "You will wait for further instructions afterwards."

Terry did as he was told, though he wanted to ask why he had to be naked. It seemed a little strange.

He didn't argue. There was never any use fighting with adults. He removed his clothes and set them on the floor and entered the chamber. The glass door shut itself behind him, locking in place.

Terry waited a moment. *Now what?*

He almost asked the question aloud, but then the vents kicked on. In less than a minute, Terry felt cold air blowing all over his body, emanating from the walls. The pressure increased suddenly, causing him to waver. He leaned forward, against the air current, steadying himself.

After a moment, the vents shut off.

"Hold still and be quiet," said Archer through an intercom. His voice was amplified and distorted.

Terry obeyed and said nothing. Despite the cold air, he attempted to remain still.

"Good boy," said the old doctor from beyond the glass. "What is about to happen will be unpleasant, but you must stay calm. Do not try to escape from the room. It is impossible. At first, it will seem as though you are choking, but you must understand this is only temporary. Endure the gas long enough and your body will adapt. Struggle, however, and you may cause yourself a great deal of pain. Even death."

Terry looked at Archer. "Huh? What do you mean?"

The doctor didn't say a word. Instead, the slow mechanical hum of the vents ensued once more, only this time the cold air never came. Instead, a wave of thick, hot air filled the room, encapsulating him. Too thick, in fact. It became difficult to breathe. *Why can't I breathe?* "Hey," Terry cried. "Hey, let me out!" He walked a few steps toward the glass window, waving his hands at Archer. The old man stared at his computer screen, never bothering to answer. *Can't he hear me?* Thought Terry. *Doesn't he see what's going on?* But before he could reach the glass, he stopped and covered his mouth. Every breath he took now burned like fire in his lungs. His skin crawled and his stomach turned. He bent to his knees, expecting to vomit, but nothing came.

Terry looked at his hands. They were shaking. His whole body trembled uncontrollably, as though it were coming apart. He tried to scream, but instead he fell to the floor. *What's happening to me?*

Wheezing like a sick child, he could feel his eyes bugging out, about to burst, the blood swelling his face. *I'm going to die here*, he thought. *Right here in this room, I'm going to die and there's nothing I can do about it. Someone help me, please.* But he couldn't talk, couldn't scream a word or plea.

The room began to dim. The edges of his sight diminished bit by bit until only darkness remained. Had Archer done this? Was he doing something to the light?

Terry's body went completely limp. His face hit the tiled floor, but he barely felt it. He struggled to take a single breath, to pull a gulp of oxygen out of the toxic, burning air surrounding him. He tried to move his legs, his arms, anything. Nothing.

The twisting, burning pain of the gas consumed every inch of his flesh, invaded every cell, and he wavered on the edge of unconsciousness, craving a release.

Suddenly, the pain faded and he became completely numb. Engulfed by the dark, he lay motionless, touchless, lifeless. Pinocchio without the fairy dust.

Unable to move, he waited, lost in an empty void of quiet acceptance. His mind began to drift, shut out from all thought or sense of purpose, a battered soul released from its weary vessel. He was going somewhere else—somewhere empty and quiet—somewhere far away.

A better place.

But in that moment, the pause between realities—a light. A piercing dart inside the black, something pulling him, tugging his mind from whatever place he'd gone, back into the foul chamber with its burning gas. Back to putrid air and toxic death, to sickness and disease.

To life.

Terry felt the cold, wet tiles against his face, and without a thought, he did what he couldn't before, what had only a moment ago felt impossible: he breathed a gulp of gas, swallowed it and found it tasted pure.

He tried to keep it inside, tried to bottle it and save the taste, but he couldn't. He let it out. Threw it out. Vomited the contents of his stomach into a pile of yellow slush.

Chunks of food spilled out of him like soup. He spit

and backed away, wiping his lips, wheezing and crying. He clutched his elbows and found he couldn't stop shaking. Terry stared at what used to be his breakfast and leaned against the nearby wall, gripping the back of his neck.

And he screamed.

He pressed his forehead hard against the wall and wept. Water streamed from his eyes as though he were a river, each tear falling onto his naked arms and chest, bathing his body.

He couldn't stop gasping. The gas was so sweet. It smelled and tasted so much better than it had before. He didn't know why, didn't even care. All he wanted was to keep breathing.

The intercom roared to life, and Archer's voice came with it. "Very good. How do you feel? Quickly now, you must tell me."

Terry tried to slow his breathing, but he had little control. He could barely speak between the gasps. "I...I can't...it hurt...so much. What did you do...to me?"

"Answer the question, boy," said Archer.

Terry closed his mouth and tried to breathe through his nose in an attempt to slow his lungs. It helped. After a moment, he managed to talk. "What happened?" he asked. "What did you do to me?"

"You were exposed to Variant," explained Archer. He tapped the glass with his knuckle. "It is important you tell me how you feel so I can assess your condition."

"I...I don't know."

"How is your vision? Your other senses? I see you can stand. Try to walk."

Terry took a few steps and nodded towards the window. "I can see okay, but before it was dark. Why does the air smell so different now?"

"Describe the smell."

Terry took in a long, steady breath. "I think…pineapple. Maybe. I don't know. What is it?"

"Interesting. Some of the others reported a similar sensation. Tell me, are you still having trouble breathing?"

Terry touched his chest. His heartbeat was much slower now. His breathing was more normal, too. "It's gone," he said.

There was a sudden buzz in the room, and a green light appeared over the exit door. "Step through there. You're finished here."

Terry drifted to the door, weaving as he walked. He felt so unstable—not exhausted anymore, but like he'd just crawled out of bed after a long sleep.

The door closed behind him, sharp and quick, and a draft of wind blew up against his naked skin. He looked down at his body, frail and wet and cold. A baby, that's all he was. A little infant only following orders.

Nuber sat in the hallway, a bag in one hand and a towel in the other. "Here," he said, handing him the towel.

Terry wiped himself, then wrapped the cloth around his waist.

"You did well today," Nuber said. His voice was very

low, like a whisper. "Whatever happens after this, you did okay."

Terry didn't answer. He only stood there. He didn't know what Nuber was trying to say. All he could think of was leaving this horrible place.

Nuber gave him the bag of clothes. "Get dressed, but take your time. It's fine if you have some trouble. The shaking should stop in a few minutes."

When Terry was finally ready, Nuber placed a hand on his shoulder. "Come on," said the teacher. "Let's get you back to class."

8

Amber Project File Logs
Play Audio File 1277
Subtitled: Students
To: Henry_Nuber
Received January 16, 2345

BISHOP: *I understand your concerns. I've gone over the whole thing a hundred times in my head, maybe more. We couldn't avoid what happened. If we didn't start the exposures when we did, we would've lost more later.*

Archer has assured me without direct contact, the children's bodies may never fully develop. The exposures need to be controlled. If we fail, we risk losing the rest of them the moment they reach the surface. Then what? We'll have to start all over, and there'll be a few dozen skeletons lying topside, waiting to greet the next batch. That is, of course, if those mutated things haven't already taken the bones for themselves, dragged them off to whatever hell they come from.

So no, I don't think we should have waited on this. If they're going to die, better they do it down here with us than up there surrounded by all of them. Given your personal history, Henry, I'm sure you can agree with that much, at least.

End Audio File

January 23, 2345
The Maternity District

"Matron," said Ross as she took a seat on the other side of Mara's desk. "I appreciate you taking the time to see me again."

"Don't mention it," said Mara, turning on her pad. She brought up a list of talking points. "It's not as though your boss will see me. What choice do I have?"

"Yes, ma'am. I'm sorry about that." Ross was so stiff in her seat. She brought a bag with her as always, but this time she kept it against her thigh. She seemed to keep a hand on it at any given time. "I took your concerns to the colonel, like you asked."

Mara's eyes widened. "And? What did he say? Are you here to tell me he's reversed his decision to leave me out of the loop?"

"I'm afraid not, ma'am. He actually chastised me for speaking out of turn. I'm sorry."

"It's not your fault," said Mara, sighing. "Once the old bastard's set his mind to something, there's no changing it. I appreciate the effort, though."

"If it's any consolation, I don't agree with withholding information from you."

"You and me both," said Mara. She shook her head. "It isn't right what he's doing. As the matron, I have a right to know what's going on over there."

"Yes, ma'am."

"The motherhood has always worked alongside the other branches. An open dialogue is essential. Why is he doing this? Has he given you a reason?"

Ross looked at the floor. "He says it's because you're too close to it…the children, I mean. He says you don't understand what needs to be done."

"And what exactly *needs* to be done, captain?"

"I want to tell you, matron," said Ross.

"But you can't."

"It's complicated."

"This is why I asked for disclosure," said Mara. "Nothing's complicated when there are no secrets."

Ross nodded, slowly. She clutched her bag, squeezing and twisting the fabric. What was wrong with her today?

Mara didn't enjoy putting Ross in the middle of this mess. Mara rather liked her actually, especially now. Had she somehow, since the last meeting, caused this woman some added stress? "It's okay," Mara said. "Why don't we forget about politics for a few minutes. Now that I think about it, I realize I don't know much about you, Ross."

"There isn't much to tell, I'm afraid," she said.

"Nonsense," said Mara. "Everyone has a story. How did such a lovely woman like yourself fall into the military's service? You're one of the few, I think."

"Females, you mean?" she asked. "It's true, there aren't too many of us in the service."

"So how did you get involved in it?"

"The last time we spoke, you accused me of being a dog of the military. Are you certain you want to hear about how I got my leash?"

"I'm sorry about that. I know you're only following orders."

Ross glanced at the bookcase on the far wall. "It's okay," she said. "I'd feel the same way in your position. I understand the desire for respect. More than most, actually." She looked at Mara. "I was slated to be a mother, back when I was a little girl. Did you know that?"

The words took Mara by surprise. "Sorry, no, I had no idea."

"Yes, I was very excited about it. Any girl would be. But a few years before I graduated, Archer released his AGP. It changed everything, but I'm sure you're aware."

Better than most, Mara thought.

"We had already received our evaluations, so there was no question as to where I'd work. During the visitation week, when the students were shown their future occupations, the soon-to-be mothers were taken to the mother's lounge, introduced to a few of the veterans, and briefed on what would happen next. They made it sound quite wonderful. I remember feeling enamored with the whole experience."

Ross's smile began to fade. Her stare went cold and narrow. "But a few months later, they took us to the labs and ran their tests. Most of the girls passed, much to their delight, but not me. I had *redundant genes*. Afterwards, they left me alone in a waiting room. I suspect the doctors didn't know what to do with me. Looking back, I can see why. The AGP had only just been released, and I'd already received my evaluation. It was unprecedented.

"I waited several hours for answers. For a fourteen-year-old girl, that's an eternity. I kept expecting someone to come in and tell me there'd been a mistake…that the reason I had to wait so long was because they needed to run more tests. But when the door opened, it wasn't a doctor who came…or a teacher for that matter. It was Ava Long."

"Ava went to see you?"

Ross smiled. "I couldn't believe it. What would the matron want with *me*, especially now? She walked over, asked if *I* was the special little girl everybody was talking about. When I said my name, she hugged me and said she wanted to sit with me for a while. I told her it was fine, and we sat together until the doctors came. She asked me questions, like what I enjoyed in school, about my friends. You know, ordinary things. She was so nice to me. I loved her immediately."

Mara smiled. "That sounds like Ava."

"When the doctors arrived and told me the final results, the matron didn't leave my side. She sat there, holding my hand, and stayed with me for an hour afterwards trying to cheer me up. Despite the results, she told me I was special. She said most girls don't get to be anything else besides a mother. I had the opportunity to do whatever I wanted. She said she'd make sure of it. Whatever occupation I chose, that's the one I would get. We talked about my options. With my test scores, she said, I could be a scientist, a clerk, a contractor. But none of those things sounded very interesting."

"So you chose to be a soldier?"

Ross nodded. "Even as a child, I understood how the system worked. Only three branches had any actual power: the motherhood, the military, and the science division. I couldn't be a mother, obviously, and after dealing with the AGP, I hated Archer. The only other option was the service."

"Which you joined."

"Yes, ma'am, I did. To make what little difference I could, to do the right thing, but more importantly, to honor the woman who came to see me on the worst day of my life."

"That's quite a story," said Mara. "I'm glad it had a happy ending."

Ross frowned. "I'm not sure yet."

"What do you mean?"

"The system's broken, matron. I've tried to patch it where I can, but in all these years I've accomplished nothing."

Mara leaned back in her chair and took a moment. She examined this captain, this Avery Ross whose childhood ambition had sought to change the world. "I'm sure that's not true."

"But it is," she said. "At every opportunity, I've tried to alter the flow. No one gives a damn, though. That's why…" She looked at the bag again, her words fading.

Mara cocked an eyebrow. "Why…what?"

Ross snapped out of the trance. She took in a deep breath and held it for a moment. "It's why I'm going to help you," she said, releasing the air from her lungs. "I can't believe I'm saying it, but I am."

Mara stiffened and leaned forward. "Excuse me?"

"I've been thinking about it ever since our last meeting. After talking with Colonel Bishop and getting nowhere, I couldn't get the thought out of my mind. I debated with myself for days on helping you, but it wasn't until I walked through your door when I decided to act."

Mara was speechless. Of all the people to turn on Bishop, she never expected it would be Ross, his golden soldier. His second in command.

"Now you know why I told you my story, ma'am. I wanted you to understand my reasons." She unlatched her bag and took out a pad, sliding it across the desk. It was a report about the Variant test chamber with a list of five names below. Mara recognized them from Terrance's class roster. She looked at the captain. "Reasons for what, Ross?"

"For betraying my command," she muttered. "For treason."

April 28, 2345
The Academy, Central

TERRY CHANGED CLASSROOMS ALMOST IMMEDIATELY. Fewer desks for fewer children. The official word was that the other students were transferred, but after experiencing the chamber, it was hard to believe any of them had walked out of there alive.

Now, with seventeen students for seventeen desks, it was like the others never existed. Yet five were missing, and Terry suspected it had nothing to do with a transfer or anything else so convenient.

But he had no proof—nothing physical, anyway. He only had his own experiences in the room with the gas, the lingering thought of possibilities, of what might have been.

It wasn't just Terry, either. They were all different. Still the same people, the same faces, but with a change beneath the masks. With each passing day, a weariness grew behind their eyes saying they knew something was wrong. Yet, despite all of that, they still smiled, still joked, still made fun. There was life within them, a willingness to adapt.

They had merely given up on being children.

"Hey, you coming?" asked John.

"What?" asked Terry. He'd been so lost in thought he hadn't heard Mr. Nuber's instructions. Was class over? No, the clock on Nuber's desk said otherwise.

"Weren't you listening? We're going to the arena. Mr. Nuber wants us to run a few drills."

They arrived soon, and Terry geared up, reluctantly, preparing for the games. He quickly noticed the change in weight as he strapped the vest on. Had they replaced it since the last time? Nuber never mentioned anything about it, and no one else had said a word. "Does all of this feel lighter to you?" he asked John.

"Now that you mention it, yeah, I guess it does. Weird, huh?"

"Yeah," he said, examining his armor. "Weird." And it *was* weird, especially given the fact that only a few days ago Terry could barely *lift* the armor, let alone walk so easily. He strutted back and forth, swinging both arms, taking wide strides. Whatever this new armor was, he wouldn't complain about it.

At Nuber's signal, Terry walked to the back of the pitch black arena and took up the same starting location he always had. He turned his night-vision goggles on and waited for the buzzer.

Roland, Sarah, and Mei took their places, too. He hated fighting Mei. She always took things so seriously. *I'll let the others take her out,* he thought. *Sit back and wait.* Afterwards, he'd go for Sarah. She took to the offensive more than Roland, but she never watched her back. If he could shoot her while she was fighting someone else, he'd only have Roland to contend with. Then, he might stand a chance at winning.

Not as if it really mattered. Terry rarely won the games. He simply couldn't keep up with the others, even the weaker kids. It was all he could do to get a single kill, let alone come out on top.

But there were always those moments of luck taking place now and again. Anything could happen.

The buzzer rang, startling him. He crouched behind a cube, taking a quick moment to observe the others, their bodies glowing red and orange behind the lenses of the infrared goggles. He switched to night vision and spotted an isolated cube near the back of the skirmish—prime real estate for an eager sharpshooter. He clutched the side of the cube, his heart racing. *Here goes nothing,* he thought, and leapt into a mad sprint.

He ran, low and steady with surprising grace. For the first time in his life, he was strong and quick, limber and agile. With each step, the weight of the vest and the weapon became lighter. He couldn't believe it. Whatever this equipment was made of, he was happy to have it.

He dashed through the array of cubes scattered between Sarah and himself, taking position far beyond where she was fighting.

"Player three retired," said the computer. Sarah had already taken Mei out, turning her sights on Roland. *Good,* he thought, readying the rifle. *Just two more targets.*

Terry relaxed, taking aim at Sarah, her back against him. It was a perfect shot by any standard. He pulled the trigger and hit her in the back of the arm, missing the kill shot. He'd need another to knock her out of the game. Unfortunately, he might not get the chance.

Sarah stopped firing at Roland and turned to look at Terry. Her predicament must have become apparent, because she immediately bolted. Roland and Terry both fired at her, but she evaded, ducking behind a cube and avoiding their shots.

Terry took the opportunity to bolt toward Roland's position. He dashed through the cubes with a speed he'd never known. As he approached, he found it difficult to slow, causing him to collide with Roland's cube and fall over to the other side, knocking Roland to the ground alongside him. Terry and Roland both scrambled for their rifles, seizing them at the same time and firing.

Two shots were fired and two shots landed. A beam of light tagged Terry in his left leg; another hit Roland in the chest. Through luck or bumbling skill, Terry had won the skirmish. "Player one retired," announced the computer.

"Damn," muttered Roland. He got to his feet and ran to the exit.

Sarah wasted no time before she began her assault on Terry's position. A shot collided with the cube nearby, calling for Terry's attention. He lowered his head and took a moment.

Both he and Sarah had been grazed, which meant a single shot could take them out. It didn't matter whether it hit them in an arm or the chest. Either way, the game would be over.

Terry's heart started racing. He'd rarely done so well, not without cheating. It was so exciting. He considered looking for an exploit or coming up with a strategy, but he couldn't focus. This energy, coursing through him—it made him feel alive. He breathed quickly, his chest rising and falling with the speed of a beating heart. He felt like he could conquer the world.

Sarah's shots passed overhead—several white pieces of light trailing together at close intervals. Terry rose above the edge of his cube, preparing to fire. But before he could aim, another shot came spiraling toward him. He dodged to the side, the light barely missing his face. He stumbled, falling to the floor. He'd never moved so fast in all his life. Where had it come from?

Terry peeked over the cube and with his goggles switched to infrared. He spotted a pulsing orange Sarah in the distance. He aimed the weapon, trying to hide what he could of himself, and fired. The shot colliding with the cube wall, spooking Sarah to hide. After a short moment, she blindly fired back, holding the rifle above her mount.

Terry ducked again. He couldn't help but grin. Never before did he ever think he stood a chance at matching Sarah in the arena, not without cheating. No one would make fun of him after today.

He tilted his head back and watched the shots of light pierce the air above him like little white dagger marks. Had they always moved so slowly? He thought for sure they were faster.

He waited for Sarah to stop firing, counting the beams as they flew overhead.

One, two, three, four. The shots were beginning to slow. *Five…six.*

Was Sarah trying to draw him out? Get some kind of response? Terry didn't see how. It wasn't like the shots were far enough apart that he could do anything. *Seven.*

What a waste of time, he thought. *If she wants me to show myself, she needs to give me more time.*

Eight.

Terry felt a flush go over his chest and stomach. He felt nauseous. *It must be the adrenaline*, he thought.

Nine.

His hands tingled, pins and needles all along his skin and fingertips. He pushed his back against the cube, trying to stand but quickly fell again when another shot passed by.

Ten.

Terry shook his head as the light collided with the nearby cube. Had it really taken such a long time for the next round, or was Sarah doing it on purpose? Her last shot moved so much slower than the others—slow enough that he'd actually been able to follow it with his eye all the way to the wall.

Eleven.

There again, like the light was moving through more than just the air, like something else had slowed it. Terry's eyes widened. It wasn't right. Nothing about it made sense. Was it a trick? *No, not a trick*, thought Terry. *You can't trick the laws of physics, can you?*

Terry felt a jolt of pain in his left temple and snapped his eyes shut. When he tried to open them, he felt another. *Must be the goggles*, he thought. *Mr. Nuber said they might cause headaches. Maybe I should take them off, just for a minute.* He removed his headpiece and set it on the ground.

Terry wiped his forehead with his palm. He was covered in sweat.

Another jab hit him right away. And another. His head pulsed, the pain coming faster and faster. Before long, it became a steady migraine, which gave no sign of ending. He took in sharper breaths, his mouth as dry as sand. He needed to get away from this place, get some water. He needed help.

Terry slid to his side, rolling on his back, staring into the darkness. He tried to say something, tried to call for help, but nothing came. He was going to black out in a room without any lights so he wouldn't even know it when it happened.

As if to answer him, a single beam of light appeared, a parting gift before he left the game for good. It moved much slower than the others, only a few inches at a time, hovering like a jewel in the darkness. Pretty soon it didn't move at all, like a lantern in an empty room, a waking dream that promised it was real.

Twelve, he thought with all his strength.

Then, the light was gone.

April 29, 2345
The Academy, Central

THE WORST PART about blacking out, Terry found, was the following migraine. As he opened his eyes, the light from the room engulfed him and he flinched.

"Relax," said a man's voice. "Don't move around too much."

Everything was blurry. Terry turned his head to see the shape of a man standing next to his bed. It was a doctor. "My *head*..." muttered Terry.

"Give it time. Breathe for a moment," said the doctor.

Terry closed his eyes and tried to do what the man said. It was difficult, but after a few minutes, he was able to regain control. When he opened his eyes again, his sight was almost back to normal.

"What happened?" Terry asked, looking around. He noticed two men in the back of the room.

"Calm down," said one of them. It was Nuber. "You passed out is all. Go back to sleep."

Of course, he had passed out. It was obvious enough to him when everything went black, and he suddenly woke up with a headache in a hospital bed. What he wanted to know was *why*.

"Listen to your teacher," said the doctor. "Here, I'll give you something. You need to sleep."

"I don't want to sleep," said Terry but took the medicine anyway. He glanced at the clock on the other side of the room. He could almost make out the numbers. 0800? No, that wasn't right. Maybe 0900. He closed his eyes and slept.

WHEN TERRY AWOKE AGAIN, the lights were out, and he was alone. The clock said it was after midnight. No wonder.

He managed to stay awake for a few minutes before the need for sleep overwhelmed him again, and in those moments, he managed to think of two specific things. The first was the light he had seen before losing control. The second was whether or not it had anything to do with the room with the gas.

The more he thought about the two things, the more he wondered whether one had any connection to the other. After all, he'd blacked out in the chamber. This could simply be a delayed reaction. If that was the case, would he continue to experience it? Was he going to be alright?

But before he could dwell on his thoughts, he drifted back into a dreamless sleep.

When he awoke again, the new day had arrived, and he could scarcely recall the worries of the night before.

The doctor came to see him after lunchtime. "We're letting you go this afternoon. You suffered a mild panic attack. It's not a big deal. Take the medication we give you and you'll be fine."

Terry nodded. Was that all it was—a panic attack? Terry wasn't even sure he knew what a panic attack meant. The doctor didn't seem that upset, so maybe it wasn't a big deal. After all, what reason did he have to lie?

Then again, what reason could there be for letting a child nearly choke to death in a room full of poisonous gas? He had certainly not forgotten about *that*—the feeling he had when the gas was filling up his lungs, killing him. And for what?

"Don't you have any questions?" asked the doctor. "It's okay if you do."

Terry paused. "I have a question," he said hesitantly.

"Whatever it is, you can ask," said the doctor.

"Does this have anything to do with the room with the gas?"

The man flinched at the sound of the last word. "Of course not," he said. "You just do what I told you and forget about the rest. You had a *panic attack*. It's over. Now listen, your instructor will be here soon to take you home. Don't move until he arrives. Understand?"

"Yes, sir."

The man left without another word. Terry waited until Mr. Nuber arrived.

"Glad you're okay," said Nuber. "Pack your crap. I'm taking you home."

Terry got out of bed and began getting dressed.

Neither said a word for several minutes as they walked through the corridors between the hospital and the school. Even when Nuber spoke to him, it wasn't much in the way of actual conversation.

After they reached the school, Nuber stopped outside the classroom and looked at him. "Before we go in there, I think I should tell you something," he said. His eyes were tired, like he'd been up all night.

"It wasn't a panic attack, was it?" Terry asked.

"I think we both know it wasn't," said Nuber.

Terry nodded.

"You've probably figured it out by now. What happened to you…it was because of the other day."

"The gas," said Terry.

"What happened to you…I guess you'd call it a side-effect. No one knows for sure if it'll happen again, but the doctors all agree it's unlikely. I wish I could tell you more about it, the name of the condition, but there isn't one. I hope that's enough for you."

It wasn't, but Terry was far too exhausted to argue. Mr. Nuber had obviously taken a risk by telling him the truth. After all, if they wanted him to know, the doctor would have said so earlier.

It was also pretty apparent from the look in Nuber's eyes that he wasn't saying everything. Something else was going on, something bigger than the blackout, bigger than the gas and the children who never came home that day. Beneath the teacher's strength, beneath his honesty, there was a fear and a worry that stretched far deeper. Something was wrong, Terry knew.

Whatever it was, it had his teacher spooked.

May 04, 2345
Pepper Plaza, Central

MARA SAT on a bench at the far end of Platform Twelve near the downtown plaza, an empty shopping bag between her legs. She watched a crowd of commuters shuffle in anticipation of the arriving train.

A little boy tugged on his mother's sleeve. "I wanna go home," he whined, but the mother ignored him. The boy looked to be around five, two years shy of his first birthday. It wouldn't be long before the academy stole him away, taught him a trade, and rebranded him an honorable citizen of the city. If he was lucky, he'd be a contractor, maybe a scientist. At worse, a farmer or a cleaner. No matter his aptitude, he could at least be thankful for a normal life. It was more than Mara's own son could say.

"Sorry to keep you waiting," said a woman's voice.

Mara turned on the bench to see Captain Avery Ross dressed in civilian clothes. Her hair, usually pinned in a clean military bun, flowed elegantly below her shoulders. She looked nothing like a soldier.

Ross took a seat next to Mara.

"What kept you?" Mara asked.

"Politics," she said. "I had to play bureaucrat for a few hours today. It kept me busy. I'm sorry you had to wait."

"I don't mind," Mara said. "But I'm not used to this cloak and dagger game you politicians like to play."

"With respect, ma'am, you're one of us now," said the captain. "You'd better get used to it. I'm sorry it has to be this way, but my office can't know I'm visiting you officially. The second I arrive at your building, the locator board records I'm there. Then, they have proof. Out here, I'm only boarding the train."

"Fair enough. Now what was so important it couldn't wait until our monthly check in?"

"You asked me to keep you apprised of your son."

"Is he alright?"

"Yes, of course," Ross said. "There was a scare, but he's okay now."

"What kind of scare?"

"Do you remember what I told you about the gas chamber?"

"Of course. It's barbaric."

"Yes, ma'am, and you know I agree, but there's been some developments."

"What kind of developments?"

"The children have begun to show signs of…I'm not sure what to call it. My point is, they're changing. Many of them are exhibiting strange behaviors and physical changes, most of which appear to be positive. Enhanced strength, endurance, reflexes. It's all very impressive. The doctors don't really know what to make of it, to be honest."

"Are there any negative side effects to whatever the hell this is?"

"Yes," said Ross. "Aside from the ones we've lost, which you've already seen, some are showing strange signs of addiction."

"Addiction? You mean like a drug?"

"Yes, ma'am. They've started asking for it."

"How many of them?"

"Only a handful. The children feel exhilarated after each exposure, completely energized. It's understandable some might become addicted."

Mara paused. "Terrance?"

"Not him," she said. "It's what I wanted to talk to you about. Archer has compiled a list of the children with the highest compatibility to Variant on a molecular level. Your son is at the top of that list."

"Isn't that a good thing?" asked Mara. "It means he won't get sick from the gas, right? It means he'll be safe."

"They thought so originally," said Ross.

"Has something changed?"

"A few days ago, Terry collapsed during a high intensity classroom exercise. He fainted. They're still trying determine why it happened, but Archer believes it has something to do with his compatibility rating. He thinks Terry's genes are so in tune with Variant that it's affecting him on a deeper level than the others."

Mara felt a wave of heat rush over her face. She imagined her son in a hospital bed, unconscious, helpless. "What the hell does that even mean?"

"I don't know," Ross confessed. "But for now he's fine. He's back in his old routine and seems to be doing alright."

"And you think all this is because Terrance has a higher compatibility rating?"

"Not me," Ross said. "Doctor Archer."

Mara watched as another train entered the platform. The doors slid open and a dozen people exited. "Thank you for telling me this," she said. "I just wish I knew what to do with it."

"Sorry," said Ross. "I thought you'd want to know."

"It's fine. You did the right thing," Mara assured her. "I just need time to think."

"This is a dangerous game we're playing," Ross said after a moment.

"It's not too late to back out, captain," said Mara.

"I told you before, the system is broken. It's never going to fix itself."

An automated voice erupted from the speaker overhead, indicating the arrival of another train. The crowd began to gather. Mara stood. "Go back to your boss and tell him I want to meet."

"What's your plan? Are you going to confront him about this?"

"If I have to," said Mara. "But only as a last resort. I'll demand disclosure first…ask him for the truth."

"In exchange for what?"

"Mothers, of course," said Mara. "I'll offer him what he wants."

"Do you think he'll agree to those terms?"

"You tell me, Ross. Is his legacy more important than his pride?"

Amber Project File Logs
February 27, 2324
To: James_Bishop
Received May 11, 2345

ARCHER*: Early testing is promising, Colonel. Out of the twenty-two subjects originally exposed, seventeen remain. If you recall the original estimates, these numbers are more than acceptable. In fact, one might even call them extraordinary.*

As for the status of the seventeen, each of them appears to be adapting differently. Almost all have begun to show clear signs of physical evolution and adaptability; however, some are more pronounced than others, depending, it seems, upon the subject's personal compatibility rating. It would appear that the higher the rating, the greater the change. Of course, these changes are at their peak when the subject is under direct exposure to the gas, but the effect remains evident for several days afterwards, gradually declining as the subject goes without exposure. Naturally, further testing is required before the experiment can reach its full conclusion. But, as they say, it is only a matter of time.

End Audio File

July 12, 2345
Central

Mara sat in Colonel Bishop's waiting room. She'd promised to reopen negotiations over potential mother candidates, but that was a lie. All she really wanted was a chance to meet face-to-face with Bishop about the children. It might not be too late to talk some sense into him.

"Matron Echols," called the young soldier behind the receptionist desk. He looked about nineteen years old, give or take.

"Yes?"

"The colonel says he will see you now."

"Fine." She stood and walked to the door, grasped the cold, steel handle and pulled it open. Stepping through and standing on the other side, a flood of memories washed over her. It had been several months since she was last here, but the room was instantly familiar. She and James had spent many afternoons together in this place, talking about her son. In exchange for that information, she provided pleasant company—a mutually beneficial relationship. Too bad it couldn't last.

Bishop grew distant when Mara became the matron. He'd objected to her promotion, citing a conflict of interest, since her child was part of a critical ongoing program, but Ava had ignored him. Mara tried to contact him several times since she accepted the position, but every request had been denied. The colonel made it clear that any and all business between their offices would be conducted through secondhand personnel. His version of a tantrum.

Mara expected Bishop to be behind his desk, but instead he was facing a display case, his back turned. She approached him. "Thank you for seeing me, Colonel," she said.

"You ransomed humanity's future against me," he said. "What choice did I have?"

"So dramatic. Are you even going to look at me?"

"If I have to," he said, turning around. He held a baseball in his hand, rubbing the skin of it with his thumb.

"I'm here to talk about your proposal. You know, the one where you requested another group of mothers for your research."

"And?"

"I'm willing to work with you, but I have some questions and a few requests."

"Of course you do." He walked to his desk and pulled the chair out. "Shall we sit?"

She nodded, sitting across from him. She pulled out a pad with the original list of mothers he'd requested. "The names," she said, handing it to him. "Why these women?"

"Because Archer says they're the most compatible. The more compatible, the greater the success rate. Nothing's changed since you were in the program, or did you forget?"

"Just checking. But now that you mention it, have there been any improvements or advances?"

"You'd have to ask the good doctor, I'm afraid. All I do is run the school."

"Then, let's talk about it."

"What does the school have to do with your mothers?"

"They'll want to know what's going to happen to their children," she answered.

"The same as any other child. Education."

She crossed her legs. "If our offices are going to work together, I'd like us to have a more open relationship. You know, as far as information goes. It's better that we both understand what the other is doing, specifically with this program."

"You already receive reports," he said.

"And I appreciate them, but we haven't been receiving everything. A little more disclosure would go a long way."

"Exactly what kind of disclosure?" he asked.

"Medical reports, to begin with. We stopped receiving those a while ago."

He removed his glasses, wiping them with a cloth. "Out of the question, I'm afraid. That information is too sensitive."

"Why?"

"You know why," he said. "The nature of this program requires a certain level of secrecy. We can't risk it leaking to the public. Sending it to you would be too great of a risk."

What a load of crap, she thought. "Ava received constant updates from your office. She had full disclosure. I'm the matron now. I have a right to those files."

"Ava never had full rights to the medical files. Her clearance ended the moment the Variant exposures began." He put his glasses back on. "I'm surprised she didn't tell you."

"It's more than that, and you know it. Ever since I took this office, you've refused to meet with me. You and Archer used to hold conferences with Ava on a regular basis. The second I became the matron, those meetings have ceased."

"Archer's work with the students occupies most of his time now, the same as it does for me. We're far too busy to sit around discussing policy, especially when a simple email will do."

"Yet you refuse to give me proper updates."

Bishop laughed. "You want an update? Okay. All of the children are fine. They're doing great, in fact. The gas is actually improving their health in ways we never could've predicted."

"That's not what I hear," she said.

He raised his brow. "Excuse me?"

Oh, well. No going back now, she thought. "I know all about the experiments...those students dying from the gas."

A brief look of surprise covered his face but quickly settled. *A rare sight*, Mara thought. But the cracks were beginning to show.

"You don't know what you're talking about," he said, finally.

She shrugged. "There's been whispers. A lot of people are talking."

He smirked. "You claim facts, but all you have are rumors," he said. "Whatever happened to the young pragmatist I used to know...the girl who scoffed at henhouse gossip?"

He was trying to guilt her, to twist her mind the way he always did, but she refused to flinch. "I don't want to believe it, James, but I need reassurances. I need to be able to tell my mothers their children will be safe."

"What are these stories you're so intent on listening to?"

"Deaths," she said. "Children dying from the gas. Needless risks. That sort of thing."

"Aside from the fact that none of what you say is remotely true, any information I gave you would endanger this program." He grabbed the baseball from the table and turned away in his chair. "Especially you."

"What the hell are you talking about?"

"You can't be trusted," he muttered. "You were the one

violating regulations by coming here and begging me for information about your son, remember? A boy, which, if you'll recall, is part of *this* program, leaving you in an extremely compromised position. You can't be trusted to act in the best interest of either the program or the people of this city. Not until your boy has graduated, anyway. You're too damn close to this and you know it." He smiled crookedly, a mocking gesture.

"You might be right," she said. "But I'm also the matron, which gives me a legal right to that information. Under section thirty six of the Stone Charter, as the political representative of the motherhood, the matron is legally authorized full disclosure on all documents related to the treatment of students. That's verbatim from the text. There's no argument, no loophole. It is explicit."

"I know all about the charter," he said, waving his hand at her. "It doesn't apply in this situation."

"Of course it does! You have to comply."

"I won't," he said.

"You don't have a choice! Either you give me the documents or I…"

"You what?" he snapped. "You'll go to somebody else? Who? The third wing of the charter? That would be Archer. I hate to break this to you, but he and I are in full agreement on the matter."

"Which is why we have a judicial system. They can overrule you. Everyone's accountable when it involves the law."

"By all means," he said, waving his hand. "No one will believe you. All you have are rumors and a colonel who refuses to give in to your childish demands."

"What happens if they investigate and find the rumors to be true? What happens when the bodies start turning up? Are you really willing to go to prison over this?"

"If it means saving the future of the human race from your shortsighted, dimwitted hands, then yes," he said, coldly. "In a heartbeat."

She got to her feet and grabbed her things. "I'm withdrawing my offer. You won't have your mothers, not until you're ready to work with me."

"We'll see," he said as she left.

She marched to the door and slammed it behind her, startling the secretary. "Sorry," said Mara, shooting her a glance. "But your boss is such an ass."

November 20, 2345
The Academy, Central

AFTER HIS BLACKOUT in the arena, Terry couldn't shake the feeling that he was destined for a relapse. But several weeks and a few more visits to the chamber later, the blackouts never came. To his surprise, he found he enjoyed the exposures—the purest, sweetest air he'd ever tasted. The fumes were pleasant, somehow, giving him unprecedented vigor, the likes of which he'd never known before.

In fact, Terry felt better than he had his entire life. He no longer lost his breath from walking up a flight of stairs. He stopped being afraid of looking weak in the arena. He had so much energy that he didn't know what to do with it all. When he got excited about something, he found himself rambling to his friends. He couldn't contain the energy.

But now he sat in class, during study hour, unable to move or talk. In a few minutes, Mr. Nuber would hand back their physics tests. After that, they'd study for another thirty minutes and then released. Maybe he'd ask John to go with him to the gym afterwards. He laughed silently at the thought. John always asked him to go work out, but Terry never felt up to it. He couldn't wait to see how John reacted.

Laughter erupted from the back of the class. He didn't have to look to know who it came from. Alex and Cole were always so obvious when they goofed around. It wouldn't take long before Mr. Nuber got onto them. Terry only hoped the teacher didn't take it out on the whole class. The last thing Terry wanted was another group detention.

"I'm passing back the tests from yesterday," Nuber said. "Overall, decent grades, but I'm expecting better next time. Some did fine. Others didn't. You'd better improve." He handed a stack of papers to Mei. She sat the closest to his desk and usually ended up distributing the graded assignments. "If you see a classmate struggling, help them. You're not alone here. Each and every one of you are studying the exact same material, taking the same tests, listening to the same lectures. If you don't help each other out, you aren't gonna get very far." He sat behind his desk and sighed, then snatched the pad he'd been reading and continued. "Oh, and Alex and Cole," he said. "Stop screwing around… unless you *want* latrine duty for the rest of the week."

The two boys went silent very fast.

Mei handed Terry his test. It had a few red marks, but he'd passed with an A-. Not bad.

John smiled and held up his paper. There was a circled C+ at the top of it. "Not too shabby, huh?"

"Great job," said Terry.

"Don't you guys want to know what I made?" asked Mei, standing in front of them.

"We already know what you got," said John. "You always do the same on every test."

"That may be true, but you could at least *pretend* to care. You know, like *good* friends do."

Terry and John stared at her for a moment.

"In case you wanted to know, I made an *A+*," she said, hastily.

"And there it is," said John, waving his hand at her.

"Oh, shut up," she said, rolling her eyes. She went back to her seat.

Terry raised his hand. "Sir, may I be excused?"

"Restroom or medical?" he asked. Those were the only two reasons they could leave during class.

"Restroom."

Nuber grunted. "Go ahead."

Terry left his desk and proceeded to leave the room. As he walked down the aisle, he passed by several desks and couldn't stop himself from looking at the grades on the papers. Most of them were decent enough, but there was one failure. Nicholas.

Nick had always done well, at least early on. In fact, there was a time when he rivaled Mei for the highest GPA in the class. But recently, for whatever reason, things had changed. Nick barely passed any of the tests, including the easy ones, and when the other kids asked him about it, he acted like he didn't care. John said Nick had probably snapped from studying so hard, trying to stay ahead of the class, but Terry had a hard time believing it. Despite what John claimed, Nick never spent much time with his nose in a book. So what sense did it make for him to go crazy?

Terry shuddered at the thought. He shouldn't call Nick crazy. If Terry had told anyone about what he saw in the arena—how the lights slowed, and his body went completely haywire—maybe they'd call him crazy, too.

But the gas did that. It changed him and made him sick. Is that what happened to Nick? If the gas could do what it did to Terry, why not Nick, too? Maybe Variant affected everyone differently, depending on the person.

Terry closed the classroom door and entered an empty hallway. He smiled, happy for the break. He didn't really have to pee, but sitting behind a desk all day drove him absolutely nuts. He probably could've waited for the break, but this gave him more time to stretch his legs.

He entered the bathroom and went to one of the stalls. He felt guilty for wanting to get away from everyone, even his friends, but sometimes he just needed to be alone.

Sitting there in the stall, Terry's mind wandered. He remembered his mother and sister, wishing they were still around. Despite never seeing them, he had little trouble remembering their faces.

He imagined himself in his room, reading to Janice, and it made him smile. Janice used to follow him everywhere. He never complained about it, even when she cried, which wasn't often. She was like that from the moment Mother had brought her home.

Now, she was older, probably somewhere in the academy. Too bad he'd never see her there. After the exposures started, they moved Terry's class to a remote wing of the school, close to the arena and the labs, but far from the other classrooms. The kids had to use different restrooms, a different gym. They even had their own cafeteria. They were being isolated. It didn't take much to figure out why.

Suddenly, the door to the bathroom flew open and Terry flinched, his eyes widening. One of the other students had come in. Was it break time already? He started to stand, but stopped when he heard shoes screeching on the floor.

The metal wall next to him shook, hit by something

else. A person? He looked at the floor and saw two sets of boots facing each other.

"Come on, moron," said a voice. "Think you can say what you said and not pay for it? Come on, Nicky. Let's see what you're made of."

"Stop it, Alex!" cried Nick, grunting as he scurried back against the stall.

"You think you're so much better than everyone else?" asked Alex. He slammed Nick against the stall, scuffing the tiles with his shoes.

"I didn't do anything!" cried Nick. Alex punched him hard and Nick gasped. "Stop it!"

Terry wanted to do something, but he couldn't move. Every blow to Nick was another reason not to go. *That'll be me*, he thought. *If I go out there, that'll be me. Then, what will I do?* So he stayed, completely frozen, his arms wrapped tightly around his knees.

Nick fell to the floor, crying and shaking, his head below the stall. Terry stared at him. "Don't you say a word to anyone about this," ordered Alex. "If you do, I'll kill you. Go ahead, and you'll see. I promise." He kicked Nick, and there was a loud thud.

Alex stormed off, and the door to the boys' room slammed behind him, leaving a swell of silence. After a few short moments, Nick began to weep, huffing and sniveling as he lay on the cold floor.

Terry opened the door and stepped out of the stall. A mirror spanned the entire wall, and he immediately saw his classmate in the corner of it, his arms around his sides. Terry ran to him. "Are you okay?" he asked.

Nick struggled to sit up, leaning against the wall, tears in his eyes. "He kicked me," he said, snot dripping from his nose. "It hurts really bad."

Terry hated himself. Why'd he stay in the stall? Why didn't he interfere? He was so weak. *I'm such a coward.* "I should've stopped him."

"But then he would've hit you, too."

Terry helped Nick to his feet. "You have to tell Mr. Nuber."

"No way," said Nick. "You heard Alex. He'll just do it again."

Terry didn't think so, but he knew Nick wouldn't take the risk. If Alex did attack him again, he wouldn't stop at a few kicks to the stomach. So long as Nick believed there was a chance of it, he'd never turn Alex in. The fear of pain was simply too much.

"But you can't just let him get away with it," said Terry.

"What else am I supposed to do?" he asked.

Why didn't Nick want to do anything? How could he let it go so easily? "You tell on him, Nick. It isn't right what he did!"

"He made fun of me for my test score. I got mad and argued. I shouldn't have said anything. It's my fault."

"No! That's stupid. You didn't do anything wrong, Nick."

"It's okay," said Nick, wiping his face with his sleeve.

"He hit me, and now he's done. If I went to Mr. Nuber, it wouldn't make it go away."

Terry squeezed his fist. "But…"

"Forget about it, Terry," said Nick, straightening his shirt. "It's better not to tell. Sometimes it hurts more when you do."

10

Amber Project File Logs
Play Audio File 1677
Received December 02, 2345

NUBER: Alex is getting worse. I'm running out of ways to punish the kid. Did you see the video of what he did to Nicholas?

ARCHER: We predicted behavioral changes. The boy's aggression is nothing to be concerned about.

NUBER: The hell it isn't. Eventually he's really going to hurt someone.

BISHOP: I get your frustrations, but we can't just pull him out of class.

NUBER: Then stop dosing him with the gas. Cut the problem off at the source.

ARCHER: Unacceptable. Removing the subject will hinder the results of the experiment.

NUBER: What good does it do anyone?

ARCHER: His reaction is unique. Further research may provide us with a means of preventing such a perversion in future experiments.

NUBER: And if he ends up killing someone? What then?

BISHOP: We'll deal with it. Remember what's at stake here, Henry.

NUBER: Please, spare me the speech. I've heard it so much I've got the damn thing memorized.

End Audio File

February 13, 2346
The Academy, Central

Terry slouched and stifled a yawn, dropping his head and trying to hide it. Mr. Nuber didn't like yawns during lectures. He said when you yawned, you couldn't hear anything, and he didn't want anyone to miss what was happening. "Everything I say is important," he would remind the class when a student asked about it. "And if you miss something, even just a few words, you'll be lost. No excuses." If you actually had the audacity to bring yourself to yawn and he saw it, he'd stop the lecture cold and stare until you stopped. He'd cock his head a little to the left and give a look that said, *I'm stopping because of you, you little bastard. Thanks a lot.*

Terry managed it without being seen, then watched as Mr. Nuber wrote out an equation on the board with a digi-pen.

He looked at Nick and wondered how he was feeling. Did he regret not telling Mr. Nuber? It'd been a few days since the fight in the boys' room and nothing had happened. Maybe everything really was okay.

He'd thought about telling John or Mei about it but decided against it. If Nick wanted anyone else to know, he'd tell them. It wasn't Terry's responsibility, right? Then, why did he feel so guilty? He shuddered. *Relax*, he thought. *Watch the teacher. Listen.*

"Now we're going to talk about tectonic plates," said Nuber. "We touched on them briefly in the last lesson, but today they're the focus." He pulled up a map of the Earth with large, jagged lines spread out across it. Some had names, others didn't. "They're the reason continents exist," he explained. "Or mountain ranges. Or trenches in the ocean. They grind against one another, and they push the rock up to form hills and peaks. When they pull apart, we see the land separate. Sometimes when they're grinding against each other, we get the quakes. You see, class, these plates, they're jagged and deformed, so when they do this grinding, they sometimes get stuck on each other, locking into place for a while. But they don't just stop moving. No, on the contrary, they *keep* moving, even though part of them is stuck. That's when the tension builds and then the part that's caught *snaps*, almost like a rubber band, which is where the quake comes from—that release of tension." He pointed at the screen. "Most of the time, these quakes happen on these lines here, but sometimes they're so big that you can feel them far away. We aren't on a line, but we're not that far from one, either, so sometimes we get them. They hit us and we have to do a few repairs, reinforce the supports. Those nasty plates can be a pain in the ass at times, but they're rare and we never get the bad ones."

Terry didn't care about tectonic plates. In fact, he was having a hard time caring about *anything* the teacher talked about. He leaned forward, staring at the map, trying to feign interest. It was a good lie, another to add to his list. He was becoming an expert on lies. Thanks to Alex. *No*, he thought. *Not because of Alex. It's my own fault.*

"Terry," said John, suddenly. He flinched at the sound of his own name. "Hey, it's time to go. You okay?"

"He's just daydreaming," said Mei. She and John were standing over him now. Was class over already?

"Well, snap out of it. We have to go back to our room and study, remember? You promised to help me."

"Right, yeah."

"Let's go," said Mei. "Most of the class is already gone."

He followed after them, trying to shake the thoughts that kept circling his mind.

That afternoon, they studied until dinner. After that, John wanted to go exercise in the gym, play in the arena. He enjoyed it more than the classroom, especially since Terry had started getting better.

But he didn't feel like going today. In fact, all he wanted to do was lay in his bed, close his eyes, and sleep. "I don't feel good," he said. "But you go ahead."

John left and Terry went to his own room. As he lay there in his bunk, he couldn't help but remember the incident with Nick, but tried his best to focus on something else. He imagined himself in the arena, holding the rifle and trying to win. He thought up strategies and acted them out again and again.

Then, he pictured himself on the surface, standing next to his friends. He wondered what kind of dangers he'd face there, what sort of wonders he'd see. Would there be animals? What if they were scary? He wondered what he'd do if one of them provoked him. Would he fight back? What if he had to shoot one of them?

An image of Alex flashed before him, and ashamed, he pushed it aside.

As he drifted off to sleep, another question lingered, and for hours it circled in his mind like water in a drain, following him into his dreams, becoming a part of him. In the night he awoke, cold and hot and wet, and there the question stood, tapping at his brain. *Would I kill to save myself?* He trembled at the thought.

Terry hoped he'd never have to know.

May 06, 2346
Housing District 01

STANDING outside Ava Long's home turned Mara's stomach. When she first brought up the idea of approaching her mentor to Ross, it sounded like a good one. The closer she got to the door, however, the more she second guessed herself. After all, Ava had left her in charge of the motherhood, given her more responsibility than any other woman in the history of the city. And what had she done with it? Practically given it away, like an antique rug, torn and unwanted. What would the first matron say to her after hearing this? How ashamed would Ava be?

But she had come too far to go back now.

Captain Avery Ross stood beside her, patiently waiting, rarely speaking. Ever the soldier. She wore civilian clothes today, a similar set to the outfit she had worn last week at the train station. Today, however, she looked even more inconspicuous. Her shirt and pants were two sizes larger than they needed to be, masking her athletic frame. She wore a pair of glasses, seemingly fake, and her hair draped neatly around her neck and ears, encasing her smile—a rare sight, normally, but a welcome change. If anyone saw her today, they might think she was a scientist or a shy intellectual, her nose stuck in a book. Mara found a shred of amusement in the physical transformation her friend had undergone, and in fact, she liked her more this way.

Mara swallowed the lump in her throat, then pressed her finger to the digital screen on the door. A series of chimes echoed from the other side, followed by a woman's voice. "Coming," she called.

Ava Long opened the door and smiled instantly. "Oh, my goodness, if it isn't my favorite daughter."

Mara returned the smile. "Matron," she said, nodding.

"Addressing yourself?" asked Ava. "I'll have you know I'm a regular citizen now, young lady."

"Nonsense," said Mara, defiantly. "You're still my matron."

Ava laughed. "And who's this?" she asked, looking at Ross.

"A friend. Avery Ross." Mara said.

"Oh, my. Yes, I know Captain Ross," she said.

Ross nodded and put out her hand. "Matron Long," she said.

"Honey, you put that hand away and give me a hug."

Ross blushed but did as Ava instructed. They embraced, Ava patting her back. "I didn't know if you'd remember me," muttered Ross, grinning.

"How could I forget about my little pioneer?" asked Ava.

Ross nodded. "You're too kind, ma'am."

"Is it alright if we come in?" asked Mara. She didn't

want to interrupt, but someone might take notice if they lingered outside too long.

Ava's smile faded. "You sound serious. Is everything okay?"

"I'll explain in a moment, if you don't mind."

"Of course, of course," said Ava. She moved aside and let them in.

Ava's apartment always smelled so lovely, a constant stir of freesia, citrus and hazelnut in the air. This was a result of her frequent visits to the farms, where she would accept donations of food and flowers from the local workers, who never denied her. She did this so that she could put together gifts for those she felt needed them, particularly new mothers who were just starting out. During her time as the matron, Ava had taken to visiting each new mother's apartment, greeting each with a basket full of gifts and a warm, wrinkled smile. She had done the same for others in the city, particularly those who had fallen on hard times, but the bulk of her hobby was aimed toward the motherhood, where her heart still lay. Looking around the apartment now, catching glances of half completed baskets, it became clear that Ava's humble hobby had finally become a full-time job.

"Sorry for the mess," said Ava. She began clearing off the dining room table, which was covered in translucent cello wrap and two half-finished baskets. "Please, take a seat. Would either of you like something to drink?"

"No, thank you," said Mara.

"Suit yourself," said Ava, gleefully, then poured herself some Earl Grey tea. "I prefer a touch of honey. Otherwise, it's bland." She took a seat across from Mara and Ross, sipped lightly from her cup, and smiled. "Now, what's got you all riled up this morning?"

"Colonel Bishop," said Mara, getting straight to the point. "He's trying to push me out of the council and block my access to the program."

"How's that, exactly?" asked Ava.

"It happened as soon as you left office. I didn't tell you because I thought it was only an adjustment period. You know, growing pains. I didn't think he was serious about cutting me out the way he has. Looks like I was wrong." She went on to describe the leaked information she received, but kept Ross's name out of it and also omitted her face to face with Bishop. Ava seemed to listen attentively to every word Mara spoke, never looking away, but she also didn't act very shocked by it, either.

Ava didn't respond immediately to the information dump. Instead, she continued to sip more of her tea, quietly staring into the cup. "I assume you're retaliating," she finally said.

"Retaliate?" asked Mara. "I don't know what you mean. I was hoping you'd step in, maybe show your support."

"Oh, of course you have my full support, dear, but you need more than the kind words of an old woman on your side."

"If your voice isn't enough, then what is?"

"You need to show your strength," said Ava. "It's the only thing boys like Bishop understand."

Mara hadn't expected this kind of talk from the former matron, but, then again, this was the woman who manipulated General Stone into restructuring the government. There were obviously sides to Ava Long that she had yet to see. "All this talk of strength," she said. "You act as though I'm sitting on an army, ready to conquer. I'm just the matron, nothing more, a glorified mother playing politician."

"You're wrong," said Ross. Her voice hit Mara unexpectantly. "The matron's influence spreads all throughout the motherhood and even to the other branches."

"But they have weapons," said Mara. "Guns and armor and gas to shut us down."

Ava shook her head. "You've already convinced yourself that you'll lose."

"I don't know what a band of mothers can do against the military," said Mara.

Ava paused, then placed her cup on the table. She took a napkin and dabbed her lips and fingers, then folded it and placed it next to the cup. Ava did all of this in silence and in no particular hurry. When she finally did speak, the room had fallen into a full and rigid silence.

"I'm going to tell you a secret today," said Ava, quite seriously. "I want you to memorize it and I want you to believe it, not because *I* told it to you but because it is the *truth*. Everyone seems to think power comes from a weapon, from something you can hold in your hands and aim at someone's skull. A bully picks up a stick in the schoolyard and makes a threat, and see how he is rewarded. The weaker children obey, not out of love, but fear. This practice doesn't change when we grow older. The only thing that changes is the stick becomes a bomb, and the bully wears a uniform and calls himself a king."

Mara leaned in, listening.

"Before the old world died, if the government threatened to take what you had, there was nothing you could do, because they had all the soldiers, all the weapons, all the bombs. The nation with the biggest guns could kill the rest of us with the press of a button, and often they would threaten to do just that. Nothing could be said for the woman in her home, holding a crying child in her shaking hands, praying to God to save her from the bombs flying overhead. Nothing but the word of a tyrant king, sitting high atop the dead-built throne, praising the works that were made in his name." Ava stared hard into Mara's eyes. "That's the illusion they preach, the trick you end up believing is real. They tell you true power is dictated by the dictator, because he lives in the ivory tower with his finger on the trigger, but the secret they keep, the part they refuse to tell you during your adolescent indoctrination…is that *none* of that is true. Real power isn't dealt in bullets, darlings, but in *words*. Words that stir a man to stand when all the rest have fled…to fight unwinnable wars, all for the sake of a thought. Every leader who made a difference didn't do it with a sword or a gun, but with a voice that might have moved a mountain. Think of all the revolutions, all the great religions whose followers once numbered in the billions, and understand me when I tell you: they started with a few delusional fools, conspiring in a room."

Mara was afraid to answer. The idea that she could ever hold the kind of influence that Ava was suggesting had never occurred to her before. She wasn't sure how she felt about it.

"I don't mean to suggest you preach a call to arms against the good colonel," said Ava. "But there are peaceful ways to protest, and history has shown them to be just as effective."

Ross's eyes lit up at the sound of this. "You're saying we should go public. Tell the city what's really going on. Get them on our side." She paused, then looked at Mara. "This could work, ma'am. With half the city against the colonel, he'd have no choice but to bring you back in or risk impeachment. The courts might be slow, but they'd snap to it in a hurry if the public's eye was on them."

A swell of tension filled Mara's throat, but she swallowed it and took a breath. The whole thing sounded crazy, but that didn't mean it wasn't true. She had tried, after all, to appeal to Bishop on a professional level, pleading for him to adhere to the established policy rather than his own egotistical ambition. But what good had it done? Where was she now, but in the corner of a room, questioning herself? "Ava, the things you're talking about…what makes you think we can do that?"

Ava thought for a moment, then quietly stood and walked to the baskets she'd moved from the table when Mara first entered. Gently, she brushed the cuff of her finger against the petals of one of the freesia flowers. Taking it in her hand, she gave it to Mara. "Smell that," she said.

Mara did. "It's very nice," she said, truthfully, though she didn't see the point.

"Do you know how difficult it is to grow flowers in the gardens?" asked Ava. "Aside from the fact that they require space, artificial lighting, and regulated temperature, the science division claims it's a bad investment because of the water it takes to produce them. 'They contribute little to the sustainment of the city's population,' I was told." Ava sat back down. Mara returned the flower, which Ava accepted. She twirled it in her hand, watching it, almost gleefully. "They don't see the point in them. I suppose from a purely logical perspective, they're right. But human beings aren't logical creatures, are they? On the contrary, we require emotional stimulation. We require inspiration. A sense of comfort. That's what these flowers do. That's their purpose." She tossed the blossom on the table. "Never mind that if we didn't grow them, they'd go extinct. But now look at how they've flourished, going out to homes all over the city."

Mara couldn't argue with her. Ava's flowers were every-

where. There were several gardens now in the plazas downtown, lining the shop corners, adding a bit of violet into an
otherwise dull world.

"You might think I did all this out of the goodness of
my little heart, but it wouldn't be the whole truth. The
reality is I needed public opinion on my side. I needed
people to like me. It's easy to get elected or appointed if
you understand the way the ladder works, darlings, but
staying in power is the tricky part. You need more than a
title and a pretty face for that. But you can't do it with fear
or violence, because in the end you'll only lose. You have to
do it with love. Show them you're a saint. Make them
believe you care, and then prove you actually do. That's
how you win the long hand. That's how you beat the other
bastards down."

October 02, 2347
Maternity District

MARA SAT in the mother's lounge next to Ava, patiently
waiting for the rest of the mothers to take their seats. Today
she would finally speak publically about the rumors
regarding the children—gossip she and Ava had quietly
spread themselves. In the months since their initial meeting,
both Mara and Ava had addressed these rumors, clarifying
and reinforcing them with evidence and leaked informa-

tion. The uproar at this had slowly grown to the point where it had reached the other branches. In response to it, Bishop had sent a representative to Mara, requesting that she put an end to whatever she was trying to prove. This representative had been, thankfully, Avery Ross, much to Mara's amusement.

Ross, of course, couldn't be in attendance, lest her superiors discover the truth about her treasonous activities. The subterfuge was why she and Mara had agreed Ross should remain as far away from here as possible. No doubt she was sitting in Bishop's office right now, unnecessarily going over matters that probably could have waited until tomorrow.

In the meantime, Mara would do what she came here to do. She would tell these women the truth, and watch as Bishop's propaganda came undone.

"Are you ready?" whispered Ava. "It looks like most of us are here."

Mara felt a crawl in her stomach. It had been a while since she had butterflies. "Yes, I'm ready."

"You seem jittery," said Ava.

Mara hesitated. "Maybe a bit."

"Been there," admitted Ava. "But you can do this. It's no different from all the other times."

The double doors in the back of the auditorium closed, sending a hard echo through the room. Mara got to her feet and the swell of open chatter from among the audience came to an end. Their eyes were now transfixed upon the matron, on Mara.

"Good morning," she said to the crowd. "I'm sorry we have to meet under such irregular terms, ladies, but as many of you are already aware, and as I'm sure most will certainly agree, there is a very good reason for it. Several months ago, information leaked from Central about the treatment of several of our children. These documents, which I myself received and evaluated, detailed several mortifying incidents in which children were either killed or, at the very least, grossly mistreated."

The crowd stirred loudly. This was the first time some had heard the news. "Please, settle down," Mara said, raising her hand to quiet the noise. Once the chatter had subsided to a reasonable level, she continued. "I sent a request to Colonel Bishop, asking for more information on these matters but was told to mind my own business. Whenever I showed up or demanded a meeting, I was turned away, dismissed outright. Since then, both the military and the science division have held secret meetings in which the motherhood is not permitted. This is a direct attack on our rights and on the Stone Charter. More than that, however, it is an attack on our children and our very way of life. We cannot stand idly by while the rights we fought so long to have are slowly taken away from us." She slammed her fist on the podium. "We are the caretakers. We are the protectors. It is our job…our privilege…to safeguard the lives of our children."

The crowd cheered at the sound of Mara's words. She waited a moment for the noise to settle, then went on. "We must take a stand today," she said, speaking louder than before. "I hereby demand the immediate resignation of both Colonel James Bishop and Doctor William Archer by the courts of our fair city."

More cheering.

"Until these demands are met," she said, "the motherhood will no longer contribute new students to the academy, nor will any new contracts be taken. We do this to secure the lives and dignity of all those who follow hereafter. We do this for ourselves, because it is the right and moral action."

"No more sacrifices!" screamed a girl from the crowd.

"No more dead babies!" said another.

Most of the women stood, their fists raised, screaming violently for action. Mara's words had stirred hysteria, but it was exactly the kind of outrage that she and her fellow conspirators wanted. After she officially released the leaked documents, the wildfire of outcry would only grow. It wouldn't take long before the courts decided they had no other choice but to act, and with so much proof on the table, their victory was all but assured.

Amber Project File Logs
Play Audio File 1327
To: John_Constein@Amber_security
From: Charles_Armstrong@Amber_security
December 29, 2346

ARMSTRONG: Sir, the following message was received twelve minutes ago at approximately 0220 from the installation's automated security system.

WARNING. UNAUTHORIZED ACCESS AT SECURITY POINT 0827. PLEASE ENTER AUTHORIZATION NUMBER TO DISPATCH SECURITY FORCES TO DESIGNATED AREA.

We are still investigating the situation, but the technicians are saying it wasn't a malfunction or an accident. That's all we have right now. I'll update you with more information as we receive it.

End Audio File

December 29, 2346
Unknown

The tunnel was darker than the city, dimly lit by the old technology running along the corners of the ceiling. Most of the lights were out now, of course, which only made traveling through the passageways all the more dangerous. At times, there was no telling what lay ahead—two centuries of negligence had left it in a broken state. Dust covered the walls like blankets, making it difficult to breathe. The smell, sour and bitter like stale fruit, was full enough to taste.

Alex slid his palm across the dirty, metal walls, flicking the grime from his fingertips after enough of it had accumulated. He wiped his palms against his coat, placed his hand back on the wall and proceeded to do it again. Most of the flakes came off as easily as they went on, but the sweat and oil from his skin mixed with the fragments that remained, creating a layer of sludge on his skin, like a natural chalk powder. The more he wiped the walls, the more grime he gathered. *Exactly what I need.*

As he came around the curve of the hall, he spotted Cole waiting for him. "I'm ready," Alex yelled, clapping his hands. "I've got this."

"Careful, Alex," said Cole, pointing to a dangling piece of steel nearby. "It's a long way down, and this thing looks pretty flimsy."

Careful? Alex rolled his eyes. "If you wanted to be careful, you should've stayed at home. The Surface ain't no place for kids!"

"Hey, I'm no kid," said Cole.

"What? I can't hear you, little kid."

"I said I'm not no kid!" yelled Cole.

Alex smiled. "Damn right you ain't." He walked to the edge of the platform and examined the hole. "Okay, so I'll leap and grab the ladder there. You follow, got it? We'll climb up together. Easy."

"Sure, yeah, easy." Cole cleared his throat and gulped.

Alex took a deep breath. It wasn't a long jump, but missing it could mean his life. He gave the order to stand back, and Cole followed it. With the area cleared, Alex walked to the back of the hall, readying himself.

He launched into a full sprint.

As he reached the edge, he leapt high and for a brief moment, flew. His chest hit the railing dead on, nearly knocking the wind out of his lungs, but he managed an arm through one of the openings, catching himself. He wrapped his body around it, doing his best to ignore the pain of the collision. He wheezed and gasped for air, trying to replenish his lungs, holding his grip with every ounce of strength his arms could wield. *Don't look down*, he thought. *Don't let go.*

"Are you okay?" Cole asked. It was a stupid question, but Alex let it slide. He didn't have enough air to waste on sarcasm right now.

"Yeah," he said and left it at that. Alex pulled himself up a few steps and waited for his body to relax. He hated how fragile his muscles were, how weak the city's air made him. Once they were on the surface, tasks like this would be easy. Their bodies would adjust to the Variant and everything would be better—more like the chamber, only all the time. He'd never be weak again. "Are you ready?" he asked. "You'll have to jump and grab my arm."

"Alright," said Cole. He reached out his hand but couldn't connect to Alex. "I gotta jump to make it."

Clinging to the railing, Alex snapped his fingers at Cole. "Do it," he ordered. "Hurry!"

Cole jumped almost immediately. Their hands failed to connect, but Alex caught the boy's shoulder. "You idiot," Alex said, once he pulled Cole up. "You realize you almost died right there?"

Cole didn't answer until they had climbed to the next platform. "Long way down," he finally said, scanning the pit below. "Maybe we're almost there."

Moronic. They still hadn't reached the midpoint yet, not according to the blueprints they'd downloaded. Perhaps the hole in the ground seemed large to Cole, but soon he would undoubtedly see what Alex already could—this was only the beginning.

He grunted and pressed on. He could teach Cole later when they had the extra time. For now, they had to keep moving.

Getting to the surface was the only thing that mattered now.

December 30, 2346
Central

NUBER STOOD in Bishop's office, along with Captain Ross and Doctor Archer. He wanted nothing more than to be somewhere else.

"There's been a breach, sir," Ross explained to Bishop. "Two boys. We have them on camera, heading through the sealed access hatch near the sewage facility. They appear to be in their teens. We think they're students."

Colonel Bishop sat at his desk and let out a long sigh. He gripped the side of his chair and squeezed. "I'm not in the mood for this. It's two in the morning."

"I've checked the boards, and it looks like it's Alex and Cole," said Nuber. He clasped his hand around his neck, sliding it against the morning's new stubble. In his rush, he'd forgotten to shave.

"Great," Bishop said. "So they've run off to do what, exactly? Where does that passage lead?"

"To the surface," said Ross. "But there was a leak a few decades ago, so the tunnel was sectioned off and closed. Some Variant seeped in."

"Can they make it through?" asked Bishop.

Ross looked uneasy. "There's a manual release valve for the quarantined section. If they manage to open it, the next compartment door will automatically lock. There's nothing to worry about."

"What are the hell are they trying to do?" asked Bishop.

"Head topside, obviously," said Nuber.

Bishop scoffed. "How do they even know how to get there?"

"It's my fault," said Nuber. "We went over the city's infrastructure a few months ago. I showed the blueprints in class, but I never handed out copies. They must have stolen them."

"Sounds like you were careless," said the colonel.

"I tried to tell you Alex was unstable."

Bishop looked at Ross. "What are we doing to fix this?"

"Sir, we are prepared to send a response team after them. We can take the Sling and beat them to the surface where the tunnel comes out."

Bishop shot a glance at Archer, who stood near the back of the room. He leaned against the wall, casually staring at the pad in his hand. He appeared to be working. "You're not saying much," Bishop said. "Any thoughts?"

Archer tilted his head and nodded. "I always have thoughts, but right now I'm waiting to see what you do. It's been a while since I had the pleasure of watching you work."

Nuber had always hated Archer. The old man was arrogant and didn't give a damn about anyone but himself. "By my count, it's been close to fifteen years since you did anything worth a shit. You should be a little more protective of your accomplishments."

"I can always make more," Archer said, still looking at his pad.

Nuber clenched his jaw. "That's some perspective you've got. Lost a person? No problem. I'll just build another one."

"Shut up, both of you," said Bishop. "I need a solution, not an argument. Nuber, you're their instructor. Give me something."

Nuber turned his back to Archer and faced his commander. "Ross said it herself. Use the elevator, beat them to the surface, bring them in. I don't see any other options."

"What about you, Doctor?" asked Bishop. "Got any *genius* ideas you'd like to share with the rest of the class?"

Archer shrugged. "You could always let them run."

"Why the hell would you do that?" asked Nuber.

"To begin with, it would show us whether or not they're capable of surviving direct exposure. The Variant we've been using is thinner and easier on their bodies than the gas on the surface. If they manage to last more than a few minutes, we'll know their bodies can handle it. If they can't, at least we don't have to risk the rest of them."

Bishop pressed his knuckles into his desk until they popped. "We'll blend the two ideas. Once the boys make it to the surface, we'll send a team up to retrieve them. Give them a few hours. Unless the doctor thinks we should wait."

"It's more than enough time," said Archer.

"Then, do it," ordered Bishop. "Now, if we've covered everything, you can all get back to work."

Ross left immediately, followed by Archer. They shut the door behind them.

Bishop stared at Nuber for a moment. "I don't need a sermon, Henry," he finally said.

"And I'm not here to give you one."

"Then, what the hell do you want? Two boys escaped, partially because of you, and I had to make a decision about what was better, not just for them, but for all the students."

"I got that."

"Then, what is it?"

Nuber took a moment before he answered. "I know it's early. Or late. Whatever you wanna call it. But I think you need to think about this for more than a few measly seconds. Have you asked yourself what could happen if this whole enterprise actually *works*?"

Bishop paused. "What are you talking about?"

"I'm asking you, what if those boys get to the surface and they're fine?"

"Then, I guess Archer's research will have been a success," said Bishop. "It should be a good thing."

"Right. But what happens next? We go up and get them, pull them back into the ground against their will. Are we gonna make them stay here? What if they don't *want* to come home?"

"They're children. We'll *make* them."

"I've spent every day with those two for the past eight years, and I can tell you right now: they're anything *but* children. They're barely even human. They're stronger, faster, and better. Try to bring them home, and you'll see. If they don't wanna go, they won't."

"You've grown more cynical," said Bishop.

"Or cautious. Either way, a couple of kids are about to do something none of our people can: walk on the surface without a damned suit. There's nothing slowing them down, no baggage to limit where they can go. And if you think a team of oxygen-reliant soldiers has a chance in hell against two unrestricted kids, you're out of your damned mind. You try to tear them away from this new world of theirs, they're gonna resist. And when that happens, with all their new strength and speed…all this in the hands of a couple of teenagers…someone's gonna get hurt." Nuber snapped his fingers and pointed at the ceiling. "And I'm not so sure it'll be them."

December 30, 2346
Unknown

THE ELEVATOR SHAFT was colder than Alex expected. It didn't have the kind of insulation the city did. The walls were different here, not steel or padded metal, but rocks and machines that ran together from one point to the next.

Alex and Cole sat together, waiting for the door to the Variant-flooded compartment to open. Containment procedures built into the tunnels by previous generations had forced the door to close, blocking off the leak. Apparently, the ventilation system in the section had stopped working, but rather than fix the problem, they simply closed the door and left it alone. All the better for Alex. The sooner he reached the Variant, the easier the trip would become.

The anticipation of what lay ahead filled him with pure elation, the gnawing eagerness of freedom. This was his moment, right now, before he found the final path—before he followed it to the end of the line, to whatever paradise or hell it might take him.

To the surface, he hoped. A world with endless possibilities, separate from the limits of this rotting grave of a place, where humans had become reliant on walls and machines to keep them alive.

He looked forward to leaving them all behind.

The console nearby let out a loud chime, indicating the

previous door had finally sealed behind them, and the next section could finally open.

The large, metal vault unlatched and a wave of dust blew against their feet. The air around them immediately filled with the scent of Variant, and Alex took a deep breath of it. "Finally," he said, grinning. "Now we're making progress."

It was only a taste, but the reward would do for now. Soon, they'd stand on the surface, surrounded by a world they could shape with their own hands—build their own lives without the burdens of the weak or the useless to weigh them down. Only the strong were allowed access; only the powerful would reign.

It would be a better world for better people.

December 31, 2347
Central

NUBER WAS COMPLETELY EXHAUSTED. The past twenty-four hours were beginning to take their toll on him. How was he supposed to manage a class full of teenagers when he also had to deal with the fact that two of them had vanished?

Bishop had a quiet, empty look on his face. He had his elbows propped against the desk, hastily rubbing his hands together. Nuber had known him for twenty-five years—time enough to understand his ticks and tendencies. The hand rubbing always worried him.

"We've lost them," said Bishop at last.

Nuber didn't bother to act surprised. He'd already prepared himself for this. "How'd it happen?"

"I'm not completely certain if the two boys are dead, but the signal from their implants is definitely gone. Ross says their vitals were normal right before they went dark, which suggests they've moved outside the safe zone. Or maybe their hearts exploded out of their chests when they got to the surface. I don't know."

"So they're missing," said Nuber.

"If they're too far for us to track, they're too far for us to go after. The oxygen tanks won't last more than twelve hours. Chances are, if they're still alive, we'll never find them. Not unless we get creative."

"Creative? What do you mean?"

"Simple. I've already sent a team, but I want an alternative. In the very real likelihood that they don't recover anything, your kids will need to be ready to follow."

Nuber scoffed at the idea. "You mean after two of them ran off and disappeared, you want to send *more?* Who's to say they won't do the exact same thing and take off, too?"

"Because I'm trusting you to choose the ones who won't. You've been with the present group since they first came here, and you know them best. Send me five who've earned whatever kind of trust you have inside that thick skull of yours. I want patriots, dammit. Get them on our side."

"And if I can't?" asked Henry.

"You tell them the truth about how you lost that arm. Maybe a little fear will keep them from doing something stupid."

Nuber ignored the insult. "This wasn't part of the timeline."

"The original launch window was eight months from now. There's no use in waiting. The next stage is direct exposure...pure, unfiltered, undiluted Variant. These runaways are exactly the kind of political justification we need."

"You can't expect a bunch of kids to play soldier."

Bishop laughed. "They do it every day in that arena of yours, don't they? Kids need to grow up eventually."

Nuber glanced at his missing arm, taking a moment to process this idiotic plan. If anything went wrong, it could cost them their lives. How could Bishop justify such a thing? Nuber took in a deep breath and looked again at his superior. "Tell me again why we're doing this, sir."

Bishop furrowed his brow. "Hm? What do you mean by 'why'?"

Nuber cleared his throat. "I mean...why are we risking the lives of these kids? Tell me again why it's worth it. I need to hear it."

Bishop took a moment, his eyes fixed on Nuber. "For

the future of the human race, Henry. It's the same reason it's always been. Don't you understand that?"

Nuber's eyes drifted to the edge of the desk. "How long will they have to stay?"

"We'll see what happens," said Bishop. "We aren't throwing them to the wolves, but we need to see what they can do. These kids represent over two decades of work. We have to make sure it was worth it. Have a little faith, Henry. Haven't we been careful so far?"

"We could've done better."

"Maybe that's true," admitted Bishop. "But mistakes happen. We've got the entire human race to consider here, and we're running out of time." Bishop tapped a pad on his desk, then slid it toward Nuber. "A list. It's organized by compatibility rating. Top to bottom. The first is the most likely to survive direct exposure. The last is the least likely. I'm not saying they won't *all* survive. The way Archer put it, every student in your class should be able to make the transition perfectly fine."

"Sure, as far as the atmosphere goes," said Nuber. "What about the other hazards?"

"I'm assuming you're referring to the animals. We haven't seen one of those since—"

"No need to revisit," said Nuber, glancing at his empty sleeve again.

"My point being," continued Bishop, "it was the only time anyone's ever seen one of those things. The only proof we have they even exist is the story you gave us."

"And the dead contractors who didn't come back with me."

Bishop stared at him for a moment. "Fine," he said. "But your incident took place near the third solar field, far from where the elevator comes out. Besides, the last signal we received from the missing kids was in the opposite direction. There's no reason to think your team will encounter anything dangerous."

"Look at my arm, James," he said, agitated. "You really want to see this on one of them?"

"They're not children. Not really. Besides, they'll have weapons, and they won't have to worry about tearing their oxygen suits, either. You may not like the idea, but you know it's necessary."

"Fine, whatever," said Nuber. He stood, preparing to leave.

"Where are you going now?" asked Bishop.

"To give a final lesson to the names on that list. If we're sending them to Hell, they deserve to know about the demons who live there."

12

Amber Project File Logs
Play Audio File 141
January 1, 2347

BISHOP: I told you I was moving on this.

ROSS: All because of the runaways?

BISHOP: No, it was only a factor. It was going to happen soon enough, anyway.

ROSS: Aren't you concerned? They're not soldiers, sir.

BISHOP: After years of training, they sure as hell better be.

ROSS: What does their teacher think?

BISHOP: He's…reluctant.

ROSS: And you're still going through with it?

BISHOP: Nuber's opinion is clouded. He's almost as bad as those sentimental mothers.

ROSS: Is that really so bad?

BISHOP: Dammit, don't you start, too.

ROSS: Apologies, sir. But you should know the mothers are talking…someone's let it slip about the launch.

BISHOP: It doesn't matter. They'll have plenty to gossip about when all of this is over.

ROSS: You're expecting it to work, then?

BISHOP: Decades of anguish for today, Ross. Decades of politics, botched science experiments, and constant public reassurances. Of course I'm expecting it to work. It has to.

ROSS: Sorry, sir. I didn't mean to imply…

BISHOP: It's fine. You've worked as hard as I have. We should both be celebrating. Hell, I've already poured the scotch.

End Audio File

January 1, 2347
The Academy, Central

Terry opened his burning, sleep deprived eyes only to see Mr. Nuber standing over him.

"Rise and shine," said Nuber.

John was already dressed. He shrugged when Terry looked at him.

Terry slid out of bed and started getting dressed. The

reason for the wake up didn't matter. He'd find out soon enough. That was how it worked.

He laced up his boots.

"Follow me," said his teacher, once Terry was fully clothed and ready. Together they left the dormitories and headed to the classrooms. It was a short walk, the same one they had taken every other day, but at this time of night the halls were quieter, more solemn. It was almost depressing.

Nuber stopped at the door to their usual room. "Go in and have a seat," he said. Terry did, with John beside him. He expected to find the rest of the class there, but instead there were only a few. Mei, Roland, and Sarah sat at their desks, bloodshot eyes on all their faces.

"Sir," said John, breaking the silence. "Where is everyone?"

Mr. Nuber ignored the question. "Sit down, boys," he said.

John and Terry took their usual seats and waited silently for answers. "Alright then," said Nuber. He pressed the power button on the desk and turned the equipment on. After a brief moment, the projector screen in the front of the class lit up and a map appeared. "I'm only going to cover this once, so pay attention." He walked to the screen, examined it, and faced the small group of teenagers. "I'm sure all of you have noticed Alex and Cole have been missing from class these last few days."

Nobody said anything.

"Well, they have, and they aren't just ditching, either. They've run away from the city. They're topside."

A few of the students shifted in their seats. Mei shot up a hand, but Nuber dismissed it with a wave, and she resigned her question. "It doesn't matter how they did it, only that they did. We tracked their movements for a while, but now it seems they've fallen off the grid. They're gone."

He turned and nodded to the screen beside him. "This is a map of the surface. It's not the whole thing, obviously, but it's the only part you need to concern yourselves with. You'll notice it's shaped like a circle. That's because it only extends about a mile from the entrance of the city. See this black spot here?" He pointed to the exact center of the map. "This is the elevator connecting our city with the surface. We call it the Sling. Everything in this circle is considered part of the safe zone, but it doesn't mean it's actually *safe*." He changed the picture. A larger map took the place of the last one. It was more or less the same, except there were a few additional structures and three red circles on the outer edges. "I'm sure you're wondering what those red marks are. They're the reason you need to stay inside the first map. Those are where our people have been attacked in the past." He walked to the uppermost one and slammed his palm against it. "This is the one that took my arm. Animals, I guess you'd call them. No one knows what they are…only that they're dangerous. If you ever start to question me, think about *this*." He rolled up his sleeve and showed them all what was really underneath it.

For the very first time, Terry saw the remnants of his teacher's arm. It was only a stub, cut off six inches from the shoulder. The skin near the end of it was cracked, a lighter shade of color than the rest of the old man's body.

"This is what you get when you aren't careful enough… when you're arrogant, and you've got it in your head to do something stupid."

"What happened?" Roland asked.

"My team got ambushed while we were investigating something up on the surface. It was only one animal, but it was bigger than me and twice as strong. Fast, too. It went after the others first, tackling them and ripping their suits apart like paper. We all ran, but only two of us made it all the way to the lift. My boss Matt Libby and myself. I asked him where the others were, but he shouted he didn't know and ordered me to open the gate. I heard a growl and turned to see the monster standing over us. I gawked at it like an idiot while it attacked Libby. I ran to help, but it saw me coming and lunged at me. It knocked me around and cut me in a few places. I could hear the oxygen wheezing out of my suit even before I hit the dirt. None of it mattered to me at the time, though. I was more worried about the giant razorback trying to kill me."

"Razorback?" asked John.

"It's what we call them. Rabs for short."

A chill ran down Terry's spine as he tried to imagine what a razorback would look like. It didn't sound like anything he'd ever seen in a book or picture.

Nuber sighed, and his eyes drifted. "Before the rab could finish me off, Libby screamed and rushed the beast, his arms raised and flailing like nothing I'd ever seen. He plowed into it, and they both fell on the dirt, tumbling away from me. Libby screamed for me to go, to get into the lift. I bear-crawled to the gate, scared shitless, closed it behind me, entered the activation code, and listened in horror as my commanding officer screamed bloody murder while the monster ripped him apart. He died in front of my eyes, his insides falling out of his belly like…noodles from a bowl.

"By the time I got to the bottom, I'd already passed out from exposure. The toxin infected my arm and should've killed me, but they managed to amputate before it spread. At least, it's the story they told me. When I woke up and saw my arm gone, I couldn't stop screaming. It didn't feel real." He shook his head, blinking. "But that was from the gas. You kids don't have to worry about it. Be thankful."

Right, thankful, thought Terry. As if anyone could feel grateful for any part of Nuber's story.

"Make no mistake," said Nuber. "The whole damned planet's still a deathtrap. You see one of those animals I mentioned, you run the other way, understand? Don't get killed for no reason. You kids take off and bolt all the way back to the Sling. I don't give a shit what your orders are. You listen to *me.*"

Everyone nodded.

"Today's the last day of class," he said. "You won't ever be back in this room again, but you don't get to rest. In fifteen minutes we're gonna leave here, and I'm gonna take you to a place with a lot of doctors and then to another with a lot of soldiers. It'll only take a few hours, but by the time it's over, you'll be on your way to the surface." He stood and proceeded to shake each of their hands.

"Congratulations," he said. "You've all graduated."

TERRY, John, Mei, Sarah, and Roland made their way along the catwalk toward the Sling, with Mr. Nuber behind. The Sling was a massive elevator, which lay at the base of a tunnel so long that the steel plated walls seemed to fold back in on themselves the farther they went. The chasm gave Terry a terrible headache.

"What's wrong with you?" asked John.

"Nauseous," said Terry, trying to reorient himself. "Not sure why."

"It's called vertigo," said Mr. Nuber, pushing through them toward the lift. He carried an extra supply pack in his only arm. "If you can't handle it, look at the ground or find something to focus your eyes on."

Mei, Sarah, and Roland followed after him.

Terry gripped the handrail and squeezed, closing his eyes.

"It'll be fine once we're inside," John assured him. "Doesn't look like there's any windows."

John was right. The Jefferson Lift, otherwise known as

the Sling, was entirely windowless. The only means of observation was the locator board inside, which tracked the Sling's progress through the five-mile diagonal chasm. Of course, the locator board served little purpose other than to give the passengers something to look at. They had nothing else to do, after all. The system was operated entirely from Central's ECP or the Entry Control Point, where a team of technicians monitored everything that went on inside. This was originally done for security reasons, back when the city still received new visitors.

"Terry, let's go," Nuber called from across the catwalk. "I need everyone inside."

"Better hurry," said John.

Terry nodded. He swallowed a few times. "I'm not sure I can hold my breakfast in until we get there."

"Hey, it's less than a two hour trip," John said, patting Terry on the back. "Be there in no time."

Nuber smacked the railing with the pack in his hand. The *ding* echoed loudly through the tunnel. "I said let's go!"

Terry and John followed the others in through the lift doors. Once inside, Nuber ordered everyone to choose a seat and strap in.

The Sling was nothing but a large, square room, with a single row of seats against a wall. Apparently, this had been the only means of transporting supplies to the city during its construction, which meant it had to carry drilling equipment and other large materials. The original engineers wanted to install faster, smaller elevators, but due to the unforeseeable calamity known as the Jolt, those projects never came to pass.

Nuber kept standing while the students fastened their seatbelts. "Everyone good? Okay. Now we've got a few minutes before this thing starts moving, so listen up. I've already told you about what's topside and how dangerous it is, so I won't bother repeating myself. Instead, I want you to use these next two hours to plan ahead. You've all been given packs with enough supplies to get you there and back in one piece." He took the pack in his arm and tossed it to Sarah, who caught it. "There's a little more."

Nuber looked at each of them. "Remember your training and don't take any unnecessary risks. You see anything you don't think you can handle, you get the hell away from it, you hear?"

They each stared at him.

After a moment, he grunted. "Alright, that's it," he said, waving his only hand. "Now go get those two idiots and bring them home."

IT HAD BEEN OVER AN HOUR, but the monitor showed they were getting close. The elevator had already begun to decelerate.

Terry and the others sat in their seats against the wall, unable to speak because of the overwhelming noise of the machine carrying them skyward. Instead, they'd taken to motioning with their hands, but only when necessary. It was a long ride, and there'd be plenty of time for talking after it was over.

Terry looked at John, who had fallen asleep on Mei's shoulder. With nothing to engage his attention, it was hardly surprisingly. Maybe it was the white noise of the elevator's machinery, or maybe it was because they had been dragged out of bed so early in the morning. Either way, Mei didn't seem to mind.

Roland had managed to sort through the extra pack Mr. Nuber gave them earlier. It contained some extra MREs and protein bars, bottles of water, and an extra box of medical supplies. He placed various items in each of the others' bags.

Terry shifted uncomfortably against the wall. The monitor displayed a map of the pit and their position in it. The map contained clearly distinguishable lines for the shaft, but the elevator was portrayed simply by a green blinking light moving toward the surface. It was remarkably similar to the locator board in Terry's old home.

The elevator jerked, slowing its speed again. Suddenly the humming of the engines was lighter, almost to the point where Terry thought he might be able to speak to someone if he tried.

The Sling shook again a moment later, the sound diminishing even further.

"Hey!" Roland shouted. "Can you guys hear me?"

They all agreed they could.

"Get your gear together and prepare to move," he said, still yelling.

Within moments, the Sling slowed to a crawl, the loud, grinding sounds of the engines settling into a low hum. Soon, there was a clicking noise or what must have been the elevator locking into place, followed by a sudden jerk throughout the lift, and finally settling into quiet nothing.

The silence lasted for only a moment, hastened by the fact that the monitor against the wall was beginning to change. The green light representing the Sling phased to red, and a nearly translucent message box appeared over the bottom half of the screen.

"WARNING. LIFT DOORS OPENING."

The moment reminded Terry of the chamber, just before the gas had come. It was the anticipation, the fear of the pain as it had been the first time he entered the place. After a while it wasn't so bad. It became easier to breathe with each passing exposure, and it took less time to adjust. But still there was the fear that one day he might go in and never come out. In those days, especially in the beginning, Terry couldn't help but hold his breath.

A buzzer rang throughout the Sling, followed by grinding metal as the doors separated. Light pierced the opening crack in the center, spreading and growing rapidly in all directions, overtaking the artificial lamps along the walls. As it reached Terry's eyes, he flinched. This light was brighter than the lights in the city, sharper in the way it cut the air. Terry reached his hand out and found it was warmer than he expected.

"Let's go," said Roland, once the doors had fully opened. He moved quickly out of the elevator. Terry could barely see him as he disappeared into the blaze of sunlight.

One by one the others followed. Sarah first, then John and Mei. Terry was the last to leave. He entered through the open door and stepped into the light, the heat covering him like a warm blanket.

He squinted, trying to orient himself. In every direction, there was so much light, filling everything. How were they supposed to survive such a wild, untamed place? Where was all this light coming from?

Terry's head sunk back and his eyes widened. The remnants of the sky were all before him, crimson and violet streaks interlaced with a variety of puffy shapes, which he knew must be clouds. Nestled in the core of the world, a brighter light than anything Terry's eyes had ever seen.

It was the sun, and its fire blazed so brightly that Terry stumbled back and to the ground.

He gasped desperately for air as he landed, huffing and puffing as quickly as his body would let him.

"Are you okay?" Mei asked, running to his side.

"Yeah," Terry wheezed. "I just forgot to breathe."

PART II

Extinction is the rule. Survival is the exception.
—Carl Sagan

All lovely things will have an ending,
All lovely things will fade and die,
And youth, that's now so bravely spending,
Will beg a penny by and by.
—Conrad Potter Aiken

13

Amber Project File Logs
Play Audio File 133
January 1, 2347

NUBER: So the chips…what's the range on one of those?

ROSS: Approximately four miles, I believe. Five if the weather's clear.

NUBER: Seriously? How the hell did you swing that?

ROSS: It's not as impressive as it sounds, I assure you. The chip isn't entirely responsible, either. We have dozens of repeaters stationed all around the safe zone. It's only four miles right now because we haven't had the capability to install more yet.

NUBER: Why not?

ROSS: Because traveling so far from the city has always been impractical, not to mention dangerous. Don't you remember your briefing the last time you went topside?

NUBER: *No, Avery, not really. When I think back to the day I got my arm sliced off, the stupid ass briefing isn't really a mental priority for me. Silly, I know, but that's just the way my brain works.*

ROSS: *Don't be so dramatic, Henry. Look, the oxygen in the suit you had only lasts for about ten hours, which limits the distance you can travel. There's also the fact that, historically, there's never been much of a reason to leave the city. Why spend the time and resources putting up repeaters that far away? We only have so many contractors.*

NUBER: *Seems like you're making excuses for a lack of foresight.*

ROSS: *Maybe I am, but that's my job. Someone has to defend those decisions.*

NUBER: *Do you really believe that?*

ROSS: *I'm a soldier, Henry. It doesn't matter what I believe.*

End Audio File

January 1, 2347
The Surface

Violence tempered the evening sky.

Purple, gray, and red bled through the haze of clouds like streaks of paint across an endless canvas. Between the many shades, a thousand beams of forgotten sunlight flitted down, like water falling through a man's fist. A hard breeze blundered through the valley. It hit Terry's face, hard and sharp, a bit of pain. He took a deep breath. The air was thicker here than the recycled oxygen that ran through the city. It wasn't even like the gas in the chamber. It was smoother, sweeter maybe, and much less bitter. He smiled and breathed again.

John and Sarah had set the fire, which took longer than anyone expected. Meanwhile, Mei and Roland broke down the packs, then remade them according to each person's assigned role. John and Sarah got the weapons and ammunition, Mei was in charge of the medical supplies, Roland had the camping equipment, and Terry took the food. They each had their part.

"We're supposed to radio in with Central soon," said Sarah, poking the fire with a stick she'd found.

"1600 hours," said Roland. "We still have thirty minutes."

"What do you think they'll say?" asked John.

"Probably give us the go-ahead to move," said Sarah.

Roland nodded. "The coordinates we have are to the west, near the edge of the perimeter."

"We'll have to cross it, same as the others," said Mei.

"Why?" asked John.

Sarah cleared her throat. "If they were in the perimeter, John, they'd have been detected."

"Maybe there's interference," he said. "Maybe their chips stopped transmitting. Stuff breaks all the time."

"Anything's possible," said Roland. "But we won't know until we've had a look."

Maybe they're dead, thought Terry, but he didn't dare say it. The truth was no one knew much about the situation or even what to expect. Everything they were saying was only speculation, nothing more. But talking about death would only make them uneasy. *Better to stay quiet,* he thought. *Just sit here and listen like a good little soldier.*

"I'm hungry," said Mei.

"Terry has the food," said John.

"Would you mind?" she asked, a pouty look on her face.

"I live only to serve," said Terry, bowing and pretending to be a butler.

"Very funny," she said.

Terry opened his pack and sorted through the supplies. "We have a wide selection of synthesized slop this afternoon. Which flavor would you want?"

"Something spicy," she said.

"Spicy slop it is," said Terry, pulling out a small bag. "I think this one's supposed to be curry."

Mei took the food and examined it. "Good enough," she said. "Can't be any worse than the stuff we get from the cafeteria."

"Says you," John said. "I think I'll wait on the food. I'm going to look around."

"Not alone, you're not," said Roland.

"Fine. Any volunteers want to go with me?"

Terry raised his hand. "My butt hurts from sitting."

"Be back in an hour," said Roland. "And don't wander too far."

"You got it, Mom," said John, jumping to his feet. "Come on, Terry. Let's head out."

"Oh, my *God*," moaned Mei, suddenly. She had a mouthful of curry.

"We'll be *right* back," said John. "Calm your little self down."

"I'm not talking about you, blockhead," she said, holding up her dinner. "I'm talking about the rations."

"What about them? Are they worse than you thought?"

"No," she said, laughing. "No, they're actually pretty good."

"And that's funny?" asked Sarah.

"I don't know," she said. "I guess I expected the food to suck as bad as the rest of this place. I mean, look around us. It's horrible."

Mei wasn't wrong. Aside from the expectantly pleasant gas, everything about the surface was awful. The harsh, gray land felt dead and empty, all its life completely drained. Had Variant truly devastated the world so badly? Was it barren now?

Of course not, he assured himself. There were still the rabs, meat-eating predators—proof that something yet survived atop this morbid planet. But every carnivore consumed, and these particular creatures were no exception. Somewhere out there, an entire ecosystem had evolved—everything from plant to beast, each surviving off the other.

With or without humanity's help, the world would ultimately move on.

Terry followed John away from the camp. After fifteen minutes of walking on the road, they stood together at the edge of a broken highway. Below them lay a vast ravine, although Terry speculated that it could have been a river once. The road, which they'd followed at John's suggestion, turned into a bridge a few yards behind them, and ended ahead.

"Nice view," said Terry.

"Do you think this bridge fell apart before or after?" asked John.

"Probably after," Terry suggested.

"How do you figure?"

"I doubt Variant would have done this. It's a gas, not a bomb."

"Yeah, but you don't know."

Terry shrugged. "Maybe it happened from an earthquake and no one was around to fix it."

"Well, it doesn't really matter how it happened, only that it did." John snagged a small stone from the pavement and threw it into the ravine. They watched it disappear into the ground without making a sound. John smiled. "It's not what I expected."

"That's for sure."

"I wonder what it was like," said John as he sat down,

dangling his legs over the side of the concrete cliff. "You know, before the world ended."

Terry joined him. "Busier, probably."

John laughed. "Less ugly, too."

Terry swept his palm against the rough pavement. When he pulled his hand up, it was covered in black dust. He wiped it on his pants. "Maybe it's not *all* this bad. We've only seen a fraction so far."

John looked at him. "What do you mean?"

"Well, how do we know the whole world's like this?"

"You heard Mr. Nuber. They have the satellite feeds from back then."

"Up until the network went down, sure, but then there's nothing. How do you know there aren't other people out there? Maybe there's a group on the other side of the planet, and they found a way to survive like we did. I'm not saying there's another underground city or anything, but who knows? The world's a big place."

"That'd be something," said John.

"Better than something. It'd be everything."

"Like you said, the world's a big place. We might never know."

"True," Terry said.

"But it's nice to think about it," said John. He leaned back and threw his arms behind his head.

Terry did the same. "Yeah."

Together they watched as the clouds overhead continued moving west into what their map told them had once been called the Sea. More specifically, the Atlantic Ocean, although in order to reach it they'd have to walk a hundred miles in the wrong direction. *Well, that's okay*, thought Terry. *It's probably just a puddle in a desert by now, anyway.*

January 1, 2347
The Surface

TERRY LOOKED on as the transmission to Central went out right on time.

"Central, this is Alpha. Do you copy?" Roland said into the transmitter.

John nudged Terry. "What's Alpha?"

"That's us. Weren't you listening earlier?"

"Quiet," said Mei, glaring at them.

"Sorry, sorry," John said, holding up his arms.

"Copy, Alpha," erupted an unfamiliar voice from the pad. "The last known coordinates of the targets are being downloaded to your pads now. Report back in at precisely 1900 hours with a full update."

"Copy that, Central," said Roland. "Alpha Team out." He clicked off the transmitter.

"Well, that was short," said John.

"It was only an update," said Roland.

"Seemed like a waste of time."

"They wanted to know if we were dead, that's all," said Sarah.

"'That's all?'" asked John. "You make it sound so casual."

"Well, it makes sense. They spent time trying to make us the way we are, and then all the training. They need to see if it was all worth the effort. If the experiment was a success." She cracked her knuckles. "I don't know about the rest of you, but I feel pretty successful right now. In fact, I feel better than I have in a long time."

"Me, too," said Roland. "Ever since we got up here, I've felt amazing."

"It's the gas," said Terry. "It's just like the chamber, except now we're stuck in it."

John took in a deep breath. "Is that a bad thing?"

Terry shrugged. "Who knows?"

"I guess we'll find out," said Sarah. "The more time we spend here, the more we'll adapt. The longer we're here, who knows what'll happen?"

Terry didn't need time to find anything out. He could already see that he was changing. His pack was getting lighter. He had more energy. He only hoped it didn't come with a price.

Roland started packing up the supplies. "I'd rather get this mission done and over with before anything bad happens."

"You're not even curious about it?" asked Mei.

He looked at her. "Am I the only one who was listening

to Mr. Nuber earlier? Don't any of you remember what he said?"

"Of course we remember," said John. "But he had a suit on and it broke. We don't have to worry."

"It broke for a reason," said Roland. "Or were you just going to ignore the seven foot tall razorback with the eight inch claws and teeth?"

"Well honestly I was hoping you'd forgotten about that," John grinned. "But nobody's seen those things in years. Maybe they're dead or gone. The tracker hasn't picked up anything."

"We can't stick around to find out." Roland grabbed the pack and continued stowing his equipment. "But don't worry. When we finish this job, they're sure to send us back. Even if they start up a steady rotation with the other students, eventually you'll all have time to get your fill."

Everyone followed by example and began gathering up their designated supplies. When they were ready, they walked along the desolate highway. Instead of heading north toward the broken bridge that Terry and John had found, they moved east, hoping for a better way.

Terry followed behind the others, staring at the ground as he went. He gripped the strap against his right shoulder and grunted as a bead of sweat fell from his forehead, plummeting into the dust below.

IT WAS ALMOST DUSK when Terry's group came upon the old gas station. Cable and Son's, the map and broken sign on the road had called it. The shop lay a few miles south of a small town called Morrisville. The roadside was littered with overgrown weeds—blue-tinted grass that rose to the hip and bent near the end. There was no trace of the grass when they first arrived on the surface, but here, miles away from their city, the earth was moving on. The soil had a fuller, deeper color to it. Terry wondered what else they might discover the longer they walked. After all, if these plants had somehow found a way, then what else?

"We're here," said Roland. "This is where they fell off the grid."

Sarah chuckled. "Like that's even a real thing."

"Well, what would you call it, then?" asked Roland.

"Not a grid, that's for sure," she said. "I mean, it's not like there are all these sensors triangulating movements throughout a certain area. It's only a few towers tracking movement and heat signatures. The system covers a specific radius, but they can only go so far in any one direction. Hardly a grid."

Roland rolled his eyes. "It's an expression. God, I can't believe we're arguing about this."

Sarah shrugged. "I'm just saying."

"Anyway," he went on. "This is where they lost the signal. I want everyone to pair up and fan out. Look for signs of life. Remember, our pads are connected so you don't have to worry about giving us your coordinates. All you have to do is hit the alert button."

"Convenient *and* easy," said John. "I like it."

"There's five of us, so that leaves an odd man out," said Roland. "Any volunteers?"

Mei raised her hand. "I'll stay. We can't leave the supplies unguarded."

"Agreed," said Roland. "John, you go with Terry. Head east for about a mile; Sarah and I'll go west. Once you think you've gone far enough, turn north and circle back. We'll do the same. Simple?"

"Simple," grinned John.

"Best to keep your weapons at the ready," said Sarah.

John nodded. "Right. No telling what's out here."

"Sure there is," said Mei. "Rabs."

John's smile faded. "I wish you people would stop bringing that up."

Terry drew his weapon and checked the safety. It was still on. He put it back in the holster. "Do you think we'll run into any of those things?" he asked.

"I hope not," said Mei.

Roland readied his gun, staring down the sight. "If we do, we'll handle it," he said. "We're armed, and we don't have to worry about exposure—not like Nuber did. We'll be fine."

Terry set his pack on the ground. He thumbed the holster on his side, the tips of his fingers coming to rest on the butt of his weapon. These guns were in many ways identical to the ones they'd been trained with, although they were completely different in one regard—when and if he pulled the trigger, whatever it shot would die. This wasn't a beam of light hitting a target; this was a bullet, aimed at a living thing, specialized in death. A true weapon, not a toy, capable of destroying anything its master put in its way. It was real.

Terry trembled at the thought of it. What did Roland know about killing? What did he know about these animals, or about this world? They were strangers here, each of them. No one had any experience. All they had were training exercises and stupid drills in an empty room. What was any of that to the real thing?

But here they stood in the open wasteland, surrounded by a two-hundred-year-old dream. Sarah, Mei, John, Roland, and Terry—each of them playing soldier, pretending to understand—each of them completely clueless.

John tapped Terry on the shoulder. "You ready?"

"As ready as I can be," he said.

"Alright, great," said John. He shot a glance at Mei. "You gonna be okay?"

"Please," said Mei. "I can handle myself. You two go enjoy your male bonding experience. I'll see you when you get back."

"Thanks, I think," said John. "Alright, Terry, let's ditch these losers."

Together they walked through the rubble of the town,

heading east. The map on their pads told them that Morrisville was a little more than sixteen miles across, although most of it used to be farmland. The bulk of its buildings lay in the center, which only took up a few square miles. Most of those structures had collapsed in on themselves, however, overgrown with the same blue grass that ran heavy in the streets.

Terry couldn't help but marvel at it all. The abandoned vehicles, rusted and collapsed, partially decayed and consumed by dust and vegetation, yet still there, still existing after all this time. He approached a nearby car, sweeping his palm over its jagged, rough body. If nothing else, they were a testament to the imagination, to the willpower of the human mind.

But so are we, thought Terry. *Even though we should all be dead, here we are, still trying to survive.* He pulled his fingers away, flakes of orange dust clinging to him. He wiped his hand on his pants and continued walking.

"This place sucks," muttered John. "It feels like we shouldn't be here, like we're breaking some kind of rule, you know?"

"You mean like sneaking out of the dorms?"

"Something like that. I don't know. Maybe I'm just nervous about the whole thing."

"We're only on the Surface. What's to be nervous about? I mean, aside from the toxic air, killer rabs, and the empty, rotten buildings."

They walked for a while after that, moving slowly at

first, but eventually picking up the pace. Most of the buildings were leveled, and the pads weren't detecting anything, so taking it slow didn't really serve any purpose. Besides, the gas had given them so much energy that the last thing Terry wanted to do was take it easy. He'd actually found it difficult to stand still back at the camp, listening to the others make plans. In fact, he wanted to run.

By the time they'd made it to the one mile marker, Terry couldn't restrain himself. "Let's race back," he suggested. "You want to?"

"You for real?" asked John. "That's not the Terry I know. You sure you can beat me? I'm pretty good."

"In my sleep. You're too big to be fast. You'll just fall over."

John scoffed. "I'll kick your butt," he said. "How far we going?"

"Quarter mile."

"Deal," said John.

They stood next to each other and got ready. Terry set the timer on his pad, counted down, and shouted, "Go!"

Together they raced, evenly at first, but after a few short moments, Terry took the lead. He moved faster than ever, hitting speeds he never could back in the gym, despite wearing all this gear. In forty two seconds, he'd already passed the quarter mile mark.

Terry slowed and stopped, glancing back at John. "You can do it!" he yelled, then started clapping his hands above his head.

John caught up a few seconds later, a clear look of disappointment in his eyes. "I can't believe it," he said, catching his breath. "When did you get so fast?"

Terry bounced in place, completely energized. "I don't know," he said. "Ever since we got here, it's been awesome. I can't shake the energy! It's like I—"

Terry flinched, a sharp pain piercing his chest, shooting through his body and into his brain like a flood of pins and needles. His hands and face suddenly felt warm and numb. He doubled over.

"Whoa, hey, hey, what's wrong?" John's voice was loud, each syllable hitting Terry with the strength of a brick. John grabbed him by the arm, trying to help him back up, but Terry pushed him away and instead lay on the ground.

"Stop screaming at me!" Terry cried, throwing his hands and arms over his ears. "It's too loud."

Even the sound of his own voice hurt, so he clutched his ears and covered himself. Every shuffle against the pavement was like a siren. His head throbbed like a drum. He closed his eyes and screamed.

Then, as the noise became too loud to bear, everything went quiet and still. The light from the sky hung in the air and the clouds stopped. John, halfway down on his knee, retained a look of panic. Absolutely nothing moved.

Suddenly, he remembered the training room and the gunfire—how the world had stopped and he thought he was going to die.

He remembered the darkness…and the empty chill that followed.

January 1, 2347
The Maternity District

"THIS IS INSANE," said Mara. "What's he thinking, sending those children to the surface? Is he out of his damned mind?"

"I'm so sorry, ma'am," said Ross. "I tried to talk him out of it, but I can only say so much without bringing attention to myself."

"I know, Ross. Don't worry. You have to look like you're on his side."

Ross frowned. "It drives me insane."

Mara and Ross sat in Ava's apartment, once again meeting to discuss their plans. Ava was listening from the other side of the table, wrapping one of her baskets. It had become a weekly tradition to hold the meetings here, always limited to the three of them. No one could know that Ross was the leak, not even the other mothers. It had become a closely guarded secret, and Mara intended to keep it that way.

"And you say they've been given weapons to defend themselves with?"

"Right," said Ross. "Their mission is to retrieve two

other students, who ran away. They were given two days."

"So the schedule's been moved forward," said Ava, not looking up. "I guess I shouldn't be surprised."

"Schedule?" asked Mara. "When were they originally planning to do this?"

"Next year," Ava remarked. She clipped a piece of wrapping tape and tied it in a bow around the top of the basket. "It sounds like the timeline was expedited. I didn't get the full report, but I knew the bullet points."

Ross nodded. "Yes, ma'am. There were a few objections, but Archer assured the colonel they held no merit."

"Someone besides you objected?" asked Mara.

"Henry Nuber, the children's teacher."

"Seriously?" Mara asked. The notion of Nuber objecting didn't exactly surprise her. What she found disconcerting was the fact that Bishop ignored his concerns. "Why would he ignore their teacher's advice when Nuber spends more time with them than anyone?"

"He tried to say Nuber's vision was clouded by sentiment, how he wasn't being impartial enough."

"Of course he did."

"Relax," said Ava. She finished tying the bow, examined it briefly, undid it and tried again. "There's no use getting worked up over what's already happened. We all knew they'd do this eventually."

"Yes, but we didn't know when," said Mara. "We've only just started protesting."

Ava finished the bow again. She tilted her head at it,

then smiled and set it aside, moving onto the next basket. "My point is there's nothing we can do about it now. Leave the worrying and the outrage to the others. It's our job to focus on the plan. Instead of getting emotional, you must ask yourself how you can use this to your advantage."

"My advantage? You make it sound so exploitive."

Ava grinned. "Exploiting situations to gain public favor is politics in a nutshell, darling."

"It's filthy," Mara said.

"But necessary. Now, what are you going to do?"

Mara considered her question, despite her own objections to the idea. "Can you get us some proof of what's happening on the surface?" she asked Ross.

"Of course," said the captain.

"Do it, then, and we'll leak it to the public. We already have the ear of the mothers and several of the farmers. This might be enough to get the rest of them on our side. Have any of the academy staff complained, besides Nuber?"

"Several, yes," said Ross.

"What about people in the science division?"

"I don't know, but I can find out."

"Okay," said Mara. "Let's tally a list of names if you can. We'll see if we can convince them to get involved."

Ava tied the bow on her basket again. "Excellent," she said, grinning. "Now you're thinking like a politician."

Mara sighed. "Now all I need is a scandal behind me, and I'll be set."

14

Amber Project File Logs
Play Audio File 164
January 01, 2347

ARCHER: While it is unlikely for the subject to experience any serious mental or physical trauma from the exposure, there is a chance the body's reaction to such an abundant supply of Variant will leave it overwhelmed. If this should happen, I can only hypothesize that the subject's cells will begin to degrade, though it is difficult to state with any true certainty.

However, given each subject has previously undergone extensive treatments and prior exposures, the body should be capable of adjusting effectively. The subject's compatibility rating should also play a factor in this. Considering each of the subjects was chosen based on his or her individual rating, the chance of an effective transition is all but assured.

End Audio File

January 01, 2347
The Surface

Terry opened his eyes to the brightest light he'd ever seen.

A sharp pain jettisoned through his skull as the blinding array engulfed him. The pain was so intense that he let out a short scream, holding up his arms in a desperate attempt to block out the light.

A hand gripped his shoulder suddenly. "Terry, what the hell's wrong with you?" It was John's voice, but Terry couldn't see him. He was so loud. Why was he screaming?

"My eyes," said Terry, rolling onto his chest. He put his face in the dirt and covered the sides of his head with his arms. "It's too bright. Why is it so bright?" He blinked repeatedly, trying to focus himself. After a brief moment, he managed to make out the ground and his boots.

"What are you talking about?" asked John, still loud. Still screaming.

"Stop yelling!" cried Terry.

"I'm not yelling."

"You are! Stop it!" Without thinking, Terry threw his arm up, hitting John in the chest and flinging him several feet away like a rag doll. He landed with a loud thud, sliding against the dirt.

"John!" yelled Terry, jerking his eyes open, filling him with pain. He looked around, half blind. He heard John wheezing for air in the distance and ran in his direction. He found him quickly. "I'm sorry! I didn't mean to!"

John turned on his side. He lifted his head, coughing, his face covered in dirt. "I'm fine...I'm fine. How'd you *do* that, man?"

"I don't know what happened! I didn't mean to hit you."

"It's okay, Terry. Calm down. It's not important." He gasped for air between the words.

"What do you mean? Of course it's important!"

"Stop it," said John. "Just stop and take a second, okay?"

Terry looked at his hands. "It wasn't me," he said. "I didn't mean to do it. I don't know what's going on."

"It's the gas. It's the only thing that makes sense."

Terry felt a flood of panic rush through him. He didn't know what to say. This was exactly like the time he'd blacked out in the arena, only a thousand times worse.

"Your eyes don't still hurt?" asked John.

Terry blinked. "They do," he said. "They did."

John pushed himself off the ground, wavering a little. "But you're better now."

"I think so…but I'm not sure why."

"I do," said John. "You stopped worrying about it. Pushed through the pain, you know? Let yourself forget. It's just like what Nuber used to say when we complained about the exercises."

"I didn't push through anything. My eyes were hurting so much. Every centimeter was on fire. My hearing, too." He touched his temple with his fingers. "God, I can already feel it coming back."

"You think you're not used to it yet?"

"To the gas?" asked Terry.

"What else could it be?"

"I don't know," said Terry. "What am I going to do?"

"Relax for a minute." John took a deep breath, using his hand to motion when to inhale and exhale. Terry did his best to mimic it, taking the breaths as they came. One at a time.

After a moment, he was breathing normally again, the beating in his chest a little softer, the throbbing in his head completely gone. "I think I'm okay," he said at last. "It still hurts. Maybe not as much as it did, but I still feel something."

"You need to tell Roland about this."

Terry shook his head.

"It could happen again. What if you don't wake up the next time?"

"Please don't say anything," he begged. "What if he

tries to send me home? The doctors will put me in the lab, and they'll never leave me alone."

"You'd rather stay here and risk getting sick?"

"I won't," he insisted. "It's like you said. I'm adjusting. The last time this happened I was out of it for days. This time wasn't even close."

John waited a few seconds. "I don't know," he muttered.

"Please, John, you can't say anything. Promise me you won't."

John stared at him, a concerned look in his eyes. "Are you sure? If anything happens to you, I'll—"

"It won't," said Terry. "I promise, John. Nothing's going to happen. I'll be fine."

<hr />

Terry and John arrived to find Mei sitting on the ground reading her pad, while Sarah and Roland studied the map, attempting to figure out the group's next step.

"Seems easy enough," said Sarah.

"If we're lucky, sure," said Roland.

Terry sat down next to Mei. "What's happening?" he asked.

She kept looking at her pad. "They're trying to figure out the best way to get us all killed," she said.

"So what are you doing?"

"The opposite." She handed him the pad. There was a map with a green blinking dot in the center. The dot was connected to a translucent red line that ran far to the west and disappeared off the edge. Terry zoomed out, revealing more of the terrain. He followed the line to its end.

"What's this?" he asked.

She pressed her fingers to her temple and rubbed them. "It's us, obviously," she said, her voice straining, breathing louder than normal.

"Are you alright?" he asked.

"Headache," she said. "Ever since we got here. Must be the light or something." She closed her eyes.

"Looks like it hurts."

"Yeah," she said, nodding slowly.

"Did you take any medicine? I'm pretty sure there's some in the packs."

She looked at him with bloodshot eyes. "I'm fine," she said.

"Hey," said John suddenly. He collapsed down on the opposite side of Mei. "What you guys talking about?"

"A map, apparently," said Terry.

"Nice, I like maps," said John. "What's it for?"

"I was just about to explain that part," said Mei.

Terry held up the pad and showed it to John. "She's drawn some kind of new route."

"Why?" asked John. "We're supposed to follow the instructions Central gave us, remember?"

"I know," said Mei. "Central told us to head to the signal's last known coordinates, but it's not going to work. Just look here." She tapped the pad again, this time pulling up another version of the same map, only this time there was much more than a mere dot and line. This time the map had an entirely new layer to it, with overlapping lines and figures. There were arrows moving east and west, circulating in the north, and even a swirling gray cloud toward the west. The more he zoomed out, the more complex the map became. "Do you know what this is, Terry?" she asked.

"It looks like a weather map," he said.

"Right," Mei said.

Terry scrunched his nose. "How can you read this stuff?"

"Because we studied it. It was three years ago for about a week. Don't you remember?"

"Not like you do," he said. "But setting aside the fact you obviously studied way more than the rest of us, how are you even getting this feed? This looks like it's real-time."

"First of all, you should be glad I studied it and stop implying I'm a nerd before I hit you. Second, yes, this is real-time feed from a few of the local towers."

John laughed. "Nerd."

"The same ones we use for the locator signals?" Terry asked. "I didn't know they could tell you the weather. That's crazy."

Mei shook her head. "No, not really. We've had these things for centuries now. They're called Pulse-Doppler Radar machines."

There was an awkward pause. "Yeah, you're totally not

a nerd at all," John said, grinning.

Mei rolled her eyes. "My hand, your face," she said, motioning with her palm.

"Anyway," said Terry. "How'd you get this stuff to show on the pad? Is yours special?"

"We all can do it," she said. "It's one of the programs. They patched it in with the last upgrade, right before we left. I've been playing around with them while you guys were gone."

"What's the big deal about the weather?" asked John. "What do all those lines and arrows mean?"

"Most of it's not very important. A cold front here, some strong winds there. It's all typical," she said. "The stuff we should pay attention to is right *here*." She tapped the gray western area of the map. "Do you know what this is?"

"A lake?" asked John.

"I'd guess some kind of storm," Terry said.

"Really, John? A lake?" she shook her head. "Yes, it's a storm."

"How bad?" asked Terry.

"Pretty bad," she said. "But it's not heading our way. It also won't be there when we arrive."

John narrowed his brow. "I don't understand. What's the big deal?"

"Look at the coordinates Central gave us for Alex and Cole. They're right there in the storm. There's no mountains, no towns, or anything nearby—nowhere for anyone to hide. What do you think they did when they saw the storm coming?"

"They moved!" snapped John. "Right?"

"That's what your line is for, isn't it?" asked Terry. "It's your best guess for where they went."

She nodded. "Yes, exactly. Now you're getting it."

"What if they go another way?" asked John. "How do you know this is the right path?"

"Like Terry said, it's only a guess. Look at the map again, though. The storm's here, with nothing nearby, but there's also a road. See where it goes?"

"Looks like a few buildings," said Terry.

"If they were smart—and I'm *not* saying they were—they would've stayed on the road and hid in one of these buildings."

"Good guess. Every other direction is empty. Why haven't you told Sarah and Roland yet?" asked Terry.

"Tell us what?" asked Sarah, standing only a few feet away. "What are you three talking about?"

"Mei's figured something out," said John. "She's got a plan for where to go next."

"Mei, what's he talking about?" asked Sarah. "Roland, come here for a second. Mei has something to tell us, apparently."

"What is it? I'm a little busy," said Roland.

Mei looked at the pad, then back at Roland. "I was looking over the maps and I came up with some ideas for a new route."

"We already have a route," said Roland. "Central sent us our coordinates and we're following them."

"But they're wrong," said Mei.

"I think Central knows more about what's happening than you do," he said.

Terry stood. "Listen to her. She knows what she's talking about. Mei tapped into the towers. She's got intel you can use."

Roland stopped walking and looked at them. "What?"

"I'm saying you should listen to her."

Roland approached him, stopping only a few inches away. Towering over Terry, he was almost a foot taller. "I don't know if you remember, but I'm the team leader here. I say we're following Central's orders, so that's what we're going to do."

Terry looked him directly in the eye. Roland was big, but he wasn't *that* big. Not as big as John had been when Terry threw him like a doll across the ground. If Roland pushed him now, could Terry do it again? He didn't want to find out, but he wasn't about to back down.

"Stop it, both of you," said Sarah, though she only looked at Roland. "Let's listen to what she has to say."

"Why? Our orders are clear about what we're supposed to do." He took a few steps toward Sarah.

Terry relaxed.

"We were all chosen for a reason. You're in charge, sure, but the rest of us have our uses. You think this team was random?" Sarah pointed at Mei. "Ever since we were kids, she's been the head of the class in practically every subject, except the arena. Why do you think that is?'"

Roland shrugged. "So she's smart. That doesn't mean our orders don't matter."

"Of course not, but this isn't the arena, and Mr. Nuber's not watching us. There's no scoreboard here. This is real life. This is the *surface*. If she has a better way, and it makes sense and it helps us, we should listen to it."

"Yeah," said John. "What's the harm in listening?"

There was a long pause as Roland looked at each of them. After a few moments, he approached Mei and held out his hand. "Let's see it," he said. "If there's any merit to it, I can send a call back to Central and ask permission to modify the plan. Afterwards, we have to do what they say, okay?"

"Okay," she echoed and then handed him the pad.

THE GROUP PACKED and left not long after Mei proposed her plan. Roland was able to contact Central, receiving permission to follow the new course. He didn't tell them who came up with the idea, but it hardly mattered. Everyone knew it was Mei.

Terry walked behind John on the road as the group headed west. After a short while, they all fell silent, and Terry's eyes dropped to the ground ahead of him. He watched as John's boots slammed into the mud, one after the other. John took such wide steps, but there was no clumsiness to them. His boot didn't waver or shake, nor did his feet curl or shuffle. He walked with the confidence of a soldier, of a man. He walked with absolute control.

I could never be like that, thought Terry. Even before, when he felt the surge of adrenaline and energy, when he threw John in the air like a stone, when he had known absolute strength. Even then, he was afraid.

Afraid of what? He wondered. Afraid of himself, perhaps, or afraid what he could do. And in that moment, when he actually did have that strength, what did he do with it? He freaked, panicked, but above all, he hurt his friend. And what would happen next time? What if the next person couldn't take the hit? What if he really did end up hurting them?

Terry trembled, afraid of his own thoughts. *Stop it*, he told himself, squeezing his fists. Panicking wouldn't solve anything. Hadn't John told him as much before? *Just breathe for a second*, he told him. But it was easier said than done.

Terry lifted his eyes from the mud, meeting the clouded light of the distant firmament. Beyond that, the sun lay hovering like a drop of yellow sweat on the backside of the purple sky. He had dreamed for years of what this place might look like, never imagining how beautiful it could actually be. Yet, despite himself, all he could do now was focus on his feeble little problems, his faults and petty weaknesses.

"It's not far now," said Mei, running beside him. Her

skinny legs were having a hard time with the mud, but she didn't seem to care.

"What does your map tell you?" asked Terry.

"A few more miles," she said. "We've been walking for four hours, and we're making decent time."

"Great," he said.

"Oh, come on. Don't act like you aren't excited to see Alex's smiling, pretty face. I bet he'll give you a big bear hug as soon as he sees you. Won't that be nice?" she asked, teasing.

"Apparently you know a different Alex than I do."

Mei laughed. "Nope, he's the same one. I can't imagine why you'd think otherwise. Maybe you're just a pessimist, Terry. Ever think of that?"

"You're really laying the sarcasm on thick today," he said.

"He'll be even happier when we tell him why we're here. I'm sure he won't resist us at all." She giggled.

"Can I ask you something?"

The look on her face shifted from a smile to a concerned frown almost instantaneously. "Everything okay?"

"I was thinking about what Sarah said. You know, about the gas. Do you think we'll be okay? No one's ever been exposed to these levels of Variant before or for this long."

"Yeah, I've been wondering the same thing," she said. "But I don't think there's much to worry about. So far nobody's had anything serious happen to them. Everyone feels great."

"Yeah, I guess so," he said. "I don't know. Maybe I'm thinking too much about it."

Mei stared at him, tilting her head. "No, I don't think so. There's something you're not telling me." She punched the side of his arm. "Come on, out with it."

He sighed. "Do you remember back in training when I ended up in the hospital?"

"Sort of," she said. "It happened a long time ago. Mr. Nuber said it wasn't a big deal, right?"

"They said it was a panic attack," he said. "They tried to tell me the gas had nothing to do with it, but I didn't believe them. After Mr. Nuber got me from the hospital, he told me I was right. I had a bad reaction to the gas, and it almost killed me." He lifted his hand toward the sky, covering the sunlight over his face. "But it never happened again. I went back to being me, and I figured that was the end of it." He lowered his hand and stared at it. After a moment, Mei grabbed it, and he looked up at her. "It happened again," he finally said.

"You mean you blacked out?"

"Hours ago," he said. "It was exactly the same as before, except I woke up in minutes, rather than days."

She dropped his hand. "You've been walking around with this all day?"

"Sorry."

"Does John know about this?"

"He was there when it happened."

"Dammit!" She snapped, kicking the mud. "I swear he's such a jackass."

"I didn't want to worry anyone," he said.

"Well you're an idiot," she said. "And stupid."

"I know."

"Do you really?" she asked. "Because if you'd told me earlier, I could've checked you to made sure you were okay. You're such an idiot!"

"Alright, alright," he said, trying to keep her quiet. "You're right. Keep it down so the others don't hear. Promise you won't say anything, okay?"

"To who? Roland?" she asked. "You think I'm as stupid as you are?" She shook her head. "I'm not going to let him send you back to Central so those doctors can study you. We'd never see you again!"

Terry smiled. "So what should we do, then?"

"When we stop, let me use the med kit's scanner on you. I'll run it on everyone so Roland and Sarah don't suspect anything. It's not the best piece of medical hardware out there, but it'll get the job done. If you start feeling sick, tell me and I'll give you some meds. No more secrets, Terry."

They started walking again, and after a moment Mei turned to him and nudged his shoulder. "Don't take any of what I said back there to sound like I'm concerned," she said. "It's not like that."

Terry looked at her. "It's not?"

"I'm worried about John, that's all," she said, looking forward. "He acts tough, but we both know he's soft. If anything happens to you, he'd be devastated, the big baby. I'd have to carry him home. I can't do that. Do you have any idea how much he weighs? I didn't sign up for that."

MEI DID AS SHE PROMISED. She took Terry's vitals, but everything came back fine. No abnormal heart patterns, no blood pressure issues, no fevers, no rashes; nothing was present to indicate a negative reaction to Variant. Terry let out a sigh of relief when Mei gave him the news.

"We'll do this again tomorrow," she whispered to him, before moving on to the others. "Try not to overexert yourself."

They were only a mile from the town now. Roland sat with the radio, talking to Central and requesting further orders. While they waited, Terry unpacked the cooking supplies and began handing out the rations.

"What'll it be?" he asked John. "We have a fine selection."

"Another bag of slop, I think. Those seem to be popular right now."

Mei sat next to John on the ground. "Doesn't bother me."

"Oh, come on," said John. "Don't you want a nice juicy

soy burger? How about some fresh fruit? Man, I'd even take a salad right now."

Mei laughed. "Do you guys remember the food back in the maternity district? My mother used to make the best tomato soup."

"Yeah," said John, his eyes wandering. "Apple pies for me…best you ever tasted."

"Sounds great," said Mei. "I never had pie until the academy, but I liked it."

"Thinking about it makes my mouth water," said John.

"What about you, Terry?" asked Mei.

Terry thought about it for a moment. "Sandwiches," he said.

"Ew, that's it?" said John.

"That sucks," said Mei, frowning.

"It wasn't bad," he said.

"Then what was it?" asked John.

"It's boring," he said, shrugging.

"So what?" said Mei. "Not like we've got anything better to do. Just tell us."

"Yeah, tell us about your sandwiches," laughed John.

"Okay, fine," he said. "Every Sunday, before the teacher from the academy came to visit, we used to sit in the living room together. Mother would make sandwiches and tea, while me and my sister played checkers on the floor. My mother never played with us; she only watched and smiled. We did that for a while…I don't know how long…but then it stopped one day." He pressed the base of his boot into the dirt, sliding it back and forth. The rocks crunched together, almost mechanically, like the noise the Contractors used to make when they repaired the city walls. "It wasn't anything special," he said. "But I liked it."

"Sounds special to me," said Mei. She put her hand on Terry's shoulder, smiling. "And I bet the sandwiches were pretty good, too. Don't you think so, John?"

"Sure," he said. "I mean, you can't beat apple pie, but I bet it's a close second."

"So there you go," said Mei. "Even John thinks so."

"What do you mean 'even John'?" asked John.

Mei fanned her hand at him. "Nothing, let it go," she said. "It's time to eat, anyway. Terry, hand out the slop, and let's all pretend it doesn't suck."

"Not sure I can," said Sarah, suddenly. She and Roland were finally finished with the transmitter. "What are you guys talking about over here?"

"Just food," said Mei, smiling.

John scowled at her. "Don't think we're done with this 'even John' business," he whispered.

Mei snickered. "Stop living in the past."

Roland sighed and sat on the ground. He twisted his back, cracking it several times. "I'm starving," he finally said.

"Well, there's bags of slop for everyone," said John.

Terry tossed one of the meals at Roland, then to Sarah. "Eat up," he said.

They each set the plate timers to warm their food.

Once it was ready, they all ate. Roland finished first and took the opportunity to talk about their new orders.

"Central wants us to check these three zones," he said, pulling up the map on his pad. The image had three red circles on it, roughly half a mile away from their current position. Each circle's size was different, but they all covered areas where the buildings were still standing. "They said these are our best options."

Sarah nodded. "Let's not forget these two probably don't want to be found. We need to use the goggles."

"God, I hate those things," said John, sighing. "The straps hurt my ears."

Sarah raised her brow. "John, you've been wearing them for years."

"Doesn't mean I liked it," he said.

"Well, this is the mission, so deal with it," said Roland. "Pack the food when you're done. Remember, we didn't come up here just to look around and smell the Variant. We came to find those two and bring them home."

Terry shook his head. "What if they don't want to go?" he asked. "What do we do then?"

Roland stared at him for a moment. "We were given weapons," he said, matter-of-factly.

"I'm not shooting anyone," said Mei.

"Central's orders, not mine."

"Doesn't mean they're right," said Terry.

"No, it doesn't," said Roland. "But they're *our* orders, and right now they're all we've got."

15

**Documents of Historical, Scientific, and
    Cultural Significance
Open Transcript 616
Subtitled: The Memoires of S. E. Pepper –
    Chapter Nine
March 19, 2185**

PEPPER: *It's strange the way our memory works. I can barely
remember my father's face without having to look up an old picture, but
I know he had a crooked nose and big ears, and I know his favorite
food was the catfish from our cousin's ranch down in Florida, back
where he was raised. He had red hair and freckles, but he could get a
tan as fast as anyone. He loved my mom to death, and his favorite TV
show was Marty Kroker's Survival Show, and it aired every day at six*

pm. He was a Presbyterian, a carnivore, a wrestling fan, and he'd choose dirty hands over a necktie any day of the week.

I remember things about him, all the little details we use to define people when we talk about them. I can tell you all of it. But it's been thirty-seven years since my dad died, and I can't remember his smell. I can't remember his voice or his laugh. I can't remember his face.

Now, don't get me wrong, I know what he looked like. I have pictures, so I know his eyes were larger than most, and I know they were blue with brown spots in them. I know he had a mustache and my mother made him shave it. I know he loved me. But when I try to remember the way he looked at me on the scary nights, back when I was a little girl and I'd cry out in my sleep from all the nightmares, all I see is a shape—a blurry thing that ought to be a man, that ought to be my father, and it's nothing. Just a shadow. So in this moment I grab his picture and I look at it and I stare at it and I wait. I wait for the memory, the one I'm sure is somewhere deep inside me. Sometimes I wait for hours.

So after a while, I put the picture down, and maybe I cry a little bit if I have to, and close my eyes and think quietly to myself. I start reciting things I know about him, all the little facts of the man I used to know, and I tell myself they're true. I tell myself they're enough, even though I know they're not.

That's the trouble with memory. It doesn't always work the way we want it to. Sometimes we have to take what we can get from it and move on.

I was six years old on the day of the Jolt. We'd recently moved here. Dad had taken a job with the Ortego Corporation, and they paid him to uproot the rest of us and live underground. 'It's just for a little while,' he told us. 'Six to eight months—that's easy. And think of all the fun you'll have.' I didn't want to go. Not again. We'd only just moved to Montana, and I was starting to make friends at school, so why would I want to go? I fought him so hard on it.

It's ironic now, of course. If he'd listened to me, we'd all have died up there, choked on fumes of purple vapors until our insides melted away. Instead, he chased the job and packed our bags. Before I knew it, I was standing on the edge of the largest elevator shaft I'd ever seen.

I have two regrets in life. The first is the argument I had with my father the day before the accident, when he suggested I accept an invitation to dinner from a young soldier, and I was having none of it. The second is that when we descended down into the earth all those years ago, I didn't stop and look up, far into the light of the deep, blue sky, one last and final time.

End Audio File

January 2, 2347
Unknown

Alex swept his palm back and forth against the surface of the wet dirt, flattening it. He dipped his fingers into the mud, letting its coldness slowly cocoon him. He smiled, even as the pain of the wound in his stomach ached like a fire in a stove.

He lay inside a dark and narrow hole, soaking wet and aching. The smell of blood ran heavy through the air as drops of rain fell softly on the ancient planks above, like a thousand tiny fingertips beating gently to their own private rhythm. The walls, made up of rotting wood and hardened earth, leaned crooked from the passage of time, and at their base lay a pool of mud and filth. Centuries in the wilderness had overtaken the half-sunk hole, which had once served the purposes of men, but now remained abandoned as the drops of poison rain fell from a violet sky. For so long, this place had been without purpose.

But not anymore. Now, this hole would become Alex's grave. He was going to die in this place, alone and in the dark, the same as if he'd never left that cursed city. Still, at least he would die in the world he was made for, breathing air only his lungs could breathe, and listening to an orchestra of rain. Even here, like this, he was still above them all. He was still the better man.

He coughed, drops of blood spewing from his throat. They tasted like salted metal, horrible and vile. He spit violently into the air, then leaned back against the wall and closed his eyes.

He awoke several times, but despite himself he could hardly keep his eyes open for more than a few moments. His body would allow for nothing more, so he absorbed all he could in the time he was given. The rain fluctuated between his flirtations with consciousness. At first it fell gently, then violently and hard. Many times the storm woke him, and many times he wondered if it would be the last thing he ever heard.

When consciousness finally found him again, the pattering of the drops above had ended, and the chaos of the storm had transformed into quiet emptiness. How long did he sleep? How long had it been since he crawled here and away from the conquering animals? He had no way of knowing, not without a pad or the sky to guide him.

He moved his hand against the ground, pulling up a fistful of partially dried earth. The rain probably stopped some time ago, he realized, or the dirt would still be mud. If so, then there was no telling how long he'd slept or how many days had passed.

Yet he was still alive, still breathing, still aching. That was what mattered. Cole may have died, but at least he did it under the light of the Sun where he belonged. Alex wouldn't die down here, not in a place like this—buried in the earth like a diseased animal, like the people in that city. Like a human.

Alex trusted his body, and right now it was telling him he'd rested long enough. The pain in his abdomen, while not entirely gone, had evaporated into something manageable. All he needed to do was move.

He edged his way to the ladder on the far wall, and pulled himself up the steps. As soon as his feet hit the ground, he collapsed, crashing into the dirt like a discarded toy.

He sat up again and blindly reached for the ladder in

the dark. When he found it again, he gripped it tightly and pulled. His wound still ached, and his legs were far too weak to make the climb. He'd have to rely on his arms for strength.

One step at a time, that's what it would take. *Don't rush it*, he thought. *Gotta be patient, same as before. I can do this, too. I can do anything.*

Alone, starving, and in the dark, Alex climbed toward the light.

January 02, 2347
The Surface

TERRY WIPED his hand across his forehead. The water was filthy and burned his eyes.

"We should go back," urged Sarah as the rain fell again. "We'll never find them in this weather. It's too erratic."

Terry shot a hard glance at Mei. "I thought you said the storm would be gone before we got here."

"It's not the same storm," she said. "Don't you remember how big it looked on the pad? The scattered rain we've seen is nothing compared to the main storm."

Terry motioned toward the sky, the rain crashing against his palm. The clouds overhead were thick and gray, blocking out most of the sun, and in the distance, he could hear the sounds of thunder. "This doesn't seem like nothing to me."

"Be thankful we didn't have to sit through the real storm," she said. "If the readings were right about the wind speed, you wouldn't be able to walk right now, let alone stand there and complain about it."

"But we're not standing, we're walking," said John. He laughed at his own joke.

Mei rolled her eyes. "Point is it could have been a lot worse."

Roland put up his hand. "Everyone stop it. We're almost there."

He was right, of course. The remnants of the town lay off in the distance. Terry could barely make out the buildings, but they were definitely there.

As they walked towards the rubble, the shapes became clearer, and the reality of where they were began to settle. Someone had built this place. More than someone: a community. Now it was gone, reduced to nothing but a pile of sticks and stones and…dust. All that remained was this place.

He shook his head. No, there were people here once, however long ago. They had names and faces. These were their homes, their work, and their lives. There was meaning here. If nothing else, Terry had to remember that.

The rain stopped suddenly, although the letup didn't mean anything. It had stopped and started so many times now it was becoming routine.

"Go ahead and get the goggles ready," said Roland when they were a hundred yards away from the nearest collapsed building. "Better now than later when the rain comes back."

"Because you know it will," said John. "God, I hate this place."

"Maybe we'll see one of those rabs Mr. Nuber was talking about," said Sarah.

John stretched his arms. "Well at least it'd be something. All these rocks and dirt are boring."

"Don't forget the weird blue grass," said Sarah.

Terry retrieved the goggles from his pack and put them on. The strap slid on easily enough, and he cycled through the different sights until he found the infrared. He glanced around, but didn't see anyone besides his group, so he switched to normal vision. Once they were closer, he'd try again.

John fumbled with his strap. Mei loosened it for him. "Here," she said.

"We should probably have our rifles ready, too," said Sarah. She and Roland had, of course, been ready with their guns the entire time. "If we run into any of those rabs, you don't want to waste time reaching for your weapon."

Terry felt for his weapon. Resting on his back, the rifle was collapsed, but expanded when he unlatched it. Both hands on the rifle, he performed the standard routine of checking the safety, the magazine, and the thermal canister.

Once he was done, he snapped, "Ready." Everyone else followed suit.

"Okay, now it's time to split up. Remember, we're checking all three locations. John, Mei, and Terry—you three head to Alpha. Me and Sarah will check out Bravo. Radio once you're done. Whichever team finishes first will head to Charlie."

"Why not split into three teams?" asked John.

"We're odd numbered, remember?" asked Sarah. "It's a bad idea to only send one person to check the mark."

"Well, here's hoping we don't miss them at the third location," said Mei.

"If we do, we'll play catch up," said Roland. "It's not worth getting killed over."

They dispersed to their designated areas. Sarah and Roland headed north, while Terry, Mei, and John went south.

Terry walked beside John and Mei, goggles covering half his face, his rifle readied at his chest. Despite having trained for this moment, the intoxicating effects of the gas, the familiar touch of the rifle's metal grip against the skin of his palm, and the company of his lifelong friends beside him, everything was at once completely and undeniably alien. Nuber was right. The training wasn't enough. Nothing would ever be enough, not when it came to preparing them to kill, to risk their lives. How could he have expected anything else?

"Terry," said Mei, her voice soft and gentle. "Terry, are you okay?"

He turned to her. She looked completely different now with the goggles on her head and the gun at her waist. She seemed taller, bulkier, but how was that even possible? Where was the girl he knew, the one with the shiny black hair and the narrow shoulders? Where had his friend gone and who was this woman? When did she get to be so big?

"Terry, your hand is shaking," she muttered.

He looked at the grip of his rifle where his hand sat. She was right. His hand was quivering, twitching. "Sorry."

A drop of rain hit Terry on the shoulder. After a moment, a thin shower fell steadily.

"We don't have to do this," she said.

"I can check it out and you two can wait here," said John.

Mei nodded. "Really, Terry, given what's happening to you, it might be a good idea."

"I'll be fine. I'm a little nervous is all."

Mei and John both looked at each other and again at Terry. "If we keep going, you have to promise to tell us if you feel sick," Mei said.

"Fine, I will," he said.

They continued on their way. Occasionally, when he didn't think the others were looking, he stole a glance at his hands to make sure nothing was wrong. The more they walked, the calmer he became. After an hour, he was fine.

The town was large, but it wasn't dense. Everything was

spread out, which meant they had to walk a while to reach their destination. Patches of blue grass and sand had over-taken most of the roads, so it became difficult to tell where anything was. Mei took out her pad constantly to check where they were. Eventually she stopped putting it away at all.

As usual, Terry continued checking his infrared. He looked in every direction, but for some reason he was having trouble with it. "I think my goggles are busted," he finally said.

"What's wrong with them?" asked Mei.

"Well, for starters, anytime you guys get more than a few yards away, you start to blur. If you're too far, you blend in with everything else."

"I've been seeing the same thing," she said.

"Me too," said John. "I figured it was the rain, though."

"What's the rain got to do with it?" asked Terry.

"Our training handbook said sometimes the infrared messes up in the rain. Didn't you read it?" John looked at Mei. "Don't tell me *you* didn't know about it, either?"

Mei scoffed. "I'm sorry, but military hardware was never something I cared about. Besides, since when did you care enough to read anything?"

John took off his goggles. Mei followed and did the same. "For your information," he said. "I wanted to see if I could adjust the stupid strap so it wouldn't kill my ears anymore. I figured the book could tell me."

"Did you find out?" asked Terry.

"I couldn't understand the instructions," muttered John. "But at least I knew about the rain!"

Mei smirked. "You sure did. Do you remember anything else about it? Like what else besides the rain could hinder it?"

John thought for a moment. "Not really. According to the book, nothing should really be able to mess it up much. Blur it a little, sure, but not completely ruin the image."

Terry strapped the goggles on again. "It's a strange new world out here. There's no telling what's true and what's not anymore."

"When the rain stops, check it again," said Mei. "We'll see if anything's different."

When they finally reached the heart of the town, they decided to rest. Roland had given the order to set their pad timers for four hours. If they didn't find anything by then, they were supposed to radio in with a status report. So far they hadn't found so much as a piece of food or a footprint, let alone two genetically engineered runaway teenagers. Still, anything was possible.

John took a seat on the hood of an old car, though it was partially buried in the sand like everything else. "Hey, get your big butt off," barked Mei. "Show a little respect."

"What are you talking about?" he asked.

"It used to be somebody's car, you know," she said.

John stood and turned to look at the ancient machine. After a moment he shrugged. "So?"

"It doesn't feel right," she said.

"It's not like it's a grave or anything," said John.

The words lingered in the air for a moment as the realization of what John said settled in. Of course there were no graves. How could there be? They all died at once, consumed by the gas and ripped apart from their insides. Even if someone had survived to bury them, there would have been nothing left. Even the bones had turned to ash.

"We're standing on their graves," said Terry suddenly. "People died all around us and they never got buried. Don't you see? Everything in this town is a grave."

TOGETHER THEY WALKED through the stalled parade of dead vehicles in the road and toward the nearest structures. According to the map on the pad, there were five standing buildings in the area, with several others now collapsed. So far they'd managed to check two out of the five, but walking between them was proving to be a pain. Thanks to the rain, the goggles were essentially useless, which meant they'd have to check every room in every building themselves. Once they'd searched all five, they set to work on the collapsed ones, but it was becoming more and more apparent that they were only killing time.

John nudged a rock with his boot, then kicked it. "Well, I'm bored."

"What else is new?" asked Mei.

Terry checked the map on his pad. "What haven't we checked?"

Mei snatched the pad out of his hand. She scanned it briefly. "It looks like there are some old bomb shelters, but I'm sure they're collapsed by now."

"Might as well check them anyway," said John. "How many are there?"

Terry looked over the pad. "In town? Six. In our section, just two."

"On the plus side, at least the rain has stopped. For good, I think." John pointed skyward and they all looked. Sure enough, the clouds were parting and the violet hue of the sky shone forth, the sun's bright rays beaming out through the myriad of dissipating gray.

"Now might be a good time to check the infrared again," said Mei. "See what's changed."

"Right," said John.

Terry flipped the setting on his goggles to the infrared and glanced around. There was nothing unusual at first, but when his eyes found the nearest patch of the blue grass, he saw it. The grass was emitting a small amount of heat. Not much, but enough for the goggles to pick up. "Hey, look at this," he said, running to the nearest patch of grass. "Quick, turn on your infrared."

Mei scrambled to his side. "Whoa," she said. "I can't believe we didn't notice this before."

"The rain was causing too much of a problem. Besides, we were surrounded by sand and rocks when we first tried using them here. Once John said the thing about the rain, I didn't bother trying them again."

"Same here," she said. "But at least now we know."

They headed to the first bomb shelter, only to find it completely destroyed. The grate had been ripped off its hinges, and the walls were collapsed, buried halfway down the shaft with piles of sand and stone. "Must have happened a long time ago," said Terry.

"Come on," said Mei. "We still have one more place to check."

The second shelter was next, though it lay near the edge of their designated circle. "Not too far," Terry said as they walked.

"Good," said John.

"It's almost time to radio the others," said Mei. "As soon as we check out the second shelter, let's make the call."

They had to move around some wreckage on the way. The pad said it was a train station, but it didn't look like any of the stations back home. This one was bigger, covered in rubble and dirt, and most of its walls were falling apart. "Probably better to go around this," Mei suggested, and they did.

On the other side lay a field, the biggest they'd come across so far. Blue grass blanketed the landscape, growing in various sizes. "Cool. That's a lot of grass," said John.

Mei took out her pad and snapped a picture, then checked the map again. "The shelter's somewhere over there. Looks like it might be the middle of this field."

Terry flipped the switch on his goggles to infrared, hoping to get some kind of reading, but the grass was making it difficult. Everything, the entire ground, was lighting up. He took the goggles off. "Useless," he muttered.

Mei pointed. "I think I see it."

She was right. There was a large piece of metal sticking out of the ground not far from where they stood. It was the door to the shelter, and it was open.

John grabbed the door's handle and pulled. Despite being corroded and flimsy, it still moved with relative ease. "Doesn't look like the other one at all."

"Can we climb down?" Mei asked, getting close to the edge of it.

Terry edged closer. "Can you see anything? How do we know it's safe?"

"I'll check it out," said John. "I can use the goggles."

"Make sure you take it off infrared," suggested Mei.

"Obviously," said John.

"No, wait," said Terry. "Let me go. You're bigger than both of us and there's no telling how stable the ladder is. What if it breaks?"

John shrugged. "Then, I'll fall, but it won't happen. I can handle this."

Mei grabbed John's shoulder. "Wait, Terry's right. Let him do it."

"Huh? Why?"

"Because John," she snapped. "If he falls in, you can pull him out. If you fall, how are we supposed to help? Did you even think about the weight? You're at least sixty pounds heavier than either of us."

John paused. "I guess."

Terry leaned over the edge and stared into the pit. "I can't even tell how far down this thing is."

"Don't worry, we can tie a rope to your waist in case something happens," said Mei.

They followed Mei's suggestion and pulled a line around Terry's chest. John tied the other end to a nearby post and wrapped part of it around his own arm. "I'll lower you in like this," he said, letting the rope slack a little. "Like we practiced in gym, remember?"

Terry descended the ladder. Each of the steps were wet, he noticed, but it didn't feel like rainwater. Mud then, he decided. It didn't matter so long as he understood that he'd have to move slowly.

One step at a time, he moved deeper into the darkness, down and down until he was engulfed by it. Finally, he could turn on the goggles.

As soon as his finger flipped the switch, the room came suddenly to life. The walls were mostly intact but slanted or broken in various places. There were a few boxes—or what used to be boxes—stacked in one of the corners but nothing else. When he finally hit the ground, Terry called up to the others. "I'm all the way down, but there's nothing here," he said. He slid his foot against the bottom, kicking up clumps of damp dirt. The floor was hardly dry, but it definitely wasn't muddy, either.

"Okay, come on back," said Mei.

He began climbing. Several of the steps were still covered in the same thick liquid as before. As he neared the top, he stopped noticing it, but it was difficult to tell if it was because his hands were covered in it or if there just wasn't any more of it left. What was this stuff? Where did it come from?

When he finally reached the top, Mei and John helped pull him up and onto his feet. He fumbled with his goggles, but managed to pull them off. He wiped his arm across his forehead, trying to keep the sweat out of his eyes. When he finally dropped his arm, he noticed both John and Mei staring at him. "What is it?" he asked.

"Terry, you've got something on your face," said Mei.

"Your clothes, too," muttered John.

Terry looked down at his hands and his eyes went wide. The liquid, dark and red, covered both his arms and chest. "What...what is this?" he said.

"It looks like blood," said John.

"Oh, God," said Mei, grabbing Terry's hand. "Where did you cut yourself? Quick, we have to patch it. There's too much blood on you!"

He pulled away from her. "I didn't cut myself," he said.

"Well, it had to come from somewhere," she snapped.

"It's the ladder," he said in a hurry. "It came from there! I could feel it going down there."

"But why would there be blood..." Mei's voice trailed off and then stopped completely as her face went long and her eyes grew big with sheer realization. "Someone was down there."

"No way," said John.

"Yes, that's the only answer. If Terry's fine, then either someone else was down there, or it was an animal." She grabbed Terry's wrist and stared at him. "*Was* there a dead animal?"

He shook his head.

At the same time, John was reaching down into the hole. When he pulled his hand back out, his fingertips had blood on them. "Gross," he said.

"See?" asked Terry.

"Thick, too," said John, rubbing his fingers together.

"If this is really blood, then they can't be far," said Terry. "It's not dry, and it's thick enough that the last rain hasn't washed it away yet."

"So it happened after the last storm," said Mei. "When did it rain last?"

"A few hours, maybe," said John.

"Right, which means they have to be nearby," said Terry.

"There," suggested Mei, pointing to a building across the field. It lay in the opposite side from where they had entered. "What do you think?"

"Good place to start," said Terry.

They moved through the grass a little faster than they'd arrived, though there was no need to rush. Anyone injured enough to bleed so much couldn't have made it very far.

The building was small, its ceiling collapsed, and its stone walls overwrought with weeds. As they neared its isolated corner of the long forgotten field, Terry tripped over a tall bundle of blue grass. He stumbled at first, but caught himself before he hit the ground. He paused, hovering inches above the weeds, his eyes wide and his mouth agape as he stared blankly into a pool of the same red blood he'd seen moments ago. As he looked back toward the shelter, he could see a trail of other drops.

It led him forward in the direction of the building, confirming Mei's prediction. There was no question about it now. Whatever crawled out of that hole in the ground had also struggled defiantly into this corner of the field.

Suddenly, right as Terry was about to tell the others about the blood in the grass, he heard a loud, piercing scream, coming from nearby. He froze, then looked at John and Mei. None of them moved. The voice, while obviously in pain, was definitely human, but who could it be?

Everyone readied their weapons at once, their bodies suddenly tense. Terry gripped the butt of his rifle harder than he ever had in the training room, and for a moment he could hardly feel it in his hands, his fingers were so numb.

John motioned silently to flank the building. Terry nodded and moved to the other side, taking wide steps. He reached the side wall, pressing his back against it and trying to stay as quiet as possible. He moved gently around the corner, his weapon at the ready. Below him trailed a thin line of blood, and he followed it around the corner. As his eyes rose to meet the source, Terry cringed at the deadly sight—a boy, lying broken and exhausted, nestled against the wall, clutching his wound as though it were a prize. Slowly, the boy's head rose, his familiar grey eyes catching the light of the day in a brief, yet distilled moment. As he stared at Terry, the boy smiled. "Hey," he whispered. "You missed all the fun already."

"Dammit," said Terry, dropping his gun.

It was Alex…and he was dying.

16

Amber Project File Logs
Play Audio File 172
January 2, 2347

ROSS: *If he were human, he'd be dead.*

BISHOP: *So he'll live?*

ROSS: *Archer seems to think so, though he did complain about the quality of the scans.*

BISHOP: *Good enough for me. Now, what are we doing about the second one?*

ROSS: *According to the report, he was dragged away by the animals.*

BISHOP: *So he's probably dead.*

ROSS: *Probably.*

BISHOP: *But we don't know.*

ROSS: *No, sir, and there's something else.*

BISHOP: *What is it?*

ROSS: *It might be nothing, sir. I mean, he could be dead. He probably is dead.*

BISHOP: *Spit it out, Captain.*

ROSS: *Right after the team made contact with Alex, his chip's signal popped back up on our feed. It happened shortly after the storm dissipated, of course, so it makes sense. No more interference.*

BISHOP: *What's your point?*

ROSS: *It's not only his chip, sir. There's a second signal coming from the north. We think it might be Cole.*

BISHOP: *Or his chip, at least.*

ROSS: *Yes, sir, but it's coming and going. We aren't sure.*

BISHOP: *Ah, decisions.*

ROSS: *As I said, there's a good chance the other one's dead already. Despite their weapons and training, there's the risk that more of them might die up there.*

BISHOP: *Still…it could be worth a look.*

ROSS: *Archer keeps remarking on the data he's receiving from the chips. He wouldn't object to further exposure. The real question is whether or not we want to risk their lives to satisfy the old man's curiosity.*

BISHOP: *Yet that same curiosity has brought us this far.*

ROSS: *How far are we willing to go, sir? I can't help but think there has to be a line somewhere.*

BISHOP: *There is a line, Avery, but we left it behind some time ago. All we have left is the goal.*

ROSS: *What difference could a few more days make?*

BISHOP: *Maybe none.*

ROSS: *Then, why risk it, sir?*

BISHOP: *Because, Captain, the opposite could just as well be true.*

End Audio File

January 03, 2347
The Surface

Terry sat several feet away from Alex. A day after they found him, he still hadn't woken up. Terry couldn't help but watch as Mei gathered the bloodied bandages to burn them. Sarah was the one to suggest it. After all, carnivores lusted after injured things, so why leave evidence around for them to find? Burn it all, they'd agreed. If everyone died in the middle of the night, it wouldn't be because of bandages.

The fire wheezed and danced as Mei dropped the bloody rags into its flames. Terry had only seen a few fires in his life, each of them controlled and handled with care, but never one so wild. Despite the tools doing most of the work, the fire cracked and whirled chaotically and naturally. It was its own animal, dancing here in the open world under the moonlit sky.

At first, Roland had been against it. "It'll attract something," he said, but Mei and Terry argued.

"It's freezing here," Mei said. "Plus, they say it keeps the animals away."

"These aren't normal animals," said Roland.

"Two guards, then," suggested Terry. "We'll work in shifts. Two guards at a time instead of one. With our rifles, we should be fine."

Roland agreed, reluctantly, and so the fire was allowed to burn.

It was a good thing, too, because Alex was barely moving. *What happened to him out here in the wild?* Wondered Terry. And what would happen to him when they returned? *Maybe they'll look at his stomach and say he suffered enough,* thought Terry, but he doubted it.

"Hey," said John. He scooted to Terry's side. "What's up?"

"Watching the fire," said Terry.

John hesitated. "I was wondering if you were okay. You know, after your..." he looked around, lowering his voice. "After what happened with you."

"You mean when I blacked out?" said Terry.

"Well, yeah," he said. "Anything else happen?"

"Not yet," said Terry.

"Good. Maybe your body's getting used to it."

"Maybe," said Terry.

Sarah approached the fire. She'd been talking with Roland for a few minutes, trying to figure out the safest path home. "Who's taking first watch with me?" she asked, glancing around the camp. "Don't everyone volunteer at once."

"I'll do it," said Terry. He wasn't tired anyway.

"Good," she smiled. "Second watch will be Mei and John, then."

John cracked his knuckles. "Don't worry, Mei. I'll protect you."

Mei placed her hand over her mouth, like she was about to gasp. "Oh, sir, you're so kind to me. I'm such a helpless, tiny thing. Thank you *so* much for your chivalry."

John put his arm on her shoulder. "You all heard it, right? She needs me."

Mei elbowed him in the stomach. "It's the other way around, and you know it."

"Okay, okay," said Sarah. "You two go to sleep. Terry and I will wake you in three hours for your shift."

John and Mei agreed and did as they were told. Roland soon followed their example, briefly checking on Alex, who slept near the fire, before going off to bed. Within half an hour, they were all asleep, except for Sarah and Terry.

The two of them took up places on opposite sides of the camp. Sarah instructed Terry to wear his goggles and to occasionally cycle through the different sights. "Leave it on night vision for the most part, though," she said. "Infrared is nice, but with all these plants around here, it's just not very reliable."

Terry sat on a large rock with his back to the camp. He

palmed the side of the goggles until he could see the field in front of him and then held his rifle tight against his chest. The field was vast and largely empty, save a few patches of grass. If anything was out there, it wouldn't be able to sneak up on them.

An hour ached by with the speed of a mathematics lecture. Terry stood and stretched, cracking the small of his back as well as his shoulders. He removed his goggles and let his eyes air out, wiping the sweat from his nose and brow. He took a deep breath, and the cold Variant air filled his lungs and he smiled.

He turned toward the camp and stared at the fire, which blocked him from seeing Alex.

Terry shook his head. It was a pity about Alex. All he wanted was to live free. He did all the work of escaping the city, risking life and limb in the process, only to discover an empty, soulless world. Along the way, he'd lost his only friend, and now he had nothing but the wounds in his belly and the smell of death on his breath to show for it. Did he even understand what was happening now? Was he aware enough to know he was going home?

I better check on him, thought Terry, grabbing his gear. It would be a shame if Alex died now that they'd gone to the trouble of finding him.

As Terry walked, he kept expecting to see Alex on the other side of the fire. But the closer he approached, the more concerned he became. After a few more steps, he began to fear the worst. Where were Alex's legs? Could he really have left the camp? How could he do anything with wounds like his?

As he drew close to the fire, it became clear Alex had vanished. At some point after Terry and Sarah had taken to guard duty, a wounded Alex had somehow managed to stand and walk away, all without anyone noticing.

Terry reached for his pad and pulled up the communicator. "Sarah! You there?"

"What is it, Terry?"

"It's Alex," he said, putting his goggles on. "He's not at the fire. I think he ran off."

There was a pause. "What?" she said. "Are you sure?"

"I'm standing right next to where he was, and I don't see him, so yeah, I'm pretty sure." Terry flipped over to night vision and scanned the area. There was nothing.

"I'm coming back. Hold on," said Sarah.

"Sure thing." He hit the switch again and brought up the infrared. There were the plants, of course, and even the fire behind him heating the nearby earth, but out there in the distant field, taller than all the other little warm dots, stood one light that was taller than the rest.

The more he stared at it, the more he was convinced it was alive.

TERRY CLASPED his rifle at the ready and ran briskly toward the pillar of warm light he saw in his infrared. Part of him expected to find a razorback or some other wild animal. Thankfully, it was nothing so dangerous.

Alex stood in silence, staring at nothing, saying nothing. He didn't bother looking at Terry.

Terry kept his distance. "Hey, Alex. It's Terry. You okay?"

Alex didn't answer.

Terry took a step closer. "I was worried about you. Hey, why don't we go back to the fire? It's really cold out here."

"I'm fine where I am," said Alex, finally.

"Terry?" Sarah's voice erupted from the pad. "I'm at the fire. Where are you?"

Alex finally turned to look at Terry.

"I found him," said Terry. "He wanted to go take a piss in the field. We're coming back in a minute."

"Oh, thank God," she said. "Bring him here right now, Terry. It's dangerous out here, and he's injured."

"Sure thing," he said.

"Thanks," said Alex.

"Yeah, sure."

Alex turned back to the same position he'd been in when Terry arrived. "Give me a minute."

"What's the real reason you left camp?" asked Terry.

"The fire's too hot. I wanted to feel the cold for a minute."

"Oh."

"Also I was tired of lying down," he said. "Being there like that, I couldn't stop thinking about certain things, you know? Like there's a vid in my head, and it keeps replaying over and over again."

"What keeps replaying?" asked Terry. He stepped closer.

"When I got this," he said, motioning to his stomach. "And those animals. Huge things with massive teeth and claws, silver-gray hair and black eyes, like something out of a story. You wouldn't believe they existed unless you saw them for yourself. I still can't believe it."

"Yeah," said Terry. "Nuber told us about them after you left. He said they were pretty scary."

Alex scoffed. "Scary? I've never seen something so beautiful."

"Beautiful? They almost killed you, Alex."

"And that's *why* they're beautiful. Terry, look around you, look where we are. Don't you see what's going on here?"

"All I see is a desert full of nothing."

"The sky is purple. The grass is blue. The animals here are vicious and wild, like monsters from a fairy tale. This isn't Earth, anymore. It's something new. Look what you're breathing. It's Variant...and it's everywhere. You're breathing a toxic gas which is supposed to kill whatever it touches, whatever's too weak, and all it does is make you stronger. You know what that is?"

"Genetic engineering?"

"Evolution!" he snapped. "That's why we were made—to do what they can only dream of. We belong up here...

don't you get it?" He kicked the ground. "I don't want to go back."

And there it was. Alex wanted to stay. Despite everything, despite all the pain he'd already endured, he still didn't want to leave this place.

Except he had to go. It was the mission. Terry couldn't leave Alex here to die, no matter how stubborn he was or how much he argued about it. One way or another, they were taking him home. First, though, they needed to go back to the camp.

"Maybe you're right," said Terry after a moment. "About all that stuff, maybe you have a point. It all makes sense." He let the words settle before he went on. "But right now you're only telling *me*, and we're all the way out here by ourselves where no one else can hear it. Don't you want to tell the others, too?"

"Of course I do," said Alex.

"Then, let's go back to camp," he said. "We'll talk about it in the morning. You can tell the others what you think. They'll listen, I promise." They wouldn't listen, not really. Alex was acting crazy, talking about running wild in the desert, like they were animals or something. But Terry needed to play along with it, let Alex think he was on his side. It was the easiest way to get him to go back.

"And if they don't?" he snapped. "I'm not going back there. I'm not!" He kicked the ground again and dust spewed high into the air. Before Terry could speak, Alex kicked the ground again. And then again. And then again.

When he was finally done, Alex collapsed, out of breath and clutching his side.

Terry didn't know what to say. This entire situation was out of his depth. Then again, so was everything else here in this place, this shattered wasteland of a world. How could Alex truly believe he belonged here? How could anyone?

When the dust finally settled, it brought the smell of the wild earth with it. Terry coughed, covering his face with the neck of his shirt. Alex on the other hand, didn't move at all. He kept staring into the wild, beyond the light of the moon.

When Alex finally stood again, he was completely calm. Looking at Terry, his eyes reflected the moonlight, turning them ghost white. "Okay," he said at last. "I think I'm ready to go back now."

Together they returned to the camp. Terry followed closely behind Alex, his finger covering the rifle's trigger guard, prepared for action. Alex appeared to be calm, but how long could it last? Better to be ready in case he decided to run, or worse.

Sarah waited for them at the fire pit when they arrived. She was holding her pad in one hand and her gun in the other. She had a troubled look on her face. "Everything's fine," said Terry. "We're back now."

"We've got another problem," she said, darting her eyes toward the other tents.

Roland stood over Mei's tent, calling for her. He shook the side of it. In a moment, Mei opened the zipper and stepped out. After a brief exchange, Roland moved on to John.

"What's going on?" asked Terry.

Sarah kept watching Roland. "Central called while you were gone. We're getting new orders."

"What kind of orders? And why so late?"

"I don't know yet," she said.

Together with Mei and John, Roland approached the fire. Standing there, the light reflecting off his deep, brown skin, he looked exhausted. The lines around his eyes had grown long and heavy, as though he'd aged another decade or two, and the sweat lingering on his forehead and neck made it seem as though he'd awoken from a vivid nightmare. Perhaps he had.

"I got the call a few minutes ago," said Roland. He wiped his bloodshot eyes with his fingertips, sliding his palm over his face as it fell. "There's a signal coming from the north. It's faint, but Central thinks it might be Cole's. They need us to check it out."

Sarah closed her eyes. "I can't believe this."

Roland nodded. "Looks like we're not going home quite yet."

January 04, 2347
Housing District 03

AVERY ROSS AWOKE in the middle of the night to the alarm on her pad. It lay on the nightstand nearby, illuminating the room with a red, pulsing glow. She blinked mechanically in an attempt to discharge the fatigue from her eyes. They burned defiantly, calling her back to sleep.

She pulled the pad in close. The screen came alive when she tapped it and a message appeared in bolded red lettering: SECURITY ACCESS, ALPHA POINT. COLONEL BISHOP, JAMES M. The time and date were stamped below.

She had set up the alert system a few months back in order to keep tabs on when the colonel entered the academy. Most of the time she didn't need it, because he rarely went in without calling her first. There had only been a few instances, and none had occurred since she installed this new system.

Ross's heart began to race, replacing her fatigue with adrenaline, giving her the strength to get to her feet. She leapt out of bed and threw her uniform on as quickly as possible. Within moments, she was out the door.

Because she only lived a block away, it didn't take her very long to reach her work. She badged into the side entrance, which was rarely used and hastily crept through the halls toward her office. She wouldn't go near the colonel. She didn't have to. Before installing the alert on her pad, she'd also installed a helper tool on Bishop's desktop, giving her remote access from her own computer, allowing her to listen in through his microphone. She could only do this from her office, which increased the risk of getting caught, but that was necessary. Anything worth doing required a certain level of danger. Spying on her boss was no exception.

She made very little noise as she entered the office, locking the door and taking her seat. She booted up the desktop, validating her credentials and finally running the helper tool.

She wasn't sure if it would actually work, given she'd never even tested it before. But to her surprise, the program ran flawlessly, and she was quickly met with the sound of men talking. She grinned wildly at her amateur success, but quickly shook the celebration off, forcing herself to focus on the job instead.

"So we're set," said Bishop. His muffled voice was more like a whisper. Ross leaned in close.

"Sure," said another voice, raspy and deep. Ross didn't recognize him. "The protest tomorrow. I'll be there."

"Good," said Bishop.

"And the money?" asked the man. "This kind of job ain't cheap."

"So long as you do it, you'll get paid."

"I better," he said. "Killing a politician is risky business."

"I promised you didn't I?" asked Bishop. "Follow the plan and you'll be fine."

"Yeah, yeah," he said. "Wave my arms, make a scene, shoot her dead. No problem."

"You have to do it while everyone's watching," said Bishop. "They all need to see you."

"Why can't I just off her while she's asleep? You never had a problem with it before. Why the change?"

"It's about sending a message. The people going to this protest, I know a lot of them. They're cowards. If they see the matron take a bullet in the chest, they'll back down."

"You ain't worried they'll come after you?"

"It's the reason you have to yell what I told you."

"Right."

"Don't screw this up. I can't help you if you get caught."

"Never botched a job yet," said the man. "I ain't gonna start now."

Ross could barely breathe, her heart was racing so fast. It was like all the air in the room had suddenly been sucked out. She fumbled with the controls on her desk, trying to hurry and disconnect the line. She never expected to overhear something so malicious, but it was too late. The truth had come out, and she had an obligation to act.

She ran swiftly to her personal bathroom, got out her pad, and waited for the alert that Bishop had left the building. She sat there, clutching the pad in her chest with her arms wrapped around her body, shaking uncontrollably. What was this horrible feeling overtaking her? Was she afraid for her life? No, she had already learned to manage personal fear. This was something else, a concern for the matron, for Mara, her friend. The thought of something happening to her filled Ross with a powerful dread. She couldn't let anything happen to Mara, even at the cost of herself. She had to stop it. She had to warn her.

The alert sounded on her pad, and she quickly left the bathroom and her office. She departed through a different exit than the one the colonel had and quietly made her way back to her apartment, where she changed her clothes to something more inconspicuous. In less than an hour, she was on the train, traveling to Mara's apartment.

Things were about to get extremely complicated and more than a little dangerous. The man with the raspy voice —he was going to make an attempt on Mara's life. He had to be stopped. If only she knew who he was. But she didn't know, nor could she. What's more, even if she convinced Mara to stay away, or she came forward and had Bishop arrested, the killer would still carry out the plan eventually. The pieces were already moving. She couldn't stop it.

A sudden realization swept over her, and she began to consider an alternate plan. What if she let the assassin take his shot? What if Mara Echols died?

January 05, 2347
The Mother's Lounge

THE PROTEST WAS GOING SPLENDIDLY. Thanks to Ross and Ava's efforts to bring in new protestors, the mother's lounge had filled to capacity. The crowd no longer consisted of only mothers but people from all across the city, including farmers, contractors, factory workers, counselors, scientists, and a handful of crudely disguised soldiers. It was a far cry from a complete success, but things were certainly progressing in the right direction.

Mara stood with Ava and several others near the back of the lounge. Among them included Dr. Timothy Rhodes, a medical doctor, Freddy Winehold, one of the farms' head operators, Patricia Stockholm, a judge, and Emmitt Clawson, owner of Clawson's Goods, the largest shop in the city's plaza. They had each shown up for different reasons —some for genuine concern, others out of curiosity. Mara suspected Clawson in particular had only come to appear empathetic in an effort to better promote his business. Still, the fact that they had all shown up was itself worth celebrating. The more people who showed their support, the louder their voice would become.

Ava nudged Mara's elbow. "You did well," she whispered. "It's quite the turnout."

"Thank you, Ava. But you deserve the credit, too, along with our other friend."

"Yes, the silent conspirator," nodded Ava. "Speaking of which, are you ready?"

You mean am I ready to die? She thought, though she didn't say it. Of course, the murder was only an illusion—a devious little plan engineered by Captain Ross. She was in no real danger. Aside from the bulletproof vest she wore under her dress, the podium was encased with translucent BB-Glass for added safety. The BB-Glass and the vest had both been a gift from Ross, of which Mara was now most thankful.

Mara gave Ava a wink. "I'll never be ready, but I'm doing this anyway."

Ava nodded. "Whatever happens, I'll be right here."

Without another word, Mara made her way to the podium at the head of the lounge. She tapped the microphone and cleared her throat. The commotion quickly subsided. Everyone's eyes were on her.

"Greetings, my dear friends," she began. "Today is an important day for all of us. Today we are, for what almost feels like the first time, gathered together under a common banner. We stand united in the opposition of tyranny…a direct attack on our way of life. Several years ago, General Stone, along with the first matron Ava Long, decided that no government could operate under the guise of a monarchy, that no single individual should have the ability to control the rest. It's why the Stone Charter was created and with it, a system of checks and balances. This system, represented by the council, has fallen under direct opposition by the other leaders. They have chosen to ignore the policy of our fathers in favor of their own. This is something that we, as citizens of our fair city, cannot abide."

A fleet of whispers swept through the crowd and lingered, rising and collapsing. Mara continued. "I'm sure you all have questions and concerns," she said. "If you look at your pads, you'll see I have forwarded all related documents to this discussion. But if you have additional problems or would like more information, my staff and I are here to help."

A woman in the front row raised her hand. Mara recognized her as being a biologist in the labs. "Yes, I was just wondering, how did you first learn of this information?"

"We have a source. That is all I can say."

"And we're supposed to believe in the reliability of this source?" asked the woman.

"Believe in the facts," said Mara. "I have not come to you today with rumors or baseless accusations…but with proof. As a scientist, I'm sure you can appreciate that the evidence is the most important part of any investigation."

"Of course," she conceded.

Mara looked around the room. "Are there any other questions?"

A hand shot up from amid the crowd. It was a dark haired man, his skin quite pale. He was wearing a large jacket with his other hand inside. "I got a question," he said. His scraping voice cut the air like a knife, demanding attention.

"Go ahead," said Mara.

The man stared at her for a moment. "You happy to be where you are?"

"Happy?" Mara asked.

"You know what I think," said the man. "You got a taste of the good life. You got a bite of the power. Now you want some more. You and all them other boys, you think you got more of a right than the rest of us. You think you're better."

"Sir, I don't think…"

"People in the slums, they're working every day like dogs and you're sitting there complaining about how you want more scraps. You ain't special, lady. You don't deserve nothing more than me…and I'm gonna prove it." He swept his jacket open and pulled his other arm out. There, clutched between his boney fingers, he held a pistol. "No more slaves! Equality or death!"

He aimed and pulled the trigger. The bullet pulsed from the barrel of the gun and sped in the direction of Mara's chest, hitting the BB-Glass and fracturing into a thousand tiny pieces, which it absorbed.

Mara fell, and the crowd scattered, filling the room with screams.

17

Amber Project File Logs
Play Audio File 183
January 05, 2347

NUBER: *What's so important you had to call me in the middle of the night?*

ROSS: *I'm sorry, Henry, but I need to talk to you. It's important. Have you been paying attention to what's going on?*

NUBER: *You'll have to be more specific. Between what's happening on the surface and the insanity in the city streets, I'm having a hard time keeping up.*

ROSS: *The assassination.*

NUBER: *Ah. Yeah, I heard about it. You arrested the guy, right?*

ROSS: *We caught him fleeing the scene. I sent a few guards to monitor the protest. You know, to be on the safe side.*

NUBER: *Sounds like you got lucky. Nice job.*

ROSS: *Yes, very lucky.*

NUBER: *Did you get anything out of the killer?*

ROSS: *Nothing substantial. The colonel pulled me away before I was able to complete the interrogation. He said it could wait and to focus on containment and public reassurances.*

NUBER: *He doesn't think it's important to question the killer?*

ROSS: *Have you spoken to the colonel?*

NUBER: *Sure.*

ROSS: *Then, you know what he's planning on doing.*

NUBER: *You mean take control over the motherhood?*

ROSS: *Yes. What did you say when he told you?*

NUBER: *I complained, but he stopped listening to me a while ago.*

ROSS: *So you don't think it's a good idea?*

NUBER: *Hell no, it's not. Since when is martial law a good idea? It's ridiculous.*

ROSS: *He says it's temporary.*

NUBER: *Sure he does.*

ROSS: *You don't believe him?*

NUBER: *He was having trouble convincing Echols to donate mothers to the project. He and Archer need them, though, so he's bound to try to manipulate this situation. It's how he operates.*

ROSS: *That's what I thought you were going to say.*

NUBER: *Sorry if I disappointed you.*

ROSS: *On the contrary, Henry. You've said all the right things. It's the reason I came to you in the first place.*

NUBER: *Avery, what's going on? You call me up in the dead of night, ask me a bunch of questions. I'm not sure what to make of it.*

ROSS: *I'm sorry. I know it's strange. I had to see if we were on the same page.*

NUBER: *Same page? Can you elaborate?*

ROSS: *I swear I will, but not right now. Can you meet me tomorrow at Virgil's Diner? There's something I need you to see.*

End Audio File

January 06, 2347
The Surface

Terry and the others traveled through dawn and into the hard light of the afternoon sun, sticking closely to the road—as close as one could get to something which came and went so often. Dust and time had worn the paths enough so they vanished randomly only to reappear an hour later. The only true point of reference was the map on their pads, which showed their location by way of a steady red dot. Their destination lay in the north, which the map displayed in calmer blue. It blinked periodically like a steady, beating pulse. It was Cole's chip, of course, and in all the time they walked, it never moved an inch.

A dozen thoughts circled Terry's mind as to the fate of his former classmate. If Alex's story were to be believed—

and he had no reason to lie—Cole was probably dead. But if he really did manage to survive, maybe he'd found himself a hiding place somewhere and was waiting for the chance to come out. Alex hid in a hole in the ground, after all, so why couldn't Cole do the same?

However, even as he thought it, Terry knew it could never be true. This new world was no place for hope, nor for life; it was a place for all the other, nastier things—the kind of things a mother tells her children to scare them into brushing their teeth or eating their vegetables. The only difference was now the nightmares were real, and they didn't stop to check a child's personal hygiene before they clawed or sneered or barked at them. The world belonged to *them* now. Humanity's time was at an end.

At least the human race kept trying. Terry and his friends were proof enough. Even after the apocalypse, people refused to give up. Maybe the same could be true of Cole, however impossible it might seem.

"Hey," said John, who had been walking a little behind Terry. "Mei says we're stopping soon. You doing alright?"

"Yeah, fine," said Terry. "I was only thinking."

"About what?"

"How Cole must be doing," he said. *And that he's probably dead.*

"We'll find him soon. No doubt about it."

Terry nodded. John was right—they'd find Cole at some point. No matter where he'd been taken. No matter what ditch or hole or cave, they would eventually find him.

The real question was whether or not he was alive. If not, what would it mean for the rest of them?

Guess I'll find out eventually, thought Terry. *One way or another.*

The day dragged on as they marched, but Terry kept himself occupied. He watched the map on his pad, monitoring the brightly colored dots on the screen and their ever-decreasing distance from one another. The map magnified as they drew nearer to the signal, keeping both their location as well as Cole's within the screen's borders. Terry looked as often as he could to see if the map had changed, hoping to catch it before it actually performed the magnification. Over the course of the next few hours, it became a sort of game for him—a way to distract from the sour thoughts of what lay ahead.

As the map continued to zoom in, however, the terrain morphed. At first, the changes were negligible, and for a moment, it seemed as though the map was simply becoming more detailed. A few boulders disappeared or moved, vacant sections of the road became clearer. But the more time passed, the more detailed the map became. Suddenly, the buildings on the map transformed into piles of stones and rubble, while the blank and empty landscape surrounding the roads filled up with abandoned automobiles and shattered highway railings.

"Wait a second," Terry said when he realized what was transpiring. The rest of the group stopped quickly alongside him. "Something's happening to the map."

John stood behind him, glancing over his shoulder. "I don't see anything."

"You have to keep watching, but it keeps changing."

Mei pulled out her own pad. "He's right. It's zooming in the closer we get."

"So?" Asked Sarah. "It's probably doing it so we can navigate better."

"That's not all," said Terry. "The details are changing, too." He pointed to a blank area near their current location. "See this? There used to be a building here. Now there's nothing."

"What's it mean?" asked Alex.

"I think the map's updating itself."

"How's such a thing possible?" said Roland. "I thought everything on here was supposed to be completely up-to-date? Isn't that the whole point of the radar tower?"

"Normally yes," said Mei. "But we're outside the towers' reach. Our pads have been going on old data." She flicked the screen of her pad, zooming back out. "Look here. See those buildings in the city? They're obviously gone now, collapsed or whatever, but if you look on the map, they're still here. The reason's because we have outdated maps of this area from before the Jolt."

Sarah scratched behind her ear. "So why is it updating? Shouldn't we still see the outdated map?"

"Maybe the towers really *are* doing it," said Roland. "Central could have increased the range on them or sent an update. They know we're going this way, right? So maybe they didn't have much of a reason to do it until now."

"I don't think so," said Mei. "Don't you remember the diagram they showed us when we went over weather patterns?"

"Not meteorology again," said John, moaning.

She rolled her eyes. "Yes, meteorology. Mr. Nuber showed us a map of the area covered by the towers. We're outside of it. Ever since we went beyond the towers' reach, we've been going based on a two-hundred-year-old map. A lot can happen in a few centuries, so of course the land's changed."

"But we still have maps," said John. "If we can't get anything from the towers, where'd they come from?"

"Could be saved data files on the hard drives. They're probably meant to be a backup in case the towers went down or we got out of range. They're not a hundred percent accurate, but better than nothing."

"The teachers most likely thought the same thing," said Terry.

"What about the updates we're getting?" asked Roland. "Where are they coming from?"

Terry thought for a moment. "It's the pads. It has to be."

John looked at him. "Huh?"

"Think about it. What else could be doing it?"

Mei smiled. "You might be right."

"How?" asked Sarah. "Don't you need to be pretty far

up in order to do that? It's the whole point of the towers, right?"

"It's not updating very far," said Terry. "There seems to be a limit. Maybe a hundred yards."

Mei nodded. "I'm thinking these pads are operating by line of sight, and since we're so close to the ground, they can't see very far. Like you said, a hundred yards, maybe less."

"So it's hardly useful," said Alex.

Mei shook her head. "If we can get to a high enough area, it might be *very* useful."

"What? You mean like a tall building?" asked Roland. "I don't see any of those around here."

"There might be up ahead," said Terry. "And if not, at least we're getting something out of it, even if it's not much."

Sarah nodded. "You're right, Terry. It's better than nothing."

"Wait a second," said John, furrowing his brow. "If the maps are updating and we're out of range from the towers, how's Cole's signal reaching us?"

Roland spoke up. "It's not a steady signal, for starters."

"Still, how can the towers reach it at all?" John asked.

Everyone paused at the question, seemingly clueless.

Mei suddenly clapped her hands. "I know!" she squealed. "The chips are transmitting. Don't you guys see? Cole's chip is sending intermittent signals to the nearest tower. It's the only thing making any sense."

"Doesn't it mean he could've moved by now?" asked Terry.

"He's probably still there. The biggest issue for us is we might have to deal with some unforeseen terrain changes."

"Could be bad," said Sarah. "We'll be walking in blind."

"The pads give us a hundred yards, right?" asked Terry.

Mei shrugged. "Maybe. It could be less."

"Still, it's something," said Terry.

Roland started walking. "As long as we're careful, we'll be fine. Remember, we're armed and trained. We can handle whatever comes our way."

***

AFTER SPENDING most of the day on the road, Terry's group finally stopped in a clearing beneath a large hill. The highway they were following merged effortlessly into the hillside, where the grass took hold and covered everything. "It's like a carpet," said Terry.

"Pretty annoying if you ask me," said John. "I'd rather have the road."

"Listen up," said Roland. He tapped the pad in his hand and pulled up the local map. The red and blue dots each appeared. They were very close now. "It's less than three miles before we get to where we need to be. This incline might slow us a little, but we should be fine. Everyone grab something quick to eat, but don't take too long. We're pushing forward in fifteen minutes. Hopefully, when we reach the top, our pads will pick up more info about what's ahead. If not, we'll still have our eyes." He unslung his pack.

"Sounds good to me," said Mei. She immediately sat down. "Terry, toss me a bag, please."

"Sure thing," said Terry. He knelt and started unpacking. "Bags of slop for everyone."

"Slop?" asked Alex.

"Best you've ever had," said John.

"He lies," said Sarah. "But it's not as bad as chewing dirt, I guess."

"Or grass," said Mei. "Can you imagine trying to survive up here without the food we brought?"

"Hey, yeah," said John. "Say, Alex, what were you planning to live on when you got up here, anyway?"

"We brought food," he said.

"Like what?" asked Mei. "You didn't have any supplies when we found you."

"We used some. The rest got destroyed during the attack."

"So what were you gonna do afterward?" asked John. "Eat the grass? Because there's nothing else around here."

"I had a plan."

"Which was?"

Terry handed a bag of food to Sarah, but Alex snatched it away.

"Hey," snapped Terry

"It doesn't matter anymore, does it?" barked Alex. "It's not like we had time to do anything." He tore into the bag, spilling bits of wet cabbage all over his jacket. He swore, but started eating anyway.

"Sorry for asking," said John.

Terry handed out the rest of the food. "Let's just eat. We have to get going pretty soon."

They hurried and ate, barely speaking. Terry packed the remaining food and hoisted the pack over his shoulder. The weight of it was hardly noticeable—nothing like it used to be, back before all of this.

So much had changed for him, but even more since he arrived on the surface. He was never tired anymore, not at all, and every day he felt stronger. But where was it all going? Tomorrow, when he awoke, would he feel better than he did today, or would it finally level out? How strong could a person become before the body reached its limit and collapsed in on itself?

A chill ran down his back. *Oh, well,* he thought, buckling the strap around his chest. *I guess it could be worse.* But when he tried to think of how, nothing came to him.

They marched along the hill, leaving a trail of flattened grass behind them. The blue weeds waved back and forth, reflective in the light, and they danced as though they'd been waiting their whole lives for someone to find them. "It's so beautiful," said Sarah. "Why can't everything be so wonderful?"

They climbed the hill for nearly two hours. After a

while, John turned around, asking how long everyone thought it would take for him to reach the bottom if he fell.

"It won't matter, since you'll break your neck," said Mei.

"You'd like that, wouldn't you?" he said.

"Of course," she smiled.

As they grew closer to the peak, Sarah started running. "We're almost there," she shouted. "Finally!" It didn't take long for her to reach the top. When she did, she didn't say a word. She only stared, her mouth agape.

"What do you see?" called Roland.

"Probably nothing, same as everything else," said Mei.

Sarah didn't answer right away, but when Roland called to her again, she flinched, like she hadn't heard him until now. "Sorry. It's…definitely something."

"What is it?" asked Roland.

"Come and see," she said, refusing to look away.

As Terry approached the crest, the sky beyond the hill peeled back. In the distance, a building appeared. With each step it grew larger, and around it several others showed themselves. Before long, a slew of broken structures larger than anything else he'd ever seen filled the distant sky. "It's a city," muttered Terry.

"Not anymore," said Sarah.

She was right. Nearly a fourth of it had been obliterated, broken apart into nothing more than a massive pile of debris. The remaining towers, while still standing, were jagged remnants of their former states. They looked like giant knives coming out of the earth, trying to pierce the sky.

Much like the rest of the planet, everything about this place had come undone.

Standing high atop the hill, Terry stared intently at the pad in his hand. The map was filling itself with details faster than it ever had before. He and Mei were right to expect as much. The elevation allowed for a far greater line of sight. "Check it out," he said.

"What's the damage?" asked John.

Mei frowned. "Uh, oh."

"Something wrong?" asked Terry.

"The map changed more than I expected."

"So what?" asked Sarah.

"So there's a problem now. Look at Cole's signal. See how different the area looks."

Terry pulled up the map and zoomed in on it. The landscape had changed drastically. The signal now came from beneath what appeared to be several layers of stone at the edge of the city. "Not good."

"No, it's not," said Mei. "It looks like he's been buried. Or he's in a cave now."

"Could be anything," said Sarah.

"Awesome," said John. "Because things weren't hard enough before, right?"

It took less time to reach the bottom of the hill than to climb it. The road reappeared near the base and continued unhindered for as far as they could see. "The map says it's this way," said Roland. He pointed down the road toward the city. "Not much farther now."

As they drew closer to the city, the collapsed walls and highway roads became more apparent. A dried up river basin stretched from within the confines of the desolate metropolis, twisting and bending out along the stone and into the endless expanse of desert sand.

Beyond the once-river, the tattered concrete jungle remained.

The city's towers looked as though they might collapse at any moment—a shattered visage of accomplishments, slowly breaking apart like dust from a dry stone.

The tallest of these monuments lay near the center, its steel frame the only evidence of its once mighty legacy. After two hundred years, it had become nothing more than a skeleton, its concrete guts eroded by rain and wind and natural decay. Someday, possibly soon, this antique goliath would wither completely, joining its fallen brethren in the sand. It might not take much—a gust of wind, perhaps, or a tremor, or simply time—but in the end it would dissolve and die, absorbed back into the earth that birthed it, the same mud that had given life so generously to both men and beast, tree and insect.

For now, though, it continued to sleep, the same as it had for so many years, ever since the Jolt came and wiped out all the spectators—no more eyes to marvel with, no more necks bent back with gaping mouths to awe.

Until a group of mutant offspring from below the crust

of the deep, dark earth came up for some decidedly fresh air. "What wonders would befall us, children?" Dr. Byrne had said so long ago. "A whole new world of stories."

In that moment, staring out across the wasteland sea, Terry imagined what the good doctor—what all of the teachers—would say if they could see what their new world had wrought.

January 06, 2347
Virgil's Diner, Pepper Plaza

AVERY ROSS SAT with her hands on her lap, waiting in a booth inside Virgil's Diner for Henry to arrive. The two of them had often come here for lunch once or twice a week in their earlier years. It had become quite routine, but after Ross received her promotion and Henry started teaching, they met less and less frequently. They tried to maintain the tradition for as long as they could, but after a while they simply stopped going.

Still, Ross considered Henry to be a friend, no matter how far apart they had grown in recent years. Part of the reason had come from the fact that Henry frequently disagreed with the colonel, while Ross's job required her to defend every decision her leadership made. She couldn't blame this single factor entirely for the growing divide between them, but it certainly hadn't helped.

Now, here she sat again. When she watched him enter the swinging glass door at the front of the diner, it felt for a moment as if nothing had changed.

"Sorry it took me so long," said Nuber.

"It's okay. You're always late. I don't mind."

He chuckled. "You order yet?"

"Coffee for me. I ordered you a beer."

"The cheap stuff, I hope."

"Nothing but," she said.

A second later, the waitress approached and set their drinks on the table. Henry took a swig from his glass. "Ah."

"Can I get you two anything else?" asked the waitress.

"Not yet," said Ross.

"Let me know when you're ready," said the woman. She returned to the counter, leaving them alone.

Nuber took another swig. "Is this where you tell me why we're here? Don't get me wrong, I'm not complaining, but we haven't done this in years."

"I know…and I'm sorry for it. We've both been so busy with the program and our jobs. But I needed to talk to you outside the office."

"Sure. It's a tough job."

"There's more to it."

He nodded. "I figured as much, judging from the call you made to me last night." He set the glass down. "So tell me, since we're away from work, what's got you so worked up? Ready to spill?"

"It's like I said on the phone. There are things

happening in this city I've never seen before. Things threatening to destroy everything our government represents."

"You're talking about Bishop."

"There's a lot you don't know, Henry, and I won't presume to get you more involved than you already are, but…"

"Hey," he said, leaning in. "It's okay. I'm here, Ross. You can tell me."

Ross hesitated, though she didn't know why. She had asked Henry here for this exact reason. Why was she second guessing herself? He wasn't like the rest of them. "How long have you known me, Henry?" she asked, finally.

"Twelve years, give or take. Why?"

"After all this time, do you trust me?"

"More than most."

"In a moment, I'm going to walk through the back door. You can follow me if you want," she said, staring him in the eyes. "But if you aren't completely certain…if you'd rather stay out of the coming storm…by all means, walk out the other door and return to your life. I won't think any less of you. We'll never talk about this again."

"And if I follow you?" he asked.

"Then you'll have your chance to make a difference, not only in the lives of those children, but for everyone in this city."

January 06, 2347
The Slums

MARA SAT in a tiny room with no windows, sipping a glass of wine, playing solitaire on her pad. She wasn't alone, but she might as well have been. Poor Ava lay in the corner, hugging the sofa. She was fast asleep.

Mara sighed, then set the pad on the table. Pretending to be dead was so incredibly boring, especially when it meant being stuck in this closet of a room, unable to show her face. She had absolutely no control over what was happening out there. The wait was killing her.

Not to mention the pain in her from wearing that vest all day, constraining her and weighing her down. Thankfully, she was still alive and breathing. The whole scene could've gone much worse.

When Ross came to her with news of an assassination, she was speechless. Part of her couldn't believe Bishop would actually do it. Had he truly strayed so far? What could provoke a once honorable man into becoming such a sadist?

But when she actually took the time to think about it, she could see it. Bishop's determination for the end result, for the ultimate prize, was without equal in his life. This obsession of his had become a crusade with no end in sight. It didn't matter if someone had to die in order to make his dream come true. He was saving humanity, after all. It was the only thing he cared about. He sacrificed those children in the chamber and again on the surface. He didn't care whether or not they lived, because the data from their deaths could help him find a faster solution. If Mara or anyone else should stand in his way, Bishop would do what he had to. Nothing but the prize mattered.

Upon learning of the plot, Mara's immediate reaction had been to go into hiding, to run and slip away like some poor, diseased rat. But like Ross had told her, canceling the venue and locking herself away wouldn't stop the threat of violence. At best, she could only postpone it. Even if she came forward and openly accused Bishop of conspiring against her, she had no evidence. While Ross could have gone on record, testifying against him, the plot she over-heard that night hadn't been recorded. It would only be her word against his. And who was Ross compared to Bishop? An insubordinate girl plotting against her superior, trying to seize the throne for herself. They'd laugh her out of the room.

Instead, Ross came to Mara with a different plan—a plan calling for her to die. Her death, in turn, would create a power vacuum, which Bishop would undoubtedly attempt to fill.

If Bishop did what she and Ross predicted, then the entire city would finally see how power hungry the colonel truly was.

It would be their chance.

There was a knock at the door. Mara flinched at the sound, but soon relaxed, reassuring herself that she was, after all, expecting company. She glanced at Ava, who was still asleep. "Ava," she whispered. "Wake up."

Ava stirred, opening her eyes. "Hm...?"

"Someone's at the door."

"Oh," she said, gently rising to her feet. "Let me see who it is. Get ready to hide if you have to, dear." She went to the door and peered through the looking hole. "It's Ross, pretty as ever."

"Correct," said the captain from beyond the panel.

"Her ears are impressive," said Ava. She opened the door and Ross hurried inside.

"Sorry I'm late."

"How did everything go?" asked Mara. "Did the teacher agree to help?"

"About that," she said. "I didn't get around to telling him about you. Sorry."

"Oh," said Mara. "So what did you tell him?"

Ross started to answer, but stopped and went back to the door. She opened it and signaled. "Come inside," she said. She looked quickly back at Mara. "I hope you don't mind, but I brought him here to see you."

Ross stepped aside. A man appeared behind her. Mara recognized him from his picture. It was Henry Nuber, the one-armed teacher from the academy. "You brought him *here?*" asked Mara, a little shocked. It was unlike Ross to do things without consulting her. "I thought all you were going to do was talk with him."

"Aren't I right, Henry?"

Nuber stared at Mara, then Ava. "That depends. Are you finally gonna explain what the hell is going on? Why's the damned *matron* here?" He blinked at Mara. "You're supposed to be dead, lady."

"You'll excuse me if I don't apologize for that," said Mara.

"So what happened?" Nuber asked. "The assassination attempt failed? Did he miss?" He looked at her stomach. "I don't see any blood, so he must have."

"We knew he was coming and prepared for it. Captain Ross here was able to procure a bulletproof vest from the armory, along with some other protective things."

"Okay, so ignoring Ross's unprecedented skills for thieving, how did you know you were being targeted?" He looked at Ross. "And why couldn't you tell me about this instead of bringing me here?"

This time it was Ava who spoke. "The answer to both of those questions is the same, I'm afraid," she explained. "Your commander."

"Bishop? What about him?"

"He hired the man who tried to kill me," said Mara. The words lingered in the air.

Nuber hesitated before answering. "This is ridiculous. Ross, tell me you aren't buying into this. Bishop might act like an idiot sometimes, but he wouldn't try to murder anyone."

"It's true," said Ross, bitterly. "I overheard the colonel

with my own ears. You might not want to believe it, Henry, but everything you're hearing is the truth."

"But I've known the man for twenty years!"

"So you know better than anyone," said Mara. "Bishop is a determined man. He's spent over a decade planning for a very *particular* future—climbing the ladder, making alliances, starting the program. He's dedicated his life to this dream of saving the world. Don't you think he'd kill to protect it?"

"I don't know," he admitted. "Maybe."

"Look at his recent decisions," said Ross. "The way he's endangering those students on the surface. He and Archer justify the risks, saying they're necessary. You know as well as I do how careless it all is. How long before he kills the rest of them?"

"You think he's capable?" asked Nuber.

"The bullet he bought for me is proof enough," said Mara.

"But why would he kill you? Why take the risk?"

"Because I disagreed with him," she said, bitterly. "And I was loud as hell about it."

18

**Private Audio Exchange
January 07, 2347**

ECHOLS: What do you have for me?

ROSS: Not much, I'm afraid.

ECHOLS: Not much seems better than nothing.

ROSS: Depends on your outlook.

ECHOLS: I'll pretend to be an optimist for a few minutes, if it helps.

ROSS: The team's moved beyond the range of the towers. We're still getting the occasional signal, but it's intermittent and doesn't last long. The farther away from us they go, the worse it gets.

ECHOLS: How often are you getting something?

ROSS: Right now? Every two to three hours. The gap will only grow as they continue moving north.

ECHOLS: *I guess it could be worse.*

ROSS: *Pretty soon it will be. Our technicians are estimating we'll lose them for good in less than twelve hours. Once we do, we'll be completely in the dark. The clock is ticking.*

ECHOLS: *We'd better move quickly, then. Are you certain you can do this?*

ROSS: *Yes, ma'am. Henry and I are standing by on your orders. We're ready.*

ECHOLS: *Alright, do it. It's time we showed our hand.*

End Audio File

January 07, 2347
The Surface

"How'd it get like this?" asked Terry, as he walked alongside John and Mei. The city was before them, though still a few miles away. "It's like a bad dream."

"Nature's taking it back," said Mei. "Without people around to fix it, everything they built fell apart. The more time goes by, the more it'll break down. Eventually there won't be anything left."

"I thought Variant did it," said John.

"Variant doesn't hurt inanimate objects, dummy," she said. "It only goes after living stuff. You know, animals and plants...those kinds of things."

"So…?"

Mei sighed. "So once the Jolt killed off everybody, no one was left to take care of the city. No more maintenance."

Sarah shifted uneasily. "It'll be a wonder if it doesn't collapse right on top of us."

"I don't think we'll have to go all the way in," said Mei. "The map says Cole's not far in."

"That's not so bad," said John.

"How do you figure?" asked Sarah.

John gripped his rifle, pulling it close to his chest. "We could be unarmed," he said. "Going into who-knows-what with nothing but our fists and wits to protect us. Think about *that*."

"Some wits are less useful than others," said Mei, rolling her eyes and smiling.

"That's why they built me big and tough," John said, smacking his chest. "Someone's gotta protect you little geniuses." He nudged Mei's shoulder. "Right?"

Mei grinned. "Right."

"We're almost there," said Roland. "The map shows an entrance through the tunnel. Our target's on the other side. Not far, though. We're in and out, understood? No sight-seeing this time around."

Most of them nodded. John shrugged.

They continued walking on the road toward the city, which was fast approaching. They'd be there soon—within the hour, probably. "Won't be long," said Alex, who was walking beside Terry. "Yep, not long at all, now."

"What are you talking about?" asked Terry.

Alex stopped and looked at him. "Well, we're all gonna die for starters."

"Geez, Alex," he moaned. "Why would you say something like that?"

Alex laughed, and the sound of it turned Terry's stomach. "You've never seen these things," he said. "I barely survived the first time."

Terry held his rifle closer. "Well, we've got *weapons* this time."

"Mid to long range rifles," Alex corrected, "and you're about to walk into a confined tunnel. I'm sure it'll work out great for everyone."

"You're acting like we didn't train for this."

"Realism versus optimism," Alex said. He clutched his side and coughed. "You're all idiots if you think those rifles will keep you alive."

"You've got a better idea?"

"You mean other than not going in there?" he asked. "Nope. There ain't no point to any of this, you'll see. They've sent us here to die."

"What are you talking about? You're not making any sense."

Alex laughed again. "They know what I know," he said. "They see how strong we are. Every time we went into the chamber, we got stronger. We got faster. We were *better*. You thought they didn't notice, but they did. And it scared them. They didn't need to send you idiots up here after me. They did it because you're dangerous. We all are. Don't you get it, Terry? If we're so perfect, if we can live up here without them, it means they're useless. They can't give up the power. They're afraid of you."

Terry tried to bite his tongue, but he couldn't stay quiet anymore. "You're talking crazy, Alex!" The words fell out of him before he could stop himself. "It's absolutely insane. Listen to what you sound like!"

To Terry's surprise, Alex didn't flinch. He was totally calm. "Say the words all you want, but you know I'm right. Deep in your soul, you know it's all true. We're not going back, not even if we make it out of that tunnel, not even if we get all the way to the elevator. They won't *allow* it."

"Don't you even care if Cole's alive?"

"He's not," said Alex. He continued walking.

"How do you know?" asked Terry.

"Because I know," said Alex, without looking back.

"What's that supposed to mean?"

But Alex didn't answer.

Terry felt a surge of anger, but he swallowed it and clenched his fist, digging his nails into his palm. Alex always complained, always pushed the rest of them to fail. He didn't care about anyone, not even Cole. Every word out of his mouth was hateful and mean. He only cared about himself.

Still, some of what he said rang true. It'd be tough to

maneuver in the tunnel with rifles. There was no getting around it. But they had to try, didn't they? Even if Cole were dead, even if they didn't find a trace of him other than that chip, it didn't mean they shouldn't try.

Terry spotted a rock on the ground and stepped on it. The stone let out a loud crunch and fell apart. Terry's foot went straight through the rock and hit the ground, nearly tripping him. He slid his foot to the side, and saw only a pile of dust remained.

As the wind picked up, the ash of the rock filled the air and floated out, dissipating. Terry slid his foot back across the pile of sand, kicking up more of the dust, and then again. The rock must have been so brittle and hollow, so lifeless and empty, that all it took was a little outside pressure to break it down.

But Terry shouldn't have been surprised. The land was either dying or dead. Why not the rocks, too? Even the air was gone. Even the sky.

So much for moving on. So much for a revival. Could anyone ever hope to turn the clock back now? Was it really possible to reverse a single ounce of it? Maybe Alex was right. Maybe the world had moved on.

Terry kicked the ground hard, and he watched as the last fragments of the stone scattered its guts far and away into the afternoon winds—the same winds that carried Variant, the disease that filled up the sky and had become the most hated thing in all creation. The ashes of the stone rose and danced around him like a cloud of gray steam, hovering gently, momentarily, until they finally disappeared, as though a great, invisible hand had come and guided them away.

THE COLLAPSED TUNNEL stood before them like a monster, filled to the brim with shadows and debris. Empty cars lined the inside, crammed so closely together that it was a wonder any of them had made it as far as they did. Quite a few of the cars had crashed, undoubtedly due to the overwhelming sense of panic the drivers felt to flee the city, as though leaving could actually save their lives. The traffic appeared to be jammed far into the tunnel.

Terry wondered what all those people must have thought as they watched the sky turn into a hellish purple and crimson hue, and they were completely unable to comprehend the meaning behind it all. It must have been the most terrifying sight any of them had ever seen, and it was only the beginning. Soon, the gas would surround them all, rip the oxygen right out of their lungs and quickly replace it with fire.

Terry knew exactly what it felt like, the same as any of the other students.

Out of everyone who had died to the gas, out of all the rest that hadn't, only Terry and his classmates had gone through death and come out the other side still breathing.

They were the only ones who could possibly understand what any of these people had endured.

That was why they lingered now before the wreckage of the tunnel, before the ancient piles of metal tombs.

"I wonder how many there are," muttered Mei.

"Must be hundreds," said Sarah, setting down her pack. She got the radio equipment out. "Maybe more, depending on how far it goes."

Terry sat on the ground and examined his pad. He went over the map. The tunnel stretched beyond the limits of the pad's sensors so there was no telling how far it extended. It didn't really matter, though. Sixty-seven yards beyond the entrance, the wall had collapsed, blocking them from their goal.

Alex shrugged. "Doesn't matter how many there are."

Mei glared at him. "You *would* think so…"

"It's true," he said. "A hundred cars or a thousand…it makes no difference. The Jolt didn't stop at the end of this tunnel. It killed everyone all over the planet. A hundred or a thousand—what's it matter how many died in this little spot? Why waste your time sitting here all quiet when the rest of the world's no different?"

"It's out of respect," Mei said.

Alex snickered. "None of them can see you. None of them care. Dead is dead."

Roland pushed through the two of them. "Enough," he said, walking to one of the cars. He examined it for a moment, reached into his pack, and pulled out a flashlight.

He shined it on the nearest wall, then followed the wall as far as he could before the light disappeared into the dark. "We'll have to find a way around. At first I thought we could find a way through the rubble, but with all these cars in the way, I'm not so sure."

Terry continued examining the map. The closer he zoomed, the more detailed the tunnel became. There were several rooms adjacent to it, and they were all connected by hallways and smaller tunnels throughout the infrastructure. He searched for the closest access door.

"So we're leaving?" asked John.

"There's bound to be another entrance" said Roland.

"Do you have any idea how far it is to the next tunnel?" asked Mei.

"It's our only option," said Roland. "We have to follow the mission. There's no other way."

"Actually, there is," said Terry.

"You just don't like the idea of giving up," said Mei. "We could turn around now and head home, but you'd rather we kill ourselves than go back. Am I right?"

"Of course not, but we're not giving up."

Mei grabbed her pad and shoved the screen in Roland's face. "Have you *looked* at the map? It'll take us a day to reach another tunnel!"

Terry stood. "Guys?"

"Or maybe you don't like hearing my ideas," said Mei. "You tried ignoring me when I said we should change the route Central gave us. You wouldn't even listen to me until Sarah told you to. This is the same thing."

"Stop whining," snapped Roland. "If there was another way, don't you think I'd consider it? But all you've said is we should give up. That's not a plan!"

"It's better than blindly going in there and risking our lives!"

"Shut up!" snapped Terry. "Shut up, both of you!"

Everyone looked at him, their eyes wide with surprise.

"I found a way in, okay? Stop yelling at each other for two seconds and I'll show you."

"What are you talking about?" asked Sarah.

"There are maintenance tunnels connected to this one. Look at your pads."

"I saw those already," said Roland. "None of them connect to where we are."

"Not all the way out here. You have to look closer. There's an access door about a hundred feet into the tunnel. See? It'll take us all the way around. It's faster than the alternative, don't you think?"

"It's not a bad idea," said Sarah.

"How do we know those rooms are even safe?" asked Roland. "The pads can only show what's in front of us. Those old tunnels might not be there anymore. We'd be going in blind."

"All true," agreed Terry. "But it's still better than the alternative."

"If things get hairy, we can always go back," suggested John.

Roland seemed to consider this. "You're sure the tunnels lead to the other side...to where we're supposed to go?"

Terry nodded. There was a long pause.

"Fine," said Roland, finally. "But everyone stays close together, and I don't want to hear any arguments when I give an order." He looked at Mei. "Do we understand?"

Mei stared back at him.

"Everyone understands," assured Sarah.

"Good," he said, turning to face the tunnel.

Sarah continued unpacking the radio gear. "I'm almost done with the equipment."

"Can we really reach Central from way out here?" asked John.

"If our chips are getting through, it's possible. But there's a big difference between optical feed and an actual voice transmission." She opened the box housing the radio and turned it on. After a few seconds, she checked the display. "Signal's really weak," she said. "We might get something through, but I don't know."

"Fantastic," muttered Roland.

"What's the big deal?" said John. "We'll finish the mission and tell them after. They've gotta know we're out of range by now."

"We can't assume they'll understand," said Roland.

"Besides, if something happens to us, they won't know where to look."

"Then, what do we do?" asked John.

Alex spoke up this time. "Come on, isn't it obvious?" He rolled his eyes. "Leave her here with the radio."

John scoffed. "Leave Sarah? Why would we do that?"

"Because, moron, if something happens to the rest of us, at least she'll be safe and can send word to Central. If we all die, who's gonna tell them? Use your brain, man."

John squeezed his fists and took a step forward. Terry grabbed John's arm, and he stopped.

"I could stay," suggested Terry. "You'll need Sarah. She's a better shot."

Roland shook his head. "Which is why you have to come. It's too dangerous to leave you by yourself. Sarah can handle things on her own."

Terry wanted to say he could take care of himself, but decided against it. He didn't know whether or not he could control his abilities one way or the other. If things went sour and he failed, everyone would pay for it. *Maybe Roland's right*, he thought.

"I don't know," said Sarah. "It's a solid idea, but you'll be down a gun. You might need me in there."

"Relax, Sarah," said John, smirking. "You're acting like I'm not even here."

She smiled. "Sorry, John. It could be dangerous. Those animals could be anywhere inside."

Mei shook her head. "We've got four armed soldiers.

Sure, Terry and I aren't as big as John or Roland, but you don't have to be in order to pull a trigger. We can handle it."

"Oh, so I don't get a gun?" asked Alex. "I see how it is."

"Of course you don't get a gun," said Roland. "You didn't even graduate."

Mei arched her brow. "And you kinda committed treason a little when you ran away."

Sarah nodded. "It's true, you did."

Alex scoffed. "All I did was leave! How is it treason?"

Mei threw her hands up. "Hey, I said *a little*, didn't I?"

January 07, 2347
Central

AVERY ROSS STOOD in Colonel Bishop's office, listening to him go over his plan to relieve the tensions caused by the recent assassination of the matron Mara Echols. She couldn't help but feel disgusted.

"The city's in a panic," he said. "Something has to be done."

The colonel had invited Doctor Archer as well as a couple of Public Affairs officers—Lieutenants Anderson and Jones.

Nuber was there, too, standing in the back as usual.

"We need people to stay calm, so I want an official

investigation underway as quickly as possible." He started to pace. "It also might help if we send a few guards to patrol the city streets. It probably won't do anything, but seeing the uniform may help calm them."

"Yes, sir," said Jones.

"In the meantime, we can't let the government fall apart. Work still has to get done. Until the mothers have time to sort things out and elect a new matron, we'll need to step up and do the job ourselves. Captain Ross, seeing as how you have more experience dealing with the mothers than anyone here, you'll take the lead and act as our representative."

Ross nodded. "Yes, sir."

"This is a very delicate situation. We have to avoid panic at all costs. Doctor Archer, can I count on the science division's support on this matter?"

"Of course. Whatever you need."

"Thank you."

"Sir," said Anderson. "What about the murderer? Witnesses said he made threats against the entire council, not just the matron. He might come after you and Doctor Archer."

"Good point," said Bishop. "Increase security to level four. Full searches and badge checks on anyone entering the building. The labs, too."

"Yes, sir," said Anderson.

"Will that be all, sir?" asked Ross.

"Yes, Captain," he said.

"You two," she barked at the lieutenants. "You have your orders. You're dismissed."

"Yes, ma'am," said Jones. They both saluted and rushed out of the office.

After the door shut, Bishop nodded at Nuber. "You've been awfully quiet."

"Nothing to add, I guess."

Doctor Archer smirked. "First time."

Nuber glared at him. "Say again?"

"You heard me, boy. You complain so often it's become predictable."

"At least I have something to say. All you do is sit there, like some senile old man."

"Better than rambling like an imbecilic fool."

"Keep talking," said Nuber. He took a step closer to Archer. "I may only have one arm, but I can still use it to break your wrinkled, arrogant face."

"Typical Neanderthal."

"Relax, both of you," said Bishop. "Henry, you're acting like a child."

"Am I?" he asked, turning toward Bishop. "I've known you for twenty years, James. *Twenty years*. If you'd asked then if I thought you had it in you to shoulder up with a clown like this, I would've said you were nuts. But now look. It's like every word you say is coming from him, this psychopath. Like he's controlling you. Is this what you've become, James? A sadistic bastard's puppet?"

"Alright, that's enough!" snapped Bishop. "I don't care

how long we've known each other. I'm still your superior, and you'll show me some respect!"

"The hell I will," said Henry. "Time and time again you've given me your word about those kids, and each and every one has been a lie. You don't give a damn about their lives!"

"Quiet!" ordered Bishop. "You're relieved. Leave now, and I won't have you arrested."

"Arrested? God! Are you listening to yourself? You'd throw me in a cell for nothing but...but *words*!"

It was all Ross could do to stand there, watching.

"Simple words," he raged. "Since when is that enough to damn a man?" Henry rose his hand, pointing at Bishop. "But you've killed for words already, haven't you, old friend? Shot that woman dead in front of hundreds. I should count myself the lucky one!" He looked at Ross, his face red. "It's time to end this farce, now before the insanity begins."

Bishop looked at her and again at Henry. "What are you talking about? Have you lost your mind? Captain Ross, arrest this man!"

Ross clutched the gun at her side and flipped the holster open. She took the safety off and aimed it at her commanding officer. "I'm sorry, sir, but I'm afraid I'm unable to follow that order."

Bishop stared down the barrel of the pistol. "What the hell is this?" he asked, rattled.

"Arresting you, sir."

"Under what charges?"

"Conspiracy to commit murder, attempted murder, and abuse of power," she said. "We have eyewitness testimony linking you to the assassination."

"I had nothing to do with that!"

"Hands on the desk, sir," said Ross. "I don't want to incapacitate you, but I will if you refuse."

He did as she said, and in a moment she had him on the floor, a pair of handcuffs tight around his wrists.

"You too," Nuber said to Archer, once Bishop was restrained. "You're both in this together, remember?"

"This is ridiculous," said Bishop. "As soon as this gets out, you'll both be executed for treason!"

"Maybe so," said Nuber. "Hard to say at this stage."

Bishop looked at Ross, a pleading terror in his eyes. "I didn't do this, Ross! I could never kill Mara. You know that!"

She walked to Nuber and handed him the gun. "I heard you," she said, not bothering to look at her former commander. "The night when you met with him in this office. I heard every word you said. You broke the law before, back when you cut the matron out of council matters. But murder? I never believed you were capable."

"You spied on me?" he asked.

"And Mara Echols is better because of it," she said.

"What do you mean? The woman's dead."

"Not quite," said Nuber. "It seems the bullet you sent wasn't quite up to the job. The matron's alive and kicking."

Ross went to the door and called for a handful of guards. They were soldiers she had personally assigned to the outer halls on this specific day, each of which she trusted. She ordered them to take the prisoners to the brig and to await further orders. They did as she commanded, despite Bishop's complaints to the contrary.

She walked alongside them the entire way to the cells, through several levels of offices and other faculties. The eyes of her fellow soldiers fell upon her as she marched, and she heard whispers throughout every corridor.

There would be questions and unforeseeable problems soon, which she would have to deal with. But Ross knew she could handle them all, the same as she always had. The people would know the truth about their would-be king, and soon they would renounce him. Ross watched silently as the soldiers placed the two most powerful men in the city into cells no larger than closets.

She kept on watching long after the doors had shut, until the deed was done and the monsters were caged.

January 07, 2347
The Surface

TERRY STEPPED from one piece of rusted metal to the next as he made his way through the graveyard of cars and toward the tunnel wall. Nearly every car required careful

336

balancing and foot placement, making the goggles and their night vision a necessity.

The sunlight from beyond the tunnel was bright enough so they didn't need to use the goggles immediately. Only after several yards did Terry flip the switch, lighting up the tunnel with a dozen shades of green.

Roland went first, of course, followed by Mei and Alex, with John and Terry bringing up the rear. Roland insisted that John, the largest of the group, protect their backs, and in doing so shield the weakest of the students from whatever dangers might present themselves.

He'd made this decision without knowing the truth about Terry's condition or the newfound strength and speed accompanying it. Part of Terry wanted to say something, to shout he was no longer the same weak child they had left the city with, that he could handle himself now. But he quickly pushed the thought aside. He didn't know *what* he was, or if this condition was even manageable. If he ended up in a fight, there was no telling what might happen. He could pass out again, hurt someone, or worse. With so much adrenaline and blood pumping through him, anything was possible. What if he gave himself a heart attack?

A flush ran through Terry's chest as he imagined himself collapsing, his friends standing over him as everything went dark. *I'm sorry,* he thought. *I've failed everyone.*

But if it happened, so be it. All Terry could do was move forward alongside the others and try his best. If he ended up in a fight, and if his friends' lives were on the line, he wouldn't hold back, even if it meant his own life. He'd do whatever he had to do.

Terry gripped the side of a nearby pickup truck. Flakes of metal rust fell to the ground as he slid his hand along the railing. Deciding to wear gloves had probably saved him from several infections, given the state of the metal. Then again, given the drastic biological changes he'd recently gone through—he was *still* going through—maybe he couldn't get infected at all.

Even if that were true, it didn't mean he needed to find out firsthand. Better to play it safe with the gloves than to take an unnecessary risk.

Terry stepped over the cab of the pickup truck and onto the hood. The flimsy metal sank in as he leaned forward. The hood crunched. He pulled his other leg over the cab, carefully setting it next to the other one.

The metallic sound grew louder as Terry shifted his weight. He inched forward, the music of the decomposing metal echoing his every movement. Probably a bad sign. None of the other vehicles had made such awful sounds. *Better hurry*, he thought.

He took another step, crouched, and made his way toward the next vehicle. Stretching out his hand, he reached for the trunk, but then froze as the hood below him shuddered.

Suddenly the steel around his feet collapsed, pulling him in. He fell forward, catching himself on the rail of the next vehicle. He looked back at his feet, which had both sunk into the hood of the truck. He could feel what was left of the engine beneath his legs, and he searched blindly for something to push himself up from. "I'm caught!" he yelled. "I fell!"

"Are you okay?" called Roland.

"I think so," said Terry.

"Hang on. We'll be right over."

How pathetic, Terry thought. *Even with all the extra strength, I still manage to fall down like a little baby*. He kicked both feet against the engine.

Terry looked around for the others. They were still pretty far away, with Alex the closest. John lingered far behind him, moving slowly to avoid the very situation Terry now found himself in.

Terry pushed and kicked, trying to get himself free, but it was no use. His leg was stuck, caught on something he couldn't see. Where was all the strength he'd shown before? Why couldn't he muster it now, when it mattered?

He closed his eyes, trying to remember the moment when his body went into overdrive. He thought about how time had slowed down, and when the light had grown too bright to bear, and how he'd flung John away with nothing but a wave of his hand. Still, nothing came. No surge of energy, no heroic rage. Only Terry, the tinniest soldier, dangling there like a child in need of his mother.

He kicked the back of the engine. So much for showing Roland and the others how strong he'd become. How could any of them respect him now? What use could he possibly be? He imagined Alex standing over him, mocking. It was all Terry would ever be good for—a good laugh.

He kicked again, and this time the truck shook. The vibrations made his jaw shudder. What would Terry do when they made it to the other side? If the rabs were there, waiting for them at the source of Cole's signal, would Terry be as helpless as he was now? Would someone have to protect him or rescue him again? He pressed his forehead to the cold metal before him and gasped. He tried to take a deep breath, but failed, anxiously wheezing. All he wanted to do was get out and run away. He squeezed the railing in his hand and felt it bend. A wave of heat filled up his chest, rising from his gut and up toward his face and arms. He kicked the back of the engine again, ramming his foot through whatever lay there, freeing his other leg in the process. With both his feet planted on the back of the cab wall, he pushed himself out and toward the other car.

After managing to stand, he was still shaking. He looked down at his hands, unable to relax. The artificial green light from the goggles was becoming too bright to bear, so he removed them. Surprisingly, the darkness of the tunnel was nearly gone. He saw everything—the cars, the tunnel walls, and finally his friends. They were all looking at him, watching through their goggles and calling to him, though he couldn't make out the words. *It's happening again*, Terry yelled inside his head. *I need to calm down. I have to.*

He closed his eyes and placed his hand on his chest,

slowing his breath as much as he could. After a moment, his friends' voices became much clearer. They were asking what he was doing, if everything was okay. "It's fine," he said. "Give me a minute."

When he finally reopened his eyes, the room had gone dark again. Whatever had made it possible for him to see the others was gone now. He strapped the goggles back on and continued taking deep, methodic breaths.

"You alright now?" asked Roland.

"I'm good," replied Terry.

Roland nodded. "Talk more when we get inside, understood?"

"Sure."

He followed after the others, moving from one vehicle to the next, although this time he was extra careful. When he finally caught up, the rest of the group was waiting for him at the hatch.

"Let's see if we can get it open," said Roland. "Might have to put some muscle into it. John, you mind?"

"Easy," said John. He gripped the handle and planted his feet, readying himself. Straining, he pulled towards his chest with the strength of his whole body. With a heavy click, the door slid open. A cloud of dust scattered in the air as John swung it back, catching everyone off guard.

They all covered their mouths, but a few weren't fast enough. Terry breathed in the dust and choked, coughing violently as tears filled his eyes. He staggered backward, catching himself on the side of a nearby car.

John leaned away from the door, bending over and spitting out whatever he could of the fumes. "Gross!"

"It smells awful," said Mei through a muffled sleeve. "But at least it didn't get in our eyes." She tapped the goggles. "Should've made these things so they cover your whole head. It could've doubled as a gas mask."

"They have those," said Roland, clearing his throat. His voice was strained. "They didn't think we'd need masks."

"Oh right," she said. "I forgot, being able to breathe Variant automatically means we're immune to every other toxin." She rolled her eyes. "Idiots."

"There'll be time to criticize later," said Roland. "Grab a rag from your pack or rip something off your clothes to cover your mouths. We need to keep going."

Terry filtered his breaths with his arm while he searched through his bag. There weren't any rags to speak of, but he did find an undershirt and some socks, each of them having been previously worn. Out of the two, the shirt seemed like the easy compromise. Better to smell sweat than feet, he wagered.

Terry tied the shirt around his mouth and head, securing the sleeves in a knot behind his ears. He was never any good at knots, but this time he'd done alright. The shirt felt snug and secure, but not so much that the pressure got to him.

"Move in," ordered Roland, leading the charge.

Mei, Alex, and Terry followed, with John bringing up the rear.

The tunnel felt neglected, like a long abandoned store-room. It smelled dank and earthy and was surprisingly cool.

The goggles made the darkness bearable, but the air was full of dust particles. There weren't so many that Terry couldn't see, but because they kept hitting his goggles and accumulating, he had to keep wiping them off.

Terry looked back at John. "This sucks," he said.

"Your idea," said John through a ripped piece of cloth.

"Sorry," said Terry.

John shrugged. "Better than climbing cars, right?"

They were approaching an open room near the back of the corridor. Roland stopped and threw his fist up. Everyone stopped, waiting. He readied his gun and leaned in, looked around, and then waved the others in.

The small room was filled with electrical equipment which no longer functioned. "Where to next?" Roland asked.

"The map's on the pad," said Mei. "One sec." She turned it on and proceeded to take her goggles off.

"What're you doing?" asked John.

"Can't see the display with those on," she said, tucking the goggles under her arm.

"Well?" asked Roland.

"We go out there," she said, pointing to another door at the far end of the room. "Follow the hall nearly to the end, take a left, then straight. That'll bring us pretty close to Cole's signal."

Roland struggled to take his goggles off. "That can't be

right," he said. "The target's on the other side of the tunnel outside. It's supposed to be in the city." He set the head-piece on the ground. "Let me see."

Mei handed him the pad. "Then, it must have moved," she said, referring to the target. She and Roland both hovered above the light of the pad, waiting. "Look!" screamed Mei. "See there? It's moving again! Oh, that's so weird."

"Wait a second," said Roland. He stared at the pad, blinking and wiping the dust out of his eyes. "Are you sure this thing isn't acting up? Let me check mine." He pulled out his own and turned it on. Once it booted, he sighed. "Looks the same."

"See?" said Mei. "We're not as far off as we thought."

"Great," said Alex. "Tell me you idiots understand what's happening here."

"It means Cole's alive, doesn't it?" asked John.

"Hey, yeah," said Mei. "He must have escaped!"

"What a relief," said John.

"No!" Alex said. "Cole's dead! How many times do I have to say it? I saw him get ripped apart…torn to pieces, do you understand? There's no way in Hell he's breathing, let alone running around. Don't you idiots get it? The only thing we're gonna find when we get to the source of this signal is a pile of bones, and the only reason it's moving right now is because one of those rabs has it. One of them's got a piece of Cole around its neck. That's what you're seeing on your stupid pad—a monster with a trophy, and it's coming this way." He laughed. "Don't you get it? They've caught our scent! They're coming for *us*. They're coming for their *food*."

TERRY WATCHED as the signal moved through the corridors and rooms, stopping occasionally at an intersection, only to continue a moment later. If it really was one of the rabs, maybe it was stopping to smell the air—trying to figure out which direction the team was in before finally moving along. He didn't like the idea of the rab hunting them—the same, twisted kind of animal that nearly killed both Alex and Mr. Nuber. Terry had never seen one himself, but the image Mr. Nuber painted was a frightening one. *Please let it be Cole*, he thought. *Please let him be alive.*

"It's gotta be Cole," said Mei.

"No," insisted Alex. "I'm telling you. There's no way he could've survived."

"*You* did. Or don't you remember almost dying?"

"That was different."

"Why, exactly? Because you're you? Don't be silly. Variant did it. Cole's got the same stuff running through his veins that you do—that we *all* do. The truth is you don't have a clue if he's alive or not."

"Don't tell me what I know, bitch!" screamed Alex.

"Excuse me?" demanded Mei. She took her goggles off, marched to Alex and pressed herself against him, staring at his face. He was almost a foot taller than her, but she didn't seem to notice or care. "Call me bitch again," she said, almost whispering. Her voice was cold and still.

Roland snapped his fingers. "Both of you, stop it. Are you hearing me?"

Neither backed down. "What'll you do?" asked Alex. "You're half my size, little girl. Look at you. You're not even a woman yet."

"Shut up!" said Mei. Her voice echoed through the room. "I'm sick and tired of you bullying everyone. You're nothing but a scared little kid."

"Says the baby," Alex teased.

Alex was so much larger than Mei. What was she thinking? Even with his injury, he'd overpower her with ease. John quietly stepped next to Terry. He tapped Terry's leg, the nonverbal signal for "get ready." Terry didn't respond. He didn't need to. If Alex so much as breathed on Mei, they'd show him the definition of excessive force.

Alex looked at Terry and John, then at Mei. He grinned and took a step back. "Relax," he said with a smirk. "You kids take everything so seriously. I was only joking."

Mei didn't laugh.

Roland still had the pad out. He handed it to Mei. "Looks like whatever it is, it's not far now."

Terry calmed himself. At least Alex wasn't completely stupid.

Mei tapped the screen, zooming in, and stared at it for a moment. "You're right. It's moving pretty fast, too."

Roland pointed at the screen. "There's a larger room along the hall. If it keeps heading this way, it'll run right through there. Might be a good idea to wait in that spot."

"Sounds good," said John.

"What do we do if it's not Cole?" asked Terry.

"They armed us for a reason," said Roland, matter-of-factly, then walked toward the hall.

Most followed, although Mei stayed back and away from Alex this time. It broke the formation, but Roland didn't complain. Maybe he understood that it was better this way. Instead, she filed between Terry and John, as though it were her natural place.

They made space. She didn't even have to ask. She never would.

The walk to the large room was a quiet one. No one spoke, though the sound of heavy breathing and all their shuffling feet filled the hall without much effort, destroying any hope they might've had for a stealth approach. Still, it hardly mattered. They were nearly there.

When they arrived, Roland went first. A moment later, he gave the signal to follow. They filed in, one by one, gathering away from the other door on the opposite side of the room. They each took a position around the walls. Roland settled near the front, nearest to the two doors, while everyone else waited at various spots behind him. "You'll be able to see me from here," he said. "I'll give the signal to fire if we have to, so be ready."

The room was filled with crates and equipment. "Looks like military," said John.

Mei shushed him. "Quiet," she whispered.

Terry took his goggles off and glanced at the pad. Indeed, the beeping dot grew closer with each passing second. It appeared to be entering the tunnel connected to the opposite door that they'd entered. Terry swallowed hard as the dot made its way along the hall toward them.

Quietly, he slid the goggles on and flipped from night vision to infrared, staring in the direction of the oncoming enigma.

An odd hum filled the room, followed by a flutter of hard clicks in waves. Terry clenched the stock of his rifle, raising his eyes to the archway.

From behind the stone, an arm stretched out, gripping the side of the wall. Long quills covered its skin, which rose and fell to the rhythm of the clicks. At its end, a set of eight-inch claws pierced the rock wall, chipping away dust and pebbles with ease.

The rest of the razorback soon followed. The same barbs from its arm covered the rest of its body, scratching against the doorway as it entered. The only exception was the face, which appeared to contain the snout of a dog and the eyes of a deer, though the details were difficult to make out through the infrared. The rab stopped walking a few feet into the room, leaned back, and stared blankly into the dark. After a moment, it rustled its quills again, a series of clicks soon following. Finally, it opened its long snout, letting out another ominous hum, filling the room and gently vibrating the walls. Terry felt a crawl inside his stomach.

On the opposite side of the room, Roland sat alone against the wall, behind a metal slab. He raised his hand, giving the signal to ready their weapons.

But the creature stirred at the sound of the movement, shifting its weight. It snapped its head in Roland's direction, tilting it sideways. There it waited, staring expressionlessly toward him.

Roland didn't move, but neither did the rab. It continued to stare at him, humming gently—clicking its barbs over and over again.

Roland gulped.

Suddenly, the animal charged, lunging at Roland faster than its weight should have allowed. Roland scurried back, firing wildly. At the same time, the others began their assault.

Terry took a deep breath and fired his rifle, aiming at the rab's backside. A barrage of light filled the room immediately, making it difficult to see through the infrared. Still, Terry kept his aim steady.

The creature let out its arms and extended its quills, inflating its size and sending endless rattling clicks throughout the air. It hovered over Roland, who now found himself against the far wall, still firing. In an instant, the monster's body overtook Roland, making it impossible for anyone to see if he was okay.

"Move forward!" yelled John, who had already taken it upon himself to reposition.

"No, wait!" screamed Mei. She stopped firing. "Look! Something's breaking!"

Terry eased off the trigger, flipped the switch on his goggles to night vision, and very quickly found the massive crack that formed high above Roland and the monster.

"There!" Mei yelled, pointing. "It's going to break!"

Terry jumped over the crate he'd been using for cover and moved closer to the fight. "Roland, get out of there!" he screamed.

But Roland's firing had stopped, and there was no answer.

Terry took another step, but a hand gripped his shoulder. "Wait," said John.

Terry shook the arm away and dashed toward the slaughter. His body began to pulse wildly, and as he ran, every step he made grew longer. The light from the rab grew brighter in his goggles, so much that he could no longer see. He threw the headpiece aside, and suddenly he saw the animal clearly. The entire room, in fact, was clear as day. He saw it all.

As he neared the hunching beast, he fired a quick burst of bullets at its back. The rab turned, revealing its bloody face and chest. Terry leapt from the ground, shooting directly at its empty, distant eyes. He dove toward it, firing shot after shot until the barrel of his gun smashed into its forehead. Terry collided into the monster, flinging it against the wall. With its snout riddled with blood and bullet holes, the monster rattled its quills a final time, and then fell lifelessly to the floor.

Roland was nearby, motionless and covered in blood. Terry lifted his body on his shoulder and started moving.

"Hurry!" yelled Mei. "It's collapsing!"

Sure enough, the rocks began to break apart, falling like an avalanche. Terry ran, Roland on his back, toward John and Mei, each of whom had started toward him. As he fell into their arms, the boulders collided all around him, shaking the walls with thunder.

Terry let Roland down, then staggered back as his knees buckled. John and Mei were quick to catch him, but not before he vomited.

Mei pressed her hand to his chest. "It's okay. Try to breathe, alright?"

When he tried to breathe, he gasped. His stomach felt scrambled, like it was on fire. He touched his gut with his hand, it felt warm and wet. When he pulled his hand away, he saw the blood, and it scared him.

John must have seen the panic in his eyes. "Relax. It's not bad. Remember how Alex was? He still made it, didn't he? And that was way worse than this."

John was right. The pain wasn't even very bad. It felt more like a pinch than a wound. Roland, on the other hand, wasn't even moving. "Check him," said Terry. "Quick, see if he's alright."

Alex leaned over and checked his pulse and his breathing. After a moment, he shook his head.

"No," whispered Terry, his voice trembling. He pushed John and Mei away from him, and then crawled to Roland's side. He clutched Roland's jacket, drenching his hands in blood. "This can't be right. I saved him. I stopped that thing before it got to him."

Alex backed away from the body. "We have to get out of here," he said.

Terry ignored him, checking Roland's pulse again, but the blood on his fingers and palm made it difficult to find the right place.

John bent beside him. "Terry, he's right. There could be more of them."

"We're not leaving him like this. We can't…" Terry wavered a moment. The room was beginning to fade. He felt around for his goggles, but then remembered how he'd left them on the other side of the room. "I can't see," he said, quietly.

"Hold on," said John. He left Terry's side for a moment, then returned, placing the back strap in Terry's hand. "Here."

Terry started to put them on, but stopped. He clutched his stomach. The pinch was beginning to feel more like a burn, quickly rising and filling his gut. He dropped the strap and pressed his hands against his ribs, tears rushing down his cheeks. "Ah!" he cried. The pain moved its way through the rest of his body, up toward his eyes. He reached out a hand in the darkness, struggling to grasp at something, anything.

He found a hand. Mei's hand. "Calm down," she said, squeezing his palm.

But Terry couldn't keep from panicking. He was getting dizzy, and there were spots everywhere. His legs went numb and in a flash of pain that consumed his entire being, he cried out again. "Fire! I'm covered in fire!"

Then he passed out.

19

Amber Project File Logs
Play Audio File 209
January 08, 2347

ECHOLS*: Any news from the surface yet?*

ROSS*: I'm afraid not, ma'am.*

ECHOLS*: Then, we were too late. Dammit! We should have acted sooner.*

ROSS*: I don't think we could have. The opportunity had to be right for us to move.*

ECHOLS*: Regardless, there's got to be something we can do.*

ROSS*: I've considered alternatives, but they've gone so far out of range that the only way to contact them would be to send a search party. Unfortunately, we don't have the capabilities to man an expedition for the length of time it would require.*

ECHOLS: *Is there anything you can do?*

ROSS: *I can try to boost the signal, but it would require us to send a team to the surface.*

ECHOLS: *Would you mind?*

ROSS: *Not at all. Henry's already talking to a few engineers right now. They're working on a way to amplify the tower's signal strength. Hopefully, I'll have better news soon.*

ECHOLS: *Good, thank you.*

ROSS: *If we're lucky, maybe something will come of it.*

ECHOLS: *Anything's better than silence, right?*

End Audio File

January 08, 2347
The Surface

Terry awoke in the darkness, except it wasn't dark—not to him. He could see everything nearly as well as the daylight. The cracked stone walls, full of dust and grime, stretched high above the floor into a vast ceiling. It was a different room than the previous one, at least three times the size. Mei and John sat nearby, with Alex several feet removed, each with goggles on. No one seemed to notice him stirring.

He touched his wound, but instead of blood or flesh, he found a bandage, wrapped several times around his torso.

He must have been asleep for a while if they'd found the time to move and mend him. For a long moment, he searched the room with his new eyes.

There were supply crates, worn and filthy, all throughout. A few had been pried open, their guts spilled onto the floor. Tables stacked the walls across from him, still supporting long unused equipment. To their left, and several feet away from anything else, a pile of oddly shaped bags lay stacked atop one another.

"Someone want to tell me what happened?" he asked, though he already knew the answer.

"Oh, thank goodness," said Mei, scurrying over to him. "You're finally awake."

John followed. "You passed out. I had to carry you."

"Thanks, but where are we?"

"Somewhere farther in," said John. "Looks like some people gathered here at one point, hoping to ride out the Jolt. They didn't make it, but they left a bunch of equipment. Mei's been trying to get some of it working."

"Don't hold your breath," she said. "Most of the electronics are fried."

"What do you mean, 'they didn't make it'?" asked Terry. "Are the bodies still here?"

Mei looked at the oddly shaped pile in the corner. "We moved them out of the way...but yeah, they're here."

"Gross."

"Hey, tell me about it, but at least *you* didn't have to move them," said John.

"Lucky me."

"We wouldn't have bothered, but they were all over the place, and I wanted to salvage through the equipment to see if anything was worth keeping. So far, nothing," said Mei.

"Where are we, anyway? I don't remember seeing this place on the way in."

John sighed. "Yeah, about that…"

"We're trapped," said Alex from across the room.

Terry looked at John. "Seriously?"

John nodded. "When those rocks fell, they blocked the exit. It's the only way back."

"Yeah, good going," said Alex. "I always wanted to die in a hole. Oh, wait, no I didn't. That's why I left in the first place."

"Shut up," said Mei. "We all get it. You're pissed. Deal with it like an adult."

Alex waved his hand and muttered an obscenity only he and Terry could hear.

"Basically," continued John, "we've gotta get to the city. Then, we can find another way out. There's plenty of roads leading away from the city, according to our maps. We just don't know which ones are still usable."

Mei nodded. "Right. And even if we manage to find a road out, it'll add at least a day or so before we can make it back to Sarah."

Terry sat up a bit. He expected pain, but there was surprisingly very little of it. Had his body healed already? It took Alex over a day before he could walk again and even that was impressive. "How long was I out?"

"Six hours," said John.

"What about Roland?"

Mei and John both hesitated, which could only mean one thing.

"Dammit," muttered Terry. He pressed his fist into the floor, cracking his knuckles.

Mei bent down and clasped his fist with her hands. "It's not your fault. You did more than anyone else."

"She's right," said John. "I've never seen anything like it. You were amazing."

"It didn't make a difference. He's still dead."

"And if you didn't do what you did, the rest of us might be, too," said Mei. "So stop it, okay? We don't have time for doubt right now. We don't' have time to wonder what we could have done differently or what we should have done. There's four of us here…five if you count Sarah…and I expect us all to make it home alive. Do you understand?"

He didn't answer.

"How do you feel?" asked John after a moment.

"Better," he answered. He looked at Mei. "We should tell Sarah what happened."

"I already did. Hours ago."

"She's refusing to leave," said John. "Said she'd wait for us to come back."

Terry tried to move, but Mei stopped him.

"Hang on," she said, unwrapping the bandages. "You

didn't bleed much. I only had to change the cloth once." The last wrap stuck to him before coming off. The air felt cool against his newly exposed skin.

Mei took a moment to examine him. "Wow," she muttered, almost inaudibly.

"What is it?" he asked. "How bad?"

John leaned in and examined it. "Now *that's* cool."

"It looks good," said Mei. "*Really* good. It's not anything like before. I don't understand it…"

"Explains the lack of pain," said Terry, looking at his gut. There were several scratches, but many of them were scabbed. "How long before I'm back to normal?"

Mei shrugged. "How should I know?" She reached for the medical kit and grabbed some swabs and disinfectant spray. "I'm not a doctor. Even if I were, this is uncharted territory."

"You still think he needs the spray?" asked John.

She applied the disinfectant. "Better safe than sorry." The spray stung when she used it, but he didn't flinch. She wrapped a fresh gauze around him. Once she finished, he relaxed.

"What do we do now?" asked Terry.

"Stay here for a bit," she said. "You need to rest, and we have to see if we can find a better way out."

"Why not move the rocks? You know, go back the way we came."

"We could try, but we might risk another cave-in. For all we know, the whole ceiling could collapse. It's a big risk."

"So is going farther in. There's bound to be more of those razorbacks somewhere."

"You're right. What do you think we should do?"

He hesitated. "Did you...get Roland's weapon? We might need it."

"Mei saved his pack, but the rifle didn't make it," said John.

"It was crushed by the cave-in," said Mei.

"At least you got the pack," said Terry. "What's the plan?"

"We don't know yet," said Mei.

"It's okay," said John. "Together, we'll think of something."

"Right," said Mei. "And in the meantime, I'm going through the rest of the equipment. There might be something we can use or take home. This trip doesn't have to be a total loss."

"What can I do?" asked Terry.

"It'll be hard for you to do anything without your goggles," said John. "Here, I saved them for you." He reached for his pack and took out the battered headpiece.

"Don't bother. I don't need them."

"But it's pitch black in here," said John.

"I know, but I can see you fine."

Mei leaned in closer, examining his face, her goggles nearly poking him in the nose. "No *way*..."

"So you can see everything?" asked John.

"Yeah. It's all sort of a dark blue-ish color. Not as good as normal, but better than wearing those things."

John held up his hand. "How many fingers?"

"Three," said Terry.

John looked at his fingers. "Lucky guess."

Mei touched the side of his left eye, sweeping her fingers across his brow. "When did all this start, exactly?"

"When I tripped and fell on that car. It happened again when I tried to kill that *thing* earlier…right before I passed out."

"No *try* about it," John assured him. "You killed it *dead*."

Mei pushed John away. "How long are these…*episodes*, usually?"

"A few seconds, I guess, but I've been sitting here for ten minutes, and it's not going away."

Mei seemed to think for a moment, though it was tough to tell with the goggles on her face. "It must have something to do with your reaction to the gas. All the stuff happening to you—it's the only thing making any sense."

"Hard to say," said Terry, though he was more certain of it than anything. Still, he no longer wished to talk about it, nor did he see the point. He couldn't stop breathing Variant, no more than he could sprout wings and fly. What-ever was happening to him would continue to happen, he decided, no matter what he did or said or hoped.

For now, he was stronger, better able to help his friends if they needed him. That's what really mattered, wasn't it?

That's what all of this was for.

Mei squealed and Terry opened his eyes. A dim, gray light glowed in the distance. It seemed to be coming from her lap.

"I did it! I got it to work!"

"Got what to work?" asked John. He was close by, combining Roland's pack with his own.

"The pad I found," explained Mei. "It's the same as ours, except older and in much worse condition. I tried swapping parts with the extra one we had from…Roland's pack, and it didn't work either. But when I started disassembling it, I found an Ortego disk inside." She held up a thin, translucent disk roughly the size of a thumbnail. "This is from the other pad. I swapped it with the one I found. Looks like it works, but it's still booting. See?"

Terry got to his feet and walked to where they were sitting. Alex joined them. They all watched the display come to life.

The home screen was exactly the same. A series of chimes rang and a capital "O" flew onto the display, extending into the word "Ortego." Immediately following the logo, a fancy-looking subtitle appeared, which read, "Building A Better World."

Mei tapped the screen, and it changed to the desktop, which was littered with files. "Hang on, while I open the disk folder."

Several dozen files appeared, one after the other. They

were mostly text documents, but there were a few audio and video files as well as some spreadsheets. "Wow," said John. "I can't believe it still works."

"Of course it works," said Alex. "Those disks last forever. Longer than any of the hardware they made to read them."

"True, but most pads have enough space already. It's rare to see a disk," said Mei.

"Maybe the person who had it before filled it up," suggested John.

"Yeah, could be," she said.

"Doesn't matter," said Alex. "Seems useless." He walked away. "I'm gonna take a nap while you kids play. Wake me when you're ready to get out of this hole."

Mei sighed. "He's right. We should go. This place is dangerous."

Terry sat next to her. "Is this the only pad you found?"

"Oh, no way! There's several. I don't know if we'll find another Ortego disk, but who knows?"

"Okay, so let's pack them all and get out of here. I feel good enough to walk now. What do you think?"

"You're sure?"

He nodded. "I feel totally fine."

John used the empty pack to house the pads and gave it to Alex. Since he didn't have a rifle and therefore couldn't fight, it made sense.

The team left the area and headed in the direction of the city. Terry had been placed in charge of the map, since he could look at it without having to remove a pair of awkward goggles. "Left up here," he said as they made their way through another tunnel. "Only a few more passageways and we're there." He and Mei had plotted the best route they could think of before leaving, making sure to stay away from open areas or places where animals might make a nest. They got lucky with the last room, which Mei admitted was probably a mistake, seeing as it was huge and could've easily housed a dozen of those things.

Surprisingly, they didn't see any other rabs in the tunnels, or evidence they'd been there at all. If there were any others, Terry was glad to avoid them.

After an hour, they found the exit door. It was latched tightly, the same as the one they'd entered through. John and Terry lifted the bar and pushed together. It opened easier than the last time.

The access door came out onto a stairwell, which led them to the edge of the highway. Back in the light of day, Mei, John, and Alex were free to remove their goggles, which they did immediately.

"Finally," said John, rubbing the back of his head. "That strap's a killer on my skin."

"Be happy you had one. We would've died without them," said Mei

Terry took a deep breath. After spending nearly a day in the tunnels, the change in Variant quality was noticeably refreshing.

The city was all around him, though he could barely tell one building from the next. When he'd looked at this place from atop the hill, it was easy to see how big or small each of the towers were. But now that he was close enough to touch them, they all looked exactly the same.

Thunder rang in the distance. The clouds were moving this way. "We need to find some cover before the storm gets here," said Terry.

"One of the buildings?" asked John.

Terry shook his head. "Somewhere more open. There's no telling if there's any animals in there. It's better if we can see them coming."

Everyone agreed. They packed their gear and hustled forward. There was a large clearing adjacent to a nearby intersection, which the map called *Starlight Park*. It was mostly dirt by now, but a few occasional clumps of blue grass appeared the farther in they went.

They managed to find a standing gazebo in the park before long, though once the rain started, it became pretty clear it wasn't entirely without its problems. Still, the leaks were manageable, and the shelter afforded them a chance to rest.

Mei grabbed the pack with the pads in it and unloaded a few. John asked if she wanted help, but she declined. "I'm only passing time. You guys relax," she said.

John and Terry sat at both ends of the gazebo, their rifles in their laps. Terry tried to do as Mei suggested, but the thought of more razorbacks—what they were capable of—kept him on edge. He began to think he wouldn't get any rest until they left this horrible place.

Alex, on the other hand, seemed oblivious. He was lying down, using one of the packs as a pillow. Terry envied him.

The rain fell for hours, tasting bitter, but it cooled the air. The sun climbed to its zenith, only to disappear behind a pair of gray, thunderous clouds that stretched far away. The leaks in the roof of the gazebo dripped and splashed, pooling and then streaming through the cracks in the floor. Everyone had to reposition periodically, but it didn't take long to learn where the water was going.

When the rain did end, the sun had already gone, replaced by the night's clear and starry skies.

John and Terry agreed to take shifts. They wanted Mei to rest and Alex couldn't be trusted with a gun.

Through the long night, the gazebo shone with the glow of Mei's pad. Terry made a few attempts to talk to her, but she didn't seem very interested. In the end, he left her to the task. She worked silently, methodically, as though there were nothing else in all the world.

Hours later, shortly before the new dawn, Mei began to tremble, sobbing quietly in the corner. Terry, still on watch, heard her whimpering and went to her.

"Are you okay?" he asked, touching her shoulder.

Her eyes, bloodshot and glazed from lack of sleep and sheer exhaustion, stared deep into the ground. She clutched the pad between her hands, pulling it close to her chest, and swallowed hard.

There, in the middle of a *Starlight Park* gazebo, surrounded by darkness and with streams of tears gliding down her golden cheeks, Mei told Terry the truth about the Jolt.

20

Ortego Disk 21
Play Audio File 0017
Subtitled: Gas Origin
Recorded February 22, 2157

GIDEON: I'm sending this message out to anyone with ears to hear it. It's about the gas. Before you ask, the answer is no, I don't know how to stop it. I don't even know what it is. All I can tell you is how it got here...or at least where it came from.

This morning at around 0730, we attended a video teleconference between our office and the home lab. They were getting ready to launch the first live test of their new project, a matter transmitter, while we watched through a little camera on the other side of the room. The test was supposed to run for approximately three minutes—safety reasons, I think. They planned to transport a small device from one containment unit to the next, both of which were within view and being observed by local personnel.

Everything appeared to go off without a hitch, the same as it had in the hundreds of simulations prior to the launch. But when the rift appeared, and they sent the beacon through, nothing came out the other side. After three minutes, Doctor Bell gave the word to shut everything down, then started apologizing to the government officials nearby. I heard someone yell back that the machine was unresponsive. Bell apologized again and went to check it out. I couldn't see where, but the cameras were still pointing at the machine, so I kept watching.

A few more minutes passed, and the rift or tear or whatever the hell it was, started growing—not huge, but bigger than it was supposed to be. Then, it fluctuated, which seemed natural when you took into account the time limit they set for the devilish thing. We all thought it was simply going to collapse. But it didn't. Not at all. It only got worse.

Then, it stopped. I don't mean that it shut down, only that it wasn't fluctuating anymore. I thought maybe Doctor Bell had fixed it.

That's when the screaming began. I couldn't see who it was, but it scared the hell out of me. People panicked and ran, but they didn't go very far. In a few seconds, every person in the room was on the floor, crying for help. Someone screamed, "Gas! Gas! Gas!" And another yelled, "It's burning!" After a moment, they were dead, and the gas… well…you've seen what it does to the bodies.

The reports came in. People everywhere were dying, the same as they had in the lab. We tracked the news coverage and monitored the path of the breakout. Whatever it is, we're certain it originated there.

My name is Doctor August Gideon, and I work for the Ortego

Corporation. *I wish I knew more about what went wrong, but I don't. All I know is in an hour the gas will be here, and I'll be dead. There's no running from it, no getting away. All I can do is send this transmission with the hope it'll help.*

I've attached the blueprints of the facility, along with detailed instructions on how to theoretically turn off the machine. I say "theoretically" because I have no idea whether or not Doctor Bell actually tried to do this before he died. If he followed procedure and it failed, there may be no way to recover this situation. But if not, we may still stand a chance.

Good luck.

End Audio File

January 09, 2347
The Surface

The four teenagers from under the earth sat in a circle listening to a dead man talk about the end of the world.

"I can't believe what I just heard," said John when it was over. "How's any of this possible?"

"I don't know," said Mei. "But there it is."

Terry stared at the blank screen. He'd listened to the recording a total of four times. Two before he woke the others and two after. He still couldn't believe it. All his life, he'd been told that the Jolt was natural—how mankind wasn't smart enough to create something as brilliantly complex as Variant. Sure, there were theories here and there, but no one ever offered any proof. It was always a guessing game, and eventually people got tired of playing.

But now Terry knew the truth. Humans started it. They built a machine and it did something it wasn't supposed to. It killed them all.

"So people did it," said Alex. "It doesn't change anything."

Mei scoffed. "Are you kidding? Of course it does! We actually know what happened now. Don't you get it? Maybe we can do something about it."

"Yeah? What are you gonna do, huh? Bring back the dead? Good luck."

"Don't be stupid," she said.

"Then, what? Run home and tell your masters? Show them your disk? Hey, maybe Nuber will give you a gold star for this one. A nice pat on the head."

Mei gripped the pad with both her hands. "This is important! It's a way to fix everything."

"Bull," said Alex. "It'll never work. There's no *fixing* this."

"You don't know for sure."

"Sure I do. All your recording says is to turn off the machine, right?"

She didn't answer.

"How long's it been since this message was sent? A hundred and fifty...no...two hundred years? Look around you. There's no way the building is still standing. Even if it is, you really think the machine's still on? Open your eyes. It turned off or ran down years ago." Alex glanced around and held out his arms. "Look at this," he said. "Still a wasteland."

"You're wrong," she said, staring at the ground.

Terry was tired of listening to them. "If we go home and turn this stuff in, it won't make any difference. They'll listen to the files, store them away, and that'll be the end of it. We'll get debriefed, and they'll probably run some tests. Alex will get thrown in prison for trying to escape." He didn't know if his prediction was true or not, but it might be worth mentioning. After all, Alex valued his freedom. It was the reason he left in the first place. "But if we do like Mei suggested," he continued. "If we find this place Gideon was talking about...even if the only thing left is a pile of dirt...it'll be *something*. They'll forget about what you did. They'll forget about how we all screwed up."

Alex laughed. "Save all the crap for someone more gullible, like John over here."

John frowned.

"Those bastards don't give a damn about me," said Alex. "First chance they get, they're throwing me down the biggest hole they've got."

"Fine," said Terry. "Then, think about this like an extension."

"A what?"

"An extension," he repeated. "You get to stay here for a

little longer. No going back until we're done. It might only be a day or two, but it's better than what you were talking about. Isn't it?"

"Whatever," said Alex.

Terry looked at Mei. "How far a walk are we dealing with?"

"Less than a day. It's on the far edge of the city. Maybe sixteen miles from here. It's a hard run, but we can do it."

"We need to radio Sarah," said John. "She's waiting for us to come back."

Terry nodded. "Mei, send a message on your pad and tell her what we're doing. Send Gideon's files, too, just in case."

"Sure you don't wanna run home?" asked Alex. "It'd be a lot safer for you."

Terry ignored him. There was no point in arguing now that Alex had agreed to come along. Instead, Terry helped John pack the supplies.

It didn't take Mei long to contact Sarah. "She's not completely in agreement about whether or not this is the right thing to do," she explained to the others. "But she said she understands. She wanted to meet us there, but I told her not to. If something happens to us, she's the only one who can tell them what we found. I think she gets it."

"Good," said Terry.

"But she also said she's not going home without us. She'll go far enough to get a signal through, along with a confirmation saying they received it. Then, she's waiting for us to meet her."

"Sounds about right," said John, throwing his pack over his shoulder. He fastened the buckle around his waist and gripped both straps. "So you guys are sure about this?"

"Aren't you?" asked Mei.

John shrugged. "Doesn't matter."

"Huh?" she said. "John, of course it matters."

"Not to me," he said, grinning. "I don't care either way. I'm following you guys."

Mei groaned. "Great. Thanks, John. Go ahead and put *all* the responsibility on us."

"We've each got our jobs," he said, as if it were settled.

"What are you talking about? What jobs?"

"You two make the plans," he explained.

"Oh, I get it," said Mei, giggling, as if she'd finally gotten the joke. "If something goes wrong, you're not responsible, right?"

He nodded. "Yup. Pretty much."

Terry laughed. "Nice plan," he said. "But if we're doing the planning, what's your job?"

"It's like I said back on the hill," he explained. "Someone's gotta look out for you. It might as well be me."

THEY MADE it to the end of *Starlight Park* and on through most of the city before evening. Mei insisted they stick to the outer roads, which ran along the edge of the city like a wide oval. This meant adding half a day to their journey, but everyone agreed it was safer than the alternative. There was more open space along the road, more fields and parks like the one they'd slept in the prior night. The more direct path had been the city's downtown, followed by residential areas. Both meant narrow streets riddled with cars, debris, and potential surprises they couldn't see coming. Out of the question.

Mei's directions had them follow the road for five miles, until it hit the riverside. Once there, the road ran parallel to the river for several miles before finally curving around. They wouldn't need to go that far, however. The facility lay across a quarter mile bridge and then several miles beyond the opposite shore. Before they could reach it, the sun began to set and they agreed to make camp.

They slept near the river's shore, once again taking shifts.

Nothing came, but through the night, they heard distance cries of life, erupting screams echoing violently from within the city's concrete jungle. Terry imagined it must be the same animal as the kind they found in the tunnel, but the more he thought about it, the more he wasn't sure. The monster he'd slain made clicks and hums, but nothing else. Even amid the gunfire as its blood poured out of its chest and face, it never screamed or cawed. Only more clicks, more hums. But if not them, then what? The monsters' victims? It made sense, Terry supposed. If he remembered Mr. Nuber's lecture on evolution correctly, and he wasn't sure he did, every predator needed its prey. For every eight-foot quilled razborback, there had to be a weaker, juicier thing for it to eat. Why hadn't they seen it yet? Why didn't they hear those sounds the night before in the park? They'd traveled several miles since then, of course. Maybe the other animals weren't near their previous camp. Maybe that place belonged to the carnivores. He had no way of knowing.

The screams came and went through most of the night, but eventually they subsided, replaced by the howling winds and the cold dew of another morning. By the time they reached the bridge, the sun had climbed high into the clear, violet sky, and the midday heat covered them in sweat.

As expected, cars littered the bridge, though the tunnel had been much more congested. The bridge was twice as wide, after all, with plenty of room for walking.

John insisted on taking point. With Roland gone and Sarah left behind, he was the closest thing they had to a good shot. Of course, Terry was stronger now, and probably faster, but someone had to guard the rear, too.

The bridge was sturdy enough, though there were a few scrapes and cracks along the sides. "I'm surprised it's still holding together after all this time," said Terry. "After looking at those buildings, I wasn't so sure this thing would even be here."

"Because it's not made from the same stuff," said Mei.

"What do you mean?"

"It's FlexCrete," she said.

"I swear," said John, leering over his shoulder. "You're like a walking dictionary, you know that?"

"I know how to use my pad, you mean. You two should try it sometime."

"Tell us what else is says," said Terry.

She tapped the pad a few times. "Um…oh! It says here, FlexCrete was created by the Ortego Corporation in 2125, but didn't see any practical use until June, 2140, when they built a new parking garage with it. Then, in 2146, they used it to redesigned their offices. Afterwards, Ortego licensed it to an architectural firm named Maddison Hills, which in turn designed this bridge…which is called the Maddison Bridge."

John groaned. "Oh God, make it stop," he begged. "And I thought Nuber was bad."

"Very funny," she said, dryly.

"Hang on," said Terry. "You said 2146, right?"

She nodded.

"That's only eleven years before the Jolt."

"Yeah, they finished the bridge in August, 2150. It only took four years. Maddison Hills built a few other structures, but nowhere near here. Hey, you think they're still standing?"

"Probably," said Terry.

He tried to imagine such a building. Surely, they existed, if this bridge was any proof. But in a world encased in grief—with absolute destruction—such a thing would stand alone. Like this bridge, everything around it would echo morbid decay, the same as the wasteland they now traveled through, the same as the half sunk city behind them. It hardly seemed a pleasant thing, and so he pushed the thought away, choosing instead to focus on the goal.

Once they crossed the bridge, Terry suggested they keep moving. The facility lay only a few miles ahead, after all. They could rest later.

There were many signs along the road, though most had fallen to the wayside, rusted or covered in dirt, claimed by the new world. *Thank God for the pads*, thought Terry.

Things could always be worse.

Their path soon took them into the countryside, far from the highway. There had been a forest here once, Mei told them, but no longer. Now, it seemed the trees had rotted, fallen back into the earth that spawned them. In their ruin, a thousand blades of teal stalks grew, dancing as a gust of wind trailed by.

As Terry came upon the plants, he hesitated to move forward. The field was thick, an easy nest for predators, but the stalks stretched on in both directions, like the farms back home.

Their class had gone to the farms once, several years ago. Mr. Nuber had said it was important to see where things came from and how they got made. If everyone knew, he had said, maybe people would understand each other a little better.

Mei examined the map. "There's no way in except through here. It's the only road."

"Then, we'll have to go through it," said John.

"This is different from the blue grass. We don't know what's in there. It's too tall to see."

"We don't have any other choice," said Terry. He reached out and touched the tip of a plant, swept it aside, and walked in.

The others followed, staying close. Mei kept ahead of John, who had once more taken to the rear. Terry hated being in such a compromised position, unable to see if something was coming, but there was no other way. They had to press forward, which meant taking risks.

He wondered what Roland would have done. *He probably would've ordered us to go home. What the hell am I even doing?*

But before he could give himself an answer, Mei took hold of his shoulder. "Wait," she whispered.

"What is it?" asked John.

"I hear something."

They waited for a moment, but there was nothing. "She's making it up," said Alex. "She's scared."

Mei shushed him. "I'm serious!" There was a thud in the distance. "There it is," she said.

They each stayed quiet, waiting for the sound to reappear. Terry tried to focus. He closed his eyes and listened. It was difficult to hear anything besides the others' breathing and the wind as it blew through the field. He thought back, remembering the moment in the tunnel when his burst of strength had come to him and his senses flared, where the dark had become the light.

Then, at once he heard a beating sound, low and steady and deep.

Thump. Thump. Thump.

There it was, the sound Mei had heard. It was soft. Maybe if he concentrated…

Thump. Thump. Thump.

The beats were louder now and heavy. He tried harder, slowed his breathing. It wasn't close. He'd have to try harder.

Thump. Thump. Thump. Ksst.

There, a new sound. Something different. What on earth could it be? He could feel the pounding in his skull now.

Thump. Thump. Thump. Kisst.

Thump. Thump. Thump. Ksst.

He should stop. It was getting to be too much. He had his answer. Anything more would be too dangerous. He didn't want to black out again…or worse.

Terry pushed the noise far from his mind. It left him slowly, in pieces, but after a moment he felt the closer sounds return—the wind and the plants, John gripping his rifle's holster, Mei's breathing.

When he finally opened his eyes, a bright and blinding light consumed him, and he dropped his head, squinting.

Mei looked at him. "Terry?" she whispered.

But he shook his head. "Hang on."

It took a few seconds for the world to get back to normal. When he could see again, he raised his head and told the others what he'd heard.

"How could you hear those sounds?" asked Alex.

"It doesn't matter," he said. "The noise wasn't nearby. I don't think there's anything to worry about, but we should still be careful."

"Terry's right," said John. "Whatever it is, we'll be fine if we keep moving and avoid it."

As they walked, the distant sound became much clearer, and it wasn't long before Terry could hear it without trying. It didn't sound like any animal he'd ever heard before, whether in a recording or here in the wild. There was far too much rhythm to it, like the engines that ran the city's ventilation systems.

By the time they left the grove, each of them could hear the pounding noises. It seemed to be getting louder the farther they advanced, which could only mean one thing: whatever this thing was, they were marching toward it.

January 10, 2347
The Surface

TERRY DIDN'T KNOW how the temperature could drop so quickly, but the air was freezing, and he could see his own breath. The Variant felt strange in his lungs but not unpleasant.

Mei seemed to be having a different experience. She was shivering, rubbing her hands together. John noticed her and demanded they stop so she could put on another layer of clothing. No one objected, but as soon as she was ready, Terry insisted they keep going.

The sound had grown quite loud, which meant they were closer to its source.

They traveled far in the cold, but the plunging temperature leveled out before long. It didn't get any warmer, but it stopped getting colder. A good thing, Terry supposed.

Soon they found the compound gate, rusted and buried in the dirt. On either side, brick walls stretched far, eroded and covered in weeds. Before them on the ground, a series of cracked, stone letters read: ORTEGO.

And below, the subtitle: Building a Better World.

They had arrived.

In the distance, a light shimmered in the field, reflecting sun and open sky. Terry and the others ran toward it, stopping once they were close enough to see. The field was littered with glass—solar panels, Terry soon realized. The very same the city still used. But there were so many more here than the fields back home, at least a dozen fold. What did a single location need with so much power?

Mei pushed through the others. She retrieved her pad immediately.

"What is it?" asked John.

She didn't answer, so they went to her.

"Everything okay?" asked Terry.

"Those panels," she said, her voice quivering in the cold. "They're the power supply. I knew there had to be *something*. Solar energy. It's so simple."

"This is good news, right?" asked John.

Mei nodded. "Very good," she said.

Across from the solar panels in an area all to itself, a separate machine stood alone—tall and cylindrical and encased in silver rings. After a short moment, it slammed into the ground again and again, matching the noise they'd first heard back in the field. Once he was certain it was the source of the sound, he told the others.

"Maybe the pad has more info on it," said Mei.

"It hasn't led us astray yet," said Terry.

"Do you think it has something to do with the power? Like the solar panels?" asked John.

Mei jumped. "Found it!"

"What's it say?" asked John. He tried to snatch the pad, but Mei deflected him.

She pushed him, laughing. "Stop, and I'll tell you!"

John frowned. "You know, for once I'd like to sound like the smart one."

She cleared her throat, paused to look at John, and continued. "The Framling Coil, otherwise known as the fever killer, is a device designed and distributed by the Ortego Corporation. While originally intended to assist farmers with managing outdoor temperatures, the device has found greater success in power generation and distribution. The coils absorb local heat, converting the energy into electrical power. However, because of the effect it has on local wildlife, there have been many protests and petitions against its use. As a result, companies have largely abstained from using it, or in some cases, such as with Ortego, restricted it to emergency use only."

"What's all that mean?" asked John.

"I think we found the reason it's so cold here," she said.

Terry scanned the area. He could already see more of them. They were spread far apart, but still close enough to see. 1, 2, 3…6…9…there were over a dozen, at least.

"But you said they only use these things in emergencies," said John. "So why are they active?"

"Maybe they kick on when the power goes out," said Terry.

"I don't think so," said Mei. "The solar panels are still working. See? They're moving."

Sure enough, Mei was right. The angle of the panels had changed in the short amount of time they'd been standing around. They seemed to be following the sun.

"I think," continued Mei, "this experiment of theirs needed all the power it could get. I think it still does."

"You mean it's sucking power from both the panels and the coils?" asked Terry.

"I bet it takes a lot of energy to keep their crazy experiment running. Remember how they only wanted it to last three minutes? Maybe these..." she looked at the pad. "Maybe these *fever killers* are the reason why."

"You said there was public backlash over their use," said Terry. "Makes sense there'd be a time limit."

"Exactly," she said. "But before they could shut it off, the gas stopped them."

"Everything you're saying is a guess," said Alex. "You've got no clue about any of it."

Mei gave him a nasty look. "If you've got a better idea, let's hear it."

He bit his lip, twisting it in his teeth, and stared at her, a contemplative look on his face. But before he had a chance to say anything, Terry answered for him. "We'll know more once we're inside," he said. "Let's get going."

The rage on Alex's face faded, but not completely. Never completely.

They soon entered the field, following the road. As they passed along the rows of panels, several spots of color appeared near the glass. At first, Terry dismissed them, assuming they were nothing more than broken equipment. But the farther they went, the more abundant the piles became.

John took it upon himself to investigate. He retrieved a clump of the material, which came apart in his hands. It looked like crystals or jewels.

"It's ice," said Mei.

"But it's red and blue," said John.

Terry took off his glove and felt the cold frost on his bare skin. "She's right, but I've never seen ice like this."

"Out of everything Variant's changed, I like this the most," said Mei.

They kept moving, steadily pushing forward, and it wasn't long before they found their destination, a lone building high atop the hill. Seemingly oblivious to time's destructive hand, the facility was tall and wide, its windowed glass reflecting purple light.

"I can't believe it," said Mei, a dumbfounded expression on her face. "It looks brand new."

"Looks aren't everything," said Terry.

The glass doors didn't open, so John tried smashing through them with the butt of his rifle. They didn't break, so he cautioned everyone to stand back. He fired at the door, cracking the glass, then kicked it several times until the whole sheet fell in.

"Fantastic," said Mei.

They stepped through the opening and entered the building. The room wasn't very wide—seven or eight feet at the most—but the walls seemed to go on forever. Every floor from the first to the last was visible from the foyer, each marked with large numbers, the farthest reading 12. A long desk lay at the center of the room, with the company name stretched across the wall: ORTEGO.

To the left of the desk lay a set of double doors, which easily swung open. There was no other way except to go through them, so they did. A musty wave of hot stink hit them immediately. John scurried to the window, coughing. Mei ran to him.

"Sorry," wheezed John. "Breathed in at the worst time. What the hell is that smell?" He wiped his mouth.

"Dead people," said Alex, calmly.

"What makes you think so?" asked Terry.

"Not a lot of exposure here. No rain getting in. No bad weather. The bodies are still here, probably mummified."

"Gross," said John.

Terry looked at Mei. She was rubbing John's back. "You agree?"

She nodded.

He eyed John. "You good?"

"Yeah," said John, standing. He pulled out a piece of cloth and wrapped it around his head to cover his mouth. He handed another strip to Mei. "I'm ready this time."

Alex didn't filter his mouth or nose. When John offered him a piece of torn shirt, he dismissed it. "I don't need it. I'm used to it by now."

"But it's rancid," said Mei.

"Maybe to you." There was a swell of pride in his voice.

Terry didn't find the smell unbearable, either, but he took the cloth, regardless. He liked to think his body was adjusting, but the truth was that he didn't know. Then, Alex's words repeated in his mind. *I'm used to it.*

Maybe I'm used to it, too, he thought, solemnly.

Then he opened the door.

21

Amber Project File Logs
Play Audio File 215
January 10, 2347

NUBER: Are you going to tell her?

ROSS: I promised I would.

NUBER: But the transmission…you heard what Sarah said. Roland's dead. The others are scattered. We still don't know anything.

ROSS: We can't keep secrets, Henry.

NUBER: All it's going to do is hurt her. Hasn't the poor woman been through enough?

ROSS: I can't argue with you there, but we have an obligation to the truth. I won't repeat my predecessor's mistakes.

NUBER: I understand, but you should tell her we're not giving up. The retrieval team is standing by. The second we get a signal from the kids, we'll be on our way.

ROSS: *If it comes to that, save a spot for me, will you?*

NUBER: *You'll be the first one out the door.*

End Audio File

January 10, 2347
The Surface

As they soon discovered, Alex was right.

Bodies littered the nearby offices, though the meat was mostly gone. Variant had the nasty habit of ripping the flesh apart so that it could no longer cling to the bone. It made it almost impossible to visually identify someone, especially since the face was the first thing to go. In any case, the building was full of corpses.

The end of the hall opened into a common area, with a few dozen tables scattered around, though several had been turned on their sides. Overhead, an arched glass pane filled the room with a natural dim light. Hanging signs pointed to different sections, such as the cafeteria, gym, and something called the creativity enhancement room.

Mei informed them the machine was on the ninth floor, so they found the stairwell near the back and started climbing.

When they finally arrived at the door and opened it, they found the place completely darkened. "Must not be any windows," said John.

"You know what that means," said Terry.

"Yeah, yeah," said John. He unpacked the goggles. "You're so lucky. Why couldn't I be the one with the super eyes?" He sighed and fastened the straps.

"Don't feel bad. At least you've got your dashing good looks," said Mei. She snorted. "Oh, wait."

"You're a riot," said John, stepping inside.

Terry held the door for the others. Mei followed next, a triumphant grin on her face.

Then, it was Alex's turn. He started to walk in, but stopped a little shy of the door. "So it's true," he said to Terry.

"What's true?"

"You're changed," Alex said. "I figured as much back in the tunnel, but I wasn't sure." He looked Terry up and down. "What else?"

"Else?"

"Variant gave you better eyes, but there's gotta be more."

Terry hesitated. He forgot Alex didn't know. He should've put the goggles on and faked it. Now he had to lie again. "Nothing else," he said, hesitantly.

Alex stared at him. "We'll see," he finally said, then went on.

Terry followed and shut the door. The room was pitch

black, except for the cracks of light coming through the door they'd entered from.

Terry's eyes adjusted almost immediately. There was a flash of black, but within seconds, the place came back alive in hues of blue light. He saw desks and computer terminals, glass walls separating offices and monitoring stations, sixty-inch televisions hanging overhead, and a few dozen bodies lying dormant on the floor. Halfway through the room, a massive railing stretched from one end to the other. When he drew closer, Terry could see the floor dropped a good ten feet, expanding into what appeared to be another area. The rail's purpose became instantly clear.

Terry looked over the railing, surprised to only see a group of servers, each about three meters high, encased in glass. Behind them lay a console, which took up most of the back wall.

"Is this it?" asked John.

"Nope," said Mei. She started descending the stairs to the server area. "But we have to go here first." She went to the console and took out her pad, then removed her goggles and set them nearby.

John followed quickly behind her, but Terry and Alex stayed near the rail, watching overhead.

She examined the pad, which lit up most of the area she was standing in. She hovered over it for a moment, then turned her attention toward the console.

"What's up?" asked John. "You need some help?"

"I'm looking for a switch. It's kinda big, I think. Should be here somewhere..."

John peered around, his goggles still on. He walked to the far left side of the table. "This it?"

She grabbed the pad and ran to him. Angling the pad's light, she examined the switch. "Yes!" she yelled, her voice echoing. "Okay, guys, get ready." She grabbed hold of the lever, getting ready to push it forward, then stopped. "Oh, you might want to take those goggles off."

A short moment later, Mei pulled the switch. There was a deep hum, vibrating the walls and floor, and finally the lights flickered on. Mei grabbed John's arm and tugged him down as she jumped. "Yes! Who's awesome? Right here!"

"Calm down, spaz," said John.

"How'd you know the lights still worked?" Terry asked.

She smiled up at him. "I didn't," she said. "But I thought since the solar panels were still working, there was a chance. I didn't want to say anything until I knew for sure, though."

John put his goggles away. "I'm just glad the goggle phase of today was short lived."

"Where to now?" Terry asked.

"There's another set of doors behind you to the right. They lead to the main lab. You see them?"

"I do," he said, looking behind him, but he also saw the dead body lying there, propping them open. Its bones, still clothed in rags and clumps of dried flesh, lay upon the tiled floor. The skeleton reached with clawed fingers. It must have been running when it died here, breathing fire into its lungs. Died without knowing the reason.

It was the same in the old videos. Everyone always ran in the end, when there was no other option and every plan had failed completely. On that day, every soul on the surface of the Earth had run, unified in fear. In place of reason, an evolutionary instinct had taken hold and forced a panic in their chest to make them move. If they'd thought it possible, they might have run into the open sea, tried their hand at growing gills and fins.

Then, somehow, through happy luck and circumstance, a handful of savages managed to survive, clinging to life like leeches on the back of a dead whale, sucking blood that wasn't there. Even then, buried in the dirt and miles below the gas, the people never stopped running. It was why they had meddled in genetics; it was why they had insisted on creating hybrid children. They ran from the idea things could get back to the way they were before. They never thought they could stop the gas. Not really. Their only answer had been submission. Adaptability. But it was all the same thing—the same tired, old instinct that put one leg in front of another and pushed a man to run: the fear to stand and fight.

Today would be different. Today there would be no more compromising. No more frightened children going to the chamber. No more sacrificial lambs. They would stop it here, together, under their own terms, so that no one else would suffer for the sake of a broken world.

Today they would stop running.

THEY FOUND THE OBSERVATION DECK, where Dr. Gideon watched the government officials die before his eyes. It was safely tucked behind a sheet of thick, protective glass, far above the lab. The nearby camera was still there, mounted on a table in the corner, surrounded by monitors. Above one of the monitors, there was a picture of a white duck with blue clothes. An inscription read, *To all my favorite quacks, especially Jenny.*

It was signed *G.*

Near the camera lay two bodies, which Mei insisted must be the officials. Their uniforms, if that's what they were, looked like simple rags now, shriveled and cracked to pieces.

Through the glass, a massive chamber stretched in all directions, above and below. The place was ovular, like an egg, rising high through several floors. At its center, a long catwalk hung, leading from the observation deck to two smaller, thick translucent tubes.

John wiped the lens of the camera with his finger, then flicked the dust into the air. "It's exactly like Gideon said. Hard to believe it hasn't changed in all this time."

"It's changed," said Mei. "Maybe none of the furniture's been moved, but things are different."

She was right. The decomposed bodies on the floor

were proof enough of that. Even in a place like this, untouched by the elements, microscopic changes were still happening. Flesh decayed, skin flakes broke apart to form dust particles. Eventually, even the bones would be gone. In all corners of the world, time made memories of everyone.

"Let's get to it," said Terry.

Mei pointed to the end of the catwalk where the tubes lay. "That's where it's coming from," she said. "The power's down below. We have to fix it, then pull the switch up top to shut it down."

"Why can't we do it the easy way and cut the power?" asked John.

"We could, but we shouldn't. It might cause problems. I think my plan is our best bet."

"But you're not sure," said Terry.

"God, no," she said. "I don't know if this will work. I'm best guessing and that's it."

"Pretty good guesses so far," said John.

"Most of it wasn't a guess. This time I really don't know what will happen. The only people who might are dead."

"I'd take you over them any day," said John.

She smiled.

There was a ladder at the far end of the observation deck which led to another catwalk. Once he made it down, it was easier to judge the scope of the room. The ceiling and the floor were at least a hundred yards apart. Terry was currently closer to the bottom, of course, but still nowhere near it.

Using Gideon's instructions, they followed the catwalk to another section. It opened into a separate room full of servers and computer systems. "We need to reset the power cycle," said Mei. "It's one of the server boxes. Should be marked."

Upon first glance, it seemed impossible to find anything. There were cables running all along the floor and into the walls. Nothing seemed to be marked. Even it were, dust had accumulated to the point you could hardly tell what was written on the box.

Terry made his way past the others, starting his search near the back. The room was quite long, more like a hallway than a server room—thin and cramped. Terry stepped over piles of junk, wondering how the hell these people had ever managed to get anything done. As he neared the latter half, he stopped to find that Alex had followed him.

"I need to talk to you," said Alex, quietly.

Terry sighed inwardly. No doubt Alex was getting ready to criticize or lash out again. "Sure."

Alex took him by the arm. "This is a waste of time."

"Relax," said Terry. "I know it's a mess in here, but we'll find it."

"Junk's not what I'm talking about. I mean this whole thing, fixing the world. It's stupid, and you damn well know it."

"I know you don't think it'll work, Alex, but we have to

at least try. Sure, it might be a pipedream, but we'll never know until we try."

Alex sneered. "Oh, I get it now," he said. "You have to put on a show, is that it?" He nodded in the direction of John and Mei, who were both wiping the dust off the sides of server boxes. "Can't let the little kids down. I get it. Used to be the same for me with Cole. People look up to you now." He leaned in close. "Don't think I don't know what's going on with you, Terry. I've been paying attention. You're changing, aren't you? More than you were supposed to."

"Everyone is. The gas does it to us, remember?"

"Don't play dumb with me. You killed the rab in the tunnel, you healed overnight, and now you can see in the dark. You'd have to be blind not to see there's something happening to you."

"Even if that's true, what do you care?"

"Let me ask you a question, Terry. Did you like who you were before? Do you even remember it? I do. I remember the little kid who was too small and pathetic to do anything by himself, had to get a little girl to stand up for him. What about you? You remember?"

Terry didn't answer.

"Yeah, I thought so," said Alex. "Now think about what's going to happen when you go up there and shut that machine down."

"It'll save people. That's what'll happen."

"And you'll be weak again. A tiny, little baby kid crying for his mother. You looking forward to John protecting you like he used to? You're stronger than he is now. You're stronger than all of them."

"It's not worth the cost."

"Cost," he scoffed. "What cost? You think what's happening to us is a *bad* thing?"

"Of course it is," he said. "The whole world's turned into a nightmare. If we've got a chance to fix it, we have to take it."

"And you really think you can? Okay, fine. Maybe you pull a switch and manage to change the sky. Hell, maybe the air turns back to what it used to be and people can start leaving the city and come to the surface again. What do you think's going to happen when they get here? Did you forget about how the rabs are so strong they can rip your face clear off? How about the fact there isn't any food? How do you expect anyone to survive?"

"We'll find a way."

"Oh, you think so, huh? Well, let me tell you what I think is going to happen. No, scratch what I said. Let me tell you what will *definitely* happen. First, the people in your city are lazy. They grew up with beds and pillows, plenty of food and water. There's no way they'll leave their nice, little cage if it means they have to work. Second, the government's never going to let it happen. They have control down there. They can police a city, easy, but not a countryside. No matter what you do, those people are never going to leave."

"Then, why create us? Why waste their time all those years on making us?"

"Because they only want a few of us. We're easier to control. You really think they'd mass produce people like you and me—people who can go anywhere and do anything? They're not stupid. Better to have a few you can control than an army you can't. They need us to do their dirty work. We're the new soldiers, Terry."

"Even if you're right, it doesn't matter. The city can't last forever. People will eventually leave. If we learned anything in school, it's that things change. It's why we have to do this now, while we still have a chance."

"So you're willing to bet it all on a chance?" asked Alex.

"Better to try than do nothing," he said.

Terry spied a panel behind Alex. It had the Ortego symbol for electricity on it—two lightning bolts in the shape of a circle. They were faded and covered by dust. Terry barely recognized it. "Excuse me," he said, walking around Alex.

He swept the dust off the lightning symbol, making sure he wasn't mistaken, then called for Mei and John.

"Good job," said Mei. She opened a hatch on the side until she found a port. She plugged her pad into it and began working. "Should only be a minute."

"After this, it's back to the control room," said Terry.

Mei nodded. "We flip the switch and call it a day." A loud pop erupted from the machine, startling them. It was followed shortly by a rising hum. "Sorry," said Mei. She unhooked the pad. "This should do it."

John helped her up. "Are you sure it'll be that easy?"

"Why wouldn't it?" asked Mei.

"I'm not saying it won't, but I've been thinking..."

"Dangerous territory for you," said Terry, snickering.

"Never leads to a good place," agreed Mei.

John rolled his eyes. "No one's ever turned this machine off before. We don't know what's going to happen when we do it. What if it explodes or something?"

Mei hesitated. "Oh, I didn't consider that."

"What's wrong?" asked Terry.

"John's got a point," she said. "We don't know what will happen. It's possible the machine could react...um, negatively."

"As in, blow up?" asked Terry.

"Which would be bad, right?" asked John.

"Only for us," said Mei.

Terry thought for a moment. "Is it possible to trigger the shutdown program from outside this building? You know, like a remote control?"

"Maybe," said Mei. "I'd have to look at the console back in the control room to make sure. Our pads could probably do it if we set up a program."

John grimaced. "Probably, she says."

"Story of our lives," said Terry.

ATOP THE GRATED platform suspended in the air, Terry stared through the paned glass cylinder and deep into the void of the rift. The edges pulsed gently, almost rhythmically, as though to some unsung melody. Inside, a vast and empty dark lay still, lingering on the edge of its reality, begging to be free. Yet Terry knew without knowing that behind the dark there must be something—the birthplace of the Jolt, the spawning grounds of Variant—and for a moment, he let his mind wander at the thought of stepping through the door and to the impossible truth beyond.

He pulled himself back, blinking at the sight of the machine and the miracle within. He turned away, both ashamed and half afraid of the place his mind had taken him.

Mei crouched beside him, fiddling with her pad, preparing the receiver. John and Alex stood at the end of the platform, waiting. "How much longer?" asked Terry.

"I've almost got it," said Mei. She was using John's pad in conjunction with her own. One to send, another to receive. They were lucky to have the pads. *Always lucky*, thought Terry.

Alex had asked for Terry's pad a few moments prior so that he could, as he put it, find the way home. There had been a taste of disdain in the words, but Terry was glad to hear them nonetheless. After their last conversation, Terry didn't know what to think of Alex. He was glad to finally see him contributing, but the sour look in his eyes was unsettling.

Mei grabbed Terry's arm, pulling herself to her feet. "I think I got it."

"How's it work?" asked John.

"I took care of everything. All we have to do is clear the building, type and send the command, and we're done. John's pad does all the real work."

"*Yeah*, it does," said John, smirking.

"Once we send the command," she continued, "the second pad relays it to the console here, beginning the shutdown. It should only take a few seconds."

"Then, the boom happens," said John.

"Hopefully not," said Terry. "If we're lucky, it'll shut down nice and quiet." He looked around at everyone. "We ready, then?"

"Back the way we came," said Mei. She started walking.

"Hang on," said Alex. He was looking at the pad. "There's a better way. If we take the catwalks, we can bypass a few floors. There's a staircase below that'll take us straight to the ground floor. Should be faster."

"Good idea," said Terry.

"I don't know," said Mei. "It could be obstructed or dangerous."

"I'm telling you, this way's faster. It'll save us half an hour."

"But if we get down there and have to come back, we'll waste even more time," she said. "Terry?"

Terry looked at John, who shrugged.

"Fine," said Alex. "That's what I get for trying to help."
He looked almost defeated.

Terry paused before answering. He wasn't sure what to
make of Alex. Half the time it felt like all he wanted was an
argument, a reason to divide people. Wasn't it the whole point
of their talk from earlier, when he urged Terry to keep the
machine running and to leave this awful place? He seemed so
determined about it, so insistent he was right. Then there was
the fact he never once offered to help them along the way,
always chastising or mocking their decisions and opinions.
Why help now? Had Terry's words actually gotten through to
him? Did he somehow reach the part of Alex that cared
about others? Or was he simply creating conflict now, the
same as he always had, trying to feed whatever part of
himself enjoyed the misery of others? No, of course not. For
all his faults, Alex usually took the direct approach. Maybe his
offer to help was genuine. Anything was possible.

"Okay, Alex," said Terry finally. "It sounds like you've
put a lot of thought into it. Let's do it."

Alex shot a crooked grin at Mei. She turned and rolled
her eyes. "We take the catwalks," Alex said, pointing below.
"There's a hatch about halfway down. Leads to the emergency exit on the east side of the building."

"If it was faster, why'd we take the other way?" asked
John.

"Because the emergency doors only open from the
inside," said Alex.

"We also had to get the lights on," said Mei.

John nodded. "Totally worth it."

They started to leave, but Terry stayed a moment longer. He looked again at the anomaly in the glass tank, at the miracle with no name, and suddenly found he didn't want to leave. It looked so gentle, hovering behind the glass. Hardly the stuff of nightmares.

A part of him, buried beneath the responsibility and guilt, wanted to leave and never look back, run far away and forget about fixing the world. It would be so easy, exactly as Alex had said. He wouldn't have to give up his strength.

Then, he thought about the city, back to his mother and sister and Mr. Nuber and all the rest. They deserved more than a hole in the dirt. More than a cage of a life. They deserved blue skies and open country. They deserved to be human again.

If he could give it to them, maybe the cost didn't matter.

———

Stepping off the ladder and onto another catwalk, Terry offered his hand to John. "Watch your step."

John chuckled. "Watch your face. I got this." He jumped off the ladder, but stumbled, catching himself on the railing.

Mei giggled. She was following behind. "Unlike the ballerina over there, I'll welcome the help, Terry."

"How long to this hatch?" asked John, changing the subject.

"Pretty close," said Alex, who was right behind Mei. "It's at the end of this little stretch here, down another flight. Pretty easy."

He was right. The path led them directly to the hatch. It didn't open when they pulled, so Terry and John put their strength together. Still, it didn't budge. Mei pushed them aside and plugged in her pad to a nearby terminal. After a short moment, it opened, warm air oozing out. "Great," said John. "Another hotbox."

"Worried about your hair?" teased Mei.

"It's more about how all this humidity is making us sweat, which makes us thirsty. If you haven't noticed, we've only got so much water."

"One thing at a time," said Terry.

The hatch led directly into a crawl space, which took them to a metal rafter overlooking the stairwell. It was a long drop to the top of the stairs—a dozen feet, at least. Beyond that, it was nine floors to the bottom.

"How do we get down?" asked John.

"Here," said Alex, sidestepping to a little black box on the the wall. He snapped it open. "This drops the ladder."

The grate shuddered, and the ladder slid, clicking into place once it met the top of the stairs.

"How'd you know how to do that?" asked John.

"It's Ortego tech," said Mei. "The same as back home. Alex, did you figure it out when you left?"

"Sure. Now, hurry up and go down."

She did and John followed. Alex looked at Terry. "After you."

Terry paused. "Thanks."

He gripped the bar and started moving. He watched Alex move away from the ledge, probably for his pack. Then, as he neared the bottom, he saw John raise a hand to help him. He took it, laughing. "So it's okay for you to help me, but not the other way around. I see how it is."

"Yep."

Mei was sitting on the uppermost stair, rummaging through her pack.

"Forget something?" Terry asked.

"No, of course not," she muttered, though her tone said otherwise. Then she whispered, "Dammit."

John went to her. "You okay?"

"I can't find my pad."

"But you had it like two minutes ago," said Terry.

"I know," she said.

"You used it to open the hatch," said John.

"I *know*," she repeated.

"It couldn't have gone too far," Terry assured her. "Look around. We'll go back up if we have to."

"It's not down here," she said. "I looked while you were climbing." She waved her arm around. "There's nothing here, not even a pile of trash to look through."

"You sure you didn't drop it?" asked John, motioning to the edge of the stairs.

Mei opened her mouth, but Terry answered instead. "We would've heard the crash," he said. "Come on, we'd better check the hatch."

"Ask Alex," said John. "He's still up there."

Terry looked around, surprised Alex wasn't with them yet. Sure enough, he still hadn't come down. What was taking him so long? "Alex," called Terry. "Alex, you there?"

No answer.

"Hey, Alex!" yelled Mei. "You see my pad anywhere?"

Still nothing.

"What's he doing? Think maybe he heard us talking about it and went to check?" asked John.

"Could be," said Terry.

They waited a few minutes, but nothing happened.

"Maybe we should go back," said Mei, hesitantly.

Clank!

Terry jumped at the sound. "What the hell was that?"

"Oh, no," said Mei, frantically. "It sounded like the hatch."

"Alex must have shut it," said John, gripping the ladder. He started to climb. "Hang on while I check." He scurried up the bars, pulled himself over the edge, and cursed loudly. "It won't open!" he yelled.

"Do you think it was an accident?" asked Mei.

John banged on the hatch, screaming for Alex to open it.

Silence.

John poked his head over the side of the platform. "He's not answering."

Mei and John both looked at Terry, waiting. He didn't know what to do. Why would Alex lock himself inside? What was going through his head?

Then Terry remembered the look on Alex's face when he had tried to talk to him about the machine—a passionate plea at first, then indifference, a look of acceptance. At first, Terry thought his words had reached him. Maybe he finally understood. But he had only played the part, put a lie on his face and said the words Terry wanted to hear.

"He's trying to stop us," Terry said. "He has been since the start."

"Stop us?" asked John. "You mean the plan?"

Terry nodded and looked at Mei. "Your pad. I'm betting he took it."

"But why?" cried Mei. "What the hell is wrong with him? Doesn't he understand what's at stake?"

"He understands plenty," said Terry. "We're trying to fix something he thinks is perfect. He wants the world to stay the way it is. He always has. It's the reason he ran away in the first place, and it's the reason that door up there is locked now."

"What are we going to do?" asked John.

"Stop him," he said, though he didn't know how.

Terry and Mei climbed the ladder to the top of the

platform. They set their packs down, and Mei unlatched the panel near the hatch to look for a switch. She couldn't find any.

"Brute force, then," said John, nudging Terry and stepping back. "Time to get mean."

"Aren't you going to help? I can't do this on my own."

"Sure you can," he said.

"Try," said Mei. "Dig deep, the same way you did before. You can do this."

Terry sighed. "Okay, but take a step back. I need some room."

They did.

Terry closed his eyes, breathing harder and faster. He shook his arms, smacking them into the grate below his feet and tried to focus on what was at stake. He felt his adrenaline kick in, and his heartbeat quickened. He opened his eyes.

Terry gripped the door and pulled it hard, straining momentarily before the handle snapped in his hands. For a split second, he thought he failed, but then he saw that the door was open, too, and part of the wall had been destroyed in the process. He looked down at his hands, at the metal lock, and cast it aside. It fell behind him, cascading off the platform and plummeting down the stairwell, filling the room with thunder as it went. He looked at his hands, then at John and Mei, who were staring at him.

He looked away and closed his eyes again, trying to

calm himself. John touched his shoulder and it made him flinch. "You did it," his friend said. "You okay?"

"Yeah," said Terry, and it was true. Whatever was happening to him, it was getting easier each time. "Come on," he said. "We need to hurry."

WHEN THEY ARRIVED BACK at the machine, Alex was nowhere to be found. In his place, the remains of a pad lay shattered on the floor. "Dammit!" screamed Mei. "The rotten bastard. I'll kill him for this!"

Terry bent over the broken shards of glass and plastic, scanning them. "There's only one pad here," he said. "He could still have the other two. We need to find him."

"Alex!" called John. "Where the hell are you?"

There were three paths leading away from the machine. They had already covered the one to the hatch, so two remained.

"Split up," said Terry. He didn't know what else to do. "Mei, go with John and take the other catwalk. I'll head this way." He pointed toward the observation deck where they had originally entered from.

They agreed and parted ways. Terry raced through the observation deck and through the connecting hallway. He peered through the rooms as he passed them, his heart pounding and his blood racing. But as he searched, he couldn't help but wonder if perhaps Alex had already gone, run out and far away. How would Terry know? He couldn't see through walls.

Then a thought occurred to him, suddenly, and he came to a dead stop.

He closed his eyes, prepared his mind. In an instant, the world began to speak, and he listened.

An orchestra of noise cascaded through Terry as he tried to filter the madness. The walls moaned like a whale singing. The air between his ears blew with the intensity of a maelstrom. A dripping pipe a hundred yards away pounded like a drum.

One-by-one, he put the sounds to bed. All the drips and drops and creaks and whirls—one at a time, he let them fade, until at last it was quiet again, and all the music had gone. He waited, unwavering, for the sound that brought the answer.

And then it happened.

Bu-bum. Bu-bum. Bu-bum.

It was coming from before him, somewhere distant, but close enough to reach. He started walking, his eyes half opened, his mind floating in a cloud as he listened for the path.

The beating pattern begged him for a name, screamed for recognition, and he craved to give it one, begging it to come and stay a while.

Bu-bum. Bu-bum. Bu-bum.

There was familiarity to the noise. A heartbeat, yes, of course, pounding intensely, anxiously. Nervously. He edged his way forward through the hall, turning at the fork to the eastern wing.

Bu-bum. Bu-bum. Bu-bum.

It was growing closer, as though it were seeking him. Could it be Mei or John, come to find him? Had they failed to locate Alex? Had he been following the wrong person?

Bu-bum. Bu-bum. Bu-bum.

No, they weren't the source. Mei and John were still behind him. He stepped through a doorway, into a storage room filled with boxes and equipment. The beating was intense now, strong and quick and powerful.

"Alex," he said, opening his eyes completely. "I know you're here. Come out."

No answer, so he stepped inside. He considered flipping the light switch, but realized his chances would be greater if he was the only one who could see, should he find himself in a struggle.

He kicked aside some broken metal and a set of bones beside them, jerking dust into the air. It made the air smell dry and old. He scrunched his nose and held his breath, waiting for it to settle. When he breathed again, there was something else still lingering—a living scent that echoed sweat and blood and flesh. He turned to his side, to a cluster of tall computer towers and storage crates, and cautiously stepped forward.

Suddenly, from behind the darkness of the equipment, Alex lunged toward him. Terry swung his rifle around, shooting wildly into the walls, missing him. Alex grappled the weapon, throwing Terry back against the wall, holding him down. He was so strong—as strong as Terry, but how?

Terry pressed his foot into the corner of the wall behind him and pushed forward. Alex reacted immediately, redirecting Terry to the wall again. The force of the impact staggered him, knocking a bit of air from his lungs.

Alex pressed the side of the gun to Terry's neck. He leaned in close, matching his eyes in the dark. Could he see him? Was it even possible?

Alex smiled. "Don't follow me," he whispered. With both his hands on the stock of the rifle, he snapped it in half, casting the pieces of it to the side. "Next time, that'll be you," he said, gripping Terry by the arm, and flung him like a rock into the wall. Then, he ran.

Terry slid into the pile of bones on the floor. He coughed as the dust scattered but quickly composed himself and followed Alex.

In all the time since they'd found him on the surface, Alex had never displayed such raw strength before. Nothing like what he'd just done, nothing like Terry's. No one had.

Could he have been hiding it? It seemed so unlike him…that he should shy away from arrogance and show of strength. To think in all the time that he had been with them, keeping this secret to himself, acting as their prisoner, he could just as easily have run. Why had he stayed with them? Why go on pretending?

Terry rounded the hall and dashed toward a sprinting Alex in the distance. He was heading back to the observation deck, back to the catwalks and the machine. Mei and John might be there. Maybe they'd be fast enough to down him.

Terry reached the end of the hall and entered the deck. Staring through the looking glass, he saw John and Mei had returned, but something was wrong. Mei was screaming.

As he drew closer, Terry saw Alex had seized Mei's rifle in one arm, holding her by the neck in the other. Atop the metal grate, John lay on his back, his gun missing, and Alex's boot pressed hard into his chest. A wicked smile and crooked eyes peered down at John before finally rising to meet Terry. "I told you not to follow me," said Alex. "I was going to let you go."

"Stop it, Alex!" yelled Terry. He stood at the door to the observation deck, several yards from them. "Whatever you're doing isn't the way. We can talk it out. Put down the gun and relax."

"We already talked it out, remember? You didn't give a damn what I had to say."

"I'm sorry," said Terry. "I made a mistake. But I'm listening now, see? Let them go and you can tell me again."

"You think I'm stupid? I tried talking to you the other night in the field. I tried again today. None of you want to hear the truth. All you care about is your friends and your precious city!" He pulled Mei close and stuck the barrel of the rifle in her neck. "But I can fix it for you, Terry. We can get rid of all your distractions right here and now."

"Stop it!" he cried. "Don't do this!"

"You did this to them when you refused to listen," snapped Alex. "It's on you!" He clutched the rifle close, then leaned into Mei. "This one's for forgetting your place, little girl," he whispered in her ear. "Enjoy the bullet, bitch."

John screamed and latched hold of Alex's leg. "Get off her!" he yelled, then bared his teeth and bit Alex's ankle.

Alex cursed at the pain and fell, pulling the trigger before dropping the rifle over the railing. Mei loosed a terrifying shriek as the bullet grazed her cheek. A stream of blood slid down the side of her face as the bullet hit the console near the machine.

Alex fell backwards and onto the scaffold, letting go of Mei. She ran, tears in her eyes, toward Terry and the observation deck. She passed him, shaking, spouting incoherent cries from having nearly died. Terry ran in the other direction, toward the others. He had to make it to John before Alex got back to his feet.

John scrambled to stand. He saw Terry and started toward him, but before they met, Alex was back up and charging.

The three of them met in the middle of the platform. Alex plummeted into them both, screaming. He grabbed hold of John's shoulder and flung him away, then looked at Terry with wild, mad eyes, his chest heaving, and went at him.

Again, they clashed, and Terry could feel the weight of Alex's fury pressing down on him, forcing him back. He struggled, desperately trying to fight, but it wasn't enough. Alex cast him down, knocking him into the railing. Then, holding him by his gear, he lifted him over the side and threw him from the railing.

Terry fell into the pit, landing hard against another catwalk, knocking every ounce of Variant air from his lungs. Blood dripped over his eyes, splashing into the metal grate like a crimson waterfall. He felt numb, cloudy, almost empty. He tried to lift his head, only managing to turn over on his back, trying to see what was happening on the platform high above him.

But he couldn't see a thing. The room was blurring, evaporating into nothing. Darkness replaced it, a fraction at a time, until everything was black and all the light had gone. Was this the moment, then? Was this where he was going to die? Killed so far from home, deep inside a grave, staring up toward the end...

He drifted, lost in a sea of memory.

He thought of the moment he first entered the academy, when he stood in Bishop's office all those years ago and listened to a towering man tell him his future—how this was his home now, and there was no going back. He thought of the baseball on the wall. He'd never seen a baseball before, except in pictures. He wondered where it came from.

He remembered Mr. Nuber, the one-armed teacher who called him a baby. The only man in the city to kill a rab and live. Terry used to think Nuber was the toughest person in the world. Maybe he was. Terry thought about his bald head. Did everyone lose their hair like that?

Terry thought about Sarah and Roland, born soldiers and natural leaders. None of this would have happened if either of them were still here. What would Roland say when Terry saw him again?

John, his best friend, always looking after him. Always noble and brave and selfless. All Terry wanted was to repay that debt, to protect everyone the same as John had. Now, he would never have the chance.

He thought of Mei, so smart and kind, filled with an overabundance of love. She could put adults to shame with her intelligence. She'd been born in the wrong century, her natural gifts wasted. She was like a sister to him.

Like Janice. Oh, how he wished he could see her, wherever she was. If he could only speak to her again, hug her, scream that he was sorry for breaking his promise. He hoped she was happy, that somehow she'd found a way to forget him. *I wanted to fix it all*, he thought, alone in the darkness. *I wanted to fix the whole thing for you, Janice. I'm sorry I couldn't. I'm sorry I'm too weak.*

Too weak and small, too lacking in the strength that makes men great. And now, because of his weakness, countless lives would suffer. An entire city filled with people would stay buried in the desert, far away from the world, and there they would remain until they died, dwindling like stars in the new dawn.

And the answer to everything, to all of their pain, to his

race's salvation, to his sister's survival, was a button on a platform, floating high above his head.

He longed to reach it now, to fix it all so he could just go home again. To find his sister and repeat the last words he spoke to her all those years ago: I love you.

But how could he ever tell her from here? How could he let himself die in a place like this without speaking those words again? How could he break his promise?

No, he thought. *I have to go home. I still have things to do.*

He curled his fingers, felt tingles in his hands and arms like they were asleep. He kicked, but his feet didn't move. He screamed, but nothing came out of his mouth.

He kept screaming, deep inside his mind. He screamed forever, over and over, filling whatever world he was in with every ounce of rage that came to him, and suddenly he felt the adrenaline begin to swarm, felt the churning, rising flame in his veins and heart. It grew intensely, uncontrollably, and for a moment, he could barely breathe. As he came out of the dream, out of the nightmare, the raw pain of his body filled him, and he screamed an awful cry into the ancient place. The pain washed over him, wave after wave, until it dragged him down, suffocating him. He gasped, sucking the Variant in, and felt the air leave his lungs and evaporate through his pores.

Then, suddenly, the light came back, and it filled him with such a force that it nearly blinded him. And in a single moment, for all there was to see, he saw everything.

The room, so simple before, so empty, became a jungle

of substance and microscopic life. There, floating in the Variant-enriched air, suspended in a beam, a thousand colors in a thousand patterns flickered, dancing on a single particle of dust.

The world echoed with hundreds of sounds, bouncing off of one another like an orchestra of life, and it was beautiful. He heard his heart pounding gently, slowly, and he felt the blood in his veins flow.

In the distance, Alex and John fought, and a pounding, beating thunder erupted from their chests, vibrating through the air and filling Terry's mind. He could feel their hearts inside his own, though they were slow, ticking an eternity apart. The moment stretched on like an unbreakable band.

Everything was moving slower, including Terry. He tried to move his hand, but it barely went anywhere. The only thing that seemed to act normally was his own mind, though he knew the reality was far different. He was actually thinking much faster than he could physically react, or that anyone else could, for that matter.

He pushed it aside, not knowing how to do it, but doing it nonetheless, and suddenly, time normalized. Alex had John by the arm, getting ready to throw him. Terry jumped to his feet. He had to get there quickly. There was a ladder on the wall, several yards along the catwalk. He started running.

He felt lighter now. Much lighter. Each stride grew longer as he went, until he was leaping several feet, several yards at a time. Before he reached the ladder, he jumped, catching one of the bars high in the air, then he climbed from one to the next until he was level with the other platform.

He jumped, easily landing above on the grate and sprinted to the far end towards the fight. All things considered, it took him six seconds from start to finish to reach the fight.

When he arrived, Alex was standing over John. He stopped to see Terry fast approaching. Alex opened his mouth to speak, but before he could say the words, Terry plummeted into him with the force of a small train. Together, they slammed into the railing, snapping it apart. Alex kicked Terry in the chest, knocking him clear and back a few feet. Midair, Terry pivoted his body so he landed on his feet, then pressed off the metal and aimed himself back at Alex like a bullet, hitting him in the face with his skull.

Alex staggered back, clutching the railing, blood dripping down his broken nose. He screamed madly, then charged again. Terry deflected him, stepping to the side and letting Alex fall onto the metal flooring. Alex caught himself, sweeping his leg under Terry's and causing him to fall. Alex leapt on top of Terry, gripping his throat and squeezing, his hands like steel bars. Terry jabbed the tips of his fingers into Alex's lower abdomen, the same spot his deadly wound had been a few days prior. There must still have been some damage, because Alex's grip immediately loosened and he let out a short grunt. Terry leaned in, grabbing Alex by the chest, and flung him back.

Alex stumbled to his feet, clutching his side. He looked around, his eyes wide with desperation. He ran to the broken railing, grabbed a piece of the bar, and snapped it clear off. With a loud cry, he started swinging. Terry raised his arm to block the pipe, but the metal hit his wrist, and he heard a crack that sent a wave of pain up his arm and through his chest and both legs. He deflected the blow, and responded by slamming his fist into Alex's chest, which sent him flying in the direction of the observation deck. He collided with the glass window, shattering it to countless pieces. He landed between two consoles.

John stood nearby against the wall. He looked at Alex, then back at Terry. "This is crazy," he said.

Alex coughed, followed by the sounds of glass cracking as he stood. His clothes were torn in a dozen places where the glass had cut him, and there was blood everywhere.

"It's over," said Terry. He took a step forward. "Let it go, Alex."

Alex didn't answer. His chest was heaving as the blood dripped from his forehead, streaming down his eyes and cheeks like tears. He looked at John, who was still standing near the wall, then back at Terry. He gave a wicked grin.

"No, wait!" yelled Terry, but it was no use.

Alex dashed at John so fast that there was no time to react. He jabbed John's face with his fist, then kneed him in the stomach. With John doubled over, Alex stomped on his leg, shattering the bone. John cried out in pain.

Alex gripped John's wrist and threw him through the window frame towards Terry, who caught him. Together they fell back in the direction of the machine, smashing into the nearby console. Terry turned John over on his back, but before he could check him, Alex was already there, lording over them. He bent down, grabbed Terry by the shoulder, and struck him in the belly. The pain was enormous, and Terry could feel blood pooling out of him. He looked at the wound, only to see a six inch shard of glass sticking out of it.

Alex grabbed John before Terry could react. He dragged John to the broken rail and dangled him over the edge by his neck. Alex stared at Terry as he got to his feet. "Move, and he's dead."

John squirmed, clawing at Alex's wrist as he struggled to breathe.

Blood began to fill Terry's throat, and he coughed, spraying it into the air. He touched the glass in his stomach, and for a moment it hardly seemed real. "Stop it, Alex. Please…"

"I gave you a chance," said Alex. "I was going to let you go because you're like me." He squeezed John's neck tight. "But it's too late now."

"It's not too late," insisted Terry. "Just put John down. We can fix this."

"Fix it?" he asked. "That's all you care about, isn't it?

You think you can fix everything. Me, the planet, the city. It's all you can think about. It's all you *talk* about. Well I'm sick and tired of listening to you ramble on about it. *I don't want to fix anything!"*

Suddenly, Alex's chest tore open and spewed a stream of blood into the air before him. A jagged piece of metal slid through his ribs. His jaw quivering, he peered down at it. He let go of John, who grabbed hold of the railing and clung to it with what little strength he had.

Alex blinked repeatedly as he staggered back, trembling at the sight of the blade in his body. He opened his mouth, but instead of words there came a river a blood.

Mei stood behind him, her terrified eyes looking up at him, her hands still in the position they were when she stabbed him.

Alex stumbled towards John, then collapsed to his knees. He continued to stare at Mei, who stepped back from him, still shaking. "B-bitch," he said, gargling his insides. "You...bi..."

Alex, his eyes cold and empty, fell lifelessly past John, careening into the empty chasm below.

Mei bent down and grabbed John's hand, trying to pull him back up. Terry went to them and helped, and together they managed to secure him. John fell on his chest, then rolled over.

Mei grabbed John's sleeves and pulled him close, wrapping her shaking arms around him. She screamed intensely until she couldn't anymore, until she was hoarse.

Bloody and broken, John held her, and in an instant there were tears in his eyes, too, and they glided along the edges of his rough cheeks, down the curve of his broken lips, and disappeared into her charcoal hair. He swayed back and forth, rocking her gently. "It's okay," he kept repeating. "Everything's okay now."

Terry watched in shock, not knowing what to say or do. His bones ached and his eyes throbbed—his body felt submerged in pain—but none of it mattered right now. All that mattered were the people sitting before him, and they were in agony. Complete and utter torment. All he wanted to do was fix it, to take their pain away—carry it on his back and bury it far from here—but all he could do was stand there.

He turned away, grief in his throat, ashamed at what had happened, at what he had *let* happen. How could he do this to them? What sense did any of it make?

His eyes drifted through the room, eventually falling on the machine and the rift. It was still in the same position it had been since they found it, quietly hovering behind a layer of glass, spreading death and singing silently. But as he watched it, mercilessly looming over him, a fire in his heart began to grow, and it wasn't long before he hated it completely. *It* was to blame for all the hurt, for all the death and moral decay. Everything wrong with the world stemmed from that initial moment, the single press of a button that spawned an eternity of horror. Right here.

He stepped to the panel, sliding his hand along its

surface. The pads were gone, so there would be no shutting it down remotely. They'd have to pack it up and go home. They'd brief the people back home, tell them the story, and who knows what would happen?

Alex might still win, after all.

Terry looked at Mei again. She'd stopped crying and had gone to examining John's broken leg. "How's it look?" Terry asked.

"Not good," she muttered. All the energy in her voice was gone.

"Can you make it out of here, John?" he asked.

"Yeah," he answered. "Might be slow about it, but I can do it."

"Good," said Terry. "Because I need you to leave now."

They both looked at him, their faces lost at the statement. "What's that supposed to mean?" asked John.

"I'm staying here to finish the job."

Mei stood up. "No," she said.

"I'm sorry, Mei, but someone has to do it."

"No, someone doesn't. No more. Let's just go home. Please." She sounded exhausted.

"If we don't do this now, it might never happen. You know there's no choice."

"What about the pads?" asked John. "Aren't they still the plan?"

"They're gone," said Terry. "All except the one Alex left over there, and we need at least two."

Mei stepped closer, took him by the arm, and tried to

pull him away. He didn't move. "I won't let you," she said. "You can't. I won't let you!"

"Let me go, Mei."

"If anyone's staying, it's me," she said, frantically. "You don't know what you're doing!"

"Mei…"

"Shut up!" she said, her voice cracking. "Shut up, please."

He pulled her back, and she fell into him. He felt the warmth of her wet face on his neck, and he embraced her for as long as he could. "I'm sorry," he whispered. "But you've saved us already. It's my turn now."

"But you could die," she said. "What if something happens?"

"I'll be fine," he assured her. "As soon as I shut it down, I'll get out of here. You've seen how fast I am, right? Nothing to worry about. Besides, you have to take care of John. He can't make it back by himself. He needs you."

"I need you both," she pleaded. "You're the only family I have."

He pushed her back and looked into her eyes. "And you're mine, too," he said. "That's why you need to leave."

She let go of him, nodding slowly. "All you have to do is press a few buttons." She showed him which ones and in what order. He thanked her and said he understood. "I don't know what'll happen next," she said.

"Most people don't," he told her. "And that's okay."

She hugged him again, then silently went to John and helped him to his feet.

"You're sure about this?" asked John, wrapping his arm around Mei's neck.

"Yeah."

"How will you know we're clear of the building?" he asked. "We don't have our pads anymore."

"We have the one," said Terry. "It can track your chips. I'll wait until you're far enough away."

"Good luck," he said. "You'd better get out of here. Don't make me come back to get you or I'll be pissed." He smiled. "You hear me?"

"Loud and clear."

John nodded and with Mei's help, left. Terry watched them go, hobbling slowly through the observation deck and into the nearby hall. He grabbed the pad, set the display to follow their signals, and sat with his back against the machine. He waited.

It took John and Mei nearly an hour to escape the building, then another ten minutes before they finally stopped on the other side of the solar field.

Terry sighed, relieved, and shut the pad off. He then turned his attention to the final task.

Touching the console before him, he swept his fingers over the dust. The buttons emitted a soft hue of red, reflecting off the surrounding metal.

Terry began the process as Mei had described it, shutting down one system after the next. There were seven in all, and it took a few minutes. After the sixth, before the final step, he hesitated.

He thought about the improbability of success in what he was doing, the risks he faced—how he might never go home, never see his friends again—and suddenly his heart began to ache. He imagined his sister's face, not the one who existed now, because he didn't know that young woman, but the girl from his memories, beautiful and innocent and loving. He might never see her again, but...she would have a chance, wouldn't she? All of them would.

And perhaps that could be his gift, something to make up for the promise he broke and the years wasted and the memories which never came to be. He hoped to see her again, somehow, wished she could love him again, there in some distant place.

Terry stared into the abyss, deep within the darkness of the void. A tear streamed down his face, and then another. He felt warm and tired and alive, but most of all, he felt loved.

Then he pressed the kill switch...and suddenly he was gone.

22

**Documents of Historical, Scientific, and
   Cultural Significance
Open Transcript 616
Subtitled: The Memoires of S. E. Pepper –
   Chapter 35, page 187
March 19, 2185**

PEPPER: I attended a botany conference last September. We convened to discuss the possibility of building yet another farm— number thirteen, if memory serves.

I'm sad to say I had very little to contribute and usually don't in situations such as these. I hate politics, and the thought of debating the merits of growing one plant over the other bores me to no end.

When I was in my twenties, nobody questioned the possibility of growing more food. You had to be crazy to say no to that. Not so anymore. Now, it all comes down to votes and handshakes, a tabletop of politicians, smiling niceties for cash.

I sat through it all, drifting, justifying my existence with the same six words I always had—I came here for the drinks. I wondered if it was enough anymore.

As it happened, I was sitting at the table, sipping my glass of delicious rosemary wine, still deciding whether or not to write this book, actually, when I overheard a man and a woman talking shop nearby. The woman had recently developed a new cooling method for the energy capacitors, which would reduce the city's overall energy consumption by about 3%.

For reasons that should seem obvious, I couldn't help but feel a touch bored by their celebration. As I was losing interest, I heard the man say something that I'll never forget. He said, "And the new capacitors won't need to be replaced for forty years, at least. What an improvement! You're bound to get a promotion off this."

Imagine that. All of their excitement over a trivial 3%. As far as I could tell, this particular oddity of capacitor design did absolutely nothing to solve the current predicament of living underground in an isolated bunker. It made no attempt at improving the conditions on the planet's surface, no progress toward a state of normalcy. Instead, it was a letter of acceptance, bound in the conviction that there could be no going home.

That was when it hit me. The people are beginning to forget.

Instead of planning for the trip home, instead of looking for ways to leave this place, we've settled into staying. They've resigned them-selves—all our brightest minds—to work on better ways at hiding. Better capacitors, better air conditioning ducts, better street lamp bulbs.

There's no point, they think, in solving the air problem on the world overhead when we can extend our stay in this lovely little hovel to some indefinite end. Why take the risk? Let's not worry about the problem when the alternative is so much easier.

Humanity has forgotten in a single generation the joys and splendor of a thousand more before it. When all the old ones are gone —myself soon to be among them—not a single soul still living can say they knew the world before the fall, before violet covered blue, and the Earth turned inside out.

Futile as it may be, and with a shadow of a childhood dream, I would ask whoever reads this book, whoever cares enough to listen… that you would not forget. There is more to the world than these hollow walls of metal, encased in stone and mud. The sky, the sun, the stars —each is a miracle, built for eyes that cannot see them, screaming out for us to come. There are cities a hundred times the size of this one, built by kings for millions more, their towers raised as tall as gods. Beyond them lies an endless sea with fleets of ceaseless waves, bending at the neck. And higher still, a myriad of stars, blanketing the heavens.

The universe exists, I tell you! And it's waiting for the artists to come back.

End Audio File

January 10, 2347
The Surface

John stood in the open field, two hundred yards from where the world had ended, where the new one might begin, and where his oldest friend had stayed behind.

Mei was beside him, shouldering his weight because he wasn't strong enough to stand on his own. His body throbbed with the pain of a broken leg and several bruised ribs. It was all he could do to breathe.

Mei shuddered in the cold air, though she never complained. It was clear that her concern for Terry overshadowed everything else. John loved her for that. He loved her for a lot of things.

A small gust blew through the valley, numbing his cheeks and neck and filling his lungs. It made the pain slightly more bearable. No matter how bad the situation seemed, there were always positives, no matter how small.

John watched the entrance to the facility, waiting for Terry to emerge. *Any minute now*, he told himself. *Then we can go home.*

He chewed his lip impatiently, imagining the relief he was going to feel when he saw his friend. He'd belt him in the arm for taking so long. Tell him he knew he could do it. Tell him how proud he was. *Yeah*, thought John silently, *It's exactly what I'll—*

Loud thunder erupted in the distance, echoing through the field, lingering a while. John scanned the building, but there didn't seem to be anything wrong. "What the hell was that?" he asked.

Before Mei could answer, they heard another one. It

snapped like a whip, making them flinch. The sudden movement caused Mei to drop John's arm, and he fell backwards. She tried to catch him, but he only pulled her down with his weight.

Overhead, high in the sky, the clouds swirled, quickly moving toward the field and the facility. Lightning flashed between them, randomly, chaotically. Mei hugged his arm and he held her close.

The wind blew hard against them, fettering the grass and shaking the solar panels so hard John was sure the glass would shatter. Before their very eyes, the sky transformed into a miniature hurricane, its eye directly over the Ortego building.

"What's happening?" screamed John.

Mei, still clinging to his arm with all her strength, buried her face in his shoulder. "It's the machine!" she yelled. "He's done it! It's happening!"

The chaos grew and built upon itself, bellowing streams of thunderous cries. Soon the sky was set ablaze—a hurricane of madness.

The second Jolt had come. It was the end of the world all over again.

John tried to sit up so he could see the Ortego building, but the force of the wind was strong. If he got to his feet, there was a very real possibility that it would carry him away. Still, he managed to lift his head enough to see the building still standing, though he feared it wouldn't be for long.

John felt the ground begin to shake beneath them. The shockwaves rattled his wounds and he clenched his teeth and squeezed his fists, ignoring what he could of it.

A sharp pop came from behind them, and John looked to see one of the fever killers collapse, its coils snapping like rubber bands, flying apart and into the storm. Another one from across the field soon followed, then another, until there were no more left. The bodies of a dozen metallic monsters circled the distant building like a halo of destruction.

This is the end! Cried John, silently. *God, what have we done?*

As if to answer, the wind suddenly died, and the debris it carried fell to the ground. At the same time, the tremoring ground began to slow, finally stopping altogether.

Mei got to her feet, then helped John to his. "Are you okay?" she asked him. "I thought for sure we—"

An earsplitting *BOOM* shook the earth, as though the very land itself had split in half. A bright light filled the sky above Ortego, sending a shockwave back so hard that it nearly knocked them down again. John shielded his eyes, catching himself on his broken leg, and he screamed something terrible. Mei managed to get under his chest, holding him with the strength of her shoulders. "I've got you!" she cried.

Within seconds, the light dissipated. John clutched Mei by the arms, trying to focus his eyes. "Are you okay?" he asked, desperately. "What the hell was that?" But before she could answer, he saw it for himself.

The Ortego building was gone. Only a crater remained.

___

THEY STAYED and searched the field for hours, but there was no sign of Terry or any major section of the building. They only found a few scattered scraps of metal and FlexCrete, hardly enough to warrant much hope.

Without a word, they got what they could and left. John created a makeshift splint for his leg, while Mei managed to find a fitting crutch for him to use. It was fashioned from part of a broken fever killer. The crutch was adequate, and it nearly doubled their speed, though it wasn't saying much.

Mei suggested they make camp at the base of the hill. There wasn't much food left, so they ate what they could and rationed what little water still remained.

John awoke several times throughout the night. He could hear Mei sobbing to herself, curled in a ball, her face buried in her arm. He went to her eventually, saying nothing, and held her in his arms. She wept longer than he cared to measure, her tears running down his arms and chest, drying on his skin. After a time, her sobs began to fade, replaced by heavy snoring. This time she didn't wake until the morning.

January 11, 2347

The Surface

JOHN WAS RELIEVED when Sarah found them. She approached the camp as they were packing the supplies. She'd kept her promise and followed after all.

"We didn't know if we'd see you again," Mei said.

"Neither did I," she admitted.

"Did you get through to Central?" asked John.

She nodded. "They ordered me home. Unfortunately, the signal cut out before I got the order." She winked.

"Lucky for us," said Mei.

"Don't know about lucky," said Sarah. "But I'm here to help. Whatever you need."

They started home again, and on the way, Mei replayed the events in the order they occurred. She told Sarah about the tunnels and the city, then talked about the night they spent in the park, the journey across the bridge and up the hill and into fields. When she finished explaining what had happened inside the Ortego building with Alex and the machine, Sarah's eyes sunk to the ground, and she was quiet for a long time. When she finally spoke again, it was to ask John how he felt and to suggest they stop and rest.

They did, and John took the opportunity to rewrap his splint. Nobody ate, though Sarah insisted John drink some water. When they finally left, the sun had risen to its peak, and the afternoon heat consumed them.

THEY CHOSE to walk around the city, rather than go through it. There was little point in taking the tunnels, subjecting themselves to its dangers, especially given John's injuries. They had barely survived that place the first time around.

Unfortunately, with the open road came the heat. Mei suggested they only travel at night, which the others agreed to. They waited under the FlexCrete bridge at the river and then went on after dusk.

They found that traveling under the light of the moon was far less tiring, which, considering their water supply was nearly depleted, seemed like a good thing.

Because of his injuries, the girls insisted John drink what he could of the water. He didn't argue, but whenever they handed him the canteen, he only pretended to sip from it, and they believed it. Still, despite his best efforts, by the time they reached the first transmission tower, the rest of the water was gone.

JOHN PASSED out on the road. He had never fainted before. He was surprised to find his body so useless, walking along and suddenly collapsing because his legs stopped working. It scared him. After he fainted the third time, Mei insisted they stop.

Sarah tried radioing Central a few times, but it was no

use. The equipment was fried. They'd have to make it home on their own.

John passed out again. He barely had the energy to stand, and sleeping felt like a tremendous relief. He dreamed a few times, though they were mostly nightmares. He imagined Terry with the machine, all alone, and screaming for someone to help him. John heard his cries and ran to him, but no matter how fast he went, he could never get there in time. Terry always died.

He awoke screaming. Mei was nearby, staring at him, mud around her eyes and cheeks. She looked exhausted. "I'm here," she whispered. "It's okay." She placed her head on his shoulder and massaged his chest with her palm.

Sarah lay on the ground, facing the other direction. She didn't seem to be moving. John watched her for a while, wondering if she was still alive. Sometime later, her foot twitched. He relaxed.

It wouldn't be long now.

They slept.

WHEN JOHN AWOKE, he was terrified to see animals standing over him, clad in reflective, white skin. They kept poking him, moving his arms and legs, repositioning his body. "Check his vitals," said one of them.

"This one looks dead," said another.

"Not yet but almost."

"Get them on the dirt cab."

One of the animals snapped its fingers a few inches from his face. "John, can you hear me?" it asked him.

"Who are you…?" he could barely keep his eyes open.

"My name is Avery Ross," said the fading voice. "I'm here to take you home."

John and the others were placed on gurneys, needles and tubes all over their bodies. He could barely feel any of it.

It only took a few hours to reach the Sling. Ross sat next to all three of them for most of the ride, constantly asking the other soldiers to check the children's vitals or to refill their I.V. bags.

The soldiers lined each of the gurneys onto the elevator, one at a time, pushing John in between Sarah and Mei.

John reached out and touched Mei's wrist. He didn't have much strength, so it was all he could do to comfort her. She clenched his finger in her tiny palm, though he barely felt it.

He didn't care. It was enough just knowing she could still feel him—that she was there. The world had taken so much from them, but at least they had each other. For what little it mattered, he could be thankful for something, at least.

As the Sling began its descent, John stared into the sky above. A vast array of silver clouds moved gently through a red and violet firmament, like waves colliding in a slow and gentle sea.

And as he watched, those waves began to part, pushing back the darkened clouds like curtains, and the hues beneath them changed. That was when he thought he saw it, right before the elevator took him down into the ground —the claw mark of the gods, a window back through time.

A streak of cerulean blue.

And he smiled.

EPILOGUE

TERRY OPENED HIS EYES.

The air was cold inside his lungs, and below his hands, he felt the sting of ice and snow. His head throbbed with the dull pain of too much sleep.

He pushed himself, resting for a moment on his elbows before finally twisting around to sit. He needed a moment before he tried to stand.

Terry stared into the rainbow colored snow, infused with Variant, riddled with signs of his movement. He'd never seen snow before. The closest had been the clumps of frost in the solar fields outside the Ortego building. He wondered if that's where he was now, somehow thrown from the blast to an undisclosed section of the field.

He scanned the area. Shards of broken metal from the building had blown all over the place, buried in the snow and rocks. There was a large stone ridge nearby, stretching far into the sky.

Sliding in the snow, he inched a few feet toward the rocky edge, surprised to find himself atop a cliff. There were trees below him, their leaves concealing all that lay beneath. He'd never seen trees before. This certainly wasn't the solar field. So where exactly had the blast propelled him?

He took a deep breath. The air was so sweet, so refreshing and full of Variant. Perhaps the elevation had something to do with it.

He got to his feet with the aid of the stone nearby, stumbling at first, but quickly finding his balance. With his hand against the rock, he moved to the other side of the ridge in hopes of finding a better view.

With a new vantage, looking out into the valley below, he saw a wide expanse of blue jungle trees and glowing grass as far as his eyes could see. Several birds chirped loudly amid the leaves, squeaking and cawing at one another, until finally they flapped their wings and set their minds to flight.

Terry's eyes followed them, rising high into the sky above. The clouds, long and full, were much lighter than any he'd seen before. The light of the sun beat against them, which Terry followed, and then his eyes went wide.

He nearly stumbled at the spectacle before him—a brazen truth beyond compare.

There, shining high atop the distant horizon, two

foreign suns danced quietly together, deep in the heart of another world.

TERRY, MEI, and JOHN will return in *Transient Echoes*, available right now, exclusively on Amazon.

For more updates, join the Facebook group and become a Renegade Reader today.

STAY UP TO DATE

Chaney posts updates, official art, previews, and other awesome stuff on his website. You can also follow him on Instagram, Facebook, and Twitter.

Search for **JN Chaney's Renegade Readers** on Facebook to join the group where readers can come together and share their lives and interests, especially regarding Chaney's books.

For updates about new releases, as well as exclusive promotions, sign up for the VIP mailing list. Head there now to receive a free copy of *The Other Side of Nowhere*.

https://www.subscribepage.com/organic

Enjoying the series? Help others discover the Variant Saga by leaving a review on Amazon.

ABOUT THE AUTHOR

J. N. Chaney has a Master's of Fine Arts in creative writing and fancies himself quite the Super Mario Bros. fan. When he isn't writing or gaming, you can find him online at **www.jnchaney.com**.

He migrates often but was last seen in Avon Park, Florida. Any sightings should be reported, as they are rare.

You can also actively engage with him on his Facebook group, **JN Chaney's Renegade Readers**.

The Amber Project is his first novel.

Made in the USA
San Bernardino, CA
16 February 2020

64561538R00285